FATE OF A BLOOD MOON

D.L. BLADE & C.M. LOCKE

Editing by Courtney Caccavallo

Book design by Laura M. Morales

Proofreading by Jamie at copyediting.by.jamie@gmail.com

Content proofreading by Anja Cota

Formatting by Diana Lundblade

Printed and bound in the United States of America.

First printing edition, March 2025

Published by Blade and Key Publishing

D.L. BLADE'S DEDICATION

I dedicate this book to my dog, Walter.
To keeping me company in my office while I wrote this story.
Best dog in the whole damn world.

C.M. LOCKE'S DEDICATION

This is dedicated to all the girls who grew up reading books in their closets when they were supposed to be in bed.
If it's 2 a.m., one more chapter and then go to sleep.

SOCIAL MEDIA

To follow D.L. Blade & C.M. Locke, visit:

D.L. Blade

linktr.ee/dlblade

www.dlblade.com

C.M. Locke

linktr.ee/cmlocke

www.cmlockebooks.com

AUTHOR'S NOTE

This is the second book of a trilogy. For full content warnings for *Fate of a Blood Moon*, visit D.L. Blade's website, www.dlblade.com.

GLOSSARY

The Black Onyx Coven: An ancient coven founded shortly after Kylan turned Valentina and vampirism began spreading worldwide. They kidnapped Rachel shortly after birth and raised her within their ranks. Their goal was to study the dhampirs' biology, strengths, and weaknesses to gain information on how best to kill them.

The Lemurian Quartz Coven: This is the sister coven of the Black Onyx Coven, which is based in Europe. Over the years, it has also taken part in the slaughter of dhampirs.

The Burning of Angels' Key, also known as the Fire Key: An antique bronze key imbued with the power of the Fire element.

Five-Point Order: The supernatural government established two years after the Battle of the Devil's Uprising. They maintained law and order between all the species after the knowledge that vampires, witches, and werewolves existed became public. In the

United States, each state has a division leader, and the central branches are based in Salem, Massachusetts.

The Witch of One: An entity of unknown origins. She has been called Hecate Incarnate, Daughter of Ceridwen, or Goddess of all Magics. The Witch of One is the creator of the Amavasya's Tear, a powerful stone stolen by the Daughters of Dusk.

Daughters of Dusk: A former coven of female witches turned into vampires against their will. They continued to practice different forms of magic using rituals, potions, and enchanted stones.

The Amavasya's Tear: A stone created by the Witch of One.

Ezrylos (Eh-zuh-rye-los): An Upper World angel. Guardian of the Summoning Circle.

The Academy: Founded by Darius Cruca in 1818 along with the Daughters of Dusk, it was a school for the Daughters' dhampir children to learn how to use their powers and blend into human society.

The Sanctum Order: An elite hunting group based in Boston, Massachusetts. They answer to the Five-Point Order's primary leadership. It is a team comprised of two military-trained humans, a former coven leader, a vampire mercenary, and an Alpha werewolf. This ensures no bias exists when searching for criminals in the supernatural and human societies. They apprehend anyone who violates the Four-Fold Accord, and either bring them in for questioning, or execute the offender on sight.

Four-Fold Accord: A treaty created to keep the peace between humans and supernatural creatures. Violators of the treaty result in execution or imprisonment ordered by the Five-Point Order and enforced by Sanctum.

Kylan (mentioned): He was a Nephalem, a creature born from a demon and angel. A curse prevented him from ever taking a human life, but his possession powers allowed him to turn one person who would go on to spread the vampire species... Valentina Vasile.

CHAPTER I

Valentina

Fiskardo, Greece, 1823

The man in my arms tensed as my fangs sank deeper into his neck, his flesh warm with blood. He made a low moan, his body writhing against mine as I drank from him. Sensual pleasure flowed through me, soothing my burning thirst and causing gentle goosebumps across my pale skin. I withdrew my fangs from the man's neck and pushed him away, his breathing labored. I savored the salty taste of his blood as I licked my full lips.

Though frozen in terror, the man's dark brown eyes moved to the older woman standing by the dock. She must have been his mother, locked in horror, unable to move or speak. She could only watch as I drank from her son.

I placed my hand against the man's cheek and pulled his attention back to me. His bloody lips trembled as he looked into my eyes and saw the dark power within.

"Why are you doing this to me?" he asked.

Humans always seemed to ask that after the exchange.

"Why can't my mamá move?" His eyes widened, but he couldn't escape power; my control over his mind and body was too strong to break. "What kind of magic is this?"

I chuckled to myself. While I was born a witch, that was not the power I used to hold his mother in stasis. Kylan had given me many gifts when he turned me, which I then passed on to my progeny. One of those was to control the mind.

I gave him a warm smile. "Don't worry about your precious mamá. She would have tried to stop me, so I used a simple power my maker bestowed upon me. I will keep it in place until I'm done with you."

He strained to look back at his mother. I frowned and gripped his jaw, forcing him to stay focused on me. My eyes flared, and I pushed more energy into his mind.

"Tell me your name," I commanded. I knew it already, but having him say it aloud gave me even more power to control him. There was a weight to a human's name, a value I stole from each person I turned.

"Andrei," he replied. He reached up and touched the drying blood on his lips. "What did I just do?"

"We drank each other's blood."

Andrei blinked in horror. "Why would I do something so vile?"

I smiled wickedly. "Because, my dear, I have watched you for a while, and I know your darkest, most desperate desires. You long for eternal life, for power, to be more than a simple village doctor. I can give that to you."

"Andrei, don't listen to her! She's a demon!" Andrei's mother shouted. She then pleaded with me to let her son go, but I brushed her words aside.

Andrei was *mine.*

His father, however, was sprawled on the small boat, gasping for air, more dark blood dribbling from his mouth. It wouldn't be long before death came to claim him.

"I want a companion." I kept my voice calm and gentle, even as the raging beast beneath my skin fought to break free, eager to slaughter the entire family and be done with it. "Being immortal is a lonely existence. I don't want to walk this earth alone anymore. So, I have chosen *you.*" Gently, I placed my hands on each side of his head to keep him steady. "I am giving you eternal life and power. I suggest you embrace this gift and serve me well." Then I snapped his neck and let his lifeless body fall to my feet.

His mother screamed, fell to her knees, and wept, but I ignored her.

I didn't have to wait long; my victims never took more than a minute to resurrect after the killing blow. Moments later, Andrei's eyes opened, and he sat up, a confused look crossing his handsome face. I helped him stand and smiled, but he flung his arm free from my grip and stepped back. I frowned at his defiance and pushed my compulsion back into him.

"That's enough!" I snapped. "Now, drink. Your father rejected my gift of immortality. If you don't feed, you'll die just like him. Drink his blood and become like *me.* Your desire for eternal life and power is right here, Andrei. Take it!"

I saw from the corner of my eye that the compulsion on Andrei's mother had worn off. She held up her hands, as if trying to ward off the inevitable. But then, I noticed something. A red-orange glow danced across her fingertips, morphing into flames.

The moment I stepped back, Andrei sprinted toward his father in the boat. When he reached him, his father struggled to escape, but he couldn't. He seized the man's frail body and pierced his fangs deep into the flesh of his neck. He only drank for a few moments before he ripped the man's throat open, pieces of spinal vertebrae and flesh falling into the sea.

His mother screamed for her son to remember who he was; all traces of the Fire magic I had seen flickering away. In the throes of bloodlust, he charged toward her. I didn't intervene; it had to happen his way. His mother would only become a nuisance, and it was clear that Andrei still needed blood to quench his thirst. Desperate to escape her son, the woman scrambled to her feet, leaped into the water, and swam against the current.

She didn't get far before Andrei took hold of her hair, dragging her back onto the dock and sinking his teeth into her neck. The woman only screamed once before blood strangled her voice. It would be over quickly.

The demon I had created was finally alive, his face contorting into a beautiful monster like me. He leaned in one last time and ripped his mother's spine through the back of her neck.

Suddenly, a cry echoed from the shed. The teenage boy with jet-black hair and soft green eyes was still in there, too afraid to flee. I had intended to spare him—he couldn't be more than fourteen. But with his parents and elder brother dead, killing him now would be an act of mercy.

"Kill him, Andrei. Save your brother from years of grief and pain. He will never see you as his family again."

Without hesitating, Andrei nodded and hurried toward the shed. I stayed behind, standing beneath the tree as its branches swayed gently above the dark water.

I didn't hear a scream, though; it was only silence.

Did he change his mind? He shouldn't be able to break my compulsion.

There was a noise, and I ducked to stay out of sight. The boy burst out of the shed, his face a mix of terror and desperation as he disappeared into the forest that led to the village.

He's getting away.

Andrei looked over at me as I came back around, and we locked eyes with each other. "You didn't kill him?" I asked, irritation laced into my words. Anger burned in my chest. The compulsion didn't work. He *disobeyed* me. "If you're to be my companion, I demand submission. Am I clear?"

Andrei's eyes widened as he looked around. The sight of his parents' disfigured corpses caused him to groan and collapse to his knees.

"Why does it hurt?" He pressed his hands into the lush grass. His shirt, now covered in blood, almost appeared black in the moonlight. He started pulling at the soaked fabric. "There's so much mess. So much blood."

"Yes, that will happen when you feed for the first time." I kneeled beside him and placed my hand on his back. "Relax. It's just blood. Soon, blood will be all you think about. You will learn control, and this 'mess' won't happen again."

Andrei's breath quickened. "It's so messy. It's everywhere." He stripped off his shirt and tossed it across the grass, then looked down at the blood coating his bare chest. "It's everywhere."

His breath grew more frantic, so I clutched his hand, resting my other against his cheek. "Eventually, this pain will disappear as you embrace what you are. I promise. But if you'd like, I can help the process move faster. I can compel you not to care right here and now—to never care about anyone else but us."

Andrei looked at me then, horror and sadness in his dark eyes. He nodded slowly. "I have a wife and a child. They'll learn of my parents' demise and come looking for me. My brother, Jasen, he'll tell everyone what I've done. My family will know."

A child?

My stomach dipped. I was a monster, but I would never harm a child. I forbade my followers from turning or injuring children, and those who disobeyed me were met with a swift death.

Other vampires didn't follow my orders, but that fell on their own maker's failures. The responsibility of spilling a child's blood was something I refused to bear. However, if Andrei were to leave them behind, he would remember them. He would always wonder where they were, and his devotion to me would suffer.

I must make him forget.

It was clear that I needed to increase my compulsion over Andrei. He was still too willful. I summoned more energy and wrapped it around his mind. As I stared into his eyes, I felt mine burn with an ice-blue glow, a physical manifestation of my strength over him.

"I demand that you erase them from your thoughts. Free yourself from them, Andrei. It's the only way you'll survive this." I focused my power on his will. *"Erase them."*

Andrei blinked as if clearing his vision, giving me a subtle nod before clambering to his feet. Before I could take his hand to escort him away from the slain bodies, he rushed past me at vampiric speed.

"What are you doing?!" I shouted frantically, catching up to him. He paused once I stopped beside him, his eyes blazing crimson.

"What you asked of me," he said. "I'm erasing my family."

I reached out to stop him, but Andrei slammed his heel against my knee, breaking it with a sharp crack. I fell to the ground, gasping in pain. As my body began to heal, he broke into a sprint and vanished into the dark trees.

"Andrei! No, stop!" I screamed and pleaded into the night. "That isn't what I meant."

The tingling sensation of my body healing washed over me, finally allowing me to stand. But Andrei was gone. Just then, the ringing of bells and the faint shouts of villagers filled my ears. The younger brother must have gone to a neighbor to find help. Even if vampires were a myth to humans, Fiskardo had a few witches who knew my kind existed. If someone killed one of their own, they would come.

"No!" I gasped and spun around. I had to leave. Now.

A sharp pain ripped through my chest, causing me to fall back to my knees. My hands grabbed the fabric of my bodice as if to quiet the horrid pain seizing my dead heart. Another wave of agony crashed over me, and something inside cracked. Human emotions that I had long forgotten in my thousands of years of existence came flooding back: regret and shame.

I clutched my chest, half expecting to feel my heart beating again. But instead, another wave of emotion overtook me: sorrow.

What is happening? What have I done?

CHAPTER 2

Valentina

Four months later

After weeks of traveling, I ended up in Rome, Italy. The city had been in turmoil, which helped in my favor—no one in the supernatural world was looking for me. They were all busy hiding from the Catholic Church and the rebellion.

I made a quick stop to pay tribute at the grave of an old poet friend, then headed to a cozy taverna near the coastline, about twenty miles from the city. It was the only place I wanted to be. The endless flow of wine and other spirits wasn't enough to smother the painful emotions that burned my dead heart. I couldn't understand what was happening—vampires feeling remorse or even grief over their kills was unheard of, especially if you were 'She Who Walks with the Devil.'

It's impossible.

My heart had been devoid of emotion or care for others for thousands of years. I demanded obedience and loyalty from my progeny and, sometimes, to satisfy my sexual appetites. But to regret and even feel sorrow for my actions? No, that was never a possibility. I was what Kylan made me to be—a soulless demon. How I came to break free from my maker's control was an enigma. One that I didn't question. But I still killed without shame. What was happening now felt like nothing I had ever experienced.

Something was shifting.

I took another long sip of red wine, enjoying the oak richness and feeling the burn slide down my throat. I placed the glass on the counter, swirling the liquid. Within hours of turning Andrei, word had spread across the nearby villages of what had happened to him. Despite my best efforts to avoid the news, a local boatman taking me back to the mainland shared it with me.

News of the esteemed village doctor's crimes had spread like wildfire. Jasen, Andrei's youngest brother, had survived, but unfortunately, Andrei had slaughtered his wife and child because of me.

The details of that brutality roiled in my mind, making me feel sick. I needed more wine to drown this guilt and pain. While I cared little for the wife's demise, the child was another matter. It was something that weighed heavily on me.

Let it go. I drained the rest of the wine quickly.

"Più vino, per favore," I called to the barkeep. I watched him pour another glass and slide it toward me. "Grazie, signore."

The instant I lifted my glass to my lips, a firm hand landed on my left shoulder. I turned around quickly, wrapping my hand around the arm and twisting it until the wrist bent. After seeing that it was a man, I slammed my knee hard into his inner thigh, causing his knees to buckle, and he fell to the floor.

"You think you can place your hands on me without my permission? That's quite rude where I come from and calls for a swift reprimand. Wouldn't you agree, stranger?"

I looked down at the man kneeling at my feet. He had wavy, shoulder-length dark-brown hair that framed his angular face, with olive-toned skin that caught the light from the lantern above us. There was a hint of a beard covering his sharp jawline, which added to his roguish charm. When he looked up, his hazel eyes caught mine, and his lips tilted upward into an amused, sheepish smile.

Well, isn't he beautiful?

There was something else about him as well. Something very familiar in those eyes and that smile, but I couldn't place him. I'd encountered hundreds of thousands of humans over the years, so it would take some time to recall the memory if we had met.

"My goodness, are you always this vicious toward someone who merely wants to talk to you?" The man, who spoke English with a Romanian accent, nodded toward his twisted arm in my hand. "I'd say you're close to breaking my limb."

"Do you honestly believe you're not in the wrong for sneaking up on me?"

He offered his other hand in a gesture of surrender, so I released my hold on him. The man rose to his feet, rubbing his wrist gingerly. "That's quite the grip you have there, signorina."

I scoffed and sat back in the wooden chair, taking another deep gulp of wine. "Well, I think someone like you could withstand the punishment," I quipped. The man's skin was ice cold. "What do you want?" I glanced over my shoulder. "... vampire."

It wasn't the first time I had pulled a cloak over my head or tried to disguise myself to avoid the eyes of other vampires and witches. But after centuries, it was nearly impossible to stay hidden. My face was too well-known—the first vampire to ever walk the Earth.

But I wasn't the first *true* immortal. That title belonged to Kylan, a creature whose angelic face masked a truly corrupted demonic entity. I was his first and only bite, channeling the power of demon and angel into my witch blood and creating the perfect weapon the Devil had desired for so long. My kind had worshipped me, but as time passed and more bodies piled up in my wake, I made far too many enemies. My followers and progeny wanted to see me destroyed. I was a fallen idol of darkness.

I eyed this man, who was grinning at me. He could very well be either an admirer or an enemy.

"Do I know you?" I asked, watching his smile grow wider.

"We crossed paths at one point in time," he answered. "And I would very much like to speak with you for ten minutes if you please."

Considering his presence momentarily, I nodded and gestured to the empty chair beside me. "You have ten minutes. Choose your words carefully."

I struggled with the instinct to leave the taverna and disappear, but my curiosity pulled at me about who this man was. Suddenly, he slapped a faded yellow parchment on the countertop and slid it under my gaze.

I looked down to see the sketch of my face and let out a deep sigh. "They got my nose wrong," I said with a smirk, bringing the glass of wine to my lips and taking a slow sip. I let my fangs slide down past my lips.

If he's here to kill me, I'll rip his throat out.

"'Wanted,'" he started, reading from the paper. "'Valentina Vasile, She Who Walks with the Devil, enemy to all. One thousand lire for whoever captures or drives a stake through her heart.'"

"Hmm." I swirled the last of my drink. "That's a bit violent. What the hell did I do to warrant my death?" With a slight smile, I tipped the glass back and emptied it. The barkeep wordlessly poured another as his gaze glanced at the man.

"Well, if you're here to kill me, I suppose I at least deserve your name."

His name may trigger a memory.

The charming man placed his finger on the flyer and slid it back to me. "Darius Cruça."

No, not a familiar name.

"Darius Cruça," I repeated. "Would you prefer to attempt to stake me here or outside? The owner is a loyal friend of mine, and I'd hate to destroy his livelihood on your foolish ... and *greedy* impulse."

Darius leaned on the bar and chuckled quietly. "On the contrary, Signorina Vasile, I'm not here to kill you." He smiled again, painting his rugged face with innocence.

My goodness, he likes to smile, doesn't he?

"There's no need to lie, sir." I paused, letting my eyes briefly look over him and his ragged clothes. "That's a lot of money, and you ... you look like you could use it."

Darius threw back his head and laughed aloud. "You wound me," he said as he grabbed my wine glass and brought it to his lips. "I have no desire for wealth anymore. But I *do* have a proposition for you." He then drank my wine. My jaw dropped at the brazen behavior.

The nerve of him.

I raised an eyebrow. "A proposition for *me*? Well, that's pretty bold of you, considering you haven't done anything to earn my trust."

"I figured since you're running now," Darius said, his voice a mere whisper, tapping his finger lightly on the wanted flier with my face on it. "I can offer you a safe place in exchange for your power and knowledge." He leaned in a little closer. "And perhaps something else you may want. I can even tell you how we first met."

I stiffened at the words and felt a flash of irritation burn across my neck. "What knowledge are you speaking of?"

"For one, you were born a witch."

I nodded, watching him closely.

"And second, you are the only being in this world whose blood is witch, demon, *and* angel. You hold a power unlike any other—one that could be the key to protecting that which we hide behind walls. A future for you and your heirs."

"My heirs?" I scoffed, a bitter chuckle escaping my lips. "I'm a vampire, Darius. Any chance of passing on my heritage died the day a Nephalem decided to strip me of my humanity."

He leaned back in his chair, his eyes never leaving mine. "What if I told you there was a way to save your bloodline? A way to pass on *all* your gifts to a single person?"

I clenched my jaw; he was speaking in riddles. "That's it. I've heard enough." As I started to stand, he seized my wrist. "How dare you!" I hissed, my voice low and dangerous as my eyes burned red. "Let go of me."

Darius didn't flinch. Instead, his eyes bore deep into mine with such intensity that I froze. "Dhampirs."

I blinked. "What did you say?"

"Twelve dhampirs born over the span of twenty years," he said quietly.

My breath caught in my throat. Dhampirs? That isn't possible. The legends spoke of them, sure, but no one had ever seen one to verify those claims. Vampires *couldn't* have children.

"You lie," I growled, shaking my head. "Dhampirs don't exist."

"That was my first thought, too," Darius said, his grip loosening, but he didn't release me. "But I've seen them with my own eyes—humans mating with vampires and giving birth to children who can feed on both blood and human food. They even have immortal powers. But unlike us, their hearts still beat."

I blinked, disbelief sinking in. What Darius said seemed impossible, yet the look in his eyes suggested he wasn't lying.

"Why are you telling me all this?" I demanded. "Regardless of my *reputation*, I'm still a stranger to you."

"Because right now, as I speak of this, I see so much pain behind your eyes," Darius said softly, his gaze staying locked on mine. "I've seen the same pain in vampire women who cannot bear children. But you can."

I felt a chill crawl up my spine.

Darius reached into his pocket and pulled out a dark, sparkling jewel. The deep hunter green stone was roughly the size of a large coin and wrapped in gilded metal cords. He placed the stone on the counter between us, and I leaned a little to examine it better. "They call this stone the 'Amavasya's Tear,'" he said.

"My, it's ... it's beautiful," I said, picking it up. "But if this gem can do what you claim, aren't you being a little reckless having it out in the open?"

He shrugged. "Probably."

"Where did it come from?" I asked, raising a brow.

Darius leaned in, his voice dropping to almost a whisper. "The Daughters of Dusk summoned the Witch of One, an ancient and powerful entity. Some called her Hecate Incarnate, Daughter of Ceridwen, or Goddess of all Magics. I mean, no one *really* knows her true name. The gem formed from her womb holds unmatched power over all elements. It even surpasses *your* abilities. They stole it from her, harnessed its magic, and cast the spell that made it possible."

When I heard the name "Daughters of Dusk," I remembered the legends passed down among witches. The Daughters were a coven who lost their power after a vampire turned them centuries ago. Even when that happened, they still practiced ritual magic with potions and enchanted gems. Their story had always been a mystery to me of power gained and lost.

Though Darius's words seemed improbable, the stone in my hand felt all too real. I felt its power humming within.

"The Daughters of Dusk ..." I said, my thoughts racing.

Darius nodded. "They were desperate. A vampire took their ability to have children. They'd do anything to get it back. However, they had to run and hide for over a decade. The consequences of what they had done kept them in exile. If the ancient covens found out about the dhampirs, they'd hunt them down and kill them. You know those witches have no qualms about killing innocent babies. The Daughters needed a place to teach their children how to survive in this cruel world. So, five years ago, they sought me out."

"Five years …" I whispered. "And you've been hiding them all this time?"

"Yes," Darius said. "It's not much—an academy, a school, whatever you want to call it—but everything I had gone into it. We've been running it for five years, but soon … it won't be enough."

My gaze returned to the stone, and doubt washed over me. "So, say I believe you. How exactly does the stone work? What's the ritual?"

"The magic of the stone activates during a Fool's New Moon," he explained.

"Wait," I interrupted. "The Fool's New Moon was just a few days ago."

"Yes. The Daughters will need our help until the next one, which will happen in another ten years. That's how long it takes for the energy to renew and the Witch of One's power to be at its peak. The ritual requires aligning the new moon with Venus and Earth before speaking the incantation over the stone." He gave me a side smirk. "Then the witch has to mate with a human."

My mouth tugged upward at the heat beneath those words. Then I ran my thumb over the stone, the cool surface comforting in my hand. "What exactly do you think I can do for them, though? I don't have my magic. The ring that would've allowed me to access my power is long gone, taken by a man I once trusted."

Darius reached out to take my hand suddenly, and I let him. "Teach and protect the dhampirs, so we can someday revolt against the Black Onyx and Lemurian Quartz Coven. These children have the power to change everything. But they can't do it alone."

I thought about something else. "The Daughters lost their powers when they turned into vampires. How are they able to pass that magic to their children?"

"The Tear is a powerful anomaly. As long as they harness that power during labor, the magic that went into the stone during the Fool's New Moon nine months prior will tether their lost essence and pass it down."

Good God.

If other immortals could harness elemental magic, we would finally defeat the ancient covens. They've always been my enemies. If there were a way to stop them, to protect these children and use their power against them, then I could finally destroy those witches once and for all.

But trusting Darius? I didn't know the man, but if there indeed was a way for a spell to help impregnate a vampire, I had to see it for myself. I had to see these ... dhampirs.

He was also right about one thing: I was indeed running. Saving the lives of others would help me feel that small moment of peace that I lost that night in Greece.

The night I let my victim kill his wife and child.

"I'll think about it," I said, removing his hand from mine. "Give me a few days, and I'll meet you at the Arch of Constantine."

"I hope you *do* think about it, Valentina. I hope you won't continue down the path of cowardice, spending eternity doing the same thing you're doing now—hiding. It's beneath someone of your power and legacy."

I raised my brow. "You better watch your tone. I might rip your tongue out."

Darius only grinned at my threat. "Don't be fooled into thinking that though the covens have left most of us alone all these years—the pure-blooded vampires—they won't take up arms against us again. Covens like Lemurian Quartz and Black Onyx will never stop trying to kill those they deem a threat, even when we haven't provoked them. Soon, we will use those dhampirs to destroy them all. Together, you and I can change history."

He suddenly reached out and brushed my long locks behind my ear.

"What the hell are you doing?" I gasped, but when his icy fingers touched the tip of my ear, my stomach leaped. Even though I had initially rejected him, every fiber of my being right then longed for a sensation to replace the guilt I felt.

"I'd like to buy you a drink now ... since I drank your wine," he said, stepping back. "And then later we can enjoy a warm glass of red liquid together."

The corner of my mouth turned up in a predatory grin, the alluring taste of warm blood invading my thoughts. No thirst was truly subdued, no matter how hard vampires tried to ignore it. "And you think you can buy a lady's time with a drink or two? Don't flatter yourself, Signore Cruça."

"Darius," he corrected me. "And I promise to make it worth your while—especially after I just gave you an overwhelming amount of information."

I let myself laugh that time before giving him a nod and ordering a bottle of wine for us to share.

For the next two hours, we sat in the taverna, talking. Darius told me more about the dhampirs, giving me a clearer picture of how he was helping them. The school—a tiny building tucked away in the forests outside Venice—remained hidden from the world, cloaked in concealment magic to ensure its secrecy.

Darius made another point: the world would reject the idea of vampires bearing children. Once they learned about the Tear, the coven would go to any lengths to steal that valuable gem for themselves. They would even kill all those who stood in their way, innocent or not.

I pushed away what I assumed was my tenth glass of wine and leaned back against the chair. It had also been years since I had drunk as much as I did; the room had suddenly begun to spin. Even for the first vampire, that was a lot of alcohol so quickly.

"Your eyes look like blue topaz," he said. "They're stunning, you know."

Darius touched my leg as I leaned back against my seat, sliding his fingers slowly up my thigh. His eyes lingered on mine like he was asking permission to keep it there. It was sudden and unexpected ... but I allowed it.

It had been a while since a man had touched me like that, too; however, being so close to such a handsome one made me not care about anything else. I wanted him to touch me. I wanted to forget about the guilt, to forget about whispers in my mind that murmured a child was dead because of me.

I was ready to give in to it all. My knee brushed against his leg, daring Darius to move closer, and I slightly urged my hip. My eyes settled on his, and I spotted it, then—a shift. The lust in his eyes turned into conflict, pain, or a mix of both. Looking down at me, he paused, contemplating whether to continue. I wanted him to, but the pained look in his eyes told me he was about to pull away.

And he did.

"What is it?" I asked, watching him turn from me and fiddle with the cuffs of his coat.

"It's nothing. I … I should probably go." Darius stood up, folded the sketch of me, and placed it in his pocket. "Think about everything I said earlier, and I'll hopefully see you in three days with your decision."

He tried to walk past me but swayed a little.

"I think you've had too much to drink. Perhaps you sit down and finish what you started under the table." His eyes looked down at me, and he bit his bottom lip. I didn't come here with the intention of sleeping with a man, but right then, the desire throbbing between my legs clouded my judgment, as well as the wine.

"Goodbye, Valentina."

Goodbye?

He tried to pass me again, but I grabbed his elbow. "What the hell is wrong with you?" I asked, rising to my feet to look at him.

He hesitated momentarily, and then he pulled free and walked toward the door.

I wasn't about to let him slip away that easily. I tossed a couple of lire on the counter and hurried after him. "You show up out of nowhere," I started, following closely behind, "offer me a position, touch me like a lover would do, then recoil like I disgust you. What aren't you telling me? You said we've met before—where?"

I glared at him as Darius finally stalled in his steps, wrapped by the night in the taverna alleyway. I had to crane my neck to meet his eyes; he was a head taller than me, adding an intimidating aura to his stature.

His eyes never wavered from mine, but he reached out again and took hold of a few strands of my hair. "I was hoping I didn't have to tell you because I wanted you to remember me."

I shook my head, more confused than I was five minutes ago.

"Romania, the seaport of Tomis in the year 912," he said, and my jaw dropped. "You walked onto the dock, watching me grieve after I buried my wife and child in the nearby graveyard, their candles still lit in my hands. You told me you could read my mind, feel my pain, and that you wanted to take it all away." A slight smile touched his lips. "I've been blocking your powers all night, shielding my thoughts."

My eyes widened, and I took a small step back. "I'm sorry. I don't know if I remember. That was long ago. I've met so many vampires throughout my time. I—"

"You took my pain away that night," he spoke over me. "And for that, I'll be forever grateful. You may not have remembered me, but I have thought about you every day since that moment on the docks." He bit his lower lip. "From the moment you sank your teeth into my neck to the final moments when I bid you farewell days later—after fucking in an inn for three nights straight." Darius leaned forward, and a slight smirk met his pink lips. "You *really* wanted me to forget my grief."

I swallowed. There had been many lovers I had shared my bed with, so this specific memory might have faded amidst the others. After all, I only remembered those that left an impression on me. The rest were merely a blur.

I stepped forward and placed my open palm on his cold cheeks. "Why? Why would you keep thinking of such a monster like me?"

He reached out and placed his finger on my chest, slowly gliding it down my cleavage. "Because I wanted to die ... and you gave me a second chance at life, a chance to do something worthwhile, even as a soulless demon." His eyes turned soft. "That one day, years later, I'd protect other children after I had failed to save my own from illness. I never forgot that act of kindness. Let me help you forget your pain tonight ... like you did mine."

"Darius," I said, reaching out and stopping his finger from going any lower. Though I somehow managed to force my body to halt him, every fiber in me wanted him closer.

Something primal unleashed between us at that moment, a thread of control snapping in two. Within a heartbeat, Darius slammed me back against the stone wall, which cracked beneath my weight from the brute force.

A small moan came out, muffled against his lips, as his hand snuck its way beneath my skirt, propping my leg up. I was already so soaked in arousal, aching to be taken by him. Desperate for something to dull this damn pain that consumed me.

We didn't waste any more time—we'd had hours of that already. Now desire spoke for us. I fumbled with Darius's belt, undoing his trousers until his cock sprang free, hard and ready. The wine blurred the world into a haze of dim light, but my focus sharpened as he thrust deep into me.

I grunted loudly, and his hand flew toward my mouth, dissolving the sounds of pleasure into nothing but soft whimpers.

"Be quiet, Valentina," Darius murmured against my ear, thrusting his hips back and forth as he forced himself deeper inside me with each movement. "You don't want others to hear you take my cock like this, do you?"

At that point, he felt too glorious for me to care about anything else. We had both fallen into an erotic frenzy that I didn't want to leave. Pleasure trickled through me with each thrust, threatening to unleash at any given moment. I could feel my guilt, pain, and regret fade away as ecstasy replaced them.

"You're just as I remember," he whispered against my ear, sending another wave of shudders. "Fucking sensational."

His pace picked up with his words, now borderline animalistic with the way he pounded himself into me, ravishing every part of my insides. My nails dragged down his chest, tearing through his linen shirt as he kept me pinned against the cold stone wall.

"You take me"—he slammed himself into me more brutally than before—"so fucking well."

Bliss exploded inside me at that moment, spreading through my entire body. His palm silenced another broken moan while he turned me into a quivering, soaked mess. A thrust later, Darius reached a peak of his own, emptying himself inside me with a heavy grunt.

His cock remained buried inside me while we both attempted to regain composure. His eyes burned into mine as he pulled back and dropped his hand from my lips.

"I'll be expecting your answer in three days."

CHAPTER 3

RACHEL

March 10, 2034 Mira, Italy

During the three-hour train ride from Boston to New Brunswick, Valentina told me about the academy she and my father helped establish alongside a professor named Darius Cruça.

He was an old friend and one of her direct progeny. He and his best friend, Cyrus—my biological father—built the academy on the outskirts of Venice. The three of them had recruited several witches to their cause, having them conceal the school with layers of protection magic and runes that only they could remove.

But it wasn't enough. In 1833, Lemurian Quartz, the sister coven to Black Onyx, attacked the academy. Fortunately for my mother, she and Cyrus managed to escape. As far as she knew, the school had been completely destroyed or they had spent the past two hundred years in hiding.

One of the dhampirs' fathers had betrayed them, leading the coven straight to their doorstep. If my life had a way of connecting with the past, then being taken under the wing of the Black Onyx was proof that it had all been part of their plan. When Valentina discovered they had been raising me, the truth became clear—they had been studying me. The war between the dhampirs and those who protected them was far from over. By the coven learning how I fought and understanding my kind's strengths and weaknesses, they were preparing for the day they could wipe out the rest of them.

Valentina and Cyrus wanted to stay behind and help fend off the attack, but Darius demanded they go. It was too risky for her, as she was a little over six months pregnant and wouldn't be able to defend herself. Valentina had learned the location of her stolen ring months before the attack, so she and my father left for the States to retrieve it. Little did she know that the Black Onyx knew of her arrival, hunted Valentina down, and killed my father.

"We were supposed to set sail the following night," she had said, her voice hoarse as we boarded the plane. "You would have been born on the sea, not in a desecrated church with your father's corpse."

She stayed silent for the rest of the flight.

We arrived in the Metropolitan City of Venice just before dawn. After finding a hostel in the city, she lay down to rest—not to sleep, but to recover and stay out of the sunlight. Valentina explained that while sleep was unnecessary for vampires, she relied on restorative meditation. It was a practice she had carried over from her days as a witch to help her mind heal and relax.

While Valentina recovered, I explored the city, scouting a hospital where I could easily steal blood. By the time the sun dipped beneath the sea, frustration and hunger gnawed at me.

Blood wouldn't cut it. I needed a steak and pasta.

Valentina, however, was another story. She truly needed blood, having gone over two centuries without feeding. Fortunately, I managed to secure what she needed from the city hospital. Thanks to my speed, no one noticed the blur that slipped into the storage room and vanished just as quickly as it came.

When I entered our room, Valentina was waiting for me. She had brushed out her hair and restyled it into a simple French braid. We still wore the same clothes we had stolen from the shop in Boston. While she looked put-together and elegant, I felt like a fucking wet paper bag.

"Here," I said, handing her the blood bag. "I may be fine for the next few months, but you need to feed before going back out there. There are too many humans roaming around, and we can't risk you attacking an innocent. From what I understand, vampires are a lot more accepted here than in the States. While I was out I noticed a few signs on buildings looking for night shift employees, specifically those without a heartbeat. But we don't want to draw unnecessary attention, especially from witches."

Valentina smiled softly before holding up the bag. "I remember when humans first started using others' blood, trying to save lives, but I've never seen it stored like this."

"Yeah, they started doing it this way in the 1900s to help soldiers in battle. We actually learned a lot about blood back then. That one," I pointed to the bag in her hand, "is Type O positive. The ones in the hostel fridge are Type B negative. Pretty wild, right?"

Valentina's eyes lit up with curiosity. "I always wondered why they all tasted so different. Human science ... it's fascinating."

A subtle smile crept onto my face as I showed her how to open the bag. For a moment, she stared blankly at the red liquid, as though trying to convince herself this was the only way. With one last look my way, she tilted the bag and drained it. There was a small trickle of blood escaping the corner of her mouth, but she didn't bother wiping it away.

After she placed the bag down, her face twisted in disgust, and she tightly clutched her stomach.

Yeah, I figured cold blood wouldn't cut it for her.

"I'm a little embarrassed. Sorry," Valentina said, keeping her voice soft. "I know I have to get used to this." Her eyes met mine. "Drinking blood cold and stored like this doesn't bother you?"

I shrugged. "Until recently, I didn't even know I had fangs. So yeah, drinking from these is pretty much the only thing I know."

Well, except for the Dimitriou brothers, but I'm pretending that never happened.

Valentina closed her eyes, and a faint purple glow appeared beneath her hand. "It's upsetting my stomach," she said as the magic she pulled from the ring swirled around her. "I used this water healing spell to help with nausea when I was pregnant with you."

Though I still felt disconnected from her, a small smile touched my lips, a fragile bridge in the silent space between us. After a minute, Valentina felt better and stood.

"Alright, I'm ready. I only hope Darius and the others survived the attack. When Cyrus and I fled, the dhampirs had already taken down several of the coven members, all while doing everything they could to protect their parents. Many of the dhampirs were still children then but were fast and skilled. Let's hope it was enough."

I nodded and walked to the door. "Alright, let's start looking now. When I went to the library, I didn't find any records of an attack or unusual events around when you and Cyrus left. But if they kept the school a secret, maybe news of the attack never reached the city."

"We'll go to the school itself. With you wearing that ring, I'll be able to sense the spellwork that's keeping it hidden."

I gave her a nod and gathered our things.

About an hour later, we reached the commune of Mira. Buildings and massive gardens surrounded by thick walls lined the city. I glanced around, taking in the dark streets with my enhanced eyesight. Valentina stood next to me, her arms crossed and eyes closed.

"What are you looking for, exactly?" I asked. "These houses are ancient, and I don't see any sign that an academy existed here."

"That's because it's hidden. Be patient," Valentina said, looking around. "It's so well hidden that even standing right next to it, you'd never notice a thing." A second later, her eyes opened, the blue in her irises now glowing. "Alright. Found the door."

She walked down an alley leading to the garden walls and stopped at two iron gates. She raised her left hand in front of her, and a purple mist flowed from her fingertips, morphing into strange symbols I didn't recognize. Valentina chanted a few words, and the purple symbols glowed even brighter, shifting to the vibrant blue of a protective shield spell. The symbols pressed into the iron gate, and a blinding light swallowed the entire wall. I covered my eyes until the glow finally died off. When I lowered my arm, I gasped. Valentina staggered back, her hands pressed against her chest.

The wall had vanished. Where the iron gates once stood was now an entrance leading into a grove of ancient trees.

"No ..." her voice trailed off. "Oh my God. No."

There, beyond the gate, was a building reduced to rubble and bodies scattered across the grounds. Bones and tattered cloth poked from the overgrowth of vines and grass. Broken stones lay scattered around the corpses, like crumbled tombstones in a forsaken graveyard, the lasting parts of them untouched for two hundred years.

Resembling a graveyard draped in verdant cloth.

A sudden chill went down my spine while I took in the sight. Though faded and almost imperceptible, I could still smell the blood soaked into the earth. I walked toward the closest pile of broken and decayed bone fragments and tattered garments. My jaw tightened, and I looked around for other clues. A scrap of cloth drew my eye, and I kneeled to examine it.

Valentina came to my side as I reached down to pull the fabric free from the bricks. She inhaled sharply, and I turned to her.

"That's a Lemurian Quartz cloak," she said, breathing out in relief. "See that pin? Clear quartz set inside a gold pentagram. Those monsters decimated the school, but I can't tell who made it out. There's too much destruction."

I laid a hand on Valentina's arm. "What I'm seeing here is a bunch of dead fucking witches. Let's say Darius and the dhampirs escaped. Where would they go?"

Valentina looked at me and nodded. "Darius and Cyrus had a plan for the day the witches came for us. It's not far from here."

After she walked toward the way we came in, I glanced down at the torn, dirty cloak in my hand and released it, letting it fall back to the dust of some long-dead witch.

The sprawling grounds of the villa looked like something made from a dream, surrounded by towering trees and thick brick walls covered in vines—purple blossoms blooming from every stem. We walked up to the ancient iron gate, and I pushed it open. The faint squeaking from the hinges gave credence to just how old the home was. I couldn't sense anyone nearby or their intentions, but there was also no trace of magic.

"Are you sure this is it?" I asked, scanning the bronze plaque on the left column holding the gate.

Cannaregio 4578

"I'm most certain. This was Darius's home. The academy was something they had built from the ground up, but this is where he slept."

Before we stepped through the open gate, a beam of light bounced off her toes.

"Figures," I said. "You don't happen to know the spell to get inside, do you?"

Valentina narrowed her eyes at the magical wall and caressed her fingers over the magic. Blue light trickled from her skin, and she winced. "Darius recruited a witch to create this ward to prevent outsiders from entering. If a witch were to walk through it, it would kill them."

"What about a full-blooded vampire?" I asked.

She shook her head. "Darius made allies with every clan within Venice. He dealt with those who *opposed* him. Only those with elemental magic are kept out."

I smiled at her. "Lovely. So, part of me would run into problems. Good thing I'm wearing this ring."

Valentina tried to stop me as I pushed through the magic. Immediately, I felt my heart stop beating, but only briefly. My skin reddened, and intense, burning pain shot through my body. "Fuck, that hurt!" Once on the other side, my skin began healing, and I turned around, raising my arms. "Okay, your turn," I said, slipping off the ring. Without it, Valentina would lose her powers and become an ordinary vampire again.

She moved straight toward the wall without hesitating, pressing her palm to the magic. The blue shimmer didn't harm her, and in a few moments, she stepped through the ward.

Quickly, I followed as she walked past the main gate and down the pathway, my eyes scanning the dark gardens for any signs of security. Nothing felt out of place, and no spells lingered to announce our arrival. This struck me as odd. Still, I opened up my senses to probe for anything unusual.

Our shoes crunched softly on the fine gravel walkway leading from the gate. It led toward the main house before splitting into two paths. One path led to the front door, while the other stretched under an archway of greenery and ended at a long crystalline pool. Everything about this place took my breath away. It was as if Valentina and I had stepped into a Renaissance painting, untouched by progressive modern life. I'd spend the night exploring if Valentina and I weren't breaking and entering.

"This way," Valentina said, pointing toward the home. It was a massive building, a mosaic of white stone with rough lines cut into it. Higher on the path leading to the front steps stood an ornate marble fountain carved out into the shape of a water nymph dressed in a flower-adorned robe. Sparkling water poured from the figure's outstretched hands, as if in sacrifice to some unseen god, and splashed into the bowl with a soft, musical sound. The sound blended with the rustling of leaves overhead and the distant flow of water coming from the river beside the house.

Suddenly, the hairs on my neck rose, and my skin prickled.

Alright, now I feel something, but it's not magic.

"Valentina," I whispered. "I think we're being watched."

"I sense them, too. Turn around carefully. I can hear their thoughts, and they're armed."

As we turned away from the stairs, there were the sounds of crackling branches on either side. We slowly raised our hands as two hulking figures with guns materialized from the gardens.

"Of course," I scoffed. "I thought it was strange there was no one on guard duty. Turns out the shrubs have eyes."

Valentina huffed out a laugh. "I wasn't expecting *this* kind of welcome."

I carefully turned my head to look at Valentina. "Yeah, well, we did walk in without an invitation and broke through their spell."

"Kneel and put your hands behind your head," one man commanded in English, stepping closer to my side. After we complied, the man speaking pressed the barrel of his gun against my skull. I knew that the ring on my right hand would prevent me from dying, but I didn't want the situation to escalate to the point where we'd tarnish the fountain with our blood.

"Would you two care to explain why you thought it was a good idea to break into this villa in the middle of the night?" the man standing behind Valentina asked, his voice thick with an Italian accent. "Obviously, you aren't witches, or you'd be dead by now. But we've worked here long enough to know you're something else. How about you tell us what that is, or we put a bullet through your skull?"

The metal of the gun digging into my skin was becoming incredibly annoying, and my temper began to rise. I had to grit my teeth to avoid doing something really fucking stupid. Just because I was invulnerable didn't mean Valentina would be so lucky. Of course, she could easily evade and slaughter the men within seconds, but she was trying to see Darius without unnecessary killing. So, she remained docile for their sake.

"To be clear," I said, clearing my throat. "We're not from here. I couldn't read the sign by the gate entrance. We thought this was a hotel."

The man laughed and knocked the gun's muzzle lightly against my head.

This fucking guy.

"The sign's in English, signorina."

Oops. Shit. "Ah, well ..." I started, shrugging one shoulder. "We considered it a suggestion, not a rule." I lifted my chin in an effort to appear more confident than I felt. "Look, we came here to find someone. It's not our fault you left the gate unlocked. Your alarm systems are either nonexistent or just shit."

I heard the guards cock their guns, and though we needed to stay calm, my internal beast was itching for a fight. "I can tell you more if you lower your goddamn weapons ... pretty please."

"If you gave us a minute to explain without pointing guns at unarmed women, I can clear this all up," Valentina said, her voice tight with anger.

"You have thirty seconds."

"Oh, for God's sake, is Darius Cruça here or not?"

From my peripheral vision, the guard near Valentina tilted his head to the right, lifting the gun slightly from her hair. "The padrone here is Lorenzo Marino. He's—"

"This is ridiculous," Valentina snarled, carefully turning to look both men in the eyes. "I'm trying not to slaughter the two of you, so if you could kindly put your guns down. Now."

I felt her power come to life in her throat as she spoke. The compulsion crawled over my skin as it moved between us and toward the guards. But the men shot each other a look before chuckling. It rolled into laughter that echoed across the grounds.

"Nice try, vampire. We've been trained to block such ridiculous parlor tricks."

As I went to mouth off an insult, a boot heel clicked against the stone porch. We all turned to see a man in his early thirties descending the stairs. He was tall with wavy brown hair that brushed his slightly scruffy jawline as he walked. He stopped at the fountain and paused, examining the four of us.

Valentina dropped her power and gasped. "Darius."

Oh, thank God.

CHAPTER 4

"What the hell is—" The man stepped closer, the moonlight breaking through the clouds and allowing him to see her more clearly. His eyes widened in shock. "Valentina? Oh my God, is that you?"

Valentina slumped back on her folded legs. "You're alive."

The man holding the gun to her head jolted back. "Valentina, as in—"

"My maker," Darius said, waving a hand up and down. "Lower your guns, Enzo, Charles. Unless you want to make an enemy of her. Drop them. Now."

The guards immediately holstered their guns and stepped away from us. Valentina went to stand, but Darius rushed over to help her up, taking her hand in his. I watched his fingers delicately graze her skin, treating her like glass.

The man called Charles approached my side to help me up. I waved him off and stood, brushing the gray dust from my jeans.

Without a gun pressing against my head, I looked around. The front gate was closed now and locked with a padlock. Of course, that only caused my stomach to fill with unease. I didn't like feeling trapped. All that did was make me question if we were actually safe.

Turning back to Valentina and Darius, I interrupted their little reunion. "So, you're the one my mom's been telling me about? The one who started that academy?"

Darius blinked in surprise. "Mom?" he stammered before letting out a laugh. "Dear God, of course. You have Valentina's eyes but are a spitting image of Cyrus."

I nodded. "I'm Rachel."

"Your father was my closest friend, you know?" Darius's eyes grew dark in the moonlight before he blinked again and smiled. "A genuine human being with a heart of gold."

Valentina smiled at Darius, but it faltered as she spoke. "After we fled the attack, we ended up in Boston. I went to reclaim my ring from Maurice, but the Black Onyx found out I had returned. They followed us, ambushed us in a church, and took her from me. Cyrus didn't make it. After that, they sealed me away in a crypt with a spell."

She wiped away a bit of dirt from her pants and straightened her black pullover sweater. I saw the anger simmering under her calm demeanor, like the weight of what those witches had done to her still weighed heavily on her shoulders.

He reached out and retook her hand. "I heard the news about Cyrus. What spread through the supernatural world was that you had died with him." His eyes flashed to mine briefly before returning to hers. "Come inside, and I'll tell you everything that happened that night. What matters now, though, is that you're here and safe. And I promise, no one on this property will harm either of you."

As soon as Valentina nodded, Darius took her hand and escorted us inside.

The moment we entered the house, I took a deep breath. There was a distinct scent as the breeze came through the open windows, smelling like old stone and terracotta tiles. I whistled low as I looked around. "Fancy."

The entryway was huge, much bigger than I thought from looking at it from the outside. A giant mahogany staircase stood right at the center of the foyer. The banister was covered in several ornate designs that must have taken years to carve out.

The walls were a pale cream with subtle gold accents, and a single chandelier hung overhead, resembling tiny stars as they twinkled under the overhead lights. To my left was an antique console table with a vase filled with fresh purple flowers, like the ones I had seen climbing all over the outside of the house.

"Darius," Valentina said. "Who all lives here with you?"

Darius tilted his head, motioning for us to follow him down the hall. "The night the Lemurian Quartz attacked us, we had no choice but to flee. The Daughters of Dusk didn't survive."

She exhaled softly, her lips parting slightly.

"The dhampirs fought to protect their mothers, but they couldn't hold them off. If we had stayed, they would have sent more." We stopped in front of a pair of heavy wooden double doors. "We didn't have the resources to shelter everyone, so we sent most into hiding. A few vampires and three dhampirs rent rooms here, but it's mostly quiet. Secluded." He turned to Valentina, his gaze softening. "When word spread that 'She Who Walks with the Devil' had fallen, witches and vampires who allied with us feared the covens would increase the slaughter and target them next. We sealed the runes, abandoned the bodies, and disappeared."

Darius turned the knob to an office with several bookshelves lining the walls and an open window toward the back.

"Come on," he said, and we followed him inside. He flipped a light switch, and several golden sconces lit up, bathing the room in a warm ambiance against the silver blue of the night.

"And they don't know you're here?" I asked him. "The covens, I mean."

"Oh," Darius replied. "Most of Italy and the other covens think this is just a vampire lair with human staff. We've done well to keep the legend of dhampirs a secret." He glanced at Valentina. "As far as we know, the new witches of Lemurian don't know the entire story. Those who did, died when they attacked the academy. All they know now is that a registered vampire clan operates an art restoration business. If Black Onyx discovers your location, charges in here, and begins killing and torturing, Lemurian will retaliate, deeming it an 'unsanctioned' act. That would ruin any chance of forming an alliance against you. While the covens may have a history of working together for the same cause, they are vastly different now and won't tolerate the nonsense Black Onyx has become."

"Well, now that I've awakened and taken Rachel from them," Valentina said, "Let's not be fooled into thinking that won't change."

My stomach churned at the thought of witches out there hunting those like me.

Darius continued, "For centuries, the Lemurian Quartz and the Black Onyx have hunted vampires and werewolves, erasing their existence to keep the world from discovering them. Even after vampires became public knowledge, the slaughter never stopped. They ignored the treaty because their beliefs never changed—to them, we shouldn't have been created. But after the attack on the academy, their priorities shifted. They realized dhampirs were stronger than us, not just because of their vampire blood but also because they possessed magic. Their mothers were witches. They're harder to kill." He turned to Valentina, his gaze hardening. "I made a deal with the Lemurian Coven. I agreed to cover up their crimes and keep them under the radar of the human government in exchange for their promise to leave my clan alone. So, for now, those behind these walls are safe."

My curiosity overruled my hesitancy about this place. Others like me lived here, and though he mentioned several dhampirs had escaped in the attack, three stayed behind. "Tell me about the other dhampirs here," I said.

"Yes. Who stayed with you?" Valentina asked.

Darius turned to look at her. "Luka, Giovanni, and Avaline," he said, and I watched as a subtle smile painted her lips. "We had a couple of vampires join us eighty years ago. Alessandro Faretti and Tati Volkov. They're excellent fighters, so they've made great use of the training room, helping the dhampirs. Like you, Rachel, the dhampirs have lived well among humans undetected. We each take part in running a business, restoring antiques so that we can stay here. All three of them inherited incredible gifts from their mothers. Gifts that protect them from being discovered by the wrong people."

Darius paused, a strange look crossing his face. My brows furrowed as I watched him shift his posture, walk around his desk, settle into his chair, and then gesture for us to do the same.

He seemed ... unsure about everything.

Is he angry that we've come?

He cleared his throat. "What about you two?" he asked. "Should I be worried about the Black Onyx or some other coven barging onto my property to hunt you down?"

I shrugged. "To tell you no would be a lie. The Black Onyx may not know we have come to Venice, but it's only a matter of time. They have ... *resources.* Valentina and I came to this city to find an academy to keep us safe. But since it's destroyed, I have to ask you. Are we welcome *here?*"

My eyes narrowed on Darius's face. I tried reading his intention, but I could only sense reluctance, anxiety, and something like ambition.

Darius smiled at the question, his fingers trailing along the smooth surface of his mahogany desk. "You want to stay here?" he asked, eyebrows raised. "What could I provide you that you wouldn't have back in the States?"

Valentina, who seemed to have forgotten human speech at this point, gave Darius a confused, hurt expression. This man, according to her, was supposed to be her damn bestie. Well, more than besties from the look of it.

"The Black Onyx wanted to kill me because I had the power to awaken my mother, which I did. Granted, it was against my will, but that's another story. By now, they have most likely devised a plan to hunt us down. The States aren't safe."

His expression changed again.

"The Black Onyx stole Rachel from me, raising her within their circle. They made her believe she was alone, an anomaly no one would accept. Those witches did it, intending to kill dhampirs. If those other dhampirs are out there, they're not safe. Black Onyx and Lemurian Quartz will hunt them down. Peace treaty be damned. I came back here because we need to end them. They need to pay for what they've done."

It all made sense. If the coven attacked the academy two centuries ago, only to be defeated, taking Valentina's child would give them an advantage. Lemurian told Black Onyx that she was coming to their territory. So, they lay in wait until Valentina was exposed so they could steal me. They would learn all the weaknesses and strengths of a dhampir to kill them more easily the next time the witches attacked.

While the two talked, I scanned the office. Textbooks mixed with old spellbooks and European fairy tales lined the dark wooden bookshelves. Stacks of papers lay scattered around, but from what I could see, they were invoices for repairs and supplies—nothing out of the ordinary.

"Perhaps Rachel can tell me more about Black Onyx." Darius's voice broke my thoughts, and I turned to look at his now-smiling face. "Though we don't deal with them here in Italy, I've heard rumors about their long history of unethical practices and how they handle those they deem a threat. We mainly deal with Lemurian; the descendants who weren't a part of the attack on the academy. Did Black Onyx raise you as a witch?"

I shook my head. "Black Onyx runs their group the way a fanatic cult would. No one spoke about anything that went on in their meetings, and they'd brutally execute anyone who did, including humans who were unfortunate enough to witness their *activities.* They raised me within the coven, but not as a witch. Now it's clear I was only a test subject, nothing more.... Well, I guess they also needed to keep an eye on the one person who could raise Valentina from the dead."

"There's something else," Valentina said. "Before the Black Onyx attacked us, I managed to get Kylan's ring back from Maurice at the church. I wore it before I gave birth, and in those final moments before the coven sealed me away, my powers passed to Rachel. Now, her magic has awakened, but she hasn't a clue how to control it."

Darius drummed his fingers on the table, glancing at me briefly. He seemed to weigh something in his mind, and it set my nerves on edge.

He exhaled slowly before finally speaking. "You need my help?"

"Yes," she said. "I had hoped the academy would have provided the right training, especially since it once housed dhampirs like her. She could have trained with them and learned how to harness her magic, not what the coven tried to make her into. But ..." Her words trailed off, her eyes darkening. "Now I'm finding that the academy and those who could have helped her are gone."

The panic in her voice washed over me like a wave, causing a sense of helplessness and loss. Valentina Vasile wasn't supposed to feel lost or afraid. We had traveled this far just to find the one place she depended on to protect me was no longer there.

"I see," Darius said softly, his gaze meeting mine. "You know me, Valentina.... I never stop training. If guidance is what she needs, then she'll still get it here." He swallowed and sat up straight. "Anyway. The ring. Where is it now? I don't see it with you."

She turned and pointed to my right hand. I raised it and wiggled my index finger.

"Well, isn't that a beautiful stone?" he said. "May I hold it?"

My eyes went wide. "You can try to pry it from my finger, but I think you may end up breaking your arm."

"Rachel!" Valentina shouted.

Darius held up his hand. "No. She's fine. That is exactly the correct response I'd expect from her." He smiled and turned to Valentina. "How much does she know, aside from our history?" Darius asked, looking at her as if I weren't even in the room.

There was a subtle shake of Valentina's head that I'm pretty sure she thought I hadn't noticed.

I pinched my brows together. "What the fuck does that mean?"

"Rachel!"

Darius covered his mouth and let out a small laugh. "It's alright."

"She has a god-awful mouth," Valentina remarked, "but you'll get used to her sarcasm at some point. Apologies."

"No need," he assured. "If we are to build trust between us, Rachel should know everything."

I shot Valentina a glare. "What is my mother dearest not telling me?"

Another strange look passed over his face as he looked at Valentina. But when he smiled, I realized Valentina held no sway with this man. He wanted me to know.

"We've been keeping it in the basement."

"Darius," Valentina chided calmly. "As much as I'd like to share with her—"

"Exploring your basement sounds like a good time," I cut in, anxiety swirling in my ribcage. Right before I stood, we heard footsteps approaching the room from the hall outside the door.

"Of course. But first, I want you to meet someone." There was a quiet knock at the door before it swung open. "Ah, Luka, come in." Darius gestured as a tall, skinny guy with lightly tanned skin and curly brown hair walked in. The guy offered us a lopsided grin and had something of a nerdy charm about him. Darius stood, and so we followed suit. "Rachel, I'd like to introduce Luka Novak. He can help you both settle into a couple of the rooms on the second floor."

"Hey, nice to meet you," Luka said, turning to me and reaching out to shake my hand. There was a slight crackle of energy when I took it, and the hairs on my arm stood on end. The magic he emitted was so powerful that my own sparked to life. As I held his hand, my ears homed in on the sound of his heartbeat. But he had no noticeable scent, just like me.

Luka went to Valentina and only smiled. "It's an honor to see you again." I caught a glimpse of his slightly elongated canines when he smiled. "You may not remember, but—"

"Of course, I remember you, Luka," she said, a touch of warmth in her voice. Luka smiled again in response and stepped to the side, his eyes sliding to me briefly before turning to Darius.

"Can I ask you something?" I said to Luka, drawing him back to me. "You're like me, so I gotta ask. How have you survived in the same city for so long? I had to keep moving, always worried someone would notice I wasn't aging or some idiot vampire would try to mess with me. We don't exactly pass for vampires, so they must have suspected you were something else at some point."

Luka paused, his gaze steady. "Now that the world knows about vampires, things are easier. But before that, we had to be careful. A dhampir like me had to blend in as human. Sure, people might have noticed I wasn't aging, but they never asked questions. Either they feared what I was and didn't want to risk retaliation, or they just assumed I was a witch who aged gracefully."

"In other words," I said, "they mind their business."

Luka's wide grin reached his eyes. "Exactly. I've had to use my abilities a few times, though. My mother was a Spirit witch before she was forced into becoming a vampire. She came from a long line of witches with powers that mess with the mind. If I wanted someone to see me differently or forget I ever existed, I could make it happen."

I stared, my mouth hanging open. "Okay, that's pretty badass."

Darius leaned back in his chair and linked his fingers together. "So, while you're here, we expect the same caution Luka and the others have made." His eyes slid to Valentina, his lips curving into a brief, unreadable smile.

Valentina mentioned her past with Darius and how they had once been in a relationship. But when she came to the academy to help him protect the dhampirs, they had to stop it, so the line of professionalism wouldn't become blurred with lust. But then she met Cyrus and gave her heart entirely to him—a human—and Darius had to watch it all happen despite how much he loved her.

Now, two hundred years later, it was clear he still did.

"Luka, prepare their beds in the spare room near the second-floor library. Oh, and call Alessandro. I'll have to talk to him before sunrise. I need a moment longer with them."

Luka gave me a quick nod before exiting the office, and the two of us followed Darius into the hallway with a staircase that led into the villa's basement.

The room was slightly musty, with water dripping from the side walls into a small puddle by the back boiler room. It didn't look anything like the rest of the house. This place felt more like a dungeon.

My thoughts drifted to Andrei's creepy dungeon basement, and my stomach clenched. I took a deep breath to calm myself, shaking those memories away, before walking deeper into the room. A small vault was on the right side, tucked behind some lumbar and fiberglass insulation. It was roughly six by six feet, with several cubbies and a keyhole beneath thick metal handles. Darius pulled a silver key from the keychain on his belt, unlocked the top left cubby, and pulled the box free. Inside was a small black box. When he lifted the lid, I looked down at a gemstone sitting on a velvet cushion. It was hunter green and wrapped with gilded metal cords.

"It's still intact," Valentina said, a faint smile on her lips.

"Is that the Amavasya's Tear? The gem you told me about on the train that helped create me?" I asked as she carefully picked up the stone from the box.

"Oh, but it can do so much more than that," she said, thumbing over the smooth facets. "It doesn't *just* help bring dhampirs into the world." Her voice was sharp, making me immediately unnerved.

"Okay, what else does it do?" I asked warily. My eyes focused on the beautiful stone, but I could see a gleam in Valentina's eyes. Something made my blood run cold.

"It's also a weapon," she answered.

Darius stepped forward. "We planned to use it against the covens before the attack at the academy. It can destroy even the most powerful witches—the ones determined to wipe us out."

Frustration burned in my chest. "Stop talking in circles. How *exactly* can it kill them?"

Valentina's hopeful expression sent another chill through me as Darius took the gem from her and carefully placed the stone back inside. "When a vampire takes part in the ritual to become pregnant, this gem and its spell draw your essence from Purgatory, fully restoring your soul temporarily. It allows *creation*—true creation. But it can also do the opposite. This gem harnesses the power of Spirit, Earth, Air, Fire, and Water. If unleashed, it can tear those elements apart, severing the magic that binds them together."

I stiffened. "You're saying it can shatter the elements?"

"We weren't just protecting dhampirs from the covens," Valentina said. "We were training them to launch a war against them."

"When we thought Valentina was dead," Darius added, "we stopped our operations. It was safer to hide instead."

"And now?" I asked.

Darius smiled and looked at her. "Now you're back and alive. But don't forget—it's not the nineteenth century, love. Reckless war will bring the Black Onyx and the human government straight to us. Don't undo everything I've built in your absence. But now that you are here and have that ring, we can rebuild and create that army ... strategically and in *my* way."

The air was so heavy with tension now that I had to laugh to lighten the mood. "You'd strip magic from this world to kill them? Are you crazy?" I said.

She nodded unapologetically. "Wanting to survive isn't crazy. I don't care if magic disappears," she said. "I'll sacrifice my own power forever if it means those witches die at my hands. *This*, Rachel, is how we end them."

CHAPTER 5

JASE

July 15, 2034 Atlanta, Geor-
gia

Present Day

The back of my neck prickled with irritation as Andrei fiddled with his damn phone. He had ignored my last question about the witch we were waiting for, Liam Kozlov, and completely brushed me off.

I was getting too impatient.

Jackson and Meredith muttered to each other a few feet away from me. Although I could eavesdrop on their conversation, my frustration with waiting for someone else made me ignore it.

"Andrei," I hissed, turning to him. "Where the fuck is he?"

This supposed heist at the Hall of Atlanta was taking too damn long. Now we had to wait for the one person to get us inside. If this witch from the Black Onyx held us up any longer, we would get caught. Then we'd have to kill whoever spotted us.

I wasn't in the mood to dispose of a body tonight.

Considering his usual insistence on punctuality, it surprised me to see Andrei letting this hindrance slide. Every detail was too important to my older brother, and any divergence from his plan would send him into a rage. However, Andrei was unusually calm despite this delay and my impatience to get inside.

"He's here," Andrei said, sliding his phone into his suit pocket and pushing off the brick wall beside us.

Right then, a tall, lean man in his early to mid-twenties rounded the corner of the museum. The sharp angles of his jawline, lightly tanned skin, and messy brown waves gave him a young frat boy look. He wore the attire I'd seen the Black Onyx wear—all black, with a wine-red cloak draped over his shoulders, flowing behind him as he made his way to the back of the alley.

The Black Onyx had always kept their circle small, only taking in members with blood ties to the founders. But ever since Valentina awoke, they had expanded their membership. In Atlanta, Georgia, they initiated three more members from the Spirit bloodline. Liam was the newest addition.

Even though I made an agreement with the Black Onyx to work with them, I still felt uneasy whenever their members were around.

Once they put me on trial, I convinced them that Valentina had forced immortality on me two hundred years ago. She turned me that night while they were busy putting up their shields in the church. I testified that I had been so afraid they would kill me for becoming a vampire that I fled, abandoning them right after they sealed her away.

Witnesses confirmed my story—that I intended to stop Rachel and not awaken Valentina for my own vindictive needs. Even though the court acquitted me, I still had to reach an agreement with the coven, since I had been fucking with them by sending photos of Rachel and stalking her for as long as I did.

I had no choice but to accept Andrei's offer of employment within the clan. That way, the clan could monitor my movements and report them to Gerald and his *cult*.

I furrowed my brow as Liam moved past me, gently brushing my shoulder with his, and leaned down to the keypad. He typed in the code and looked straight at me over his shoulder with warm hazel eyes. "We go in and out. Here ..."

His eyes averted from mine, and he turned to Andrei, handing him a black stone with a gold etching at the center.

"That will open the seal," he explained.

"What do you mean by 'we?' If you've already given us everything we need to get the key, then what purpose do you serve now?" I asked, raising a brow.

Liam flashed me a playful smile. "Because I'll need that back once Andrei's done with it. Though my coven is willing to work with you, you're still vampires. Get the key, return the stone, and I'm gone." Liam pressed down on one more button and stepped back.

The resounding beep and click of the lock answered. My brows knitted together, casting Andrei a brief, uneasy glance as we opened the door. "Alright, let's go."

I stepped inside the cool darkness of the museum storage area. This was the exhibit's entry point, where workers moved in and out to various locations. There were crates of unopened artifacts that would, no doubt, be valuable on the black market. I examined a few unpacked pieces in plexiglass containers.

As much as I would like to pocket a few jeweled amulets, we aren't here for necklaces.

"So, where is this alleged key hidden?" I asked Jackson, who had just finished disabling the cameras and joined my side.

"Somewhere on the second level, where the Renaissance paintings and artifacts are," he replied.

The five of us crept through the dark hallways of the museum, avoiding the windows and any sensors that might be there. As we reached the second-floor hallway, Meredith opened her mouth to speak, but Andrei held up a hand to silence her, his head cocked to the right. "Dammit," he whispered. "There's a guard up here. There wasn't supposed to be anyone on this level right now."

A faint squeak of leather shoes caused us to look over to where the sound came from, and I ran a hand through my hair, angry at this hitch in the plan. Andrei regarded me with his dark eyes and raised an eyebrow.

I threw up my hands. "Why the fuck are you looking at me? I'm not doing that."

From the moment I joined my brother's Black Blood Diamond Clan, he started singling me out for their killings. I didn't mind spilling human blood or taking out his rivals, but it irritated the fuck out of me that Andrei wouldn't do any of the dirty work himself.

Over the last few weeks, I noticed something was off. Andrei preoccupied his twisted mind with plans I wasn't privy to.

Meredith had said that Rachel's arrival had a "profound impact on him"—a pathetic excuse.

All because of one woman?

All because of *her?*

In that instant, I felt the urge to clench my fists, digging my fingernails into my palms. I needed to relax and get Rachel out of my mind so I could focus.

"Come on, Jase. You haven't had fun in a while," Andrei said, his voice low, but it pulled me out of my thoughts. "I imagine you've felt a little parched since your last feeding. Some blood will loosen you up a bit and take the edge off. Kill them and make it quick. We need to get past that entry point"—he gestured toward a small steel door across the hallway—"and reach the exhibition area by midnight."

Go fuck yourself. "You got it," I said instead, the words tasting sour on my tongue.

As I stepped toward the hall leading to the main exhibit on the first level, Andrei added, "Liam, go with him."

Immediately, my body locked up, and I bared my fangs. I didn't need a self-righteous witch hovering over me while I made my kill, but Andrei called the shots, so I had to bury my annoyance and put on a fucking smile. "After you, Liam," I said, gesturing ahead. "I'll hang back to ensure no one sneaks up on us."

"While you two are taking care of the guard, the three of us will move down the hall and make sure no other security detail is around," Jackson noted, gesturing to the second large room a few feet down the hall.

I nodded, and we moved into the room where the noise had come from while the others hurried to the second room, disappearing into the shadows.

Once inside, the sweeping beam of a flashlight moved across the floor on the east side. The white light landed on a collection of bronze goblets in glass cases and medieval swords suspended in displays along the walls.

The footsteps got louder, so we moved behind a roped-off black and gold dais and waited for the guard to come into view. After about a minute, an unusually tall man in a stone-green security uniform rounded the corner, whistling softly as he strolled down the middle aisle. As he passed us, I positioned myself behind a glass display case, and Liam attempted to grab my wrist to yank me back. The sound of my shoe scraping against a rug caused the man to freeze.

Fuck me, I don't want to kill the guy here. We won't be able to clean up the mess.

Instead of turning toward me, the man continued whistling and headed down the aisle toward a grand antique mirror on the south wall, away from the main exhibit.

I looked over my shoulder, and my eyes glared into Liam's. "Are you going to stop me when it's time to kill him?" I asked, studying his reaction.

Liam flashed me a crooked smile. "Do what you gotta do, demon. I'll sit back and watch the show. What's the life of some weak and powerless human worth, anyway?"

Something about his tone surprised me. He wasn't like the others. This witch seemed to bask in the darkness like us. Maybe that's why the coven chose him to babysit us during this mission. He wouldn't flee or try to stop us from doing what had to be done to get that key.

I quietly followed the guard, pressing myself against the wall. There was something off about his movements, and a sickening feeling in my gut warned me that something was wrong. I ducked behind a medieval wardrobe display and watched the guard look at himself in the mirror.

He ran his fingers through his shaggy silver hair before adjusting his tie. Thick sweat formed on the man's brow, and my ears homed in on the quickening pace of his heartbeat. The guard reeked of fear and anxiety.

He knows we're here, but … I think he's preparing himself.

The man's pants were too big and hung loosely around his waist. He pulled the belt tighter and double-checked everything was in order before straightening his shoulders and lifting his head.

What the fuck is he doing?

"You can come out now," the guard said, his voice quivering. Stepping into the light, I moved closer to him. I wasn't sure where Liam had gone, but if he were smart, he'd stay back while I did what I do best.

The guard turned around, leveling a small handgun right at my chest.

Cute.

"Are you fucking kidding me right now?" I mumbled to myself, holding up my hands and giving him a wicked smile, exposing my fangs. "I wouldn't do that if I were you, bud. Put that tiny gun away, and I'll make your death quick."

The guard shook his head, now panting. "This gun has sharpened wooden bullets. I wouldn't be so sure about your survival if I shot you." The man's hands shook slightly. "You weren't supposed to be here."

I tilted my head to the right. "Yet you were prepared for a vampire intruder, weren't you?" I asked.

The guard nodded. "How many of you are there?"

Like I'd tell him that....

"We'll be in and out in minutes," I said. "I can make this a lot easier for us by killing you quickly and dumping your corpse in one of those coffin displays. Or you lower your weapon, turn around, and get the fuck out of this building. Because pointing that gun at my heart is only sealing your fate as a meal for me."

"I ..." His voice trailed off, and he quickly wiped the sweat dripping into his eyes.

"Yeah, I'd say pointing a gun at a vampire and realizing you're about to die would make you feel how you do right now."

His hand trembled even more, and I could hear the audible gulp as he swallowed, his Adam's apple clicking. Then I noticed something else. It was subtle, but he pulled his hand back slightly as if he wanted to lower the weapon, but ... he couldn't.

Then the light in his eyes winked out, leaving pools of inky darkness instead, and he dropped the weapon, stepping back. My eyes homed in on each side of his neck, right at the center of his shoulders. There was a bulging movement in his skin, pushing up and down, as if something were trying to free itself from his body.

What the fuck?

The man's growling, rumbling noises echoed so loudly against the walls that I had to press my palms to my ears to muffle the sound.

Where the hell is Liam?

I watched the guard collapse on to all fours. His spine protruded upward, and black hair follicles sprouted from his skin, ripping his suit free from his body.

Werewolf … wait … no. Something else?

The pulsing bubbling from his flesh grew increasingly rapid until his skin tore apart in a shower of greenish-black blood, revealing two additional heads emerging from his shoulders. The one with the guard's face shook his head vigorously until it mirrored the movements of the others. Staring back at me were the six piercing eyes of a three-headed creature, its body morphing into that of a massive ebony-furred beast resembling a dog.

"Jesus fucking Christ!" I shouted, stumbling over my feet. I shook off the initial fear and bolted toward the back of the room. The beast leaped over me and crashed into a glass case above me, sending shards onto my head. Several bronze and iron artifacts struck me in the face and arms, causing me to stumble. The creature whipped its three massive heads toward me, revealing dozens of black, razor-sharp teeth that dripped with silver liquid.

It lunged for me.

Using my vampire speed, I rolled onto my back and delivered a powerful kick to the charging monster, sending it flying across the room and crashing into a painting on the wall. The instant the beast was prone, I charged for it. I seized its left head before flipping it over, slamming it against the floor, and jumping onto its back to grab the larger middle head. It thrashed under me and threw its body onto the floor, splitting the tile in half. The creature shrieked, but I buried my fangs into his neck, cutting off the sound. I was afraid to drink its blood. It wasn't a werewolf, but I still wasn't sure what its blood would do to me. I needed to get to an artery or the spinal cord and tear it out.

As I struggled to sever its vertebrae with my fangs, the creature seized the back of my neck with its claws, digging into my flesh until its grip forced me to release it. I wrenched free from the beast, but the right head swung around and slammed into the center of my back, sending me to my knees.

Before I could move, a crimson-red mist flowed over me and wrapped around the monster's torso and the middle head. I watched as the mist constricted, causing the beast to roar and thrash, knocking several displays to the floor.

My eyes widened as the mist severed through the head and crushed the torso. The body dropped to the ground, and the three heads vanished into gray smoke and dust. I whipped my head around, and Liam stood behind me, the red mist hovering over his outstretched fingers.

Well, shit.

"Thanks," I said, watching him shake off the remaining power.

"I've got to say, I didn't see that one coming," he said, strolling over to the beast and looking down at its remains. "It's been ages since I've seen one of these."

I blinked. "What the fuck is that?" I asked, standing up and walking over to look with him.

"That right there is a Cerberus," he said. "They rarely roam Earth, that's for sure."

"Do you think the angels sent him to protect the key?"

Liam's lip turned up. "I don't think the Upper World had any-thing to do with this."

I swallowed. The key was a powerful tool created by the elemental families centuries ago, protected by angels or whatever the fuck they're called up there. It was the power we needed to save our souls. If Liam was correct, the devil knew we were trying to break that curse, and he just attempted to stop it.

Well, fuck me.

A sharp whistle echoed off the walls as Andrei and the others entered the room, surveying the destruction. "Jase, I'm surprised at you," Andrei growled. "I would have hoped you wouldn't make things so messy. But thanks for taking care of business."

I used my head to gesture to Liam. "Don't thank me," I said.

Andrei looked down at the bloodied mess. "What is … well, what *was* this?"

"Something that wanted to stop us from saving our souls. I think this mission got a hell of a lot harder than we thought it would be," I observed.

Andrei nodded. "Well, just in case there are more, we need to get moving. We have one hour from the time we tripped that alarm. Come on."

Liam adjusted the pentagram clasp on his cloak and moved past me, giving me a nod.

Spinning on his heel, Andrei walked to the small door on the other side of the room.

It led to a tapered section of the exhibit, featuring medieval weaponry and painted vases. Andrei stood in front of a massive pottery piece that portrayed bright orange and red flames licking the bodies of shadows tied to poles.

I looked over his shoulder. "'The Burning of the Witches of North Berwick.' Andrei, this jar is over four hundred years old. Are you sure it's in this? It's too obvious."

"I'm certain," Liam said, cutting in to answer for him. "I'll stand guard in case something else comes crawling into one of these rooms to stop us. Use that stone I gave you."

Andrei picked up the jar and rotated it until it was upside down.

He placed the black stone at the center, where it hummed softly, almost like a harp string when plucked. He then traced a sharpened fingernail over the surface of the clay until he found a slight curve. As he dug deeper into that curve, the clay crumbled under the increasing pressure. Then there was a sharp crack, and I felt something ripple through me.

"What the fuck was that?" I asked. Andrei didn't answer me.

The jar's bottom crumbled into powder, leaving a heap of clay dust scattered across the floor. Without a word, he set the jar back on its pedestal. Then he placed the stone in his pocket, kneeled, and dug around the broken pieces. I moved beside him as his fingers wrapped around a cylindrical rod and pulled it free.

There's the key.

As I leaned in closer to look, I noticed the intricate details of the ornate brass key, with delicate engravings of ancient runes etched into the metal. At the top of it, nestled in the lacy filigree design, was a reddish-brown stone that glimmered in the darkness.

"What exactly are we dealing with here?" I asked.

Andrei smiled at me, a smile I hadn't seen in over two hundred years. "This right here is the 'Burning of Angels Key,' blessed by the Archangel warrior of the Upper World. That ripple you felt was the element of Fire reacting to the key's removal. All witches born under that element, including us, reacted to it."

"How can we feel magic? We're vampires."

"Our magic was briefly returned to us, remember?" he explained, slipping the key into a cloth pouch he produced from his pocket. "Now, aside from this key, which will get us into that cave, our next mission is retrieving Rachel."

My chest burned at that thought. Since Andrei shared how the spell worked with us, I was no longer on board. He wasn't just planning to use Rachel's blood to activate the spell; he wanted to bring her home to New Orleans and back by his side.

The barely concealed feral expression he wore sent a chill up my spine. "It'll be nice to have our family be complete again."

Andrei's behavior was unsettling. As much as I wanted to save my soul, this wasn't how I wanted to do it.

I buried the unease inside me and slapped a hand over his shoulder. "Alright, we better get out of here. If whoever controlled that creature realizes what happened, they'll attempt to stop us again and send another mongrel." I stood, brushing clay and drying blood from my jeans. Before I followed them out of the exhibit, I lifted the hem of my shirt, revealing the small rune on my lower stomach. It appeared shortly after Andrei and I left the train station that Rachel and Valentina had escaped from. When it happened, it felt like a hot iron brand had seared into my flesh, stealing the breath from my lungs. Once in a while, it pulsated with a strange, vibrating energy, especially when I thought about Rachel a little too much.

I may have been born a witch, but I knew next to fucking nothing about runes or symbols like these. Whatever this irritating blemish was, I wanted it gone.

Without a word, Andrei strode out of the exhibit toward the stairs where we had initially come in. Meredith and Liam hurried after him, leaving Jackson and me in the dark room, and I lowered my shirt, concealing the mark.

"Look, I may have to save my soul from being the devil's plaything, but something tells me that Andrei's persistence might get us killed in the process," I said, keeping my voice hushed after my brother disappeared down the stairwell. "You should have seen that thing back there. It was a fucking unholy sight that made every hair on my arms stand on end. And I have a feeling it's just going to get worse."

"What's worse than your soul being dragged to Hell and tortured for eternity?" Jackson asked.

I swallowed.

Nothing ... absolutely nothing is worse than that.

CHAPTER 6

ANDREI

We headed back to my Atlanta office shortly after leaving the museum. Liam and Jackson followed closely behind me as we walked through the large, empty building. Once we entered the office overlooking downtown, I locked the door and sat at my desk. Reaching into my coat pocket, I pulled out Liam's black stone and slid it across to him. He quickly picked it up and pocketed it inside his cloak. Then I gestured for both men to sit.

"I wanted to thank you personally, not only for assisting us in getting the key but also for saving a member of my clan," I said, inclining my head. Liam gave a brief nod in acknowledgment.

The Black Onyx Coven still hadn't learned that Jase was my younger brother, only that the supposed rogue vampire who came to New Orleans to stop the dhampir from raising Valentina was now working for my clan, the Black Blood Diamond.

After Rachel fled with her mother that night four months ago, the plan that I carefully crafted on the floor of that desecrated church sprang into action. The coven eventually caught up with us. And since Jase was with me, they brought us all to trial. Accused of orchestrating the resurrection of Valentina and allowing her to escape, I, as Rachel's guardian, faced a difficult position. However, we convinced those witches with our well-crafted lie. We spun a tale so convincing, so perfectly tailored to their fears and suspicions, that they bought it without a second thought.

Meredith, Jackson, and I corroborated Rachel's actions. Honestly, the witches had no reason to doubt us; after all, why would a clan of vampires defend an outcast, a stranger?

Though Jase faced repercussions for abandoning the coven two hundred years ago, taunting them with photos of Rachel and putting her on edge, as if he was toying with prey, they didn't punish him. Instead, he had agreed to work with my clan to complete every task they hired us to do. His skills as an elite predator made him a valuable asset to the coven in their mission for power, and they wanted to exploit him as much as they had exploited everyone else they had trapped in their net.

In the end, they spared Jase. Rachel was at fault, and the coven backed off.

"Look," I started, "I know you've made a home for yourself here in Georgia, but I'd like to propose that you return with us to New Orleans."

Liam raised an eyebrow.

I leaned forward, resting my elbows on the desk. "We've always had witches working with us in areas where our vampire abilities fall short. Of course, this might require some persuasion with your superiors—especially Helen—since you're one of her newer protégés. But I assure you, we'll compensate you generously, and you'll find more satisfaction with us than with them. You'll come to assist us when we need you, while still maintaining your position with the coven. It will just be in New Orleans instead of here. Black

Onyx owes us a significant debt after tonight. The key will not only save lives, but it will benefit the coven as well." I paused, meeting his eyes. "The sooner they grasp our clan's values and strengths, the quicker we can complete our tasks. They'll also be more likely to let you join us on more missions like this."

Liam folded his arms and cleared his throat. "What makes you think I would *want* to leave home and come work with vampires? Tonight was just an assignment the coven leaders forced on me. I don't give a fuck what happens to the lot of you...."

"Yet you saved Jase from the Cerberus. Why bother doing that if you didn't give a shit about ... the lot of us?"

Liam shrugged. "It was my job. Can't retrieve an artifact if everyone is dead."

"True," I said, glancing at Jackson. "By the way, Elena Kozlov, a medical student at Johns Hopkins. She's your younger sister, yes?"

Liam's eyes darkened, and his lip peeled back in a seething sneer. It was very clear he knew what I was implying. I sat back in the chair and ran my hand through my hair.

Checkmate.

"I'm not a monster. I'm just a vampire who gets what he wants. And I was hoping you could work with my clan. The coven sees me as an asset because I'm willing to get my hands dirty for them. I'm not afraid like they are. But I've done my research, as always, with anyone who enters my circle."

Liam scoffed. "Of course you did."

I shrugged. "You can't be too thorough in this business. Your bloodline is very impressive, and your magic is exactly what we need. You sign a contract with me, and I'll take care of Black Onyx, ensuring your return to their fold once we've completed each assignment, no questions asked. Why not have both the coven and a powerful clan standing behind you? I'll compensate you ten times what they pay you, and I guarantee your sister will have everything she needs for schooling. That is how we take care of our family."

Liam took a deep breath and leaned back against his chair. I could see the wheels turning, but he knew there was only one answer I'd allow.

With one nod, he said, "Alright, give me the contract." Jackson pulled a stack of papers from the folder he had tucked under his arm and handed them to Liam.

"You'll see the tabs where you need to sign and initial," I explained. "But first, I need to have a word with Jackson. Please head down the hall to the kitchen. Meredith will be waiting for you with a cold glass of whiskey."

Once Liam bowed and exited the office, I returned to Jackson across the desk and cleared my throat. I pulled out my phone and opened my tracker app. After staring at the map and the flashing blue dot for a few seconds, I slid the phone across toward him.

He leaned down to look at the screen. "Still in Italy?"

"Still in Italy," I confirmed. "She's our top priority, but I'm worried about Jase being involved."

Jackson tilted his head and cocked a brow. "And why is that?"

I ran a hand over my face. Jase had been acting oddly since I mentioned our plans to travel overseas to catch Rachel. We had too many pressing matters to settle before we could act, including retrieving the key. But Jase and I needed our magic back for our plan to work. Now that we have Liam as a part of the plan, it could be crucial: a witch who could wield Spirit magic alongside our Fire magic.

Jase, though, was against this strategy and urged me not to go. I couldn't understand why. He was the one who was so adamant about tracking them down within the first couple of weeks of them leaving.

"Just keep a close eye on him, alright?" I asked. "You'll report everything, and I mean everything he does to me." Leaning forward, I added, "Keep an eye on Liam, too. I believe he'll be an excellent asset, but he's an outsider and has to earn our trust."

Jackson nodded and rose to his feet but stopped at the door. "What about Lucy?"

I shook my head, taking my phone and slipping it into my pocket. "I haven't decided about her yet. Taking her with us to Italy would make approaching Rachel a lot easier, but she is still too wary of me and hates Jase with a passion. But if Jase comes with us, she'll learn to play nice."

Jackson nodded in agreement. "She's waiting down the hall in the smaller office. Do you want me to send her in?"

I nodded, and he left to get Lucy. We had brought her along to Atlanta because I couldn't trust that she wouldn't run away at the first opportunity she got. I needed her close by as bait for Rachel.

Five minutes later, Lucy entered and stopped at the door. She swallowed before stepping closer to my desk and sitting in the chair across from me.

"Yes?" she said, tucking her straight black strands behind her right ear. She seemed somewhat nervous, having no idea why I brought her to Atlanta. The gesture was so human. It was as if she weren't a vampire like us.

I initially hesitated to keep Lucy at the lair with me and the others after Jackson brought her back from Rachel's apartment.

Since Jase had joined the clan, she had avoided him at all costs. She hated him for turning her into a monster, and after what happened in the church, I wasn't exactly her best friend's favorite person.

But aside from that, I was the best chance she had at survival in a world that still hadn't entirely accepted us. To our surprise, Lucy had proven to be a valuable addition to our clan these past few months. Her experience managing hotel bars was beneficial for nightclub operations. Lucy still refused to embrace all of her vampire traits, and having her feed from my personal suppliers was always an arduous event. Lucy would only go to government-run feeding clubs. She wanted to ensure that the person was completely on board with it.

I did gain some trust when I agreed to go with her to see her mother, helping her by sharing with her mom what she was and how it changed nothing. Of course, Gabriela was initially afraid, but after seeing that her daughter was still Luciana Morales, her baby with the heart of a saint, she accepted her. Lucy stayed in regular contact with her mother, and I allowed her to visit whenever she wanted, as long as a member of my staff went with her.

Building loyalty and obedience is done brick by brick.

"In the next few weeks, we'll travel overseas to Europe. I'd like you to come with us."

Lucy's eyes widened, and her mouth parted in shock. "Is it Rachel? Do you know where she is? Is she all right?"

I raised my hand to stop her questions. I couldn't very well tell her how I tracked Rachel down or for what purpose. For this trap to work, Lucy must be a willing lure for her best friend.

"I received some information from a contact that she may be there," I explained. "I can't confirm anything, but it needs to be investigated."

"Then why wait weeks before finding her?"

"Unfortunately, the Black Onyx is watching us very closely, and if we suddenly disappeared, it could raise suspicions. They would find Rachel and kill her for what she's done. We must move carefully."

Lucy balled her hands into fists. "Those bastards are the reason this all happened in the first place. They lied and manipulated her; she would never do something so rash without a reason."

I nodded. "While I agree, we can't risk any bloodshed. I'm asking you to come with us because Rachel will need a friend. I may have been her boss, but we never had a close relationship. She will need you to reason with her to return home so we can protect her."

A whip of wicked desire sent a burning lust between my legs, causing my dick to swell.

Lucy went silent for a moment, clearly contemplating the information. She soon looked up, her dark eyes shining. "Okay, I'll help."

"Good. Please tell Jackson to take you back to the apartment. We'll return to New Orleans soon. Once preparations are in place, we leave for Europe."

Lucy nodded and then rose to exit the office. I leaned back against the chair and closed my eyes. I let my hand trail down to my slightly stiffened cock and growled softly.

With the window open behind me, I could hear every patron from the bar across from my Atlanta office stumbling drunkenly out into the late night. Scents of liquor, perfume, and lust lingered in the air, wafting through the breeze. I stood up and walked to the back wall, where I had the bar installed, grabbing an unopened bottle of Japanese whiskey from the top shelf. Now seated comfortably on a deep leather couch, I took another slow sip of the deep, smoky amber liquid.

While the burn of alcohol was welcoming, it couldn't take away the cold stone of my rage. I leaned back and stared at the ceiling as my left hand clenched into a fist. Thoughts of that night in the church, after that damned Hades Blood Moon—after Valentina rose from the dead, and they fled from us—filled my head.

Even though the tracker showed Rachel's coordinates, the guardian bond remained intact. I could still sense her fears and sadness, though the connection wasn't as strong as it was when we were closer to one another. It was as if she was pushing me out—unknowingly—and trying to sever the bond.

I knew I should have chased after her, even with her despicable mother just across the train tracks. I should have taken her, stolen her away after fucking her in that bathroom. But I was a coward, letting fear cloud my judgment.

I foolishly let her go.

Right now, I needed to hold on to the emotions I sensed from Rachel when she popped into my mind—the lust, the sadness, the pain—which were intertwined with mine. They all came with the bond transferred from Tony. I couldn't explain the strange sensation of Rachel existing in two planes—here with me but distant, like a ghost.

Tony and the coven had kept so much from her to keep her submissive and obedient. I smirked at that thought.

I leaned forward and refilled my tumbler with more whiskey. After taking another drink, I took out my phone and reopened the tracker app.

Zooming in on the map, I watched the little blue dot blink over a small building in Mira. I turned on the Google Earth feature and searched the grounds. It looked like a massive villa with several gardens and tall shrubs surrounding it. Rachel had been staying in that area since she'd arrived, coming and going throughout the day as she pleased.

I closed the app and clicked the phone icon. It hadn't taken long to extract Rachel's burner phone number. While Lucy prepared for her trip to see her mother, Meredith distracted her, snatched her phone, and found the number under a false name. She was careless. I tapped the number into my phone and pressed the call button.

I leaned back on the couch and swirled my glass clockwise.

Then I waited.

After thirty seconds, the call was transferred to an automatic voice, telling me to leave a message after the tone.

I hung up and tossed the phone on the table.

What the fuck am I doing? Why am I calling her when I need to catch her unaware?

My fingers reached for the phone again. I needed to hear Rachel's voice, even for a moment. The predator within me wanted to listen to her fear, her terror at the knowledge that I was one step ahead of her. She needed to know that it was only a matter of time before she'd see my face again.

Pushing aside the memory of her icy azure eyes and full, red lips, contorted in a mix of hate and pleasure, I redialed the number.

"Come on, my little dhampy," I whispered. "Pick up the damn phone."

CHAPTER 7

RACHEL

Okay, so the irritating trill wasn't a dream and was, in fact, my burner phone ringing. I rarely carried it with me, but I brought it when I went into town the day before. I only used it to check for messages from my mom to see if we needed to meet for training. Even when I called Lucy last month, I used the phone I kept stored away in my closet. We had an agreement for her safety that we would only call each other on the first and twentieth of every month. Until then, keep the phone hidden and powered off. It was too risky.

"Who the hell calls this early?" I groaned as I rolled over on the mattress, slamming my hand over the phone and dragging it to my sleepy eyes.

It was a U.S. phone number, and the area code was in Louisiana. My stomach iced over.

I knew I couldn't stay this far from home without talking to Lucy. She had promised to keep anyone from getting both my numbers, but I knew they would, eventually. She even had them saved on the phone as "Matt" to throw them off.

Not that they could track it—my number's area code belonged to a completely different country.

Still, I hoped Andrei had better things to do than call and beg for my location. He wasn't getting it. I buried my face in the pillow and groaned. At least he took four months to try. Privacy was fun while it lasted.

God fucking dammit.

I clicked the answer button, pulled my face from the downy fabric, and pressed the receiver to my ear.

There was only silence for a moment, and then it sounded like he was running his tongue over his lips. A tingle of nerves danced down my spine. "What the fuck do you want?"

I should hang up now.

There was another beat of silence before he replied, "You know what I want."

I swallowed. "You do realize it's six in the morning here, right? It's too early for this nonsense, Andrei. I need my beauty sleep."

Andrei chuckled, and I could hear him shift in a chair. "And you do realize I'm a vampire and don't sleep. It's not even midnight."

"Hmm. Sounds to me like you're bored and lonely," I said. "It was better this way."

"I miss you," he murmured, and my stomach clenched again. I never expected an admission like that. Nor did I believe it.

"Do you actually miss me, or does your dick miss his plaything now that it's gone ... or the ring?"

I flipped to my left side, waiting.

I really should hang up.

"Maybe both. I thought you could just come home and save us the trouble of me hopping on a plane and making my way to

Venice to take you back. Trust me, it would be far more pleasurable for me ... though I do *enjoy* chasing you."

My eyes widened, sleep no longer clinging to my brain. Even if Andrei had gotten my number from Lucy, there's no way he'd know my *exact* location. The guardian bond didn't work like that.

And even if it did, I, unfortunately, haven't found a way to break that magic. He has to agree to revoke the bond.

"How?" I asked, without even bothering to lie. "I mean, I figured you'd learn my whereabouts at some point, but not this soon. What did you do?"

I was met with silence and airwaves, more drawn out than before.

"Do you miss *me*?"

I laughed out loud and fell onto my back, staring at the ceiling. There was no way I could answer that truthfully. Sure, there were parts of Andrei I missed, but after he tried to kill my mother in the church and threw me aside for power, that snuffed out the good I thought I saw in him. But then again, given the horror Valentina inflicted on him and his family, was he justified?

What I felt for Andrei was confusing. It was very much lust-driven, but that kiss in the station bathroom ... I couldn't get it out of my mind.

I wish I hadn't fucking done it.

"Now, now. Surely, you didn't call me to discuss your *feelings*."

"Answer the question, love," he hummed. "Do you miss me?"

"Not really, no," I replied, yawning. "I'm finally free after two hundred years of lies, of being leashed and used. If you truly cared about me, you'd let me enjoy this freedom a bit longer before fucking it all up and taking it away from me."

No response. Just empty air.

"Right. That concludes the talk about feelings." I didn't know why I was still entertaining this phone call, but something stuck with me. "Did you actually care about me?" I asked. "Was I more than just an assignment or a good fuck to you?"

Andrei moaned that time. Truthfully, it was more like a growl.

This fucking man. Jesus Christ.

"Of course, you're more than that," he answered. "But what's wrong with craving you in the most filthy, diabolical ways? No matter what you call this, whether love or lust, the results are the same. You wanted me, I wanted you, and we were damn good at it."

"That's because you had all the control over me. You forced me to sign a contract to work with you and manipulated a deal to become my guardian. You wanted to have a firm grasp on me at all times." I paused. "Not to mention there's something else you want from me now." My right thumb rubbed the underside of my index finger, delicately circling the bronze metal of Valentina's ring. The obsidian glinted in the light, and while I could still see the veins of red within, they weren't as bright as they were in the church.

Like it's sleeping, the eerie thought clanged in my head. I tapped the speaker icon on the phone and set it on the nightstand, closing my eyes.

"That's where you're wrong, little dhampy. There are a *few* things I want from you," he replied. "What I want most right now is to bend you over and fuck that disobedient attitude right out of you."

Oh fuck.

It felt like something pulled my breath from my lungs, drying out my throat in the process. Suddenly, my body flooded with heat, and a tingling sensation rippled through my core.

"I want to remind you how good I can make you feel...." he purred. "And now that I can hear your voice and you hear mine, our bond just got a lot more interesting. You see ... Black Onyx ensured I knew all the ins and outs of the guardian bond. It seems there's more to it that the others didn't take advantage of. I thought I'd play around with it to see if it works."

Even more intense arousal burned through me like a cage of passionate flame.

What ... what the fuck is going on?

My legs clenched together, and I slid my hand down my belly to in between my thighs. I began to caress myself in lazy circles above the fabric of my linen pajama shorts. It was like my body separated itself from my mind and acted of its own accord. It was doing what it wanted, what it *needed*.

The logical part of my mind realized what was happening.

No, that's not possible.

"What are you doing?" I stammered, my hand now sliding under the waistband and resting on the thin lace of my panties. My fingers were itching to go further, to touch my growing wetness. My pussy was practically aching at that point. "How the *fuck* are you doing that?"

My breath grew heavy as my stomach twisted into something else. Andrei's deep, smoky voice, laced with those damned hedonistic purrs, was driving me over the edge. He was conjuring a dark storm of lust inside me, taking away my control over anything.

"Tony was a damn fool not to use this bond's power with you," he whispered. "I can feel your desire so much better now. My guess is that this contingency was set in place if you decided to go rogue and they needed your guardian to reel you back in."

"Bullshit. That's not how the bond works," I said. "It has a limited power range and can't work at this far away ... not like *this.*"

Or could it? With every guardian they'd assign to me, I tested those limits. The only time we felt each other was if we were in the same city.

This should be impossible.

Not only that, but I hadn't felt Andrei once since we left the train station. Not fucking once.

But what he was doing now was something I never thought possible. Our voices somehow linked our emotions together, as if he was right beside me.

Even as I pondered if this was real or just a dream, a sense of peace swallowed me whole, and my desire to be fucked by Andrei overtook any sense of morality.

"Fascinating, isn't it?" he asked, as if he'd read my thoughts. "I can push through the bond just by hearing your voice. Maybe it comes more naturally to us because your mother is my maker, and you are her daughter, along with the fact that you and I have shared blood. It enhanced the power of the bond altogether. Your feelings are mine, and mine are yours. You just have to tap into it and give yourself to me."

I didn't want to believe it, but Andrei could have been right. Tony and other guardians in the past had only ever been able to know my location but never my emotional state. Tony would have felt my terror when Andrei attacked me in the alley and came running if we were emotionally bound. Anger swept through me. Those damned witches only cared about where I was, never about how I was feeling. They didn't care that their little experiment was drowning.

"Focus on me, Rachel," Andrei hissed. "Ignore those witches and obey *me*. Go on, love. I know you want to...." His voice melted like honey, smothering my anger with more desire. Dangerous. Inviting.

"Fuck. You." I gritted my teeth. He was right. No matter how wrong it felt, I wanted to do it, and I wasn't strong enough to resist his urging. Slowly, I moved my fingers beneath my panties and between my legs. I prodded between my folds but resisted entering. Not yet.

"That's my good, needy girl," Andrei hummed. "Now, tell me, how wet are you for me?"

I squirmed, drawing my bottom lip into my teeth as I finally slid one finger inside of me. Slowly, at first, but the second thrust was more forceful. The pleasure that surged through me was so intense that I wanted it to stop. But I couldn't—until I found my release.

My thumb pressed against my clit, and my hips bucked up with the sharp shock of pleasure.

"I want an answer," he demanded. "Tell me how wet you are for me."

The rational part of me wanted to tell him to go fuck himself and hang up, but when I opened my mouth, all that came out was a breathy, "So fucking wet."

I could hear the snick of a button coming free and a zipper being dragged down. A groan echoed through the speaker. "Fuck yourself for me harder," he ordered low in his throat. "I want to hear you whimper my name as you touch that perfect pussy."

I knew he was stroking his cock, imagining himself thrusting inside of me and filling me up with his length. What was worse was that I was imagining the same, too. In my mind, he was on top of me, pinning me down with his muscular body. He had my legs thrown over his shoulders, and his chest pressed against mine as he slammed himself into me—again and again.

My breathing hitched on the image, and I bit my lower lip harder to keep the moans from escaping. I wouldn't give Andrei the satisfaction of hearing them. My rational side kept shouting for me to hang up. I *needed* to shut this call down and destroy the phone. But this arousal, this ... feeling was too good to sever. Not yet, at least. Not until I got what I wanted, too.

My fingers were no longer sufficient to bring me release, so with my free hand, I opened the drawer of my nightstand and pulled out a small vibrator. I'd purchased it for moments of loneliness that inevitably came, but I didn't think I'd be using it for *this.*

I clicked on the device, and a soft hum filled my ears. A low chuckle floated through the phone speaker. "What did I tell you? Only I can satisfy you, darling. Put that thing away."

I didn't deign to give him a response. Instead, I slid my hand away and replaced it with the vibrating silicone. My entire body shuddered at the increased intensity, my back arching as I closed my eyes.

"Oh God," I moaned, letting myself drown in the intensity of pleasure that rippled in waves. The image in my mind's eye became more real, and I swore I felt his body on top of mine.

"Your moans are going to make me come undone right here in my office," Andrei said. It seemed like he was getting close, too. "Fuck, Rachel. Fuck that tight pussy for me. I want to hear you come for me."

"I hate you," I said, but my voice lost its fierceness; it was only breathy and light. I was drowning in the pleasure and the sound of his voice in my head. The bond was pouring his feelings into mine, overtaking me. I was on the brink.

"You're such a liar, baby. Quit pretending like you don't crave my cock sliding into you and pounding you as I claim you as mine. Every single time."

"I don't. I will never be yours. The first chance I get, I'm ripping your goddamn head off. Then I'll finally be free of you," I retorted. The image became solidified, connecting us as he fucked me, and neither of us would last much longer. My body was shaking beneath his, and I felt him throbbing with each thrust.

"As long as I get to bury myself inside of you first, I don't mind dying," Andrei muttered between heavy breaths.

That was what tipped me over the edge, and my orgasm ripped through me so strongly that I dropped the toy, pressing my ass into the bunched-up blankets. The waves of pleasure dragged on and on. I decided to see if whatever the fuck was going on would allow me to do the same to him, drawing up an image in my own mind. Now, I was on top, riding his face as I came a second time, and it was his tongue that took me past the point of no return. I no longer held back my groans.

"Fuck," Andrei cursed, followed by a slight groan. He found his release as well, his sharp nails digging into my arm until I winced. "I need my hands wrapped around your throat, love. I need to *watch* you come the next time I take you."

"There will never be a next time. We are *done.* "I blinked, and the vision began to dwindle. "Leave me alone, leave my mother alone, and let it go." I sighed and ended the call, but looked at the call log before I set it down.

Shit. Lucy called me three times on this phone. She never does that. Well, I have a pretty good idea of why she's calling.

It was too risky to call her back now. *Fuck.* I dropped myself onto the mattress and looked up. That was when I felt the sting on my arm, and I looked over. The scratch marks from my vision were still there, slowly healing, as if Andrei had really done it.

I must have done that myself.

My breath felt heavy, and I lifted my shirt, suddenly feeling a burn on my stomach.

I placed my hand on the rune that had etched itself onto my stomach shortly after we fled Boston. I hadn't told my mother about it yet, not until I could figure out what the hell it meant.

Sighing, I shut my eyes, as if they would shield me from the reality of what had happened. The bond was stronger now, especially when we talked. That was fucking clear. Andrei knew I was at least in Venice, but did he know exactly where? His image was still in my mind, but it shifted as my fingers gingerly traced the rune symbol on my stomach. Andrei's dark brown eyes blurred, and sparkling emerald-green ones replaced them.

Someone else replaced Andrei.

Jase.

Ugh, not again.

CHAPTER 8

RACHEL

Falling back asleep was no longer an option, so I stared at the ceiling instead, replaying what Andrei had done during that phone call and what I had seen after I hung up. I pressed the heels of my palms into my eyes, trying to rub away the sleepiness and frustration out of them.

Slowly, I threw the blankets off and swung my legs over the side of the bed, feeling the soft fibers of the carpet beneath my feet.

Everything felt so real in the vision.

Andrei somehow used the guardian bond to get inside my head. His words pulled me into a vivid sexual fantasy, taunting and teasing me until I was soaking wet and aching. Shaking my head, I walked over to my dresser and pulled open a drawer to grab a black T-shirt, shorts, and a sports bra. As I dressed, a different face once again flashed across my vision.

Jase.

My *true* enemy. The one who tried to kill me and Valentina. Though we managed to escape that bastard, it still felt like his presence was always with me. It differed from the connection with Andrei. He felt like a tether in my head, waiting to be pulled.

Jase ... Jase felt like he was always by my side, a constant ghost. What happened after that vision wasn't the first time he'd popped into my head.

It was frustrating, to say the least. I wondered if it was because I couldn't stop thinking about how Jase had been stalking me for four fucking years. Every time I thought about that, how he had watched me, made my skin crawl. He was the nightmare I wanted to escape from ... *not* Andrei.

After brushing my teeth and splashing my face with cold water, I stepped out of my bedroom. I headed down the hall toward the kitchen, turned on the coffeemaker, and grabbed two frozen waffles from the freezer. When they popped from the toaster, I put them on a small plate, poured a large mug of coffee, and settled down at the table.

As I chewed on a piece of waffle, nerves retook hold of my stomach, turning the food into glue in my mouth. I swallowed the thick lump painfully and sipped my coffee. I was too on edge. The all-too-real phone call left me shaken, and I couldn't relax.

I turned my arm over to see where Andrei's nails had dug in. The skin was smooth now, but those angry red scratches from earlier weren't a dream. The guardian bond had *changed*. No fucking way it was like this before. Tony and I never had the connection be strong enough to where he could physically touch me down the bond. If Andrei had found a way to exploit a previously unknown feature, I would never sleep peacefully again.

Jesus fucking Christ, I'm fucked.

I took another large bite of waffle, and the sweet flavor eased my mind a little. The sound of a hedge trimmer came through the curtained window. It was going to be another beautiful summer day in Venice.

Venice ... I thought about what Andrei had told me. Did he really know where I was, or was this just a warning from my subconscious? I could have also caused the scratches in my sleep.

I'll check the call log again when I turn the phone back on later today.

When I finished my waffles and coffee, I carried the dishes to the sink to wash. Valentina spent the evening reinforcing the existing protection spells after we arrived and other security runes around the grounds. She knew we were intruding on Darius's space, so she wanted to ensure that no one here would be in danger because of us.

It would take enormous magic to shatter the spells around the villa. Valentina said she often used the same spells to repel hunters during the thousand years she roamed until Maurice stole the ring.

My thoughts returned to the intense vision from earlier as I continued to lather the dish sponge with soap. Although Andrei was still in my head, I couldn't get Jase out. Was Andrei fucking with me? Why was I seeing his bastard brother so clearly? Since I drank Jase's blood at the church, it was as if his existence seeped into me. The way his arms wrapped around me as I drank his blood, the smell of him, the taste of him on my lips. How was it that someone like *him* could have such an impact on me? My initial impulse was to tell Valentina, but things between us had become pretty intense over the last couple of months.

At first, we bonded. She'd take me around Venice for a few nights and show me where she and my father frequented, including a hideaway wine bar with an incredible selection.

But all she'd been talking about lately was the Black Onyx and how the Amavasya's Tear would bring them down. Her entire focus had been on that fucking stone, and I'd have to be an idiot not to see what it was doing to her.

Footsteps from the hallway that led into the kitchen perked my ears, but I was too wrapped up in my thoughts to acknowledge who walked in.

Did the witches of Black Onyx and Lemurian deserve to die? Maybe.... except now Valentina's obsession with killing all of them and destroying magic was getting a little too extreme. For fuck's sake, she gets revived, has her daughter again, and has access to her magic. If it were me, I'd be thrilled and focused on building a relationship with my child. Since we arrived, she hadn't asked about my life or interests other than learning what the coven did with me.

This is all too fucking weird.

"Earth to Rachel?" Luka's voice broke my train of thought, and I looked over my shoulder at him, holding a mug. I hadn't even noticed he poured himself some coffee. "Where'd your head go? I've been saying your name for over a minute. Did Gio give you a concussion yesterday?"

Shaking my head, I turned off the hot water, letting my thoughts dissipate with the steam. Then I refilled my cup. Sitting back at the table, I leaned against the chair, stretching my neck. Luka often joined me in the mornings for coffee before we parted for the day, whether going to the training facility, the library, or venturing into the city. Today, however, we had something planned together.

"Seriously?" he asked, smirking at me. "What gives?"

"Sorry." I yawned. "I slept like shit last night."

Luka shot me a skeptical look before taking a sip. So, I changed the subject.

"God, I love coffee, but I can never get the full pick-me-up that a human can, no matter how much I drink. Is it the same for you?" I asked.

Our alcohol and caffeine metabolism surpassed humans', but as we weren't fully vampires, we still needed rest to recharge. We could also gain a sense of functionality with the tasty bean juice. Lucy liked to joke that she could drink two cups of coffee and nap right after. Every year, her grandmother, or "Mita," as she called her, would visit, bringing the most amazing Colombian coffee I'd ever tasted, grown on her family's farm. Honestly, I had a hard time comparing any other brand after that.

God, I miss my best friend.

Luka offered his usual charming smile. "I can drink up to five cups of coffee a day and not feel a damn thing. But, weirdly, it does help curb my cravings when it gets close to when I need to feed. Vodka also helps."

I laughed, raising my mug to him. "Cheers, then."

As I lowered my mug, Valentina walked into the kitchen. She opened the fridge and pulled out a blood bag.

"Morning," I said.

"Good morning, ma'am," Luka added.

Valentina nodded before tearing open the bag and starting to drink. I could see the grimace on her face; she hated consuming cold blood, but she refused to hurt a human. Each time, she clutched her stomach as if she might throw up, often needing to cast the anti-nausea spell. Valentina was trying, but I knew it was only a matter of time before cold blood wouldn't be enough.

Warming the blood beforehand could help, I theorized in my thoughts. *We'll try that next time.*

Valentina had become a lot more secretive since we came to the villa. She would disappear with Darius for hours as soon as night fell, usually when everyone in the house had left to hunt or drink. It was always the same whenever I tried to sense her intention: veiled and elusive, even when she was trying to teach me magic.

Which I still hadn't learned how to fucking control properly, goddammit. Valentina's lessons were insightful.... I just couldn't put them into practice the way she wanted me to.

As Valentina sat at the table, Luka offered her a slight bow of his head. "I spoke with Darius about today's schedule," she said.

"Does he want us back on the mats for training tonight?" Luka asked. Valentina still looked serious, but her eyes were relieved.

Something had changed in the last few days.

"Yes, you'll get a chance to eat, go about your day, and then report at seven," she replied. "Before you go, though, Rachel, I'd like to speak with you."

"About what?" I asked dryly. *Here we go.*

"Aside from some magic study, your black eye from yesterday." She tapped a long nail on the tabletop.

I scrunched my face. "Gio just got the upper hand, that's all," I explained, trying not to show annoyance. Valentina was pointing out my flaws *again.* "Come on. It healed in less than an hour. I'll do better next time."

"See that you do," she said coolly. "You can't allow anyone to land a blow, not even for a moment. I know you're used to fighting against witches, and that knowledge is more than beneficial. But you need to hold your own against every kind of opponent. You can't get knocked down."

My temper flared at the implication. While I understood Valentina wanting to prepare me to fight against the covens, she was putting too much damn pressure on me. If I wasn't as strong as she wanted me to be after *two hundred* years of fighting against witches, how in the hell would training with the other dhampirs change her opinion?

"Yeah, I'm aware of your 'expectations,'" I said with air quotes. "You don't need to remind me every goddamn day."

There was a heavy silence, and Luka shifted uncomfortably in his seat before he stood. "Alright, that's my cue. I'll let you guys finish talking." He raised his eyebrows at me. "I'll meet you out front when you're ready." He bowed to Valentina and left the kitchen, leaving us alone.

I wish the ground would swallow me whole right about now.

Valentina ran her hand through her shining red hair and finished the last of her blood bag, swallowing back a gag. God, she looked so human, so typical, that you'd never think she was the progenitor of the vampire race. She, or those acting on her behalf, committed so many atrocities. When Kylan had turned Valentina, he collared her with Lucifer's ring and set her loose, letting her untamed appetite run rampant across the world. She became an uncontrollable, immortal monster.

But with how utterly bitchy she had become since we arrived at the villa, that was the only thing I had seen. Valentina's temperament was all over the place. One minute, she was kind and helpful; the next, she scolded me for my mistakes. It was like the two powers within her raged constantly, even without the ring's influence.

Maybe she's just a shitty mother.

Finally, Valentina leaned back in her chair, nails tapping on the damn table again. She wouldn't stop looking at me.

She wanted me to speak first.

I cleared my throat. "Luka and I are going into the city to grab some breakfast and supplies for the training room: hand wraps, towels, and things like that. Do you need anything?"

She didn't answer. From the slight wrinkle between her brows, it looked like my mother was trying to read my mind even though the ring prevented her from doing so.

I wonder why she still tries to do that.

"What's going on with you and Luka?" she asked, raising a brow. "You seem awfully fond of one another. *Too* fond."

"Wow," I said, sliding out of my chair, but she gripped my wrist as I moved past her. Hard. Slowly, I turned to face her, letting out a sigh. "Luka's gay. So, you can stop worrying that I'll be distracted and not do the job you seem keen on me doing."

As she stood to tower over me, I yanked my arm away.

"Oh, and just in case it hasn't clicked yet, I've been alone for a really, really long time. No one has ever understood me like Luka, Ava, and Giovanni. No matter how hard you try, you can't even comprehend what I've been through. And frankly, it's none of your goddamn business. So, if you place your hand on me again, I won't give a fuck how special you are to everyone behind these walls. To you, I'm just a child who still needs my mommy. But here's the thing: I may be *your* child, but I'm not *a* child. Never grab me like that again, or you'll see how I treat those who do."

Valentina's eyes went wide. We had been dancing around each other for weeks now. I knew she was up to something and holding back plans that she and Darius had, but her lack of drinking from the vein made her dangerous. It was only a matter of time before something pissed her off enough, and she'd snap.

As we stared each other down, Valentina's expression softened, and she stepped back. "I'm sorry. You're right. Just … just be careful," she warned.

I couldn't help but smile at that. Valentina, acting like a concerned parent, was comical. Yet I appreciated her trying to be better than her demon moniker.

"When you train with Gio again, focus on overcoming his abilities, not his strength. He's a dhampir of Earth magic, so you must counter him with Water. That's how you beat him."

I knew what I had to do, but knowing and doing were two different things. Gio fought like the ground was a part of him. My magic slipped through my fingers whenever I tried to harness it. While I could conjure up the power during training, it didn't come naturally to me as it did to the others. I couldn't control the flow.

"You inherited my magic, Rachel," she continued, as if she'd read my doubts. "You need to harness *and* control that power for what's coming. Soon, I'll tell you everything, and we'll be ready to leave this place. But I need to see the change in you before I send you out there."

She needed proof I was ready. *Sorry to disappoint you, Mom.*

I nodded, but doubt still lingered. Understanding wasn't the problem—becoming what Valentina needed me to be was.

She moved aside so I could walk past her. "I'll be back at six," I said. "Gio can wait until later."

The run from Mira onto the island of Venice was always a great way to clear my head and test my speed against Luka's. No matter how fast he was, I always beat him. He said out of every dhampir from that academy, I was the fastest one yet, and that definitely boosted my ego.

After Luka and I went to the Rialto Market and grabbed the training supplies, we sprinted over to Giardini Savorgnan, the park on the other side of the canal. We found a secluded spot, unfolded the blanket we had brought with us, and sat facing each other.

Once settled, I let my fingers brush over the blanket, focusing on the softness under my touch as I started grounding myself.

"You need to focus more today," Luka started. "I know you're distracted by how your mom has been treating you, but I can't keep fighting her off." He reached out and took my hand. "She's been attempting to read my thoughts ever since she saw us hanging out, suspecting something."

"And you've been able to kick her out every time?" I asked, and he answered with a single nod.

In the 1700s, Luka's mother, Ana, left Croatia to join a new coven. When they were turned into vampires against their will, they had no choice but to form a clan called the Daughters of Dusk, with her being the only member born a Spirit witch.

Her telekinesis abilities allowed her to repel anyone attempting to mind-read. Oddly enough, his abilities were very similar to Valentina's, and he discovered he could use compulsion just like her. Luka wondered if his vampire heritage played a role in that. So, when we started practicing, he instructed me to use my vampiric power as a source for the shield and then add my magic once I learned how to control it.

"It's only a matter of time before she uses her abilities to force me to remove the ring," I reminded him. "At this rate, I won't be strong enough to stop her."

"That's what you have me for," Luka said. "Now, just as we have been practicing since you approached me … focus. Until now, we have had limited ability to breach the walls between our minds. I think you should consider removing the ring."

I looked down at my hand and shook my head. "I can't. If I do, she'll feel her powers vanish and think something happened. She will react … *badly.*"

"But if we don't, you can't truly feel what I'm doing, so you can resist it properly. The more practice you have, the easier it will be when your mother tries to do it to you. You can say you went to a safe place to remove it to give your hand a break or something."

Removing the ring, even in this secluded place, held risks. I felt too vulnerable without it on. But if I didn't learn …

"Okay," I said, swallowing down my nerves. "We'll have a twenty-minute window after Valentina senses what's wrong and sends one of the human guards to come find us." I looked up at the brilliant blue sky before meeting his gaze. "She can't exactly come out into the sun herself."

I slipped the ring off, placed it between us, and closed my eyes. The sudden shift in the atmosphere caused my hair to dance in the wind, a swirl of power surrounding us. Luckily, we were alone in the garden so that no humans could get caught up in the spell.

Italy differed from the United States in terms of acceptance of the supernatural. We didn't have to hide our powers because of the fear of the government charging into the park and killing us. As long as the magic never touched civilians, they left everyone alone.

They didn't know dhampirs existed, so if anyone witnessed this, they'd assume we were witches.

However, if Valentina or Darius were to catch us, we'd be fucked.

Luka's hands reached out and gently touched my temples. I felt his powers come through, reaching deep into my mind to take control.

"Move your hands to the right," he commanded. I felt the desire to listen, but I fought back. It wasn't the same power Valentina had. I wasn't a puppet on a string, obeying at will, but the desire leached into my thoughts, morphing into my own to obey.

"No!" I seethed, pushing back against his magic as the surrounding void strengthened. The beast within me roared, agitated by the intrusive magic. I loosened her reins, letting the vampire power trickle into my mind. I opened my eyes and saw the effect of the magic. The bubble of power was translucent, thinly veiled with dust, and loose grass kicked up from the earth. Its energy kept us pinned so that outside sources couldn't interrupt us.

"Move your hands to the right. Now!" he ordered again. My hands twitched a little, and I fed more of my vampire self into my mind, willing a solid dark-blue wave of power to shove his away.

"Fuck you," I said with a smirk. Luka let out a slight chuckle and gripped my still-twitching right hand.

"You're losing control. Pull yourself back," he instructed. "Fight the compulsion. Forget about everything else. Fight it, Rachel."

My vampiric beast grinned wickedly in my head, but I shoved it aside and pushed harder and harder. Finally, Luka's magic broke apart with a jolt, and the compulsion to obey disappeared. Taking a deep breath, I slipped the ring back on, feeling the slight hum of power moving back into me.

Even now, the ring doesn't seem to stir so much.

"Well, goddamn," Luka said, letting go of my hands. "You did it."

"This is only the start. I have to be one hundred percent perfect on this."

I turned and looked at my phone, noting the time. "When are you meeting Alex?" I asked.

Luka blushed. "A few hours. He took the day off from the cafe to head into the city with me."

"Have you thought about telling him you're half-vampire?" I asked.

Luka nodded. "Every day. He's often told me about his acceptance of the supernatural world, but I'm too afraid he'll slip up and tell someone I'm something else. I don't need that wrath from Darius if I fuck up." He shifted and crossed his legs to get comfortable. "Just like you, we've worked hard to stay hidden. What's a few more years until we can do it right and announce to the world that vampires can have children?"

CHAPTER 9

VALENTINA

Darius's rough palm slid up my bare thigh, marveling at the smooth skin like it was a precious marble sculpture. His hazel eyes looked up at me, his gaze full of lust and desire.

"Don't stop there," I teased, biting the left side of my bottom lip. The house was empty tonight, making it easier to fool around without drawing attention. It wasn't against the rules to be fucking each other, but it would make things ... complicated.

While Rachel and Luka were off in the city doing God knows what, Tati and Alessandro were off to hunt and feed. Gio and Ava went to try a new restaurant that had opened near the eastern canals.

I thought about the vampires who lived here. I envied their ability to feed without losing themselves to the beast that lived within our kind. Hunting fueled me for centuries—the thrill of the chase was the most satisfying part of a kill. It made me feel alive and powerful, like the apex predator Kylan had made me into. But I hoped for the day when I could hunt again without killing someone.

I was so tired of needless death by my hand.

I need practice—an anchor to hold me so I don't lose myself in the blood frenzy. It's been too long.

Darius lowered his head, running his tongue over my wet core before giving it a gentle kiss. My brows furrowed together with the pulse of pleasure that coursed through me. But instead of continuing, he paused. "We need to talk," he said. I huffed, flopping back onto the mattress. Frustration creeping over me, I stared at the ceiling.

He can't be serious. Right now?

"I told you that I don't believe Rachel is ready." Raising myself on my elbows, I watched Darius shifting positions between my legs. His fingers slowly entered me, and my thighs opened wider, allowing him more access to the place that desired his *full* attention. "She removed the ring today, Darius. She said it was because some dirt got under the band, irritating her skin. But it was still careless. She trains in your gym every morning, yet she's nowhere close to where I believe she'd be ready to take orders and fight for our cause. Frankly, she's disappointing me."

Darius laughed, his fingers stroking me. "That's a bit harsh. She's your daughter."

I shrugged one shoulder nonchalantly. "I'm not trying to be harsh, but the Black Onyx were the ones to train her. They limited her to what they *wanted* her to know. Not what she was capable of. The last thing they probably wanted was for Rachel to use her magic against them someday. She'll get there, though, I'm sure. I think Luka's been training her outside of the gym. They're together a lot."

He nodded, his pace increasing slightly and making me gasp. "We're getting closer," he said. "The witch spies I've sent to infiltrate Black Onyx and Lemurian Quartz have already made contact. Of course, they'll have to go through initiation rituals; they'll be subjected to a series of humiliating and dangerous tasks to prove their 'loyalty.' They may have to offer blood, but that's not something to worry about. The witches can handle it."

"And you trust them?" I asked, my left leg trailing over his broad shoulder.

I had never made allies within covens worldwide. The distrust was swift and immediate. I disrupted the balance of life and death by creating undead creatures who killed without remorse. Why would they trust me?

When I took my life after Kylan fed me his blood and reawakened me as a vampire, he only stayed with me long enough to ensure I completed the transition and gave me Lucifer's ring, binding me to his control. After that, he disappeared, and I was all alone. My new predatory instincts drove me to slaughter or turn hundreds of humans. It wasn't until the ring's power over me weakened and some of my humanity returned that I learned to control my instincts. Still, that night in Fiskardo, where genuine remorse had stirred within my dead heart, unsettled me deeply. Though I didn't want to become this *monster,* I enjoyed not feeling guilty for my actions. I *enjoyed* the kill.

Darius gave me a slight shrug, now far more focused on how my insides clenched around his fingers than our conversation. He had his priorities straight; I gave him that. I raised my hips to meet his slow thrusts. The man knew how to hit the right spots.

"Well ..." Tipping my head back, I breathed, "Maybe we can discuss this later. We only have about an hour before the others come home. And I'd rather put our time to better use."

Darius smiled at me but said nothing. He didn't have to—his hands told me everything I needed to know. Darius wanted to pleasure me, and I couldn't argue against that. My teeth sank into my bottom lip as he quickened his pace, the strokes becoming merciless in the way he rammed them inside me. Bliss tingled over my body, growing stronger with every passing second.

"More," I commanded. "Give me more."

He obeyed immediately. It only took him a moment to remove his hand that gripped my thigh, so he could reach for his zipper and pull out his cock. His fingers were doing a fantastic job, but I needed to feel his length inside me. My core pulsed at the sight, eager for release. Darius gave himself a few strokes of encouragement before settling between my legs. He then slammed into my tight pussy.

"Oh, fuck!" I cried out, digging my nails into his back. "Harder."

He pulled out and slammed back in. A ripple of pain spread through me, causing my eyes to roll upward. The roughness of his force was delicious. God, I had forgotten what it felt like to fuck another vampire until I found Darius again.

The threads of guilt were tugging at me, though, and pulling my thoughts to over two hundred years ago. I tried to ignore it while Darius continued to fuck me, but my mind went to *that* day, regardless.

Darius and I had been intimate for a few months after that night in the taverna before deciding it was best to end things and focus on saving dhampir children. A year later, he introduced me to Cyrus, whom I initially thought of as a weak human in over his head. Cyrus later volunteered to be my blood supplier under Darius's supervision, and we quickly bonded over our shared interests in exploration, literature, and wine. Before long, I fell in love with him—against all odds, I, the scourge of all that was good, had found my mate. When the Fool's New Moon approached, Cyrus agreed to perform the ritual with me, thrilled at the thought of being a father, while I eagerly looked forward to raising our child together.

"Valentina," Darius sighed into my ear, dispelling my thoughts. His chest pressed against mine, our bodies flush. The way Darius took me was perfect, but he would never make me feel alive like Cyrus did. It was just the truth. "Your pussy belongs to me. You feel so fucking good."

Such vulgar, filthy words made my body shudder.

A slight, shaky breath escaped my lips, and the pleasure rolling through me stole my words. Darius gripped my hip and lifted me into the angle I loved, hitting that sensitive spot deep within me. Somehow, my mind released those old memories, and I wrapped my legs around his hips. Each thrust burned in the most delicious way, filling me up and drowning me in euphoria. As Darius picked up speed, my body tingled all the way up my spine. My head fell back. It was easy to lose yourself in this ecstasy.

It didn't matter that I didn't love him like Cyrus; Darius knew how to fuck.

Still pressed against me, he allowed me to dig my nails into his muscular back. I scratched down the cool flesh, piercing deep until he bled. He groaned, and the intensity of his thrusts increased to maddening levels, mixing our pleasure with pain. The room filled with the scent of blood, laced with desperation and something darker—something raw and hungry.

"So ... fucking ... perfect ..." He groaned loudly, tensing above me. He was close—I could feel it. The roughness of his grip aroused me more. I was trembling, my mind swirling, and it only took a few more thrusts for us to reach that peak together. My orgasm seized me in a wave, and I moaned as my fangs slid from my gums. Without a word, I sank my teeth into Darius's neck, savoring the richness of his blood as I came. I didn't ask for permission because I knew the answer.

"Oh, God! Valentina!" he cried out, trying to pull away from me as I drank. Our agreement not to share blood no longer mattered. I had to have his. I *needed* it. It tasted like rich, intoxicating nectar against my tongue. It made me feel so damn alive, and I wouldn't stop until I had my fill.

When Darius relaxed and allowed the euphoria of the bite, he collapsed against me.

After a few more seconds, I retracted my fangs and licked my lips. Darius slowly lifted his body from mine, using his palms to create space. His hazel eyes stared into mine as the wounds on his neck and back stitched closed. Beneath the haze after coming, there was a feral hunger there.

"Why deny ourselves?" I purred, tilting my head to the side. "Drink from me."

He shook his head. "We agreed—"

"I don't fucking care," I said. My eyes glowed icy blue. "I said, 'Drink from me.'"

Darius looked down at my pale, exposed neck and nodded slightly. His fangs emerged, and he bit down on the soft spot between my neck and shoulder.

My God.

The bite, albeit sharp and painful, soon vanished as vampiric euphoria took over my mind. Every inch of me came alive as he drank. As I felt Darius's cum drip between my legs, I squeezed his hips with my knees.

"That's right," I whispered. "Drink, my darling."

When vampires fed from me, their control would slip, so I knew I'd have to pry Darius off … but for now, this was what I wanted. I arched against him, biting my lower lip as he drank.

Though I felt rejuvenated from *his* blood, something shifted in my energy. He was draining me, causing my head to spin out of control. I tried to move, but my body struggled to respond. "You're taking too much. Enough."

Darius shook his head and grabbed my wrists, slamming them back onto the mattress to keep me pinned beneath him. He growled against my skin, lining his cock back against my pussy. He was more animalistic than coherent and had no intention of stopping.

Shit.

"Darius, that's enough!" I shouted, channeling my compulsion into my throat. Using my Water magic, I coated my wrist in ice, allowing me to slip free. I slammed my fist into his chest, cracking his sternum. The force caused Darius to release his fangs and fly off the bed, hitting the wall across the bedroom.

I jumped to my feet, eyes now burning red and fangs bared.

Darius scrambled to his knees, hands lifted in a pleading gesture. "I'm … I'm sorry. I told you this was a bad idea," he said, slowly standing. "Your blood does something to me. What we did was too reckless."

Though my temper still simmered inside me, I smiled and walked over to him, placing my hand against his cheek. "It gives you some of my vampire power. But it can also unleash the beastly nature of our predatory selves. If we are to win against the witches, you will need this power. However, if you don't get control of yourself while you drink from me, I can't promise not to punish you for it. This is your only warning. From now on, you will drink from me when I demand it, and I with you, and you will control yourself."

Darius, with fear still evident in his eyes, nodded.

"Good boy."

CHAPTER 10

RACHEL

Early the next day, Darius sent a text message to everyone in the villa, asking them to meet in the conference room within the hour. I groaned, irritated by the fact I couldn't sleep in again. So, I quickly showered and threw on a pair of jean shorts and a black-and-white T-shirt before heading to the main house.

Since Darius ran his art restoration business from home, he renovated the house's east wing into an office. Two smaller rooms were a studio and a lounge; the largest room had a projection screen and a table at least twelve feet long. Some nights, Darius would host a "family dinner" in that conference room since it could accommodate all of us.

When I walked in, Ava, Luka, and Gio had already taken a seat at the far end, closest to the wall. The moment I plopped down in my chair, Ava slid a mug of coffee over to me. I was half tempted to kiss her for it, taking a slow sip.

"What's going on?" I asked, my eyes fixed on Alessandro and Tati, the pure-blood vampires, as they walked into the room and settled into their chairs. Tati greeted us with a cheerful wave, her pink lips curving into a smile. Beside her, Alessandro looked much different; his bloodshot eyes and dark circles made him look like he hadn't fed in days. They had hunted the night before, but clearly it wasn't enough.

"Darius wanted to speak with us ... *all* of us," Valentina said as she walked into the room. The vampires and dhampirs rose to their feet and bowed to her.

I stayed seated.

Darius rarely gathered the family in the house outside of the dinners and had been too busy over the last month with "business," as he'd explained. I shifted uncomfortably.

"Yeah, something's going on. He never does this," Ava whispered, tucking her black hair behind her ear. Her curvy frame was tense, her shoulders rigid, like she was bracing for something.

Avaline Jean-Claire was originally from Versailles, France. Her mother, Juliette, was one of the first to undergo the fertility spell. Unfortunately, when the coven attacked the academy, she and Ava's father died protecting her, leaving Darius and his witch allies to help her develop her Fire magic after they moved into the villa.

Ava was an exceptional magic wielder, and her ability to manipulate flames into animals was the most incredible gift I had ever seen. My personal favorite was when she crafted a giant wolf from red fire. She lovingly named the beast "Guillaume" after her favorite romance.

Luka opened his mouth to speak, but the door swung open, and Darius strode in, the murmurs dying off. He was wearing a suit, which was unusual for him—a sleek black suit with a light-blue shirt underneath.

He had even trimmed his beard.

"Sorry, guys. I know meeting on a Saturday morning is inconvenient, especially for the humans. But a lot has happened in the last twenty-four hours."

Darius sat at the head of the table, and everyone fell silent. As he clicked on the projector, Valentina took a seat on his left, placing her hand on his arm. She and Darius had become so close over the past few months, and I didn't know how to feel about that. Valentina seemed to agree with everything he said, no matter how unethical it sounded and demanded that we follow suit. It was so fucking aggravating.

Now that Darius had everyone's attention, he pulled a small remote from his pocket and opened a slide on the white projection screen behind him. The image of an old oil painting appeared. It was of a female angel with blindingly white wings spread wide, and her golden hair flowed down to her hips. An aura behind the angel shimmered like fallen snow in the twilight. The painting was beautiful, but I could tell that it couldn't fully capture that woman's radiance.

"We're going to be reviewing a bit of history today," Darius started. There were a few teasing groans from everyone, and Darius rolled his eyes. "Oh, come on. It's the history teacher in me. You know I miss it." He turned back to the screen. "We reviewed some information four months ago when Valentina and Rachel arrived, but our plans going forward make it crucial to understand where we all come from." His voice was serious now, glancing at Valentina, who smiled and squeezed his arm again. "Now, this is obviously an artist's rendering from the library archives, but given the features, who can tell me who the woman is?"

Alessandro quickly raised his hand, and Darius pointed to him.

"Tatyana," he replied. "She was the angel who created the Chosen Coven, the witches who embodied Earth's sacred elements and bound all magic together. She also created Purgatory, where a vampire's soul dwells in limbo until the second death."

"Correct," Darius replied. He clicked on another image. It was Tatyana standing with a male demon, their gazes locked in some sort of fervor.

Whether it was hatred or love, I couldn't tell.

"Thousands of years ago, when humanity was new, Lucifer sent a demon child named Misha to Earth. He had planned for his general to live among the humans and learn their weaknesses so that he would destroy all that was good and enslave the people. Once Misha grew into a man, he had a dream where Lucifer instructed him to create more like him. He used his blood to create vampires, except they weren't like us; they were like *him*. The vampires were uncontrolled and demonic-looking. He had no choice but to kill them and start over. It would be much harder to manipulate and conquer the humans when they were afraid. Lucifer warned him that the high God, who watched over the humans, was sending an angel, Tatyana, to stop him. But instead of completing her mission, she *allegedly* fell in love with Misha."

Darius looked around the room. "Does anyone know what happened next?" Ava raised her hand. "Avaline?"

"She and Misha had a son, Kylan, the first true-born vampire and Madame Vasile's maker."

Darius nodded in approval. "Correct. Kylan was the first and only being born of angelic *and* demonic blood. He created immortality by turning his first human into a vampire—Valentina

Vasile." He glanced at my mother and winked. "If Kylan is the Father of Vampirism, then Valentina is the Mother."

Gross.

Luka shot me a look, and I chewed my lower lip anxiously.

Why the hell is he rehashing a well-known story? What's the point?

Darius stood and moved from his chair to where Alessandro and Tati were sitting to his right. He raised his hands from his sides. "Whatever horror the Devil may weave, we must overcome the threads of his evil and alter the course of history. We erase the chapters he writes. We *deny* the darkness."

When he looked over at me, I averted my gaze to look at Valentina instead, who gave me a subtle smile.

He continued. "Aside from Enzo and Charles, who are very much valued, we are vampires and dhampirs in this house. Let me tell you that despite what the humans and witches may believe, you are *not* demons. We may carry darkness within us, but we still have a choice to deny it. We choose who we become. In that, we are the same as everyone else." Darius clicked the remote again, and an all-too-familiar picture filled the screen. An icy shiver ran down my spine. It was the church I was born in—the same church where my friend-turned-enemy, Hailee, died. My heart kicked up its pace, and I swallowed hard.

I leaned toward Luka and whispered, "Where the fuck is Darius going with this? Why the church?"

"I have no clue," Luka replied under his breath. Ava and Gio looked just as confused as I did. They also knew my story.

"Two hundred years ago," Darius started, "inside that church, Valentina and her human mate, Cyrus, confronted the vampire

Maurice Tomassi. Many of you know who he was. She came to retrieve a ring that he had stolen from her. Now, what was so special about a ring? Well, this ring allowed Valentina to access the magic she had as a witch eons ago. That ring would protect her and her unborn baby—a child who would one day walk this world with great strength and power."

Everyone turned to look at me. My cheeks burned, and my entire face reddened as I sank into my chair. I took another gulp of coffee and intensely examined the table's wood grain.

Darius returned to the front and turned off the projector before leaning against the table. "After the confrontation, the Black Onyx Coven attacked, killing my best friend, sealing Valentina away, and stealing her child. Maurice escaped and later tried to create an army to enslave Earth. You all are familiar with the Battle of the Devil's Uprising over ten years ago. That man unleashed Hell onto the world, all for the goal of taking over the world himself. The Chosen defeated the demonic armies, driving them back to the Underworld, and killed Maurice," he explained. "Maurice wanted to uphold the vampire legend, depicting us as the embodiment of soulless monsters who wanted dominance over the 'inferior humans.' He believed all life needed to bend to his will as the apex predator—to destroy everything in the vampires' path to self-assured victory. Without realizing it, he almost succeeded where Misha failed."

I leaned back, rocking the chair slightly with my feet. Where was Darius going with this? Everyone knew about Maurice and the war. Others seemed to share my sentiment by the looks they were giving him.

"Since that day," Darius said, his voice commanding the room again, "they forced us to come out of hiding, sign peace treaties with every human government, and assimilate into human society. And though most vampires agreed with the treaties, Lemurian Quartz and Black Onyx still persecuted us. They disregard innocent lives for an old bias that fuels their need to kill us all, and it extended to the dhampirs, resulting in more slaughter. I say that it's time to put a stop to these self-righteous witches. It's time we wage *war* against these covens and their supporters."

My jaw dropped, and I glanced at Luka again. "What the hell?"

I raised my hand, and Darius nodded. "Uh, what happened to no 'reckless war?'" I asked.

"Well, Rachel," Valentina said, gently squeezing Darius's arm. "Things have changed. What must be done has to be on a larger scale than what we discussed."

Oh shit.

When Darius showed us the gem he'd kept hidden in the basement, I knew their plan. To live peacefully, the covens had to go. But the more I watched Valentina and Darius plan the impending attack, the more it became clear they were ready for a bloodbath. I wasn't ever on board with removing magic from the world, not even temporarily, to have the upper hand.

But I understood it would be a quiet, swift attack to finally bring peace to the dhampirs, so they would no longer have to hide. The two covens were the only ones who knew vampires could procreate, and since they operated in secret, no other witches knew about it. If we could take down the witches hunting us, dhampirs could finally live like everyone else, and no one would try to kill us. To kill a witch meant war, not just between the species but also with the human government. Non-supernatural society didn't consider vampires human, as they did werewolves and witches. We would be the first to go.

It could drag us into the public and not on our terms.

The vampires didn't have to worry about how the government would respond if caught waging war against another supernatural creature. The world was familiar with them. While hunters might want to capture them and dole out punishments, the clan's vampires were clever. Each one could escape when necessary, and society would view them like any other creature that the human government was trying to force the public to accept.

It was the dhampirs that concerned me. Ever since the government became aware of the supernatural, they had approached each creature on a case-by-case basis. The dhampirs would eventually have to come forward, and there was a real possibility that we could be subjected to experiments, just as I was during my childhood.

Others would determine if we could exist. They would round us all up because vampires weren't supposed to procreate. We would have to disclose our powers and vulnerabilities and then sign a treaty with them.

Or be killed.

If not by them, then Black Onyx or Lemurian Quartz. They would know where to find the place where I had finally found peace. Was I ready for all this to change?

Valentina rose from her seat, and all eyes followed her with rapt attention. She was the vampires' true maker and still held power and reverence among them. Her story was inspirational to them. Valentina Vasile represented the journey of falling into darkness, of being so lost in pain and death that you'd never be able to escape.

To be perceived as evil with no redemption. But she did. Valentina regained the tether to her humanity and soul, fell in love with a human, and had a child—me. She was the epitome of finding your way back from the abyss and pushing toward a better future, a chance to be more than a monster.

"According to Darius's sources," Valentina started, "the Black Onyx now lives in New Orleans and is working on expanding their numbers, recruiting witches to join their forces so they can come find me, Rachel, and all of you. But we know our numbers aren't enough. They know we are stronger. The dhampirs in the academy killed thirty members of the Lemurian Quartz within minutes, but we have learned that it will no longer be enough. They are building armies ... and so shall we."

"We will end their reign of death," Darius added.

Having recovered from his shock, Luka raised his hand and cleared his throat. Darius nodded to him. "Is it correct to assume that you want us to recruit other vampire clans to help?"

"We don't have a choice," Darius answered. "They would overrun us without more help, even if the stone can disable magic. Going to the Five-Point Order in America won't do anything. They comply with the Black Onyx's misdeeds, and no European government body has reined Lemurian in. The corruption runs deep."

"What about the dhampirs in hiding right now?" Gio asked. "Will they return after what happened?"

"That's something I'll take care of. For now, we'll continue to work and live as normal," Valentina added. "We will gather here in a few days to discuss departures. Ava and Gio, Darius would like you to remain here and work on recruiting clans. Luka, Alessandro, and Tati will travel to the States. Any clan willing to help us is the best chance to combat the witches' army. It's the only way."

"Darius," I started, my stomach twisting into knots, "there's no way to know if any clan will want to help. Believe me, the one Andrei forced me to join is full of selfish assholes who only care about money and control. You can't assume anyone will come. It's too risky."

"I understand your hesitancy. I do," Darius replied dryly. "But without vampires to help, it would only be a matter of time before those murderers come here again and execute us. *This* is the best course of action for you and your mother. You're all excused."

As Alessandro and Tati rose from their chairs and walked out, Luka, Ava, Gio, and I remained seated.

I turned to my friends. "Why do I have the sinking feeling that this is too dangerous?"

Gio swallowed and looked at me, his eyes full of worry and fear that I'd never seen him have before. "Because, mi amica, it is."

CHAPTER II

JASE

As I rested my palms on the cool, polished marble of the balcony railing, a gentle breeze swept across my face. It carried the sweet scent of magnolia flowers and grass, creating a sense of calm to wash over me—a peace I hadn't felt in decades. Under the light of the half-full moon, I could see the grounds of Andrei's estate and frowned.

The view from the third floor offered a stark reality of how far Andrei had slipped since Rachel left. A thin film of algae, dead leaves, and dirt coated the inside of the once pristine, now drained fountain. Even the lawn had overgrown, and the well-kempt ivy was now wild, consuming the mansion's walls. Since Rachel fled the place, Andrei had let it fall into ruin, refusing to let his staff maintain the property. He met those who did so with rage and a termination letter.

It was like his blackened soul now bled into the world around him.

My brother knew only anger and obsession. They fueled his every move and decision, affecting everyone he came into contact with. Now that he possessed the Burning of Angels' Key we had just retrieved in Atlanta, I was worried about how much farther he'd fall before dragging the rest of us with him.

Andrei had always been unrecognizable to me after the night he killed our parents, but this … this was a new side I'd never seen. He was becoming an entirely different man. Vastly different from the one I knew four months ago in the church, who offered me a safe haven while he devised a new plan to get the ring back.

Initially, I was supposed to play the part of a repentant figure to appease the Black Onyx Coven and prevent retaliation for unleashing Valentina back into the world. But I somehow convinced them I was only trying to help. Rachel was the *real* villain. Our plan tied up loose ends after that disaster in the church when I broke the sealing spell and awoke Hell on Earth. Andrei had manipulated the coven to spare my life and convince them to assign Liam to our clan to help us find the two women.

Andrei was losing his grip, and it felt like I was the only one in that goddamn room who realized it. He commanded such loyalty from those grovelers that no one questioned why he would want to do something so fucked up. Something that would doom us all.

He was going to ruin everything.

"Jase?" The sound of Meredith's voice behind me made me recoil a little. I didn't turn around, and when I felt her arms slide around my waist, it took all my will not to shudder with disgust.

I turned around then, forcing her to drop her hands. "Is there something I can help you with?" I asked, struggling to hide my tone.

"I wanted to check on you. You seem distant since we broke into that museum," Meredith said, hurt shining in her eyes. "Do you not trust Andrei's judgment on this? You know it's the only way."

I knew what this bitch was doing. Andrei must have tasked her with trying to poke around in my head, thinking she could seduce me into spilling my secrets.

"I don't trust anyone, Meredith," I replied. "Especially my brother. A lot changes in over two hundred years."

Meredith's brows furrowed. "He's doing this so you don't end up burning in the pits below us. Even though we're immortal, we can still die. The moment someone stakes your heart, your soul will be ripped from Purgatory and dropped right into the Underworld. You will suffer something far worse than roaming Earth as a bloodthirsty corpse."

My lips curved into a wicked smile. "Andrei isn't thinking this through," I told her. "He's motivated by his dick. While he claims Rachel is essential to all this, I know he's let his selfish desires cloud his judgment. He'll get this entire clan killed with his idiotic and reckless plan to summon the Warrior. If he accomplishes this, he'll kidnap Rachel, taking her against her will again."

"Oh, God. Why the hell do you care what happens to her? She hates both of you," Meredith reminded me, moving closer into my personal space. "I have been Andrei's friend and companion for over a hundred years. I know his intentions, and if he says this is to help you, I believe him."

I turned to her and stepped forward, closing the gap between us. Placing my right palm against her cheek, I gently ran my thumb over her skin.

The gesture revolted me to my core. I didn't want to touch a woman like her, not one fucking bit. But Meredith was the easiest to manipulate. Her loyalty to Andrei made her blind, which played to *my* advantage.

"Maybe ..." I whispered, "Maybe you're right. I probably should trust him."

I dropped my hand to move past her toward the door, but she reached out, snaking her fingers over my stomach before inching lower, lightly cupping my crotch. "When will you stop pretending like you don't want this?" Meredith purred, her green eyes filled with feral lust.

I *didn't* want it.

"I've been rather lonely the past few months," she shamelessly admitted. "Aren't you? When's the last time you were with a woman?"

I cleared my throat, shoving the boiling urge to rip her throat out down in my mind. "Meredith, you may enjoy fucking anyone that so much as glances in your direction, but I'm not interested."

With that, I broke from her hold and went inside, leaving her alone on that dirty marble balcony.

~•~

When I walked into my bedroom, I removed my leather jacket and tossed it onto the chair. I made my way to the small end table and pulled out a whiskey decanter, pouring two fingers into the crystal tumbler. After settling on the bed, I pulled my cell phone from my pocket and eyed the dark screen, ready to send some messages to my contacts.

My thoughts went to the idea of my brother using Rachel to save our souls and then bringing her back here so he could put his hands on her, claiming her as *his*. The image provoked an unwanted physical response in my stomach—my shoulders tightened, and my veins pulsed with anger. The feeling was all too familiar. Over the last four years, I had to watch Rachel take men to her bed, watch as strangers followed her as she walked past them, the lust burning in their eyes, mentally undressing her.

One fucker got a little too close. I smiled, recalling the sound he made as I snapped his neck before dumping his body in the river.

After sending my texts, I leaned back against the propped-up pillows and sipped my drink. It made sense if what Valentina told me was true. Was Rachel really my mate? Or was she still just a tool to achieve my goals of absolute power and security? I swore to kill her that night of the Hades Blood Moon after I took possession of the ring.

Instead, I hesitated.

Since then, the urge to find Rachel, to possess her, had been slowly burning these past few months, consuming my mind like a blue flame. Valentina was right; I was supposed to hate Rachel. But even after everything, I still didn't. All those years watching her, learning her routines and habits, only added to my obsession.

The burn of alcohol anchored my spiraling thoughts, and I knew in my gut what had to be done. I had to beat Andrei to Italy and take Rachel for myself. Whether it was by divine cosmic power or a bunch of bullshit Valentina spun, I needed to know.

After hearing Andrei's plan for taking Rachel back after all this, I concluded my brother was more unhinged than I was. If I had learned anything from the past, it didn't matter how much Andrei cared about someone; he wouldn't hesitate to spill innocent blood.

This plan with the key, the sword, everything, wasn't about saving our souls from the Devil's grasp. It was to claim dominance over everything and forcefully take what he wanted.

After tossing back the rest of my drink, I left my room and headed to the library. Once settling into the chair, I picked up a book from the coffee table in front of the couch. I had flipped through it once since arriving at the mansion—a dark romance with a cover depicting a skull and a butterfly tattoo. As I opened to where I had left off, my phone buzzed with an incoming text. I pulled it out and glanced at the new message.

> **Andrei:** *Jase, we need you in the dining room. The members of Boston's Black Onyx* Coven request we join *them tonight. You have ten minutes before we walk out the* door.

"What the fuck?" I whispered. Since when did they come back to New Orleans? They had left a few behind to delegate and keep an eye on us, but not the entire coven.

Did they fly down and only tell Andrei?

Knocking back the rest of my drink, I stood up and felt a slight buzz in my head. For a vampire, it took a lot of alcohol to feel its effect. I had been drinking since seven a.m., much more than I usually did. It was the only thing to help numb the chaos in my head since I arrived at Andrei's home four months ago.

I left the library and walked down the stairs toward the dining room. Jackson was leaning against the wall just outside the door. When I approached, he looked over and greeted me with a strained smile.

"Hey, do you know what's going on?" Jackson asked, worry flashing in his warm brown eyes.

That surprised me. Andrei always kept Jackson and Meredith in the loop. He trusted those two far more than he trusted his own brother.

"Not a damn clue," I shrugged, pushing the door open and walking into the room. Meredith and Liam were already inside, but there was no sign of Andrei. Meredith offered a smile when she saw me. I tried not to grimace.

One thing I learned over the decades since becoming a vampire was that no one is what they seem on the outside. Meredith's attempt to have me trust her only amplified my suspicion that she wasn't the kindhearted, loyal friend Andrei made her out to be.

I would never trust her.

"Meredith," I called, standing beside her and folding my arms over my leather jacket. "Did he really keep *all* of us in the dark?"

"A need-to-know basis," Andrei's voice rang out as he walked from the kitchen. "What I'm going to share stays between just the four of us." He picked up his suit jacket from the dining chair. "Now, has everyone fed?" he added.

We all nodded, still confused. Why the hell would that matter? It's not like any of us would dare try to attack and feed from a Black Onyx witch.

"Given the limited details from your text ... are the *original* members of the coven holed up in New Orleans?" I asked.

Andrei moved to the head of the dining table, resting his hands on the back of the chair. "They are now. With Valentina awake and hiding alongside Rachel, they're establishing new divisions across the country to hunt for them if we are to fail. That includes potential allies overseas. Their headquarters will now be just a few blocks from the French Quarter. The Black Onyx realizes this could be war, and the last time they were here, they established some key players to help with their cause."

I furrowed my brow. "Are they planning to march into Venice and drag them out of that house?"

Andrei shook his head, irritation flashing in his eyes as his jaw tightened. "Do you think I'm a fool for allowing them to reach her before I do? They don't know where she is. Their endgame was to kill them both after using Rachel's blood for the spell, but I've ensured that doesn't happen. At least not to Rachel. But the coven can have Valentina and the other dhampirs once they find them. The ones I learned about during your trial that existed before she did."

His gaze made it clear he hadn't forgiven me for that omission. *Tough shit, brother.*

"Whatever they say in the meeting tonight, know that the coven is merely a tool for me. I have my own agenda, and I expect you all to keep it to yourselves."

I met his gaze. "Where do the witches think she's gone if they don't know she's in Venice?"

Andrei straightened. "They suspect Rachel and Valentina fled to Europe. That's it. They're unaware of the tracker in her arm, so they can't demand that I disclose anything. This house they're staying at is likely one of Valentina's allies, but I want to reach her before anyone else does." His expression darkened.

Meredith frowned. "What about Liam?"

"Liam will learn everything when I'm ready to trust him. Right now, they are relying on me because of the guardian bond.

Tonight's meeting is to outline those plans. Everyone will remain silent and let me do the talking. If all goes as intended, we'll be on a flight tomorrow morning."

I narrowed my eyes at him. "What *is* your endgame, anyway?"

He smiled. "Rachel, Jase. I've made a deal with them to guarantee her return to *me*. Even if she tries to fight it."

⁓

After removing my bike helmet, I noticed a stony trail leading into the forest. Andrei, Meredith, and Jackson were already at the edge to go inside.

"What is this place?" I asked Andrei. "They're in the woods?"

"We're just north of the city. This property has been closed to the public for a few years, so the Black Onyx thought it best to hold their confidential meetings here," he replied.

"A coven of witches gathering in some dark and secluded woods … That's not creepy at all," I said sarcastically.

Jackson snickered quietly before speaking. "Don't sound too excited, Jase."

We all turned as leaves rustled under footsteps, and Liam appeared, wearing a red robe that reached his ankles and tied at the neck. "Gentlemen … Miss Meredith."

Andrei gave him a brief nod before we followed him deep into the forest, leading to an underground cave with a tall wooden door built into the rock.

Liam climbed the broken stone steps to the door with runes etched into it. He reached out and pulled out his pentagram fastener. After murmuring a few words, the pentagram glowed with a faint blue light before Liam pressed the pin into a hole in the wood. He turned to look at us before opening the door. "Once we're inside and the meeting begins, you're not to speak with each other or anyone else unless Gerald gives permission. You're not to share any information about what occurs here, or we'll burn your heart inside your body. Is that clear?"

What the hell are these witches doing?

Andrei nodded, which surprised me. He never came off as a leader who'd let anyone speak to him that way, especially a witch.

Liam spun around and gestured for us three to follow him. I glanced at my brother; I couldn't tell what the hell he was thinking, only that he had a stern look on his face.

As I stepped through the threshold, the scent of incense and sage stung my nose. A subtle click echoed through the space, and rows of gas lamps flickered to life. I let out a low whistle as the cave's interior appeared in front of us. Sunken several feet into the ground, the floor created an ideal hiding spot, its wood and stone surface easily concealed from human eyes.

Just then, a hooded figure approached us. The silhouette held out four black cloaks with silver dagger-shaped clasps, and when we took them, the figure melted back into the shadows.

What the fuck? I blinked. This meeting was nothing like the gatherings we had when I was a member of Black Onyx over two hundred years ago.

"These cloaks are to show that you are vampires, therefore outsiders," Liam explained smugly.

Dick.

"This is far more archaic than what I remember the coven being like," I remarked.

"This is more efficient than you think, *vampire.* Just watch," Liam whispered before heading to the cavern's left side.

The entire space was massive with staggered wooden pews along both sides. At the center was a tall podium with a black runner hanging over the front. I saw the pentagram embroidered into the fabric with a glimmering gold thread. Brightly lit lamps lined the ceiling, casting a warm light on the walls. There was a creaking noise, and a second door on the left swung open. A coven of witches came in, their scarlet red cloaks floating behind them as they moved to the pews. A few of them noticed me and sneered in disdain. In response, I grinned wickedly, wiggling my fingers at them in a wave.

"Don't cause trouble," Meredith hissed in my ear. "Gerald's here, and we need to play nice with these sycophants." She pointed to Gerald Madison, leader of the coven, as he walked in and headed to the podium. Andrei walked up to Jackson and whispered something in his ear. He then came to me and leaned in close.

"You three will stay in the pews while I go down to Gerald," Andrei said. "We still need to play the part of you being repentant for your actions as a would-be traitor and serving in my clan. So, you can't be foolish. Don't say a *word.*"

I snarled at him. "Fine, but I'm no one's dog, especially theirs."

Andrei smirked, then went to where Gerald was sitting and took a seat to the left of him.

"Witches of the Black Onyx," Gerald's voice boomed through the tower. "You're summoned to discuss matters most severe. But first, we have a traitor in our midst. Someone who has broken our most sacred laws and endangered our coven. Bring in the perpetrator."

The doors at the back swung open, and two more hooded figures dragged an unconscious man inside. He was pale, with reddish-blond hair and multiple purple bruises on his face and neck. The figures threw the man onto the stone floor before the podium, drawing a moan from his bleeding lips. Gerald sneered down at the beaten man.

"Wyatt has broken the laws of our coven by revealing our name to a human. His betrayal forced us to spill innocent blood. For that, we invoke his crimes as the sacrifice for the Runes of Silence."

I looked around at the witches; they all, in unison, held their left arms over small golden chalices embedded in the pews. They lifted tiny black daggers and drew the sharp edge over their exposed wrists. The scent of fresh blood hit me then, and my fangs pressed against my lips. I found the smell delicious, but my hunger had been satiated earlier that day, so the thirst didn't burn as much.

Explains why Andrei ordered us to feed from the suppliers.

As the blood flowed into the chalices, the coven began to chant.

By the wind, our words are carried away.

By the moon, our breath draws no more.

By ageless darkness, no words this night be uttered.

By stone, we are bound.

By fire, speak and become ash.

Wyatt jerked and grabbed at his chest and throat, agonized wails pouring from his bloody mouth. Between his fingers, black smoke seeped through. The smoke trickled across the floor and into the chalices, turning into dark blood. It set my nerves on edge as the cups glowed with a red aura. The witches dipped their fingers into the liquid one by one, tracing a symbol onto their foreheads. The blood seemed to crackle on their skin, and Wyatt screamed even louder.

He tried to speak, to plead, but smoke started pouring from his mouth. Finally, his scream faded to a guttural, wet sob, and then ... nothing. His smoke-stained hands fell away from his chest, and there I could see the blackened holes where his heart and vocal cords once were.

Liam was telling the truth about keeping our mouths shut. As the red light of the blood magic faded, there was a collective hiss of pain before the bloodied runes faded on the witches' skin. Gerald followed suit, wiping his hands with a black silk handkerchief before they carried Wyatt's body out the same back entrance. Once they removed the body, Gerald spoke in the same booming voice. "This meeting is crucial for the safety of our coven and all witches. It serves as a reminder of the importance of loyalty to our trust and coven."

"Yeah, no kidding," Jackson muttered quietly beside me.

"As you all know," Gerald said disdainfully, "a few months ago, our ward, Rachel Hardmann, resurrected her mother, Valentina Vasile. While we believe they have fled the country, that doesn't mean they won't return seeking vengeance. Since Andrei is still bonded to Rachel, we've tasked him with finding and retrieving the dhampir and killing Valentina so she's no longer a threat. We've also granted Andrei access to an ancient artifact that can summon magic powerful enough to rid the world of our true enemy—the Dark King of the Underworld, who has caused so much destruction."

My stomach lurched, an icy dread settling in my gut. I knew this was the plan, but if I failed to stop Andrei, then we'd be fighting the Devil and whatever demons crawl through the gates by the end of the week.

"Andrei and Jase foolishly wore Valentina's ring," Gerald started again, his eyes moving to mine, "which puts them in a unique position. Not only will they be doing us a favor, but they can also save their own souls in the process. We have given Andrei the Burning of Angels' Key and will soon provide him with the Book of Shadows. This book will guide him through the spell needed to retrieve the Upper World's most coveted weapon, the Sword of Ezrylos, which will finally destroy the Devil once and for all."

The coven's collective whispers bounced off the walls.

"He who controls the Sword of Ezrylos controls the Underworld, thus enabling the Upper World to take hold and transform Hell into a realm that erases evil souls—not tortures them—from existence." His gaze slid over to mine again. "Yes, this includes vampires, but we'll ensure to save those who ally with us. There will be no redemption for the others, no resurrection; once gone, they are truly gone. By using divine power to eliminate Lucifer, we can assume his role, merge Heaven and Earth, and ensure that no one can challenge our authority."

What. The. Fuck? This wasn't part of the plan that Andrei told us.

Andrei turned to face us and smiled. "In exchange for delivering the sword, Gerald promised to grant me complete control over the dhampir. If she's simply part of the family again, she could run. So, Rachel will remain in my possession without protest for as long as she breathes. I'll ensure she's kept far away, where she can no longer be a danger to herself or anyone else. In time, people will forget her existence, and the dhampir fable will again be just a fable. That is, once they have found and killed the others like her."

A slow, burning rage curled in my gut. Rachel wasn't something fragile to be hidden away like a dirty little secret. The image of Andrei sinking his claws into her, caging her like some helpless creature, made my hands clench into fists. He didn't deserve to be the one to control her fate.

I did.

I also hated that he'd planned to hand over a magical sword to the most notorious coven in the Western world. Fuck the Black Onyx and their power trip to control the realms. They weren't getting shit.

My plans just got moved up a notch.

"What the fuck is he doing?" I heard Jackson whisper. When I glanced over, his eyes widened in shock.

"I hope Andrei locks her in that basement cage and leaves her to starve," Meredith said. "If we don't support this, they won't save our souls when the time comes. We'll be gone just like the rest of them."

I whipped my head to her. Her green eyes, now crimson, burned with rage and disgust.

"Are you fucking crazy?" I asked. "How could you agree to any of this?"

"Your brother has fallen since that little whore came into our clan. This eliminates several problems that have harmed us." Meredith glared at me, and I pressed my lips into a thin line. An ember of panic replaced the fear and grew into a flame. Rachel was in more danger than she could ever fathom, and somehow, I cared enough to let that bother me.

My thoughts were spinning out of control. I needed to leave. "I'm going to step out and wait for these ... *witches* to finish their little chat."

As I backed away, my back pressed against a solid wall. When I turned around, the mouth of the cave we had come through was gone, replaced with stone.

"What the fuck is this?"

"No one can leave until Gerald unseals the door. Ensures that no one runs off or causes *trouble*," Meredith said, patting my shoulder before returning her eyes to Andrei.

"Then open the fucking door," I growled through my teeth.

Meredith folded her arms like a defiant child and walked down the stairs to where Andrei stood. I heard her say, "Jase needs to go outside. I'll go with him. Tell Gerald to let us out."

Andrei gave her a nod before turning to the coven leader, but my stomach still hollowed out. My brother had lost his goddamn mind, and he would destroy everything I had planned. I needed to act before he stole that sword and took Rachel away.

Away from me....

CHAPTER 12

JASE

"What the hell is wrong with you?!" Meredith shouted as we walked to the parking lot. While Andrei and Jackson hung back to wrap up that weird fucking meeting they forced me to witness, I went to my bike.

I need to get the fuck out of here.

My mind spun at what the Black Onyx was doing in this era. They had always been ritualistic in their practices, some of which I had even participated in as a member. But that? That was something twisted.

"Why did you take off like that? Do you really want to get on the Black Onyx's shit list? Do you not understand what that could risk?"

I turned to look at Meredith's furious expression, leaning against my bike. Irritated, I folded my arms tightly over my chest. "There's a reason I defied those witches two hundred years ago, so why would this be any different? *You* may want me to play repentant, but I'll *not* act complacent around those bastards."

Meredith's jaw went slack, and her eyes widened in fury. "This isn't a joke. We went to extreme lengths to keep the coven from turning you over to the Five-Point Order, and Andrei is the sole reason you're allowed to roam as freely as you do."

I stared at her, trying to choose my words carefully. Meredith would take anything I said and report it back to Andrei, and my temper was loosening my tongue too much. After what they discussed at the meeting, I knew that agreeing with what Andrei wanted to do would stop my plans from coming to fruition.

"How can we be sure that this plan of summoning the angel Ezrylos will work, anyway? If this backfires, then what? He'll leave us with an uncontrolled deity bent on slaughtering everyone and a coven with unlimited power and control." I bit the inside of my cheek, tasting iron and frustration. "Meredith, this is a plan to kill the King of Hell and deliver an angelic sword for Black Onyx to wield. There is no guarantee that those fucking witches will honor their word to spare us. And we're not even talking about the likely power vacuum that will result. Spilling Rachel's blood isn't worth the damn risk. The spell could *kill* her."

Meredith cocked her head to the right, knitting her brows together. "Well, that's an interesting thing to say. That's twice now you've mentioned her safety." Her eyes darkened a little. "I can understand the hesitancy in killing Lucifer for those witches, but why the fuck would you, of all people, care if Rachel lives or dies? She's a poison, an anomaly that we need to eradicate."

My body involuntarily twitched at those words, my fingers clenching.

She came closer, much too close for my liking. The smell of heavy perfume floated around her like a toxic cloud. I tried not to choke on it.

"If the spell doesn't kill that little rat ... *I* will. Ever since Andrei brought her into our lives, she has *changed* him. I want the old Andrei back. The one who slaughtered anyone who got in his way." Meredith pressed her hand against my chest, rubbing her thumb over my leather jacket like soothing a wild beast. "Come on. I know you feel the same. After two centuries apart, you're finally reunited with your brother, only to find him presenting you with a lovesick fool who prioritized a harlot over family. You eliminate that weakness, and you two can be lords of The Big Easy together."

I watched that infuriating hand move across my chest, and I wanted to tear it off from the wrist and throw it into the swamp. Yet as Meredith caressed my chest, slowly inching her fingers to the hem of my shirt to touch my bare skin, the idea brewing in the back of my mind finally clicked. One that would unleash chaos on the city and, if it went exactly how I planned, would pave the way for me to get out unscathed.

"Sweetheart, I'm only trying to help you," she said softly. "You know how conniving that woman is. Even now, she's causing strife within our clan." Meredith pressed herself even closer to me, her breasts brushing the zipper of my jacket. "That Wendy witch may have been in your bed for four years, but you've been alone for centuries. You can have a family again.... You can have *me.*"

The audacity of Meredith's assumption made my teeth clench, as if she had any right to know what I *needed* in my life. Wendy was not some paramour; she was a pawn who got me to Rachel and her mother.

I didn't *need* anyone. Ever.

"Meredith," I said, stopping her hand from reaching for my belt buckle. "Maybe ... maybe I need to relax first. A lot has happened, and there's too much to process. I guess we *could* unwind a little."

Meredith's lips widened into a grin. She was so foolish, so eager to get in my pants that she'd forgotten my rejecting her only a few hours ago.

"Hmm," she hummed, stepping closer. "What did you have in mind?"

I smiled back and tucked a strand of pale-blonde hair behind her ear. "I know a place I've visited often over the last four years. It was a great spot to let go a little when I wasn't with Wendy."

She raised a curious brow. "Well, I'm all for anything that takes your mind off the coven *and* Rachel. A bit of normalcy will be good for you."

I dropped my hand. "Believe me, this place is anything but normal, but given what you like to do in *your* downtime, this might be up your alley. I need to make a phone call to the owners to get you access to the inside. It's outside city limits, so we'll have to take my bike to get there."

Meredith's eyes flashed, a feral delight in the green of her irises. She looked over my shoulder at my motorcycle parked beside Andrei's Mercedes.

"Alright, make the call, and let's get the hell out of this swamp."

Rush hour was long over, so it only took us an hour to reach the club off Old Hooper Road in Baton Rouge. The owners designed the club, Blood and Envy, to resemble a Victorian-style home—a perfectly normal-looking building to anyone who might venture that far into the woods. Instead of wood siding, they built it with solid brick and painted it jet-black, which gave it a haunting Gothic feel. The front doors were bronze with crystal flower motifs covering the surface, and golden columns framed the entrance.

A bouncer stood with a leather-bound notepad in his hand. As each person approached, he would scan them over and check the notes, ensuring they were welcome inside. As Meredith and I approached the front of the line, she leaned in and whispered in my ear. "I would have never guessed an establishment like this would be in Baton Rouge. How did I not know this was here?" Meredith watched as three female vampires escorted a human male into the club. Two puncture wounds stained his neck red; the vampires had started the party early on the ride over. His high-pitched giggling confirmed it, the telltale haze of euphoria that only came from a vampire's bite. Meredith's eyes widened slightly as she licked her ruby-red bottom lip.

I knew this place would intrigue her.

"While the club's been around for a while," I replied, "it recently came under new ownership. Believe me, strict laws have kept this place running. As long as the vampires adhere to them, it'll remain open. So, no dead bodies."

"You have a wilder side than I thought," Meredith snickered. "I never would have guessed you'd enjoy a place like this."

I couldn't help but smirk as I turned back to the door. "This is where I met and recruited Wendy."

"Hmm, so witches also come here?" she asked. "That's very bold of them."

I nodded, pointing at the small stained-glass window over the doorway. It was a purple-black raven surrounded by bloody red roses, a curved dagger in its beak. "This once belonged to her coven, Raven's Blood, but the witches sold it a few years ago to a vampire clan when they moved. They transformed it into the ideal den for the appetites of the undead: fucking, blood sharing … tying up naughty humans and punishing them until they reach their peak."

Meredith's smile grew. "Sounds like my kind of party."

Clubs like Blood and Envy were few and far between across the country. In the past, they'd kept venues like this underground. Since vampires weren't open to the public, secrecy and death were much more prominent. The Five-Point Order implemented strict guidelines for clubs that involved willing donors and sex-craved vampires, and owners had to go through multiple government agencies to get licensed for these activities. Authorities executed anyone caught committing illegal operations on-site; there was no trial or fines, only immediate death.

Vampires were predators, and if the government forbade them from hunting their food in the real world and forcing humans to bend to our will, our kind created safe spaces like this where it felt like they could. Blood and Envy was a specialty blood-sharing club. Their theme was the traditional "hunt and chase," with humans signing consent forms for primal play. The club owners chose this location because of the massive forest behind the building.

The concept was simple: the humans would run into the forest to escape their vampire counterparts. They engaged in cat-and-mouse play, which ends with feeding and fucking as the human pretends to fend off the vampire.

Except some vampires couldn't resist taking things too far, causing way too many humans to get *lost* in the forest. So, they put strict laws in place. The doors stayed open as long as no one reported the business, and every human who participated checked in with the staff. If the vampires broke the rules, the employees would rip them apart and toss their ashes in the trash.

Andrei's nightclub wasn't the same. Vampires and humans mingled, but they weren't fucking out in the open. Sure, they shared blood behind closed doors, but Andrei never let it escalate past that. It would tarnish his reputation, and he needed willing clients to take part in the blood trade. But there were no contracts at Black Diamond, no forms—only pleasure, pain, and uncontrolled thirst. It was the thrill of the game.

No safe words.

"So, will I see the 'Stalker Jasen' in his element?" Meredith asked with a hint of snark. "I've wanted to see you in action these past few months, but I could never get you out of your shell at the mansion. All it took was for you to come here, find a human woman to chase and fuck, and unleash that monster inside. You spent so much time hunting and stalking Rachel but never had a chance to *have* her. A pity."

My body stiffened, but I gave my best, most charming smile. "Like I said, Rachel was merely a tool for my plans, and it was never about *that.* This is much more fun, and fewer demons are crawling through windows."

Meredith laughed and leaned in slowly, her hand inching down until she reached my crotch. "And that's precisely the sinful delight I was hoping for." Her voice had dropped to a slow, seductive hum.

This bitch is relentless.

Before I could move away, her hand started rubbing my jeans, trying to get me hard before we could even step inside. *Jesus.* Reaching down I took her hand from my zipper. "Save your lascivious energy for what I have planned for us later tonight."

Meredith pulled a sour face but thankfully dropped her hand. "I hope this is worth the effort. I'm getting tired of my leather clubs and need something new."

We approached the bouncer, and I gave him our names. The bouncer raised an eyebrow at Meredith's name but only nodded before handing us two red rose-shaped pins we fastened to our shirts. Human guests received blue lily pins. He opened the luxurious wood and crystal door and waved us inside. As soon as we entered, I sauntered to the bar and ordered a beer. With the frosted glass in hand, I turned my attention to the dance floor, where guests undulated beneath the strobing lights. I leaned against the bar, scanning the crowd and taking in the chaos. Meredith soon joined me, red wine in hand, and together we clinked glasses.

"To not giving a fuck about witches and dhampirs for one night," she said.

To the far right was a wooden staircase leading upstairs and a stage below it. As the vampires on the dance floor watched, the woman lay on a dais, with her legs splayed wide, while a man sat on top of her, keeping her arms and wrists restrained. They'd ripped her clothes—a sign of apparent struggle that preceded this scene—but even from here, the glistening arousal of her pussy was clear to me. Another vampire held the chains they bound her with at the head of the dais, smiling as they gripped the steel. She resisted as she played the game. If I hadn't known what this place was, I would have believed they were about to rape and feed from her.

The first vampire suddenly sank his teeth into her throat, and immediately her fight vanished. She arched her back underneath him, surrendering to the ecstasy of his bite. His hand snuck between her legs, stimulating her pussy and only torturing her with more pleasure. It wasn't long before the second vampire joined, and the moans of their bliss echoed deep through the club, melting with the music.

I glanced down at the time again.

"Why do you keep looking at your phone?" Meredith asked, her brows pinched together. "Is the sight in front of you not interesting enough?"

"The sight *is* interesting, but a friend is coming to meet us. Trust me, you're going to love her."

Meredith cocked a brow. *"Her?"*

The struggle not to roll my eyes continued.

Before I could answer, my gaze darted toward the front of the club, watching the dance floor part. "Ah, there she is," I said, waving Emily over.

Emily Cavalli looked stunning as always, wearing a bright-red tank top, black jeans, and matching high heels. Like Meredith, she wore crimson lipstick, complementing the long, raven-black hair framing her heart-shaped face.

"Emily, it's good to see you." I smiled, leaning in and kissing her lightly on her right cheek. "Meredith Loren, meet Emily Cavalli. Emily, this is Meredith."

Meredith offered her hand, and Emily shook it, a cat-like smile playing on her lips.

"I don't see a blue lily pin on your shirt," Meredith said pointedly. Emily smiled again and shyly tucked her hair behind her ears.

"Well, I'm not an ordinary human." She giggled. "I have *special* privileges."

"Emily was the one who introduced me to Wendy four years ago. They were both Raven's Blood Coven members before Wendy betrayed them."

Meredith's mouth parted with surprise, like she hadn't expected that.

"She may have left us for a vampire, but Jase did us a huge favor by taking that bitch off our hands. She was the most pretentious woman I ever met. Power-hungry, with mediocre magic at best."

I threw back my head and laughed. This was going all too well. I finished my beer and signaled to the bartender. I ordered two cocktails for the women and one more beer for myself, and we all clinked our glasses together.

And for the next hour, Emily played her role exactly as I instructed her to.

I wasn't interested in watching, but it was more entertaining than the debauchery surrounding me. The conversation moved from small talk to the women cuddling up to each other. Emily now had her long legs draped over Meredith's lap and was trailing a finger over Meredith's upper arm.

Meredith's fangs were out, gently nipping at Emily's neck before slowly gliding her tongue up the column of her throat toward her ear.

"I see this place is getting to you," Emily purred into Meredith's ear, her brown eyes flashing to mine momentarily. A slight smile crossed her pretty face.

"It might be," Meredith said, inhaling Emily's intoxicating perfume. I understood why. Emily was graced with a ... *unique* scent that lured vampires to her. The flow of alcohol, along with the sexual atmosphere of the club, worked in my favor. "Or it might just be you. I'm imagining all kinds of things I want to do to your body...."

"Don't just tease me," Emily whispered as she moved her hands under Meredith's skirt. I didn't have to guess what she was doing as Meredith's head fell back, and she bit her lower lip. Emily thrust her fingers back and forth, and the sound of Meredith's arousal was pretty damn clear to my ears, breaking through the music. "Tell me, what do you want to do to me tonight?"

"Fuck," Meredith said, grinding her hips into Emily's hand. Her legs spread wider, and Emily hooked Meredith's skirt up slightly. Maybe it was so she could enjoy the show. Perhaps it was for me. I couldn't tell.

I felt myself getting hard from the display, but that was as far as I would allow. The physical actions were appealing, but I couldn't get distracted. I took a long pull of my drink and tried to think of naked old nuns or something to quell my dick.

"You can pull out your cock, Jase, and join us," Meredith said, her tone a little too excited. She attempted to roll her hips against Emily's hand, but Emily put herself in control, pinning her down with her weight. Meredith's head tipped backward as she allowed Emily to have her way with her, light trembles consuming her body. "Oh, fuck, just like that. This is good. Come join us," she repeated as she continued to grind her pussy against Emily's fingers pumping inside her.

I adjusted myself as I remained in the chair, trying to tame my dick to not give a shit about the moans leaving Meredith and Emily's lips.

Naked old nuns, naked old nuns....

"I'll enjoy the view from here," I said. Meredith's breathing grew heavier as her body convulsed more against Emily. And Emily enjoyed this game. She increased her pace, trailing her tongue against the side of Meredith's neck. And soon came the point where Meredith could no longer take it.

She cried out as sweet pleasure consumed her, bracketing Emily's shoulders with her hands and pulling her in. Leaning against her, she sank her teeth into Emily's neck as she came. Emily moaned loudly, as if some of Meredith's pleasure had been pumped into her bloodstream.

"Easy," Emily whimpered. "Not too much."

Meredith needed a few moments to regain her composure before she could force herself to pull back. She licked her lips, running her hand through the back of Emily's long hair, gripping it slightly, and pulling her head back. Her eyes darkened as they locked on Emily's. "Tell me what you want," she commanded, "or I'll choose for you."

Emily was a fucking fantastic actress, and though she played the part of being afraid of Meredith, well, I knew she wasn't as she melted into feigned submission.

"Chase me," Emily said into her ear. "Hunt me until you catch me. Then make me yours for the night."

God, this was way too easy.

***

It was close to one o'clock in the morning, the forest quiet in the warm night. The previous hunt had wrapped up, and I requested the next time slot for the game. The moon hung low on the horizon, and its white light played with the shadows of the trees.

"Alright," Emily said, pulling off her high heels. "What are the rules of the chase?"

I smiled and winked at her before answering, "You start running, and we'll give you a one-minute head start." I glanced at Meredith, who grinned widely as she kicked off her shoes. "Meredith and I promise not to use our vampire speed ... to make it fair. If we catch you, we fuck you. Mercilessly, to the point where you won't be able to use your legs afterward. But if you make it to the river, you're safe."

"What if I *purposely* don't make it to the river?" Emily asked, biting her lower lip.

I took a few steps forward until I was standing beside Meredith. "Then you'll have her tongue deep inside your pussy and my cock in your mouth within the next fifteen minutes. And trust me when I tell you, it'll be quite some time before you manage to free yourself from us."

Meredith let out a drunken giggle before her eyes grew dark and red, ready to hunt down her prey.

"Keep it interesting, Emily," I said, meeting her eyes. "Now, run."

Within a beat, Emily took off, sprinting into the forest. Meredith went to run after her, but I blocked her with my arm.

"Hey, we said we would give her a head start, so we honor that."

Meredith rolled her eyes and scoffed. "You can't be serious. This was supposed to be *my* game, so I should make the rules."

"We did. But you know it wouldn't be fun without some challenges. I'll make it interesting for you. If you can wait the full minute, I'll shove my cock deep in *your* throat, too, when we catch her. Deal?"

Meredith looked practically feral at the offer. Good, the more wound up she was, the more mistakes she would make.

"Deal."

I glanced at my watch.

Thirty seconds ... fifteen ... five ...

"That's long enough. Let's catch our meal," Meredith growled as she ran off. At least she obeyed the rule of using our speed and kept hers at an average human pace.

I followed close behind, moving through the trees and dodging fallen branches in the damp earth. The rhythmic thumping of Emily's heartbeat grew louder as we approached the river. I had lied to Meredith and told her the river was a mile deep in the forest, but it wasn't. It was much closer. Hopefully, she'd be too distracted with the promise of fucking to hear the heavy flow of the water.

As we descended a small hill in a thick grove of trees, the sound of the river grew louder. But something else was running ahead of us. Heavy footsteps that weren't Meredith's ... or Emily's.

Right on time.

Meredith burst through shrubs and stopped at the bank of the river, her confused gaze fixed on Emily. Not only had Emily reached the river, but she stood on the opposite bank with a devilish grin, heat burning in her dark brown eyes. "Well, shit," Emily said. "I guess we won't be fucking after all."

"What the hell is going on?" Meredith seethed and rounded on me as I walked up. "If she doesn't play the game, we can kill her. Right?"

A bitter laugh rumbled in my throat. "Emily and I had something more fun in mind. I'd brace myself if I were you."

"What—"

A wall of deep-green light smashed into Meredith, sending her flying back ten feet as Emily unleashed the full force of her magic. Meredith's skull cracked against the flat rocks, sending a spray of blood against the bark of a fallen tree.

Immediately, Meredith sprang to her feet, fangs bared, and bolted for Emily. But her steps faltered, and I seized her by the throat, squeezing until her eyes bulged. Her legs flailed in the air as I lifted her from the ground. "Feeling a bit unsteady? Well, I forgot to mention something about Emily and her coven. They have powerful paralytic magic and spells that render vampires immobile. Emily's blood, while enticing, acts as a mild poison when consumed. So, that strange numbness in your legs. That's her gift. Now, if you behave, they may go easy on you."

I threw her to the ground, her body hitting with a loud thud. Two figures stepped out from the eastern edge of the forest and came toward us.

"Meredith, if you haven't met, I'd like to introduce Hendrick Anders, Alpha Wolf, and his new Beta, Brayden. He took over after Jackson ruthlessly killed Franklin."

Meredith struggled to her knees, her face twisted in rage and horror.

"The Bayou Perot Pack? You're working with werewolves?"

I shrugged nonchalantly. "I wouldn't say *working* with them, per se. We cut a deal, that's all. One that not only benefits my goals but the wolves can finally get the justice they've been wanting since Andrei killed the Alpha's wife, Alana. They can't bring her back, so they decided to destroy and take what he loves most away: power, his club, his reputation ... and you.”

Meredith tried to lunge at me, but Emily snapped her fingers, shooting vines of green magic to wrap around her legs and hold her down.

“Why the fuck would that even concern you, you traitor?”

“It doesn’t. But the wolves wouldn’t have agreed to help me if I didn’t provide *something*.”

Her eyes widened as Emily hopped over some stones in the river and back to our side. She splayed her fingers, and the vines around Meredith writhed, lifting her off the ground.

“What is she doing?” Meredith asked, panic growing in her voice. Emily just smiled as the vines tightened and small red flowers bloomed from them. “I can’t move!” She screamed and tried to wrench herself free. But the magic was too much for her weakening vampire strength.

Emily approached and placed her hands on each side of Meredith’s head at the temples. She chanted a spell, and a blue light formed at her fingertips. Meredith screamed even louder, her cries reverberating through the dense forest.

When Emily finally released her grip, she went to Hendrick, holding up her glowing hands.

“May I?” she asked, and he nodded. She lifted her fingers to the Alpha’s temples, closed her eyes, and chanted a different spell. The blue light flickered out, and Hendrick opened his eyes. “Did you get all that?” Emily asked, keeping a hand on his temple.

Hendrick’s gray-blue eyes glowed in the darkness, the yellow of his wolf side burning just below the surface. He nodded again. “Thank you, witch.”

Meredith groaned, "What the fuck did you do to me?"

Emily strolled in front of Meredith, just out of reach. "I pulled your memories and gave the information to the wolves. They need it to find your friend Andrei's contracts, including the one where that rival pack put out a hit on the Alpha's wife. You were chock-full of useful knowledge, including the code for the club and Andrei's safe. So, thank you, sweetie." She puckered her red lips and blew Meredith a kiss. "My vines will last for another few minutes, so I suggest you wrap this party up." She turned to the Alpha. "I'll send my witches to help with whatever you need." Emily walked past the wolves, going over to me and kissing me on the cheek. "Thank you again for getting Wendy out of our coven. She gave witches a bad name, and you know, you're not all that bad for a bloodsucker." With that, Emily walked toward the forest and back to the club. I watched as the darkness swallowed her before turning to Hendrick and Brayden.

"Every contract Andrei has ever taken is in the safe in his office at Black Diamond. You know how to disable all the security measures now. All I want is the key and Book of Shadows inside the safe. It's an antique bronze with a fire symbol etched in the center of the key head. I can't get it myself without fear of being spotted or caught. He has too many men to put down for me to do it myself."

"And what about this bitch?" Hendrick growled, jerking his head to Meredith, whose eyes were wide with horror and disbelief.

"You can do whatever you want with her. Aside from Jackson, Meredith is his closest ally. You destroy her, and you deliver a heavy blow to him. I'll be long gone by then. I'll contact Brayden and discuss retrieving the key and book by tomorrow night."

The Alpha reached out his hand, and I shook it. I could see a lot of pain behind those eyes. He lost his mate, and it left a deep scar that would torment him for the rest of his life. I tried not to think about that.

"Our deal is done, Jase Halpert," Hendrick said.

"Our deal is done," I repeated, dropping my hand. The two men went to Meredith and gripped her arms, ripping her free from the poisoned plants. Her body shook, and she had no power left in her legs.

"Jase," she panted, "please ... don't do this."

"Sorry, darling. The brother I once knew died that night in Fiskardo, the moment he slaughtered our parents without a second thought. If he doesn't wake the fuck up, his existence will drag us all to hell with him. He may believe I've forgiven him, but he's wrong. I'll never forgive the blood on his hands, the betrayal that's turned my entire life into a nightmare. Fuck Andrei, and fuck every single one of you in his goddamn new family."

Without looking back, I walked into the forest, the sounds of Meredith's panicked screams following me.

Music to my fucking ears.

CHAPTER 13

ANDREI

As night fell over New Orleans, the city hummed to life. I took a deep breath, listening in on the chaotic energy and savoring the scents of the evening. There was one scent in particular that caught my attention ... spilled human blood, reminding me I needed to feed soon.

Liam and I headed to meet my driver, Dominic, who had his phone pressed to his ear. He looked stressed. When he saw me, he spoke a few words and hung up.

"What's going on?" I asked him, my fingers curled into fists at my side. In the corner of my eye, I noticed Liam subtly shifting next to me, as if he could sense my change in demeanor.

"Alexei called from outside the club," he said, sounding uneasy. "No one can get in the building to open up. He's called Meredith a hundred times but mentioned he hasn't seen her since last night."

My stomach felt like it plummeted into ice.

"There's a spell on all the doors and windows, too, and some strange symbols written on everything. Someone's also blocked off the sewers. A few security guards were inside, but we can't get a hold of 'em now." He paused, looking to me for directions."

"What do you mean that there's a spell? Why haven't our witches been called? What about the cameras?"

"No one can get a hold of them, either, sir. Someone disabled all the security cameras two hours ago, so no one saw who entered the club to do all that shit." Dominic looked even more distressed, but I didn't care. I turned to Liam, baring my fangs at him.

"Is this your coven's doing?" I growled, grabbing his shirt collar.

Liam seized my wrist and sent a tendril of red mist down my arm, snapping against my flesh and forcing me to release him. I shoved him away, and he straightened his shirt back. "You know goddamn well we didn't do this. That den of sin is of no interest to the coven. We just want the sword and her mother dead. This sounds like a personal problem."

I snarled, feeling the threads of my self-control fray.

Yanking the car door open, I said, "Dominic, get us to the Black Diamond as fast as possible. I don't care if you have to run over pedestrians. Get. Us. Back."

Without another word, the others climbed into the car, and we sped off into the night.

⁕

Dominic deserved credit for getting us back to the club in under ten minutes, even though he broke every traffic law while not killing anyone.

During the drive, I managed to leash my anger but felt its beast roaming beneath my skin, still agitated at the disrespect and inconvenience placed on me.

As soon as I find the intruders, I'll shred them into pieces and feed them to the Mississippi catfish, I mused as we pulled up to the front door.

My head of security, Alexei, was waiting. I shoved open the car door and strode over to him. The assholes who did this had chained off the front door, and several markings covered the ornate wooden surface.

The markings resembled ancient runes but none I recognized from when I practiced the craft centuries ago.

"What the hell is this mess? You couldn't find *one* witch to help? Why do you even bother showing your face to me?"

Before Alexei spoke, Jackson rounded the corner from the alley.

"This is worse than we thought. It'd be smarter if you came through the back door. Witches weren't the only ones who sealed off the building." He paused, his eyes narrowing. "We've got bigger problems than we were told. Trust me, it's not just magic at play here."

"Then who was it?"

"The Bayou Perot Pack."

"The werewolves? Not possible. Those dogs have nothing to do with magic, and besides, we killed more than half the pack, including their Beta, Franklin."

"And you killed the Alpha's wife," he remarked. "Don't be a fool to think the wolves wouldn't recruit a coven to help them carry out their revenge. You knew damn well they'd never let that go."

"The Moon Stone Pack killed her," I reminded him. "I was just their weapon to do it."

Jackson jerked his head toward the alley, and Liam and I followed. When we reached the back of the building, a prominent symbol painted the green metal service door. Liam let out a low whistle.

It was the crest of the Bayou Perot. It was a pair of wolf fangs glinting under a crescent moon with a torn, bloody bat wing draped over the moon's curve—an old symbol of the eternal struggle between my kind and theirs. The bastards wanted us to know it was them.

I growled and walked to the door, but Jackson grabbed my shoulder before I could touch the handle. "Someone spelled the building. No one has been able to touch it. See?" He lifted his hand and touched the door. There was a loud crack in the air, and Jackson yanked back his hand, his skin blistering.

"It's a blood shield spell," Liam remarked from behind us. He closed his eyes and lifted his hand. A red glow trickled from his fingers, touching the door as if probing the shield. After a few seconds, he opened his eyes. "Well, shit. The spell's tied to you, Andrei. You're the only one who can break it and get inside." He waved a hand to the crest. "Touch it, and the shield will crack."

"Not to state the obvious," Jackson started. "But I think you'd better stay outside. It's pretty damn clear we're walking into a trap."

"Someone compromised my club, Jackson—*my* business. Fuck those wolves. I refuse to let some weak magic deter me. Liam, you'll come inside and deactivate any magic those wolves used."

Liam nodded, while Jackson shook his head and stepped back. I grabbed the door handle, and in an instant, a flash of pain and blue light shot through me, followed by a pop that echoed down the alley. I wrenched the door open, nearly tearing it from the hinges, and stormed inside. As I rounded the corner past the DJ booth, I froze.

"Jesus Christ."

My club was unrecognizable, with debris and wreckage everywhere. Broken shards of glass and liquid from every bottle of wine and liquor that was once behind the bar now spread out along the tile floor.

They'd ripped everything apart, leaving only splintered wood and torn upholstery. Deep claw marks marred the furniture, ripping through the leather sofas and chairs.

The cushion foam hung from the rafters like globs of yellow fat. They'd smashed the tables beyond recognition, scattering parts across the torn-up carpet. A wolf had ripped the red marble bar clean from the wall and slammed it vertically into the center of the dance floor. Every glass and light fixture lay shattered, the glass twinkling in the mess.

Liam walked past me and kneeled on the floor. He let his magic flow across the tile, covering the walls and broken furniture in its red tentacles. He looked at me with a grim expression. "There's no trace of other magic on this floor. No traps, nothing. They wanted to trash the place and leave the mess for you to see."

I clenched my hands and walked deeper into the area. That's when the smell hit me. Rage coated my tongue, burning my throat.

Vampire blood.

I looked more closely at the walls and saw dark splashes. Beneath the clotted blood lay piles of ash.

The missing security guards.

Jackson came up next to me, his face stricken. "What in the fucking hell?"

Hot rage boiled inside me. *I'm going to rip out their spines through their mouths.*

As I opened my mouth to bark orders, there was a muffled cry coming from my office. The three of us took off up the stairs, and I threw myself against the locked door. The wood cracked in half and fell into the dark office. An even more intense smell of blood washed over me, and I staggered back.

That scent was familiar. Too damn familiar.

Carefully, I flipped the light switch and illuminated a prone body sitting in my desk chair—a form that was dripping blood into the carpet, a form with pale, golden-blonde hair.

"Meredith!" Jackson shouted, taking a step into the office. I threw my arm out and stopped him.

"Don't," I said steadily, but my body and mind were anything but calm. "Look at her."

The wolves had bound Meredith to the chair with silver chains, an eerie glow against the links, most likely magic to keep her from breaking free of them. They also strapped a silver gag over her mouth, as if to silence her screams. The rips on her clothes showed me she'd fought back before they subdued and restrained her. Even with her head hanging low against her bloody chest, I saw she was still alive.

When I looked closer, I saw that silver staples had sliced open her arm, and dark red blood dripped down her skin, pooling on the floor. *She must have been here for hours.*

I looked over my shoulder at Liam and hissed. "I thought you didn't sense any magic." I pointed toward Meredith. They were the same chains I had used to tie up that messenger, Brayden, when we exchanged a hostage for Keith.

"The power's so faint I couldn't detect it downstairs," Liam whispered. "Just go slow, and don't touch her. I'll work on disenchanting the silver chains first."

Slowly, Jackson and I stepped into the office while Liam chanted his spell. We moved toward the chair, and at the sound of our footsteps, Meredith's eyes opened, and her head shot up. She began thrashing, muffled shrieks coming from the silver gag. Meredith shook her head back and forth, and a glint of metal around her throat caught my eye. It was a wire.

The room fell silent, as if something sucked out all the sound, leaving only the steady ticking of the clock against the wall.

I turned to grip Jackson by his shirt's collar, but it was too late. When one of his legs moved forward, his foot hit a small peg in the carpet, and a whirring noise. The wire suddenly tightened against Meredith's throat. I used my vampiric speed to rush toward her, but the moment my hand reached out to grip the wire, it sliced deep into her neck.

My eyelids couldn't even blink before Meredith's head rolled from her neck and dropped into her still-twitching lap. Liam gasped from behind me as my body went still, my breath caught in my throat. I staggered back until I felt Jackson's chest, then fell to my knees right as Meredith's corpse crumbled into pieces of ash and flesh, falling to the wet carpet.

"Fuck! Meredith! Meredith, no! What did I do?" Jackson fell to his knees with me, his breath ragged. My jaw cracked as I gritted my teeth in fury. That's when I saw the trap in its entirety.

The bloody wire had snapped away from her body and ricocheted against the wall with a crack. I jumped to my feet, leaving

Jackson behind me as I followed the wire toward my bookcase. I realized then that magic had concealed something.

My blood ran cold as I saw several stacks of C4 come into view, each stack with its detonation wire going into the walls of my office. They had rigged Meredith as a bomb, and she had inadvertently set it off. I ran to Jackson, grabbed him by the shoulder, and sprinted out of the office.

"Liam, run, dammit!" I shouted as I shoved Liam toward the stairs to run with us. Together, we crashed through the front door, where Alexei, Dominic, and two other staff members waited. "Get away from the building! Run!"

We all began rushing down the street when a roar chased us. A wave of intense heat slammed into our backs, throwing us into the dirty, rain-clogged gutters. Then the world shattered in a concussive blast of brick and smoke. As broken pieces of the club rained down on us, I threw my hands over my head. Nearby cars blared, and distant shouts of humans rang in my ears.

Once the debris had settled, I lifted my head and looked back at my club.

Smoke filled the air and climbed toward the rising moon, but soon, I saw beyond the thick black clouds. My club was gone, reduced to rubble and ashes. I rose to my feet and ran back to the shattered building.

"Drei! What are you doing? Stop!" Jackson shouted after me, but I drowned out his voice.

I only had minutes before the police started digging through the rubble. I needed to get the key and the book.

I leaped over the partially broken wall attached to my office and ran to where the vault, now surrounded by drywall and burning wood, sat smashed into the floor. The fire raged around it, and the paint started peeling away from the metal. I hurried over.

The explosion didn't do this, but someone had unlocked it, the door wide open, and the latch pulled back into the lock.

I reached inside, moving my hand around, and felt nothing. "No!" The Book of Shadows, the Burning of Angels Key, and my murder for hire contracts were all missing.

There were only three people who knew where I'd hidden them. They must have tortured Meredith for the code as she was the only one who had it.

Rage burned inside me as another thought came to my mind. *Where's Jase?*

I stumbled backward, dropping to my knees. My knuckles slammed into the concrete again and again, each blow splitting the skin open, only for it to heal moments later, then tear again with the next hit. Meredith, my friend—my loyal companion for over a hundred years—was dead. The Fire key and Book of Shadows were gone, the only hope to save Jase's and my souls from burning in the Underworld.

Like a wild animal, my screams pierced through the darkness.

Rage ... only pure blinding rage ....

CHAPTER 14

JASE

It surprised me that Tony remained in the city despite the situation with the Black Onyx. Although he had been relieved of his duties to the coven, he still worked as a bartender at Lune de Blanche.

Over the last four years, I watched Rachel and, by proxy, her closest friends. Wendy, who posed as Hailee, was also my source of information about Rachel's movements. I wanted to learn as much as I could about her before I struck. Tony, though, was an enigma. Wendy could only tell me that Tony knew everyone in the city, and while he was like a brother to Rachel, he had a little crush on Lucy, constantly watching her when she was looking the other way.

Other than that, I had no intel on him.

Given that I had turned Lucy, I was most likely on her shit list. Expecting me to show up at his doorstep wouldn't be on his radar tonight. I had to be ready for him to attack, but with his guardian bond to Rachel no longer a thing, he was unlikely to land a blow.

After securing my bike, I walked to the front of the building. Fortunately, a woman with black hair and peach-colored skin was using her keycard to open the door, while balancing a bag of groceries in her arm. The moment she pulled it open, I slipped in after her and into the lobby.

"Oh, shit. Um ..." the woman's voice trailed off as she realized I snuck in after her and didn't have a keycard. Now she wondered if she should call security or let me pass.

"I'm sorry. It's not your fault. I left my wallet in my new apartment and was running back up to grab it," I said, flashing a charming smile. "My name's Jase." I held my gloved hand out, but the woman only looked at it. She shifted the bag of groceries against her chest. "I moved into the building last week."

At times like this, I wished I had the gift of compulsion as some of those Valentina turned directly. I could be out of this situation within seconds. My gifts were a tad different. Unfortunately, Andrei had the same gifts as me, making it harder for us to fight against each other. Though we were vampires with superstrength and speed, our enhancements exceeded most of our kind. So, the only power I could use on this innocent woman was snapping her neck before she could even blink. The last thing I needed was their security detail, who were most likely viewing the camera in the foyer, to stop me before I could reach Tony's door.

Or alerting the Five-Point Order.

I homed in on the woman's heartbeat, slowly going from a rapid pace to a more calming one.

"Oh, well, welcome to the building," she said, but her voice had a slight tremor. She wasn't sure yet if she could trust me. "What floor?"

Now she was testing me.

I smiled again. "Third floor, down on the east side."

The woman smiled back and gestured her head toward the elevators. "Ah, me too. I'm on the west end, but we can ride together."

I gave her a nod. "Here, let me at least help you carry that bag."

As we entered the elevator, I went to press the button for the third floor. Before I could, the woman reached out and brushed her fingers against my exposed wrist. Her blue eyes went wide, and she jerked her hand back. "You're ..."

I let out an annoyed sigh. "Please don't panic. I'm one of the good ones," I lied, flashing her a wink. But her face went pale, and her fingers curled around the bar on the side of the elevator as if she might bolt.

"I would like my bag back, please," she said firmly, arms tightening around her stomach now. Although she kept her expression blank, I could hear the rapid pulse of her heart, each beat faster and louder than the last. Her eyes remained on mine, not even blinking, as if breaking eye contact would shatter what little control she had left.

She had none.

"No, I'll help you bring the groceries to your place."

Her nostrils flared slightly as terror emanated from her like a sweet perfume. I questioned what Valentina told me about still having a soul in moments like this when I had a human cornered. I could smell this woman's fear, her disgust, and all I felt inside was the endless craving to drink her life away.

The elevator doors slid open, and we exited into the hallway. "What's the number on the door?" I asked.

"Please, don't." That was when her eyes turned glossy. She was going to cry.

I stepped closer, reaching my right hand to her shining black hair. Slowly, I tucked a loose strand behind her ear. She had silver rose-shaped earrings. "Look, I'll make it quick, I promise. You might even enjoy it."

The tears flowed freely now as she let out a hard sob. My victim wouldn't look at me now, only nodding as she led us down the hallway to her apartment. The woman pulled out the key and unlocked the door. Once inside, I looked around and scented the air: no pets, children, or a partner.

I set the bag down on a nearby blue-gray couch and turned to her as she closed the door. She was smart for not running; it would only make things worse if she poked the beast and caused me to hunt her down. I touched her face, making her flinch away.

"I can't have you reporting me to the Five-Point Order or human law enforcement. I'm sorry."

Before she could speak, I grabbed her by the throat and spun her around, pressing her body against mine. There was so much fear coming off her that my mouth watered at the smell of it. The monster within me craved this destruction, this ending.

My lips pressed against the soft skin of her neck, wrapping my left arm around her waist. The woman gasped and struggled against me. I sunk my fangs into her neck, and she cried out, digging her nails into my jacket.

To vampires, it was second nature to feel aroused when the first taste of a victim's blood touched our tongue. Especially when they were afraid and fought against us—a sick and perverse pleasure, but addictive, nonetheless.

But as she thrashed and kicked at my hold on her, I realized something. There was no physical or sensual response in my body as I drank. I felt nothing, just a yawning chasm that bore an emotion I couldn't acknowledge. The woman's hands clawing at my arms slowed and then fell to her sides, her body going limp against mine. I released my fangs from her throat and tossed her body on the floor.

Her complexion was now chalk white, her lips the same. Although she was still alive, her breathing was labored, and I knew death would claim her within minutes. Something strange overcame me then, and I stepped back, my shoulders hitting the door. I watched as her chest rose and fell in a stuttered rhythm.

"Please, just accept death and go," I whispered. "I have things to do tonight."

While listening to her slowing heart rate, I looked around the apartment more in-depth. The place had a simple feel, with little furniture and only a handful of décor scattered on the walls. But a large, framed photograph caught my eye in the other room. I stepped past the dying woman, crossing the threshold for a better look.

My victim grinned widely, standing between an older man and a woman. I took in the details of their faces staring at me. The frame had an engraving: "The Family Trip Yosemite." The photo held so much joy, love, and purpose in their eyes. A family that knew the meaning of closeness.

I looked at the father. He and his daughter shared the same eyes, blue like the sky after a rainstorm. She shared her mother's complexion with the same shade of dark hair. The mother had striking green eyes that looked eerily similar to *my* mother's.

I glanced over my shoulder at the woman, watching the blood slowly trickle down her neck and drip onto the carpet.

What would Mamá think of all this? Of me causing so much pain the way that Andrei caused hers?

The thought jarred me. "God fucking dammit," I cursed before spinning on my heel and walking over to her prone body. I kneeled beside her and sliced open my wrist with my fangs. I held the bleeding cut over her mouth, dripping the blood onto her lips and tongue. "Drink."

The woman, barely clinging to life, tried to push my arm away. I lifted her head and tilted it back, forcing her mouth to open further.

"I said drink," I growled. "Now."

Her throat clicked as she swallowed, allowing her to consume more of my blood. I lowered her back onto the floor.

"Listen carefully. My blood will heal and replenish what you lost. I promise you'll not become a vampire like me." I pointed to the window behind us. "Just don't throw yourself out the window, and you'll be fine. In fact, try not to die for a few days."

A slow touch of color rose in her cheeks, and the woman sobbed uncontrollably. I stood straight and headed to the apartment door.

"Oh, and if you report me, I *will* come back and kill you. Be grateful I'm sparing your life."

Once I stepped back into the hallway, I wiped the blood from my face with a rag I kept in my pocket before moving toward the east wing of the building. Tony's apartment was at the end of the hall, with music blasting through the walls. I pounded on the door, hoping he'd hear me over the noise. The music faded, and the door swung open. Tony stood there; his face went from confusion to shock before twisting into a vicious scowl.

"Hey, Tony," I said cheerfully. "We need to talk."

CHAPTER 15

JASE

Tony's reaction didn't surprise me. He tried to slam the door in my face, but I caught it just in time and shot him a glare. "Try that again, and—"

Tony raced to the bedroom, slamming the door behind him before I could finish my threat, probably to find something to shoot me with. I couldn't say I blamed him. Just a few months ago, I threatened the woman he considered a sister and turned her best friend into a vampire against her will. He probably thought I was coming for him next.

I scanned the apartment, waiting for Tony to find whatever weapon he needed and return. The living room was slightly messy, with magazines and an empty bottle of Jack Daniels on the coffee table. Tony's black leather jacket hung over a kitchen chair, and his cell phone was within reach.

I walked to the phone and picked it up. Tony must have used it recently since there was no lock screen on. While waiting for him to return, I casually flipped through the text messages.

Nothing from Rachel.

"This wouldn't be a fair fight, you know? You're not bonded to Rachel anymore, so any supernatural strength you used to have is long gone. You're just a mortal going against someone like me. If you'd calm down for a second, we could talk like rational men. I'm not here to kill you."

The door swung open, and Tony came charging out, a shotgun leveled at his shoulder. The weapon had been modified, and I saw that a thick wooden stake was inserted into the barrel.

"Oh, that's cute," I derided. "Would you put down the damn gun? I'm here to talk like adults."

Tony didn't lower the weapon, only lifted it higher, steadying its aim at me. "You have some nerve showing up here," he barked. "Some fucking nerve!"

Irritation burned in my chest, but as much as I wanted to lash out, I couldn't, for obvious reasons. "I'll give you the courtesy of my patience. You just hit strike one. I'll not ask again. Put the gun down."

Tony's arms trembled, his heart speeding up to a quickening beat. I needed to de-escalate this clusterfuck before there was a trigger finger mishap.

"It's about Rachel, if that changes anything," I said. "She's in danger, and maybe we can put aside our grievances, and you can hear me out."

Tony froze when I mentioned Rachel's name. While he didn't trust me at all, he lowered his weapon slightly. "What about her? What's happened?" he asked.

"Sit down, and I'll explain everything." I pointed to the couch.

He carefully moved to the couch and sat down, the barrel of the gun still aimed at me. "Don't think I won't stake you if I don't like what you say."

I rolled my eyes and moved to the second couch across from him, removing my leather jacket and tossing it onto the cushions. I ran a hand through my hair.

"Alright, I'll get to the point. I gather you know Andrei and I came into possession of Valentina's ring at the church and what the consequences of wearing it are?" Tony nodded. "Andrei plans to save mine and his soul by summoning the warrior angel Ezrylos and using his magical little sword to kill Lucifer. Thus saving us from eternal torment, destabilizing the Underworld, and securing his power in the vampire species." Tony's eyes widened, and I leaned forward, clasping my hands between my knees. "He needs Rachel's blood to do it." I swallowed. "The spell's dangerous. It could very well kill her in the end. And if it doesn't, he's planning to bring her back to his dungeon at the mansion to make her his plaything."

"Jesus," Tony gasped out.

"Though my past actions would suggest that I have some nefarious agenda to kill Rachel and her mother myself, I don't. I want to save her from Andrei, but I can't do it without yours and Lucy's help."

Tony stilled at Lucy's name and glared at me.

"I know, I know," I replied. "I had the same expression when the revelation came to me, too."

"Give me one damn good reason why I should even *think* about helping you. If you can't answer that, get the fuck out of my house," Tony growled, tightening his grip on the shotgun.

I breathed out, the image of that night in stark detail behind my eyes. "Four months ago, at the train station in Boston, Valentina told me something right before she and Rachel took off."

Tony's brows pinched together.

"She said Rachel and I are fated mates," I said and watched Tony's brows shoot up. "That celestial magic wove our destinies together two hundred years ago, and the bond solidified the night I released Valentina. As much as I don't want to believe it ... it explains a lot. The way I've felt about her these last four years while I watched her. No matter how much I fight it, something deep in my dead heart pulls me to her. Believe me, Tony, if I could make it stop, I would."

Tony's jaw dropped, and he stood quickly, gun forgotten, running both hands through his hair.

"Yeah ... take your time with that."

I watched as Tony mulled over what I had shared before plopping back on the couch. He shook his head. "How?" he asked. "You're a vampire, and she's ... It doesn't make sense. Not you and Rachel. You tried to kill her—"

"If I wanted to kill her, I would have." I turned my eyes from his and dropped my head. "This would be a lot easier if it wasn't true. But something pulls me to her, and I need to know what it is, which is *another* reason I need to get to her. You and I now share a common goal. You want to keep her out of Andrei's clutches as much as I do, and Rachel won't hear me out unless her two best friends vouch for me."

Tony threw back his head and laughed. "Vouch for you?" he said mockingly. "First off, Lucy wants to *kill* you, motherfucker. What the fuck makes you think she will help you? She won't let you get within ten feet of her best friend. And despite what you've told me, I don't think I could either."

I bit the inside of my cheek, trying to control my anger. This went a hell of a lot smoother in my head. "Well, it's Rachel's funeral if you don't. My brother will lock her away, the ancient covens will hold the most powerful weapon on this planet, and you can kiss your freedom goodbye. Once they bury Rachel from the world, don't think they won't come for anyone who knows she's a dhampir, keeping their precious secret safe in their little culty caves. That includes you and Lucy. Tick. Tock."

Lucy had lived in Andrei's mansion since Rachel sent her to him. Though Andrei honored his word and never put her in danger, that didn't mean he didn't try to indoctrinate Lucy into his ideologies about vampirism. Andrei wanted to make her see humans as only a means of survival and pleasure for vampires. He and his men watched Lucy at all hours, waiting until she'd crack and tell them about the house Rachel was hiding in without giving away that they had her location pinned on a map. Meredith even tried the "confidant friend" role to get her to open up. Lucy saw right through the bullshit. So, if anyone can help me get Rachel to listen … it's her.

"Look, Andrei knows Rachel's in Venice. Okay? He knows. It's only a matter of days before he boards a plane and hunts her down."

Tony's eyes widened again in panic, my heightened senses homing in on his rapid heartbeat. "How does he know?"

"He put a GPS tracker in her body. On top of that, the guardian bond has grown stronger. He can sense her from here. Not where she is, but what she *feels*. Whatever Rachel experiences, he knows about it."

"Ah, fuck," Tony muttered, running a hand through his messy hair. "It wasn't like that with us. Not even close. I mean, there were times when we trained that I felt her energy so close to me. But unless she was terrified to her core ... nothing other than the faint sense of her presence. The bond lets you summon each other. Even the night she fought Andrei, she believed everything was under control, so I felt nothing. I don't know how else to explain it."

Andrei had told me exactly how strong the bond had gotten over the last few months. He had theorized that drinking each other's blood may have amplified the magic enough that he could always feel her presence. Even when Andrei wasn't physically touching her, the sensations felt real to him. The things he told me about ... what he'd done with her? It made me burn with rage, and it took every ounce of my self-control not to let it show—pretend like I didn't care when all I wanted was to tear his fucking throat out.

I wanted to kill him for touching her.

There was also the matter of Lucy. She kept her distance after we got back from Atlanta. She knew Andrei wanted to find Rachel but questioned his intentions. Smart woman.

"You know Lucy's going to lose her shit if she sees you," he said.

Lucy had been roaming the streets of the French Quarter for months, relying on the kindness of strangers to donate their blood in government-run clubs. She was determined not to become the monster Andrei was trying to twist her into, so she refused to feed from any of the suppliers.

Even with the clan keeping her on a tight leash, Lucy defied them every chance she could, making connections with everyone she met at bars and hotels. Lucy may have hated Andrei for harming Rachel, but she loathed me with every fiber of her being. She was waiting for the perfect moment where she could run a stake through my heart and rip me to shreds. Meeting with me would be the last thing Lucy would want to do.

"This is the part where you tell me where Lucy is, so we can go get her. We're running out of time and I need to get a key and book stolen from Andrei's safe."

Tony raised a brow, but then he gave me a quick nod before standing and heading to the kitchen. He opened a drawer and pulled out a false bottom, producing a burner cell phone. "What is this key and book?"

I stood and went to meet him at the counter. "I'm meeting with Brayden Whitlock to get them. I'll explain more on the way. He's—"

"Yeah, I know who he is," Tony interjected. "You're working with werewolves now?"

I shrugged. "Let's just say that Bayou Perot has a score to settle with Andrei, and when that happens, we'll be long gone." My phone buzzed in my pocket, and I reached in and pulled it out before scanning the message. "Ah, speak of the devil. He just sent the address." I tucked it back into my jeans and then looked at Tony with a knowing smirk.

He stood silent, still looking way too wary by the way his lips pressed together. Likely debating everything I had told him and trying to determine if I was telling the truth.

I waved my hand in the air like I was brushing him off. "You know, maybe I should just go alone. Dragging Rachel back while she fights me the entire way sounds ... tempting." I flashed him a wolfish grin. "But I'm sure you wouldn't let that happen, would you?" I leaned in slightly, poking the bear. "I could have Rachel chained to my car door and be in Greece by Thursday night, but hey, I'm sure you'll want to be the one to stop me. Your call."

Tony's heart picked up its anxious rhythm as he swallowed and gritted his teeth. "Give me ten minutes to pack a bag, asshole."

We met with Brayden outside of New Orleans, about an hour north on the banks of the Mississippi around ten. We still had one more stop to pick up Lucy, so we had to make this meeting quick.

The wolf was waiting on a decrepit dock when Tony and I pulled up on our motorcycles. As soon as the engines cut, Brayden hurried over to us. When he saw Tony, he stilled. While Tony knew everyone in Louisiana's supernatural world, these two hadn't met yet.

"Who's this?" Brayden asked, his fingers tapping nervously on his thigh.

I held up my hand. "Tony was Rachel's guardian before Dimitriou stepped in," I explained. "You can trust him."

Brayden sniffed the air, no doubt taking in Tony's scent. After a breath, he smiled before reaching into a black pouch that hung from his belt and pulling out the key and the small Book of Shadows. I didn't need to touch it to know it was the legitimate key. The power thrumming from it was so heavy I could feel it dancing over my blood and bones. Since I was born a Fire witch, the magic was that much stronger. It felt like it was pulling at me, reaching for the power I had lost two hundred years ago. It wanted to latch on to a ghost, to pull it back from darkness.

But then again, I wondered if my soul was still within me, as Valentina claimed. *Did I lose it?*

Brayden handed me the items, and I felt the warm metal of the key press into my palm. I closed my eyes, wrapping my fingers around it and feeling a tiny spark hum against my skin. If my soul were still somehow inside me and linked to Rachel, what would happen if she and I were in close proximity? What would awaken then?

"Jase?" Tony snapped me out of my thoughts. "We need to go. I made a few phone calls, and my contacts reported that Lucy has been at the same club every night this week. I'll give the club a call on the way to confirm she's there."

I nodded and quickly tucked the key and book into my satchel before slinging it over my left shoulder. Tony followed me to the river, and we both threw our cell phones into the deep-black water.

"By now, the wolves would have taken care of Andrei's club, so he'll be distracted for a while. We can't be sure he isn't tracking us even without the phones," I said, turning to Brayden. He nodded nervously as if trying to follow my train of thought. "If we want to get out of here, we must become ghosts."

CHAPTER 16

JASE

Tony called the club before we hopped on our bikes, confirming that Luciana Morales had indeed signed into a private room tonight. And luckily for us, she was still there. Tony led the way to the club on his motorcycle, and I stayed close behind on mine. During the trip, I kept scanning the cars in case my brother gathered his wits quicker than expected to hunt me down.

Fortunately, we arrived undetected at a small club called the Ruby Rose. It was a blood-sharing club run exclusively by the Five-Point Order. I hadn't heard of it before, but Tony gave me the rundown as we walked to our bikes. This club was more like a blood bank than a den of sin like Blood and Envy. There was no sex, no debauchery of any kind. There was just music, some wine, and monitored feedings.

It was an old brick building that once housed a sugar mill a hundred years ago. The Order purchased the land after the treaty and converted it into a haven for vampires who wanted to feed on humans but not kill them. A concept that had been growing in popularity since the Devil's Uprising. We approached the large glass entrance that bore a stained-glass rose emblem over the archway. A doorman stepped forward to meet us, his black sports jacket fitted snugly over his broad frame and a small, jeweled rose and pentagram pin on the lapel. His red hair glowed under the lamps, and his pale skin seemed almost translucent.

As we approached, his sharp green eyes watched us. "Good evening, gentlemen," he beamed. "Do you have an appointment?"

His cheerful tone irked me, and I thought about shoving past the man and walking in. Before I could, Tony moved past me, mimicking that same repulsive grin. "Are you Freddie McIntire?" Tony asked.

"The one and only," Freddie replied.

"We spoke on the phone tonight. I'm Tony Manetti."

Freddie nodded, and his face lit up. "Yes, of course. We have you on the schedule for eleven twenty. Lucy's finishing up with her eleven o'clock." Freddie looked at me, and his eyes narrowed. "Vampires have a different vetting process that requires you to speak with Rebecca. I'll need to see both of your IDs. After you check in, she'll give you a quick tour before your appointment."

This was going to take too damn long. I smiled anyway and handed over my license to Freddie.

"Alright," the man said. "Give me five minutes to get you checked in."

Freddie pulled out a radio before going inside the building. He began speaking, and when I tried to listen with my enhanced hearing, I realized I couldn't.

"Soundproof magic," Tony explained, seeing my frustration pour from me. "Keeps the secrets safe from nefarious eavesdroppers ... like yourself."

I smirked at him and crossed my arms. "I gotta warn you. I've seen Lucy like this. You haven't. Are you sure you're ready to see your friend as a vampire? I mean, you haven't seen her in four months."

Tony winced as he inhaled sharply through his nose, shoving his hands in his jacket pockets. "From what my sources have told me, she's the same. Well, except instead of struggling to lift a crate of beer glasses, she can bench press an entire car now."

I huffed out a laugh. "Lucy lost her humanity. Don't be so naïve as to think she's the same."

Tony glared at me. "I get that you've lived a life full of bloodshed and violence, but what if this entire theory about vampires not having a connection to their souls is bullshit? We know vampires' souls go to Purgatory until they're gone for good. But what if pieces of that soul stick around, letting vampires hold on to their humanity? I don't know. Maybe it's all bullshit. Or it all comes from that demon blood Valentina passed down from Kylan." Tony flashed me a side smirk. "You're not an asshole for not having a soul because it's not the soul that makes you a decent human being." He tapped my forehead with the tip of his finger. I debated biting it off. "It comes from inside there."

Tony looked over at the entrance, and then he turned back to me.

He has more to say.

"You need to feed on humans to survive," he continued, "and watch everyone you have ever cared for die while you live on. I get it. I understand why you'd use the power of a vampire to shut it all off. Vampires like Lucy, though, would welcome every moment of grief, sorrow, and joy to avoid becoming a monster."

I blinked, surprised by Tony's thoughts. Love and desire weren't entirely foreign to me. I *had* felt those brighter emotions before. The demon part of me wanted only to kill, destroy, and feed. But the other side I buried long ago wanted to rip free and smother the darkness.

Freddie came back outside before I could open my mouth and ask questions I didn't know how to ask.

"Alright, Mr. Manetti. I've cleared you to meet Ms. Morales in her private room. When you enter, head up the stairs and down the hall to the check-in desk. Rebecca will get you inside and escort you there after your tour."

Tony smiled and extended his hand to Freddie. "Thanks, man."

Freddie grinned and shook his hand eagerly before turning to me. "Behave yourselves in there. The Five-Point doesn't tolerate violence in places like this. If you touch anyone without permission, we won't just kick you out, if you catch my drift."

I curled my lip at him and raised a particular finger in the air. "Scout's honor."

Tony sneered at me. "Come on. Let's go."

We walked past Freddie and up the black granite staircase leading to the Ruby Rose.

At the end of the hallway, a woman with warm brown skin and a beautiful smile sat at a deep walnut table. Her gold-plated name tag read, "Rebecca."

"Mr. Manetti. Come on, guys. Follow me," she said cheerfully as she rose to lead us to a pair of stainless-steel double doors with a keypad and card reader.

She produced a black card with a five-point star emboldened on the surface and tapped it on the reader. She then pressed a few keys away from our eyes. There was a hiss of metal locks, and the door swung open easily.

Rebecca rounded on us. "Now, there are rules in this establishment that *have* to be followed. The first rule is absolutely no unsanctioned feedings. The vampires already have assigned volunteers, and any interference will result in immediate execution. No excuses; you're dead. We staff several wolves and witches to deter any unacceptable behaviors. Second rule: if you fight, we'll kill you. You have an issue with a vampire; you take it outside and away from here. The establishment refuses to allow any violence that could harm humans or get us shut down. The same punishment applies here—last, no inappropriate behavior."

Her dark eyes landed on me pointedly, as if I'd already been singled out for a warning.

"We're aware that a vampire bite can be euphoric, but that's no excuse to engage in sexual activity. This place isn't for that. We'll bar you from this club forever, and our witches will ensure you never return. Are you clear on the rules, gentlemen?"

I offered her my best smile. "Crystal clear."

Tony gave me a side-eyed glance before nodding. "We'll behave."

We stepped over the threshold into the club, and my mouth parted. I'd expected something clinical, like sterile white walls, shitty music, and communal wine for guests. Instead, I walked straight into the 1920s.

Elegant glass lamps bathed the main room in a warm, dusk-hued light. Mahogany and green velvet couches sat in almost every corner and wall space, and each table was dressed with vases of red roses that pricked at my senses. There was a lively buzz of laughter, too. Guests lounged on the furniture, sipping their wine and picking at plates of food as a soft saxophone solo drifted through the overhead speakers.

On the left-hand side was a bar with rows of liquor bottles across the glass shelves. Near the back were several numbered doors. Some had a red rose attached to the handles, while others were bare. I looked around and noticed a few staff members stationed around the room and near the doors. A sniff in the air told me they were all werewolves. One of them kept glancing in our direction, mainly focused on me.

The best choice to subdue a vampire if they get out of line.

The club was so unlike anything I had ever seen before. Most places I frequented were dark dens of blood, lust, and pain. Even the other Five-Point licensed businesses weren't this laid back.

"Well, this is different," I said to Tony as we crossed the room. Everyone's eyes glanced over at us as we passed and then back to their conversations, uninterested.

"The main rooms serve as meeting places for vampires and their suppliers, and witches use them to monitor the security cameras," Rebecca said, pointing to a black glass bulb on the ceiling and in every corner of the room. "They use magic to detect abnormal behaviors from either group and deal with them accordingly."

Way too many fucking rules. A place like this would drive me crazy.

Rebecca stopped before a dark red-brown door with a red rose woven through the bronze handle. She flicked her pointer and middle fingers over the handle, and the rose wilted and fell to the floor.

"Enchanted locks to keep wandering folks out of private sessions. When the pair is done, the rose will wilt and fall. I'm the only witch who bypasses the Rose Lock spell in case of emergencies—or other circumstances. From the looks of it, your companion was close to finishing her session, anyway. Just give her a few minutes, and wait until her client steps out of the room."

Once Rebecca left us to wait and rounded the corner, I placed my hand on the doorknob, but Tony grabbed my arm.

"Wait, I need to go first. Lucy might panic if she sees you right away, and we can't risk a brawl with an innocent human in the crossfire. Not to mention—" He pointed over his shoulder at the werewolves.

I sighed and stepped back, gesturing to the door. "Have at it, then."

Tony's hand shook a little as he grasped the handle and pushed the door open. The suite mirrored the main area, but it was clearly meant for a more private, one-on-one experience. The warm lighting made the dark-green walls look almost black. A couch was in the middle of the room, and Lucy and a human man were on it, propping up against several pillows.

From the looks of it, she wasn't done feeding from him.

Lucy leaned over the man's throat, her long black hair falling forward and concealing most of her face. Carefully, she wrapped her arms around him in a close embrace as she fed, her sleeves rolled up and tattoos visible.

Andrei told me that shortly after Lucy joined the clan, she expressed relief that her tattoos remained after I'd turned her. Anything new would heal too quickly for the ink to take, but those marks stayed. She saw them as a physical reminder of the humanity taken from her.

The man was in his thirties, with thinning brown hair and a lean build. His eyes were closed, and he was enjoying the euphoric effects of a vampire bite.

After a few seconds, Lucy pulled her head away from the man's throat. He opened his eyes and winced, putting a hand over the puncture wounds.

"Oh my God. I'm so sorry. Did I hurt you there?" Lucy asked frantically. She didn't notice our presence as she reached for a warm cloth beside the couch and pressed it against the man's neck. "I'm sorry. I don't enjoy doing this. Are you okay?"

"No, I'm fine, thank you," he said, looking up to meet her eyes. "I actually enjoy the pain, as odd as that sounds."

Lucy smiled while Tony's eyes filled with anguish. He then cleared his throat, drawing the pair's gaze to him. I quickly ducked out of sight and waited.

"Lucy," he called. "Sorry to interrupt, but we need to talk."

"Tony," she breathed before jumping to her feet. "How did you know I was here?"

"It doesn't matter." Tony looked at the man, who stared nervously at him. "You can leave now."

The tone suggested no argument. He nodded, rising gradually to avoid feeling faint and falling over. He grabbed his coat and looked at Lucy one last time. "Thank you, Miss Lucy. See you next month."

The man brushed past us and disappeared into the main room.

I peered around the doorframe as Tony stepped into the room. Lucy looked at him, her mouth open in shock. Within a breath, the two moved forward and pulled each other into a hug, as if they were afraid something would rip them apart again. Another nagging pull in my chest flared. I rubbed my sternum as I went into the room and shut the door behind me.

"Well, isn't that touching?" I said coldly. The two jumped apart, and Lucy hissed at me, showing me the fangs that she hadn't retracted yet.

"Demons like you don't get to enjoy places like this," she growled. "Get the fuck out of here."

Her dark eyes shifted crimson, but Tony stepped in front of her.

"Lucy ... wait. He's here because of me. Actually, because of Rachel." We both watched as her eyes grew wide. "Yeah, like I said, we need to talk."

Lucy turned back to me, her eyes boring into mine, as if her stare alone would burn a hole through them.

Since I'd turned her, we'd done our best to avoid talking or being in the same room. She'd spent most of her time outside the mansion but was still part of the family, still moving through the halls of the home and making friends within the clan. Not that I was afraid she'd stake me from behind; I just knew that I'd done something pretty fucked up to her, and I gave her the space she needed.

With me coming into the one place she felt truly safe, I was stepping on dangerous ground. Right then, I realized it was going to take a hell of a lot of convincing to get her to trust me.

Lucy turned to Tony, and her eyes finally softened. "What do you mean ... Rachel?"

Tony shifted on his heel and nodded. "I'll let the *demon* explain this one, but you might want to sit down."

Lucy's eyes widened, but she nodded, moving back to the couch. Once she settled on the cushions, she leaned forward, placing her elbows on the tops of her thighs, and crossing her forearms. Her furious gaze lifted to meet mine. "What the hell is going on?"

"This might sound fucking insane to you, and frankly, it took me a long time to accept it. So, try to keep an open mind." I exhaled slowly, trying to find the right words to explain this shitty mess. "Months ago, I was hell-bent on catching Rachel and using her for my own agenda," I explained. "I wanted her blood to awaken and take revenge on her mother. I had even planned to kill her after I inflicted as much punishment as I could on the woman who destroyed my family. She was my means to an end. But something changed. Something that solidified my thoughts about her over the four years I followed her."

"Four—" She paused, her fangs out again. *"Four* years?"

Fuck, I never mentioned that.

I waved my hand. "Again, means to an end. The wolves got a little creative in my brother's club and blew the damn thing up tonight. I don't think it'll take long for them to notice my absence."

Lucy's jaw dropped before she pressed her lips into a thin line. She leaned against the back of the couch, and Tony touched her shoulder gently. Lucy nodded at me to proceed.

"Valentina told me the reason I couldn't harm Rachel, even that night in the church, and why I feel compelled now to find her."

I ran my hand through my hair.

"Apparently, the divine magics had a plan for me from the moment she was born. Our souls latched on to each other, and she somehow pulled my soul back from entering Purgatory when Valentina turned me. At least, most of my essence stayed behind, sealing a fate under that blood moon I never thought possible."

Lucy blinked. "What the fuck are you talking about?"

"Rachel and I …" *God, why does saying it out loud make me so uneasy?* "… are fated mates. The pull to be near her was created when the Hades Blood Moon crossed the sky two hundred years ago. The bond took full effect during that same Blood Moon at the church in Boston when she fed on my blood."

She placed her palm over her mouth and shook her head.

"Look, I don't know if what Valentina said was the truth, but I need answers, and I can't let Andrei capture Rachel and lock her away forever. What he plans to do to save our souls from Hell could *kill* her."

She shook her head. "Andrei wouldn't do that."

"Yeah, he would," I said. "Andrei made a deal with Black Onyx. In exchange for retrieving a power source to kill the Devil, he gets to lock Rachel away in his lair for all of eternity *if* she survives the spell. We got wind of it once he found her living somewhere in Venice. He's had a tracker on her this entire time."

Lucy fell silent, her hand pressed against her heart like it was pounding against her ribs. The gesture was so human, and another uncomfortable emotion tried to make its way into my head. "But Andrei doesn't know where she is … *exactly*, right?"

"Some mansion outside of Venice. He never showed me where, though. We haven't entirely gained each other's trust. He just needed to gather resources to make his move. Of course, with the destruction of his club, this may delay him."

Lucy cleared her throat. "Um … but I might know where she's at … exactly."

Of course, she does.

"Care to share?" I asked, while Tony folded his arms tightly across his chest, giving her a heated look.

"Oh, come on, Tony. I'm her best friend, for God's sake. She didn't want to put you in harm's way, so I promised her I'd keep it a secret. I'd delete the call log as soon as we'd hang up. I had her saved in my phone with a different name."

"Lucy," Tony said, "especially now that you know where she is, we need you to come with us. Andrei will figure out what's happened and slaughter everyone, including you, if not to manipulate you into something you know deep down is wrong. We have to protect her from him. And we have to do it now."

Lucy glared at me, hatred still burning in her eyes. I stared back. She must have seen something because she sighed and grabbed her purse from the coat rack near the door. "You know I'd do anything for Rachel. So, consider yourself lucky, *Jase.* But it doesn't mean I like you."

CHAPTER 17

JASE

Thanks to Tony's contact, Shannon Lewis, we had quickly secured new documents and passports for Rachel. With those in hand, we took Lucy back to the mansion. She slipped inside and quickly packed a bag and her passport before sneaking back out. Most of the clan had been out of the house, likely dealing with the explosion, so no one had noticed her.

Now we faced a long flight from New Orleans to Venice. Long layovers meant we wouldn't arrive until tomorrow morning. Hopefully, the explosion had bought us enough time before Andrei realized I was missing and came after us. If we were lucky, it would slow him down just long enough.

Still reluctant to be anywhere near me, Lucy sat in the window seat, focusing on a few novels she had bought at the airport. The flight was at full capacity, so we had no choice but to sit together. Tony sat between Lucy and me and spent several hours using the phone's Wi-Fi to map out our route once we picked up the rental car and grabbed Rachel.

"Okay," Tony said, finally tucking his phone away. "Once we get the car, we'll need to stake out the house before going in. The last thing we need is Valentina stopping us before we reach Rachel. We'll have to wait until sundown, anyway." He turned to me. "But there's something you need to do, though."

I gave him a quizzical look. "And what's that?"

"When we find Rachel, you gotta stay behind and let Lucy and me approach her first."

Though a slight irritation ran through me, I nodded because their idea was less reckless than mine. It wasn't as if Rachel and I had a happy ending before she took off with my ring. I was the last person Rachel would want to see, and more likely, we'd end up killing each other before we could have a mature conversation about why I was there.

But the possibility of being around Valentina made me nervous. That bitch promised to do everything in her power to break us apart, and seeing my face would no doubt throw Valentina into a rage. As much as I hated being tied to Rachel, I wasn't ready to get ripped apart before I figured out what the hell this bond meant for me.

"Are you sure you know the address?" I asked Lucy. "How long have the two of you been in contact?"

She smiled. "Since the day she left. She made sure that at least one of her friends knew where to find her in case of an emergency. I memorized it, though. It was too risky to write it down."

"And if she's not at the house when we get there?" I asked.

Tony shrugged. "We'll just have to trust that 'bond' *you* have and hope it's better than your brother's."

I shifted in my seat and cracked my knuckles, my jaw stiffening.

Tony smiled coldly. "You know, it's funny how the idea of your brother manipulating her makes you agitated, yet you did the same thing with using Hailee as a plant in our friend circle. You manipulated Rachel to get to that church and awaken her mother. Now you're risking your life to find her and essentially save her from *Andrei's* schemes." Tony leaned back in his seat and smirked. "I'm starting to believe this fated mate story you're telling."

I let my smile slip. "How do you know I'm not using you right now to get to Rachel and kill her?" I asked, raising a brow.

Tony rolled his eyes at me. "You blew up your brother's fucking nightclub, murdered Meredith Loren, his most loyal companion, and sold his secrets to Bayou Perot. If you were acting on his behalf right now, this is one goddamn crazy way to do it."

I looked straight ahead. God, four months ago, I used every manipulation tactic at my disposal to get Rachel where I wanted her. Then everything changed when she drank my blood and saved my life when we fought those demons. Even after that, I remained the villain by hurting her, taking that ring, and trying to kill her mother. I mean, in that moment, I wanted to. I needed to. Being so close to her made me feel everything I had been trying to suppress during the four years I had watched her. My free will felt like it was stripped away, reminding me of what her presence did to me. I'd never experienced anything like that with anyone in my entire life.

Honestly, I was unsure of my own feelings about it.

"Yeah, well, I needed to send a nice little message," I said. "As far as what I feel, I don't fucking know. Ever since the church, all I've felt was jealousy, need, and lust. And something else ..." My voice trailed off before I turned from Tony and rested my head against the seat. "Valentina was right. I was supposed to hate Rachel. It would have made killing her so much easier."

"And now you're trying to save her."

I turned back to him. "Fucked up, isn't it?"

Tony nodded grimly. "So, how is Andrei going to cast this spell that supposedly weakens her after he pulls out her blood, summoning this 'warrior angel?'"

"There's a Spirit witch named Liam who works for Black Onyx, but now he's contracted to work for Andrei. I've noticed he's in Andrei's ear a lot. That can pose a problem. He'll be the one to cast the spell and use Rachel as the means to do it."

"Why Rachel specifically? She's a dhampir, not a witch or anything like that," Lucy piped in, her novel open on her lap.

That's right, Lucy doesn't know the entire history.

"Valentina was born a witch before being turned into the first vampire. Her ring, created by Kylan, allowed her to access magic. When she was pregnant with Rachel, that magic passed on to her. Not only that, but Rachel's father was human. Rachel is *unique*. She shares the blood of a witch, a demon, and a human. The blood of three realms. She's the perfect sacrifice to open a portal to the Upper World and summon their most powerful deity." I thought about one more thing. "An angel created the spell, so someone with angel blood has to break it."

Tony and Lucy's eyes widened in abject horror, and Lucy's hands gripped the book in her lap with such force that it started to tear. "I've seen the sketches in that Book of Shadows you stole, but aren't you still doing the spell to get the sword?" she asked, panic seeping into her voice. Tony reached over and grabbed Lucy's hand.

I shook my head. "Andrei plans to take the ring because he needs magic to subdue the angel and destroy Lucifer. With us, she'll keep the ring on. We would only use her blood to activate the pentagram, enter the summoning circle, and destroy the obelisk. If we destroy that magic, then he can't summon shit."

"In other words," Tony said, "if he gets his hands on the sword, he'll use it to kill the Devil, and then he'll hand it over to Black Onyx in exchange for Rachel." He ran a thumb over Lucy's hand, a silent reassurance.

I ignored their touching moment and closed my eyes. My thoughts went back to that night at the church and when I spoke to Valentina at the train station. Something had fundamentally changed, which rocked me to the core. I spent so long being burned alive by anger and betrayal at what Andrei did to our family and plotting revenge against the vampire who took my brother from me. I blamed them both for the destruction of my life and the endless nightmares in my head.

What I didn't account for was Andrei falling into madness after putting the ring on. Nor did I expect him to fall for Rachel so fucking hard. Now he was on a mission to save our souls from the Underworld while putting her at risk. Andrei was willing to destroy everything to lock her away like some prized pet for his enjoyment.

Granted, we were both monstrous men, but my motivations changed when Valentina told me about my fate.

The mark on my stomach tingled again at the thought of Rachel. I ran a finger over the raised flesh beneath my T-shirt. It wasn't the first time it had reacted when she came to mind. Closing my eyes, I pictured her face—those beautiful blue eyes.

As I conjured up an image of her in my mind, Tony let out a heavy sigh, causing me to open my eyes and look at him. "Let's not be fooled into thinking Andrei isn't already buying a ticket to head over here. Right now, our focus is getting Rachel. Once we do, we need to put some distance between us and Venice."

"What about the guardian bond?" Lucy asked. "Won't he know where she's going?"

"He can feel her emotions but can't detect where she's at," I said. "That's why he has the tracker, so that thing will have to come out when we find her."

"Maybe we get her away from the home she's staying at before we do," Tony suggested. "If Andrei shows up after us, he's using that device to track her down, and we don't want to put innocent people in danger."

"I can't believe that fucker did that," Lucy cursed and leaned back into her chair. "Once we cut it out, toss it in a bush. As long as he thinks she's still in that area, he won't know she's on the move with us."

"This would be so much easier if we had a witch like Wendy to put a cloaking spell on her," Tony explained.

Lucy winced at the name of her fake dead friend. "I wish I could have beaten that dirty cunt senselessly and ripped out her heart."

While Tony and Lucy snickered at her remark, I let my head tip back onto the headrest, remembering how close Wendy got to fucking everything up.

Soon, the hardest part would be over. Then I'd have to decide what I truly wanted. Could I let Rachel go a second time?

The thought of seeing her again after everything that happened made my chest strangely ache. I had no fucking idea how to tell her the universe fated us since that first Hades Blood Moon without sounding like a lunatic.

Fate bound her to a monster—a man she loathed.

Maybe there's a way to remove it? And if not, I'm about to turn her world completely upside down.

CHAPTER 18

RACHEL

Luka and I headed into the villa's training room around seven p.m. It was a wide-open building about the size of a small airplane hangar at the back of the property and away from the main house. Darius had outfitted the floors with top-of-the-line black foam mats. He built it to withstand everything from claws to knives to fire. Reinforced concrete walls enclosed the space, lined with metal shelves stacked with weapons and potion ingredients.

The vampire mothers who used the stone to have children passed on their powers to them, allowing the dhampirs to wield both a vampire's strength and a witch's magic. That night at the academy, the coven hadn't just battled a vampire-human hybrid—they had faced those who could harness elemental magic.

Like me.

But *unlike* me, the three dhampirs had been learning to control their powers since they could walk. Not only did they know exactly what they were capable of, but they could control it with ease. I, on the other hand, wasn't quite there yet.

Darius commissioned the training facility shortly after the Black Onyx placed Valentina in a deep sleep. Even though Darius said there would be no war with the witches anymore, he still wanted to protect his clan, so training took place once a week. Now that we were about to recruit clans in every corner of the world, he wanted us to train more often.

The two vampires, Alessandro and Tati, taught weaponry and combat during the evening hours. Magic was, of course, taught by my mother. She knew once my powers resurfaced, she'd have to start from scratch with me. I lived life like a vampire and a human, not a witch.

Today's training combined martial arts with magic implements. They paired me again with Giovanni De Luca because he beat me in hand-to-hand combat a few days ago.

When I entered the training room, Valentina and Tati were speaking in the far left corner by the water fountain. They leaned in close, completely engrossed in conversation. She must have sensed me because her icy blue eyes found mine in a heartbeat. Though I was getting better at shielding her when she tried to enter my thoughts, it slipped this time. She wanted to tell me something later.

"She seems on edge," Luka murmured as we unpacked the hand wraps. "Think she's mad at you?"

"Probably. Valentina knows I took off the ring. She tried to confront me the other day after we got back from the garden, but I brushed her off. It's going to be another argument," I replied, wrapping dark-blue strips of fabric around my wrists and knuckles. "Not that I give a shit. Defending myself from compulsion takes priority. I'll come up with a story after sparring."

Luka just shrugged. We finished wrapping our hands and went to the mats with the other dhampirs, with Tati and Alessandro instructing us.

"Alright, guys," Tati called out. "Today's training is magic combat. The drills will be like last month's exercises, except you'll use offensive tactics and face off against your opponent from yesterday. We'll start in five minutes. Please separate into your groups and get ready."

"Gio isn't winning this time," I growled under my breath. Luka snickered, giving me a sympathetic look before heading off to the other side of the mat. Jealousy coated my tongue as I walked over. He was so good at what he did. Over the last four months, Valentina helped me with my Water element. I was getting better, but I still struggled to rein it back in when I commanded it. When I summoned water, it would come out as either a trickle or a fucking geyser. It didn't come as naturally as it did for her and everyone else born with elemental powers.

In the church, when I screamed, the power surged through my body like a tidal wave, and I couldn't calm down until the energy was exhausted. That was the kind of magic I wanted again, only without the lack of control.

Maybe I was overthinking it.

Cracking a few knuckles, I began my warm-up stretches. If we were using offensive magic, I would have to up my speed to evade Gio's Earth spells. I've been on the receiving end of one too many of those attacks, and the concussions were not worth it. Not to mention, Gio's proficient magic also enhanced his vampire strength, which was why the black eye took longer to fade.

Gio was a dhampir from Naples, born shortly after Luka as a result of the spell. His mother, Lyra, was an Earth witch from the Daughters of Dusk—the very one who summoned the Witch of One and stole the gem. His father, a native of Naples, passed down a lot of the traits common to the region. Gio had often talked about how he and his father looked so much alike.

Though immortal, he looked like he was in his early twenties. He was massively tall and well-built, his medium-brown skin complementing his deep hazel eyes. His long black hair, often tied into a bun, made him look even more elegant. It was honestly intimidating most of the time. But even with his strong, muscular frame, Gio had one weakness—his love of sweets.

I guess that was the perk of being immortal; we could eat whatever we wanted and not have to worry about our insides falling apart.

"Morning, Rachel," Gio greeted me, a wide grin painting his handsome, very young-looking face. His heavily accented English was flawless, and we often joked with each other. He was immediately welcoming when Darius first introduced me to him and Ava.

"Buonasera," I replied. "Are you ready for round two?"

"Yeah, I'm ready to ... how do the Americans say 'kick ass and take names,'" he replied, followed by a playful smile.

I threw back my head and laughed. "You're absolutely correct on the term, dude," I said while I finished stretching. "Just leave my face alone today."

Gio's warm hazel eyes glittered with excitement. "Let's have fun, and may the best dhampir win."

"Alright, Hardmann and De Luca, you're on the mat. Remember, keep your powers contained to your surroundings. If there is any power overflow, you're DQ'ed. Okay?" Tati shouted, taking her position at the edge.

We both nodded and faced each other. From the corner of my eye, I watched Valentina join Alessandro and Ava to watch our match. She looked frustrated yet again.

Join the club. It's not like I haven't been trying to master my power.

I rolled my neck. Black Onyx extensively trained me to evade magic and use hand-to-hand combat for nearly two hundred years. I took a deep breath and reached within my vampiric nature. There, my beast was waiting, fangs ready. My human heart kept a firm hold on her but let the reins loosen just enough to tap into my speed and strength. My beast growled, wanting more freedom, but I soothed her fury.

Not now.

I opened my eyes, vampire power now at my command. Ava let out a quiet gasp, and I knew it was because my eyes had shifted to a black-blue color. My eyes had never turned to crimson like my mother's and other vampires'; this was uniquely mine.

"Are you both ready?" Tati asked. Gio and I nodded. "Bow."

In unison, we dipped forward in respect.

"Begin!"

Gio immediately launched the offense, coming at me with a flurry of punches glowing with a golden light. I deflected each one before ducking a haymaker. Using the muscles in my right leg, I slid my left back at an angle I knew would find a mark. Pushing off, I kicked out, slashing the air at blinding speed. My shin connected with Gio's exposed ribs, and there was a meaty thud. Gio grinned at me before grabbing my leg. He flung my body across the mat, and it took a few twists mid-air to land within the ring. I landed with one knee bent, one outstretched, and my left hand digging into the foam.

"Nice try, Gio." I hissed out a laugh.

"Good kick. That fucking hurt like hell." Gio rubbed his side, wincing slightly.

I smirked before lunging. We became a blur of fists and kicks. Gio's magic made him damn near invulnerable, and I knew it would be only a matter of time before one of those landed and fucking *hurt*. I tried to focus on drawing my magic to the surface, but I was met with silence.

I dodged another kick to my head, executing a backflip away from the blow. Glancing down at my hands, anger boiled in my gut. Everything I'd done for the last four months, I still had only felt traces of my magic. Gritting my teeth, I looked up too late to see Gio's magic coming at me.

"Shi—!" I yelped as conjured stones whizzed past my head, one the size of a softball striking me square in the cheek. My head fell back, and I dropped to a knee.

While blood dripped from the gash, the familiar itch told me it was already starting to heal. Luka, as he always did, shouted a string of encouragement, but my mother, on the other hand, glared right at me, piercing into my damn soul. Heat flared under my skin as anger rose like a tide. With a snarl, I drove my fist into the ground, the crack of splintering cement echoing through the room.

"Halt! Thirty-second pause. Goddamn, Rachel, rein it in," Tati scolded. I nodded sheepishly.

"Sorry," I called as I rose to my feet and took a couple of deep breaths.

Maybe now's the time to test out my idea.

My fingers slipped into my pocket, and I found the item I had retrieved from my dresser. I felt the jagged edges of the amethyst press against my palm as I pulled it free. The gemstone was one of the four remaining elemental magic stones Lily Winchester had given me back in New Orleans. I had used the jade stone to fight against Wendy, and it gave me the power of Earth. Amethyst represented the element Water; this should be a damn cakewalk since I was technically of the Water elemental bloodline. The magic in the stone could help me channel this better.

I closed my eyes and concentrated on the cooling power of the stone. Like last time, I made up an incantation to awaken the water's energy.

"Water to blood, I beseech thee. Let the life of all awaken within me. Waters of the sky, Earth, and sea, awaken and let your rushing power flow free."

There was a cracking sound in my head, and a cooling rush of water filled my veins, mixing with my vampire power. The beast within me roared at this new power. Unlike Earth magic, which only coated my skin, my body eagerly devoured this energy, taking it all within myself, like it was meant to be a part of me. My hands tingled with power. There was strain, however, and the mixed energies were fighting to overtake my mind. I redoubled my mental control.

"Rachel, Gio. Resume!"

I charged with my right fist cocked back. I let the magic trickle through my knuckles, coating my hand in glowing purple mist. There was a collective gasp from them, including Valentina, as they saw the mists manifest around me. Gio grinned wildly at this turn of events, conjuring a stone shield in front of his body. My power slammed into his with a flash of light and water spray. I spun around, using force to strike a knife-like blow against the shield. There was another crack as my blow left a clean gash in the rock. Gio grunted before kicking out, forcing me to retreat. The shield began to mold and reshape into a long club. He twirled it deftly in his right hand, and I flashed him a feral grin.

Even though I'd borrowed it, this magic felt natural, albeit strenuous. But if this were the way to wield my abilities, I would gladly take the burden for as long as the amethyst lasted. Gio swung his stone club at me, and we fell into a rhythm of punches, kicks, and blocks while magic energies danced around us.

As we fought, my smile broadened. The magic was making me feel punch-drunk. I wanted more of it. I wanted to see what I could do. Flipping away from another kick to my ribs, I raised a hand over my head and began concentrating. Wendy had manipulated her magic into weapons. Maybe I could, too.

I began channeling more magic into the mists, expanding and molding it into the weapon I pictured in my mind's eye. The purple fog swirled and writhed beneath my fingers, elongating into a halberd.

Fuck, yeah!

Then I made a mistake.

I added more magic, so much more that my vampiric power leeched in. My fangs pressed against my lips, and the crackle of energy only added to the burden.

The strain was unbearable.

"Rachel, stop!" Valentina shouted over the roar in my ears. "Stifle the power. It's too much!"

I didn't know how. The chaotic energy of the mists in my hand was beyond my control. I fell to my knees and cried out as magic and vampiric energies fragmented and exploded. A pulse of purple mists and dark-blue vampire power surged, forcing Luka and Valentina to throw shields around those in the room. The ceiling cracked, and drywall dust rained down. The blast threw Gio onto his back, and he coughed.

"Fuck! Are you alright?" I asked frantically, scrambling to my feet before running over to him. "I didn't hurt you, did I?"

Gio slowly rose and threw back his head, letting out a deep, hearty laugh that shook his entire body.

"Rachel, that was the most fun I've had since the academy. I've never seen vampire power and witch magic come together like that. No one here can do what you just did, not even me. We've always kept our powers separate, so what you pulled off was incredible. I owe *you* pastries tomorrow."

I sank back on my heels, running a trembling hand through my hair, and scanned the training room. Luka, Alessandro, and Ava stared at me in awe and, from what I could sense, a kind of reverence. Tati had a stern look, though, and I could see why. Large chunks of concrete and rebar steel had fallen from the cracked walls. *Well, shit.* Some lights, broken and loose, dangled from their wires. But it was Valentina's look of distaste that made me freeze. I had cheated to access magic, and it had backfired.

"Well, that was fucking wild," Luka said, finally breaking the silence. His hand gripped my arm and Gio's hand, pulling us to our feet. "I say we call it a night until we can fix this room."

Heat burned my cheeks. *Shit.* I hadn't realized how bad it was until I did a complete three-sixty.

If the ground wouldn't mind swallowing me whole right now, that'd be great.

Luka slung his arm over my shoulder. "If you think you're the first of us to damage this room, I have news for you. I do it all the time." He flashed me a smile. "This was probably the fiftieth time in the last two hundred years. Even the one at the academy had a few repairs from shit like this. Don't stress over it."

I nodded and headed toward the exit, my head hanging.

I didn't get far before I saw Valentina storming toward me, her shoes falling in my line of sight as I strode through the garden toward the house.

"Rachel? Why did you use an elemental stone?" Valentina asked in her harsh, judgmental tone.

I turned my head up to glare at her. "Why not?" I hissed, tears burning the corners of my eyes. "Every dhampir in that goddamn room is stronger than me. Even Alessandro and Tati. They don't even have magic! I know you wanna send me out there to help recruit clans and start a war, but how can I do it when I can barely defend myself?" I waved my ring-bearing hand in the air. "Just because I have this doesn't mean I'm safe. For fuck's sake. You've been harassing me for months about this. I wanted to see if the amethyst would help me control it better. Make it stronger."

"And you think cheating and destroying the training room is the right way to do it?" she chided. Valentina moved in front of me, forcing me to stop. "You have to allow magic to flow naturally, or it will backfire just like that. Not only did that magic turn on you, but your vampire powers were also uncontrolled. Who knows what could have happened if we didn't shield everyone?" She stepped closer to me, invading my space. "You could have *killed* them." Her accusation made me clench my fists. "I didn't risk everything using that stone to create a child like me just to be disappointed. You have a purpose—a purpose I gave you. I meant for you to be like *me* ... powerful ... ready to destroy anyone in our way. Not with some damn pebble. It's time to act like a Vasile!"

Frustration, anger, sadness, and self-loathing were burning in my lungs. I couldn't breathe, couldn't think behind the dark energy roiling inside of me. The edges of my vision went dark, and my breathing grew raspy.

"Rachel?"

I tried to contain it, balling my hands into fists, the muscles in my hands straining under the force. Everything came crashing down on me at that moment. *Breathe. Breathe.*

And then I screamed. I screamed from deep inside my chest, the same surge I felt that night in the church. A concussive sound wave burst from my throat, and violet mists shot out of my body, slamming into the surrounding trees and brick walls around the garden. Everything exploded into pieces, wood and torn leaves raining down around us.

Valentina used her vampiric speed to move closer, attempting to shield me from the debris, but I still felt the force of branches and rocks hitting my head and back.

Once everything settled, I looked around. Only a few flowering shrubs and trees remained standing. Everything else was a crater. My eyes widened. Though I had caused a shit ton of destruction, I didn't feel bad about any of it. Letting all of that out felt fucking amazing.

Yes, it was the same power I used when Andrei and Jase were about to kill my mother, only this time, it wasn't fear and desperation that triggered it. My gaze fell on Valentina, who surveyed the damage around us. Our eyes met, and she huffed out an impressive laugh. "Well, that's twice now that you've used that scream."

I pulled my brows together, confused. "I don't understand. How am I doing this?" I asked, no longer giving a shit that she had just reminded me I was some progeny project to carry on her legacy.

Seeing how upset I looked, Valentina gently squeezed my hand.

I honestly thought she'd be more pissed than this, like she was in the training room.

Valentina pulled a twig out of my hair before saying, "You did that without a damn stone. We can work with this development, and I think we can foster it because now we know what fuels your powers."

I blinked. "Frustration and anger?"

She nodded. "At least it's something you feel a lot."

Even though I was still annoyed with everything, I grinned in relief.

"We do need to talk to Darius about the fact that you destroyed his property," she continued, looking around at the mess I made. "And I don't think he'll be as lenient as I was with you."

Fuck.

CHAPTER 19

ANDREI

My back pressed against the wall of my office, blackout curtains drawn tight. With my legs extended on the plush green carpet, I closed my eyes and took a long, steady breath. Part of me wanted to smash all the furniture into pieces, but I had just renovated it after the last time I wrecked my home office, and I didn't want to shell out more money so soon.

The small bronze hourglass clock chimed four p.m., and I looked up, irritated. I debated crushing the clock to cease the incessant noise but stayed seated.

I was sure I had been sitting here for hours.

"Drei?" Jackson called my name as he opened the office door. I looked up at him. Despite the absolute nightmare we'd been dealing with, including Meredith's murder, Jackson still held his head high. He leaned against the doorframe and crossed his arms over his broad chest, eyes fixed on me.

I knew I looked like hell—nothing like the calm and collected vampire boss he'd known since the '80s.

He saw a disaster sitting on this carpet: my disheveled dark hair reeking of smoke, dark circles under my eyes from not feeding since last night, and the pale, cracked skin of a monster. My torn jacket lay next to me, forgotten, and my dirty white shirt remained unbuttoned at the top.

If I saw myself, I would be unrecognizable.

I caught a glimpse of my hands in my lap, still coated in ash from the fire, and my skin prickled. It was a brutal reminder of last night—the look of terror in Meredith's eyes before she was decapitated and set off the explosives in the club.

Clenching my fists, I tried to recall all the information my clan had gathered about the people responsible. We knew three things: the Bayou Perot Pack was behind the club's destruction and stealing all the files from the safe. As for why, I wasn't sure. It couldn't have just been payback for Alana's death. They would've just taken the contracts that the Moon Stone signed to orchestrate the killing. Instead, the wolves stole *every* contract I had.

It would stand to reason that the pack intended to expose all the sins of New Orleans and destroy the Accord once and for all. The truth in those documents would tear everyone apart, both humans and supernaturals alike. Bayou Perot was making a power play in which they would come out on top, possibly ousting my clan as the ruling class.

They wanted to own the city, and this was their first move.

When those secrets came to light, the Five-Point Order and the human government would come down on my clan *hard*. The Four-Fold Accord was a flimsy treaty broken a hundred times over. I was just the assassin who kept their hands clean. Everything I had built over the past century was about to be destroyed.

The wolves wanted to start a war in my city.

They're about to get one.

Second, they knew how to get inside the club and take out the security guards without triggering the alarms. Only Jackson, Meredith, and I knew the codes to enter the building, the office upstairs ... *and my safe.*

They must have tortured Meredith for that code before strapping a bomb to her. There was no way they pulled this off alone.

And I knew exactly who helped them.

Jase.

And now he was missing.

How convenient.

The Bayou Perot wolves destroyed my club and killed my closest friend, and it was my own fucking brother who gave them the information to do it.

"Have you found Lucy yet?" My expression was neutral as I asked, but beneath the surface, rage burned like the very fires of Hell. It was a ticking time bomb in my head, ready to detonate, and no one could stop it.

"Both Lucy and Tony are no longer in New Orleans. Right before midnight last night, someone spotted Jase and Tony at the Ruby Rose. A witness saw Lucy leave with them," Jackson replied, confirming what I had suspected. There was only one place those three would go.

It was a good thing I still had the leash on my little pet. They might be able to get to Rachel before I did, but I had the power to trap her in her mind.

She would never be free of me unless I *allowed* it, and I had no intention of letting Rachel go. Never. The guardian bond kept us tethered, and I'd be damned if I severed it.

And I always get what I want.

"I've arranged flights to Venice," Jackson said. "The last thing the Italian government needs is a vampire clan coming into their city and causing chaos. Which is why I booked just us, as well as Liam."

I nodded, rubbing a sore spot on my shoulder. "I agree. We have to be as discreet as possible. You'll have to inform Alexei that he'll be in charge of clan operations for now. Have him send all updates directly to me. If Five-Point moves before we return, Black Blood Diamond will need to prepare for retaliation."

I needed to keep my head clear for everything to go perfectly.

What is Jase up to?

With a groan, I climbed to my feet, picking up my jacket and putting it back on. After adjusting the black diamond cufflinks and smoothing my hair, I walked to Jackson. My legs wobbled a bit, and my throat burned viciously.

I need blood.

As if he could read my mind, Jackson said, "Nadia is waiting for you in the library. I'll have Joanna and Wyatt pack our bags and put them in the limo. We're leaving later tonight."

"What time?"

"Ten o'clock. We're taking the red-eye with two stops. We should reach Venice by nine p.m. tomorrow night."

"Beautiful. That gives you and me plenty of time to take a detour before."

Jackson grinned. "What sort of harrowing trip are you planning?"

I matched his grin. "Well, before we leave, I think punishing some naughty dogs is only fair."

"Huh," Jackson said as we walked along the dock in Bayou Perot. "I guess we should have expected this."

The pack had completely cleared out the homes lining the swamps, leaving only a couple of small motorboats bobbing in the black water. Something stirred within me—an itch of death. We walked toward the Alpha's house, and I sniffed the air, searching for any sign of a dirty wolf. The slightly open door and the overall state of the room suggested Hendrick left in haste. Only one lingering scent remained, and I growled low and deep in my chest.

Not everyone turned tail and ran.

"Let's check to see if they left behind anything we could use, and then torch the houses," Jackson said. "What do you think?"

Something faint pricked my ears, and I closed my eyes, homing in on the sound coming from the dock around the back of the row of houses.

Footsteps.

Using my index finger, I silently communicated to Jackson that someone was coming. He stiffened and slid out his fangs. We scanned the area outside Hendrick's home for the enemy.

"Where are the—" Jackson started, but I silenced him, taking only a single step before a snap and a rush of wind filled my ears. There. I saw a wooden arrow hurtling toward me. Even with my speed, I wasn't fast enough before the projectile buried itself in my chest, mere inches from my heart.

"Shit!" I fell to my knees, and Jackson quickly threw his body in front of me, potentially shielding me from more arrows.

"Jackson, run! Take cover, dammit," I ordered, yanking the arrow out of my chest and soaking my shirt in blood. Jackson stubbornly shook his head. The sound of footsteps grew louder, and we both turned to see a woman with silver hair and purple-pink streaks round the corner of the last house. Her eyes were blazing gold, and her crossbow pointed right at us, another bolt knocked and was ready to fire.

"I'm an excellent shot, Andrei. That first one was to get your attention. The next one won't miss. But I have orders from Hendrick not to kill you yet, as much as I'd like to."

My smile was charming, but my eyes heated with fury. "Why spare us, dog?"

The woman cocked her head. "Because you aren't who Hendrick wants, you pasty little bitch. We all read the contract. We know that Moon Stone ordered the hit to kill Alana and made it look like one of us did it. But what those other documents we took from your safe revealed ... *That* was something we didn't expect."

My grin grew wicked and cold. As much as I expected the secrets to come to light, it was still highly amusing. The Five-Point Order was about to get a rude awakening on how little the Accord meant to anyone.

"The Incubus Clan was the one who made the payment to you. They were working alongside Moon Stone for land and power over New Orleans. Not only that, but several covens paid you to execute rival witches, creating a disruption that allowed them to swoop in and take their magic for themselves."

A laugh rumbled in my chest. Not that I wanted the word to get out that every creature who signed that treaty was as sick and unhinged as I was, but if this created a war, we at least had the backing to fight the so-called leaders of Five-Point.

"Hendrick wants you to see the consequences of your need for bloodshed. He wants Five-Point to come for you when all this becomes public knowledge. The club was just the beginning of your retribution. So, why not punish you for your crimes instead of killing you? If my pack can bring you to justice, we'll have the city in our hands. You and your clients broke the treaty, and the Five-Point Order will thank us for handing over that evidence. Soon, this city will be ours. You forgot about that one little piece of the Accord. If it's vampires who break it, they'll release the hunters. They'll no longer accept vampires into this world, and you'll be outsiders again."

I barked out a laugh that time. "What makes you think your pack will survive my wrath before any hunter gets to me or my clan?" I hissed, climbing to my feet. Jackson stood too, his body angled for attack. "I'll hunt you all down and dispose of you one by one. Documents or not, you dirty dogs destroyed my club and killed Meredith Loren. We *will* spill blood. Let's start with you."

The deep burn within me intensified, filling my heart with black rage. This wolf would die at my hands, and I would enjoy every second of it. I started advancing on her, Jackson close behind.

"You think I'm afraid to die? I fucking volunteered to stay behind," the woman replied, shouldering the crossbow. "I've lived long enough that death would be a welcome rest."

Her scent caught my nose, and my eyes widened. "You're an old one, aren't you? Your wolf lifespan is on its last thread."

The woman's face hardened. "Like I said, I *chose* to stay behind. I was born under the moon in this bayou and will die under it. Kill me if you want, but know that everything you have yearned for is nothing but ash."

I lunged then, fangs flashing, and the woman fired the crossbow. The bolt whizzed past my head, but I heard a grunt beside me.

"I'm fine," Jackson shouted as he doubled over. "She hit my shoulder."

Continuing my charge, I sped across the dock in a blur. I ripped the crossbow from the woman's hands and hurled it into the murky water. My left hand closed around her throat, while my right plunged into her chest, tearing through bone and muscle. Her erratic heart thrashed in my grip, the pulsing muscle twitching against my palm. The stench of wet fur and iron filled my nose, and despite myself, I gagged. A wolf's scent was never pleasant to a vampire.

"This does … fucking nothing … you little undead bitch …" she gasped, falling to her knees. "You're marked for destruction. Your … end."

Growling, I ripped her heart free from her mangled ribcage, gore spraying over me. With a sigh, the woman's eyes closed, and she collapsed on the dock, silver and purple hair fanning out like a halo. The heart finally stopped beating, and I dropped it. Jackson came to my side, his right hand covering the wound in his shoulder as it slowly healed itself.

"What did she mean by 'marked,' Drei?" he asked worriedly. I waved a bloody hand and turned on my heel.

"It means we have to get the hell out of New Orleans before the human government sends its hunters. Come on. We need to change and get to the airport. Call Liam."

A few hours later, Jackson, Liam, and I boarded the red-eye to Italy. After ordering a glass of white wine, I settled into my seat, replaying the events that unfolded over the last few days. My empire would survive this setback. Yes, the contracts would expose the endless crimes of New Orleans, but the city was always a little rotten at its core; what was another bit of darkness?

Rachel was all I wanted. She was *mine.* My possession that was taken from me, and I'd be damned if I let her slip through my fingers again.

When I find her, I will follow through on my promise and chain her to my bed ... or in a little cage.

The image of her naked in my bed stirred me, and I adjusted myself. Maybe I could pay her a visit and remind her of who she belonged to. I pulled out my phone and connected to the airline's Wi-Fi. A thrill bounced in my stomach, and my body eased into the cushioned first-class seat.

Pick up, my little dhampy. I want to play.

CHAPTER 20

Rachel

My cell phone rang, and that familiar unknown number appeared on the screen. I groaned as I shut the water off in the bathroom sink. Was I ready to hear Andrei's voice this early in the morning?

Of course, I hated what had happened last time, but curiosity won.

I need to know how he's manipulating the bond to this extent. How the fuck did he project himself into my head like that?

Lifting my phone from the counter, I tapped the green AC-CEPT button.

"My little dhampy," Andrei's deep voice flowed from the receiver. "What are you wearing?"

A smile tugged at my lips, but before I could answer, there was a sharp tug within my mind. My vision swam as Andrei pulled me into the projection of a dark room filled with gray smoke. As I looked around, I let out a low whistle.

"I won't lie; this power evolution is pretty fucking cool. I am curious, though. How did I manage to take over the last time? If I were to call you, could I manipulate the visions—control your demented head and keep you at my mercy?" I asked. "If you know where I am, why not meet me here in the flesh?"

A figure manifested from the darkness, and Andrei stepped through the smoke. A wicked grin was on his face as he walked over to me. "I'm a little tied up at the moment. This will have to do for now."

Once he reached me, I stepped back, but he seized my hands, wrapping his long fingers over my wrists. The strength in his hands was real, *too* real.

"What the fuck are you doing?" I cried out, lifting my knee to strike him in the groin. But then I felt Andrei manipulate the bond, and my limbs jerked down. *What the fuck?* My body no longer obeyed me, like trying to punch in a dream. "How are you doing this?"

Andrei sized me up, a dangerous heat flaring in his eyes. "This is how the bond was always supposed to work. If my dhampir is in trouble or *causing* trouble, I need to feel her physical energy. To seek it out and control it. That's how a guardian is supposed to protect you."

"Oh, bullshit," I snapped. I didn't want to believe that the bond had *this* kind of power. I was already unlucky enough to be tied to him against my wishes. Of course, he'd weaponized it against me. "Release me, Andrei. You have no right holding me like this."

"Neither Tony nor your other guardians ever used this ability," he continued, clearly ignoring me, "but I bet if they did, they would have used it *often*, considering your rebellious nature. But I think its amplification has something to do with my witch heritage and the fact that Valentina turned me. Not to mention, you and I shared blood. So, why don't you relax, love? Enjoy that we can still meet like this despite being a thousand miles apart."

My eyes widened. Andrei was always a demanding, heartless bastard, but this ... something felt wrong. His intent was dangerous. What he projected went beyond his control-freak persona. This was pure obsession.

"I don't want to see or feel you," I said. "I'm free from monsters, remember? Let me be free."

Andrei frowned as he released my wrists. Before I could move, he lifted his left hand, and another image manifested.

Horror bathed my veins in ice as I took in the steel bars of a giant birdcage forming around me. I ran toward them, wrapping my fingers around the bars. Then I pulled hard, using my vampire strength to pry them apart. They didn't budge. I channeled more of my strength and tried again.

Still nothing.

What the fuck?!

"Something is happening in the States. A war is brewing between the supernatural species, putting everything at risk. The wolves plot to take New Orleans because the Four-Fold Accord is broken, and the covens will retaliate. They're building an army, and you're too far away for me to protect you from what's coming."

"This is your idea of protection?" I snarled, slamming a fist against the icy metal. "A fucking cage? Andrei, I don't need your goddamn protection. I am *gone.* I plan on staying gone."

Andrei looked around. "I know this cage might be scary, but think of how safe you'll be. No one will hurt you. Not the witches, your mother, *no one.* You were meant to be like this."

"What ...? You're out of your fucking mind. What is wrong with—"

His eyes rolled into the back of his head, and his mouth fell slack. I recoiled from the bars into a defensive stance. After a few seconds, Andrei's eyes returned, and they had gone from dark brown to pitch black. Dark energy pulsed in the space between us. Something cold and murky, like a lake of sludge.

Andrei was under the influence of evil. I sensed something was wrong from the last vision. This confirmed my suspicions. Malice was pouring off him. It felt like his own but more twisted and amplified. "Andrei? Andrei! Is there a witch near you? Wake the fuck up!"

My words failed to reach him. Instead, he grinned before stepping forward, phasing through the bars like a goddamn ghost. It should be impossible. But this was outside the realm of reality. He trapped me in his vision, so he could do whatever he wanted. My heel caught on the floor when I stepped back, sending me tumbling to the floor. I scrambled on my ass until my shoulders hit the other side of the cage. My attempt to tap into my vampire abilities was futile; it felt like something had smothered the power within, and whatever I did to alter the vision last time was severed.

I needed to get away from Andrei and break out of this vision. The last place I wanted to be was inside his head, especially now, but the dark magic that leaked from him left me without options. I couldn't flee as Andrei grabbed my ankles and yanked, causing me to slide across the floor toward him.

The icy sludge of power moved over me, snaking its way against my skin and freezing me in place. Fear overcame me as I felt a subtle shift of force roam near my stomach. My lips parted, and I wanted to say something—anything—but the words wouldn't come.

"Do you want me to stop?" he purred, the icy power morphing into a heated smoke as it slipped down my pajama pants. Andrei wasn't using his hands, but he controlled the power that did it. It slid over my thighs delicately, slowly parting them, while I had no choice but to take it. The smoke entered me, thrusting slowly as if to allow me to adjust to what was about to happen. My mind rebelled against this unwanted touch, but pleasure ignited my body, making me gasp.

"Oh, fuck!" I cried out, my hips bucking. It felt good, *so* fucking good. This was beyond fucked up, and I needed to pull myself together and make this stop, but when I tried to object ... I couldn't. The energy curled at an angle, rubbing against all the right spots that made my eyes roll into my head. "No ... don't stop."

Andrei's hands were on me now, ripping my clothes down the front, leaving me naked on the floor. That strange smoke slid free from me and wrapped around my limbs, keeping me prone. I looked up at Andrei and saw he was naked as well, kneeling between my legs. His sculpted abs and slightly tanned skin were on display as he held his cock, giving it slow, teasing strokes. He was thoroughly enjoying seeing me tied down by the magic.

What the hell kind of power is this? This isn't the guardian bond. No, it feels wrong ... foreign.

"This ... is exactly how I like you, Rachel," he hummed, those eerie dark eyes boring into my soul. The urge to look away and hide from that intensity was strong, but my body wouldn't obey.

"Held against my will while you violate me? Fuck you," I spat. He grinned, amused by my defiance.

"Such a dirty mouth. But don't worry, I know the perfect way to shut you up." Andrei moved his hips slowly, prodding his cock between my dripping folds before entering me with a gentle thrust. I hated that man to my core, but goddamn him, his cock felt good inside me. His hands gripped my ass and lifted my hips, thrusting harder into my wet pussy. From that angle, he stimulated me in a way that had my heart racing. I had no power to fight him off ... and part of me didn't want to.

His muscular form caged me in as he moved. My eyes tried to flutter closed, but the energy pried them open, forcing me to watch Andrei claim my body. No matter how much I wanted to escape this—I couldn't.

"You ... get off of ... Fuck," I panted. I wanted to tear Andrei's throat out, fight back, do *something*. But pleasure melted my resolve like molten lava. My body shuddered, lost in the sensations that burned through me from all directions. I was in heaven, even though a demon like him was fucking me.

Andrei's lips lowered to my collarbone, leaving a trail of angry kisses as he fucked me like he wanted to brand every inch of my skin. Each kiss was timed perfectly with his thrusts, slowly chipping away at my sanity. This shouldn't feel so good.

This is a vision. None of it is real. Andrei isn't really here.

"You can fight it all you want," Andrei growled. "But I know what you need. I know *exactly* how you need to be fucked." The words were filthy and wrong on so many levels. As much as I wanted to lie to myself, he was right.

"Go to hell, you sadistic bastard," I managed to say as a moan escaped my lips involuntarily. A wicked grin spread across his face again. Whatever image of himself Andrei had conjured in this space was sinister and brutal.

"Oh, I'm already there, love." Something shifted in his body then. His thrusts grew wilder, as if he was pounding all of his anger and fury into me. More smoke-like power brushed over my breasts, tickling my nipples like tiny needles, just short of piercing the skin. It was oddly pleasurable, enhancing the ecstasy I was already drowning in to impossible levels. My toes curled, my back arching as the sounds of my wetness accompanied his frenzy.

My teeth sank into my bottom lip as I fought to regain control, but it was so hard to think. Soon, I was shaking, hanging on by a thread as I struggled to hold it together.

Don't show him how good this fucking feels. He didn't deserve the gratification.

As if Andrei had read my mind, he spoke again, his words raspy and breathless. "Let go, my pet. I know you want to come on my cock. Show me how good I feel. How *right* I feel." Gray smoke covered my entire body now, tendrils touching every sensitive, exposed area. I felt a soft pressure against my clit—an odd contrast to how ruthless Andrei was fucking me. My feeble attempts at control shattered. A loud moan escaped my lips, melting into a broken gasp as I struggled against the magic. I was going to come—I was on the edge, even if I didn't want that prick to have the satisfaction. My hips squirmed, desperate to escape his wild pace, but to no avail.

"That's it, love," he said. "Surrender yourself and become mine again. I'm going to come soon to that house you're hiding in, kill everyone there who keeps me from you, and then bring you back to New Orleans. I'm going to keep you locked in my house, where I can fuck you how I want and when I want."

Another wave of pleasure ripped through me again, choking my voice to where I could only cry out Andrei's name. Stars burst in my vision, my brain spinning from the build-up. *Oh God.*

"Before I can do that, I must do one more thing, and I need your magic for it."

My eyes widened as a powerful orgasm tore through me, the energy holding me down as Andrei took my body for his selfish pleasure. As I rode my euphoria, he fucked me harder and harder until the pain bloomed beneath the surface. Sweat poured from my skin as Andrei continued, with no intention of stopping. He wanted to shatter me entirely.

"You're the one who will save my soul by opening the gates of Hell. But to do that, I'll need some of that exquisite blood of yours."

I blinked at his words. *What the fuck is he talking about?*

But I couldn't ask him. I could barely breathe to form the words. My legs were shaking now as I came down from my orgasm. Andrei didn't stop; he kept fucking me incessantly. He was going to push me to a second release.

"Jase is coming for you, too. Trust nothing that he says. He intends to kill you once and for all. He knows where you are, too, my pet. I'll protect you, so *wait* for me."

Something in my stomach tightened, and the threat sank into the back of my mind. Andrei came hard and fast right then, his head snapping back as he filled me up. That was when the second wave of orgasm seized my muscles. I finally closed my eyes and bit my lip to keep myself from shattering into a million pieces. The rolling sensation seemed to last forever.

The smoke vanished, leaving me chilled on the concrete floor. I carefully pushed myself onto my elbows to look at him. His naked form was now on the other side of the cage, leaning against the bars, and he smirked at me.

"By the way, you can thank Lucy for me. She was careless with her burner phone, and I was able to get your number. Not that it matters now. Soon, I'll be there in person to retake my fill of you."

"You think you have the right to me?" I snarled, scrambling to my knees and feeling his cum drip down my thigh. "Naw, I would rather die than have you lock me in a cage." I gestured to our surroundings. "I don't know what is fucking with your head right now, but it's given you an undeserved sense of entitlement."

Andrei threw his head back and laughed. "You say this even after you came on my cock *twice?* I'm insulted, dhampy."

"None of this is real. You're a projection of insecurity and obsession that forced itself on me. You're pathetic, and I would never help you."

There was a flicker in Andrei's eyes, then a surge of energy blasted toward me. The dark smoke grabbed my throat with brutal pressure. Before I could blink, his fingers replaced the magic, lifting me to my feet and slamming my chest against the bars.

"You are *mine,* love. Soon enough, you'll be right back where you belong."

Andrei's grim expression dissolved into shadows and smoke as he and the cage vanished. As the vision faded from my mind, I gripped the porcelain sink in my bathroom, dropping the phone. Its glass screen shattered against the tile.

Dammit!

My breath shuddered in my lungs as I drew air in slowly. Andrei did it again. Only this time, it was more potent, more terrifying. I hated the bond's power, even if the vision felt so damn good. I turned around and noticed a breeze brushing against me, biting against the sweat that coated my skin. That's when I looked down and realized I was completely naked, my torn pajamas lying on the floor.

Holy. Fuck.

CHAPTER 21

RACHEL

Now ... *now* I was afraid. What Andrei had done to me in that fucked-up mind game was different this time. It was straight up evil.

I slowly took a sip of coffee to keep my hands from shaking.

He wasn't just playing with me—he was trying to scare me. This was a warning. On top of that, I now had to worry about the power within me. Sure, I was glad Valentina was finally proud of me, but this magic was unpredictable. Why the hell did it have to be tied to how angry I was?

I was always angry, which made this more dangerous.

It wasn't just the power that terrified me, though—it was the revelation that this power had been dormant for so long and had only surfaced. A power that might lie within all dhampir magic. This was an ability I needed to learn how to control—and, more importantly, how to control it *safely*. I needed it to show up when I was calm and happy.

Valentina's optimism about it was obvious, and she'd been combing through every book she could find in Darius's library, hoping for answers.

"Alright, fill me in," I said, watching her walk into the kitchen with her head low. "How did it go—?"

As Valentina looked up from the floor, shock stole the rest of my words. She looked *withered.* Her skin, albeit pale, looked sickly, and her hair had lost its lustrous shine. I put my mug of coffee down and stood from the table, walking over to her. I grabbed her shoulders and gently turned her around. Even Valentina's blue eyes were dim and tired.

"What the hell is going on with you?" I asked, but she only shook her head.

"Just a bit parched," she joked with a weak smile and a playful wink, as if she were trying to make light of her condition. "It's been a while since I've had something to drink." She leaned against the counter, a hand pressed to her mouth. I hurried over to the refrigerator and pulled out a blood bag. I ripped open the plastic, poured the blood into a large mug, and set it on a warmer plugged into the wall. After thirty seconds, the blood was heated and ready. When I handed her the mug, she smiled weakly at me before taking a deep gulp.

I pressed my back against the refrigerator as she drank. After her last sip, Valentina lowered the mug from her mouth, wiping a drop leaking from the corner of her lips. Color bloomed back into her cheeks, and her sickly pallor improved.

After placing the mug back on the counter, she sighed. "Thank you."

I gave her a pointed look. "Sure, but why the hell aren't you feeding on your usual schedule? If I need to give you my damn blood, then I will. But you and I both know pure human blood is the only one that will really help you. It's ridiculous that you'd let yourself get like this." She flashed me a look of annoyance, rolling her eyes. "Oh, now suddenly, I don't know what I'm talking about. You're smarter than this. You might not care if you kill someone, but I do. Respectfully, *Mother*, get your shit together."

Valentina raised her hand. "As much as I appreciate your feigned attempt at calling me 'mother' for the first time, you're being a bit dramatic. I'm just stressed. While Darius hires a crew to clean up the mess in his garden, we're scheduling a trip to Ireland. We leave tonight."

My brows shot up. "Excuse me?" I let my arms fall to my sides. "We're leaving already?"

"Darius has arranged a meeting with the Aileach Clan. They're more ruthless than most. It'll take some *mental persuasion* to get them on board, if you know what I mean."

She was planning on altering their thoughts with her mind games.

That was risky.

"Listen," she continued. "Although I gave you that ring before we left the States, I've burned some bridges in the past with many of these clans. My life is more in danger than yours right now, so I'm going to need it back before we board our flight."

My body stilled. I *knew* this was fucking coming. Promises didn't mean shit to her.

"Naw, that's okay. I think I'll keep it on for now."

Valentina's eyes turned dark. "It wasn't a suggestion. Once we pack our bags, you're taking off that ring."

After Valentina left the kitchen, my body felt like it couldn't move. Luka prepared me for this. Once I refused, she would use her power, and I had to be ready to fight the bitch off.

Night quickly arrived, and everyone was busy. It wasn't just my mother and me leaving the villa to recruit. Aside from the human guards staying on post to protect the property, everyone had their assignments. After packing my bags, I jumped into the scalding shower, scrubbing my body clean. My mind was racing with the potential outcome of what could happen if I failed, and she did actually remove the ring. I had survived for two hundred years, so I wasn't worried these clans would hurt me, but Andrei made it very clear he was coming for me, and his threat about Jase didn't make me feel any less afraid. Both those psycho brothers were unpredictable, and I had to be ready if they tried to take or kill me. That ring was my only guarantee.

I placed my hand on the shower tile and leaned forward. "Fu-uuck," I drew out the word.

Even with the hot water pouring over me, my skin went cold at the thought. I had to tell Valentina about the guardian bond and the shift in its power—how he could come to me in dreams and manipulate my emotions into something dark and lecherous. Maybe then she'd let me keep the damn thing on.

I had to tell her the truth. She had to know *everything*.

Thirty minutes later, I stepped out of my bedroom, freshly cleaned and dressed. Valentina glanced up as I walked out, her eyes widening and her body going completely still.

A sickening feeling hit my gut, and my brows furrowed with concern. "What's wrong?" I glanced down at my outfit. "Is it my clothes?"

I had decided to wear black jeans that tapered at the ankle, a silver belt, and a deep emerald-green silk blouse. The waves in my hair flowed gracefully, reaching past my shoulders. I kept my makeup to a minimum, just a simple brown eyeshadow with mauve lip gloss.

"Your outfit's fine. It's perfect, actually. It's just ... you look so much like Cyrus; it takes my breath away sometimes. That shade of green—it reminds me of him. It was his favorite color. He would always seek out clothes or gemstones with that exact shade, actually. When we found out about you, he used his last coin to buy me a jade necklace."

"What happened to it?" I asked, watching her eyes turn glossy.

Valentina smiled. "The night in the church, it broke when it fell from my neck. I should have known it was an omen, but I was too focused on the ring and protecting Cyrus. It all seems meaningless when I think about it. I lost him and you in the end."

She took a deep breath and grabbed my hand. "Enough about that. We need to catch our flight." After a heavy breath, she said, "Take off the ring."

I bit back my need to mouth off and clenched my jaw. "Maybe not right now. Let's wait until Ireland."

Valentina's eyes turned dark but not at the level they did when she was about to go all demon bitch on someone. "You're being ridiculous. It's *my* ring."

I tried not to flash a mocking smile, but damn, I wanted to. "Yeah, I know, but ... I'm going to respectfully decline. You gave it to me for safekeeping. So, I'm keeping it safe. We're going to be late." I marched past her, but she reached out to grab my wrist. I jerked my arm away, and in the blink of an eye, she used her vampiric speed to dart in front of me, blocking my path.

Okay, now her eyes are red.

"Take. Off. The. Ring." The power of manipulation moved through me, but I fought back, using Luka's training from the last four months to push it away. I let the deep blue of my vampire power encircle my mind, my magic a secondary layer, and shoved her compulsion back.

"Well, look at you," I mocked, "you little liar. You promised not to use that power on me."

"How?" she growled through her teeth, stepping forward as she pushed more power into me. "How are you resisting this?"

Fuck, I'm going to have to fight my mother.

It was as if there was a stranger before me—an enemy. I had to treat her like one. I lifted my leg and slammed my heel hard against her gut, sending her flying across the hall.

Shit.

As I lunged at her, I felt a firm grip on my arm. "Go!"

Luka.

"I'll slow her down," Luka said quickly. "Darius is outside. Jump through the window by my room that leads to the back gate. You'll be able to get away with your speed." My heart was pounding. "Now, Rachel!"

Quickly, I hurried over to my bag and grabbed it, throwing on my leather jacket as I rushed down the hall. I adjusted it as I bolted, heading into Luka's room and over to the window. I pulled it up and leaned out, tossing my bag through and throwing my legs off before dropping into a sharp rose bush.

There was a ton of commotion going on in the house. If Darius weren't my enemy before, he would be now.

As soon as I saw the trees concealing the path to the back gate, I sprinted faster, ignoring the fading throb in my ankle from jumping out the window. The fully set sun helped me move through the deepening shadows undetected.

I reached the western gate and placed my hand over the iron lock, where the ward held the shield spell. Thankfully, I didn't have to break the spell to leave; it was only for outsiders coming in. After moving through the ward, I slipped out, closed the gate, and looked around again.

On the other side of the gate was the path leading to the neighborhood's main road. I ran toward it, keeping flush with the villa walls so no one saw me. I had no fucking clue where I was going, but it certainly wasn't Ireland with my mother, not with her trying to get the ring.

I'll return once everyone cools down.

Once away from the entrance and in the grove of trees near the road, I looked around frantically, chewing on my inner cheek.

"Rachel," a familiar voice called from behind me, and an icy shiver rolled down my spine, shock numbing my limbs.

No, it can't be.

I turned slowly to see Tony and Lucy standing near two thick trees that shielded the road. At first, I thought I had lost my mind and was hallucinating, believing I saw familiar faces in front of me. But then Tony spoke again. "It's us. We're here."

Shock overwhelmed me at seeing my two friends there, and I ran toward them, throwing myself into Lucy's outstretched arms. Her white rose perfume and vampire scent flooded my senses, confirming that my best friend was there. I felt Tony's muscular, warm arms slip around us, and his familiar scent reminded me of how much I missed home.

Missed *them*.

"Holy shit," I breathed, pulling back. "What are you both doing here?" I scanned their faces, confusion fading as I caught the worry in their eyes. But then my gaze locked on Lucy. "What's happened? How did you even leave the States without Andrei stopping you? Please tell me he's not here."

Tony put a hand on my arm. *"He's* not, but ... We can talk about what's happening in a minute. It would also be best if you braced yourself."

Lucy took my hands in hers. "I'm really sorry about this, babes. We brought someone *else* with us. You need to hear them out before you react badly ... like you usually do."

"What the hell does that mean? React badly about what—?"

Then I saw him step out from the shadows. His green eyes shone under the property lights, staring right back into mine. His hair, though slightly shorter than the last time I saw him, was intentionally messy, and he had on the same leather jacket and dark jeans he always wore. As I glared straight into the bastard's soul, an arrogant smile tugged on his handsome face. "Hey, angel."

"Jase," I hissed through my teeth, drawing my fangs out in fury and taking three steps toward him until we were within arm's reach. Without thinking about the consequences, I pulled my elbow back and slammed my tight fist into his left cheek, a sting pulsating in my knuckles, and I winced. "You fucker, that hurt!"

Jase's eyes widened, and he held his hand to his cheek as if my reaction surprised him. Instead of lashing back at me, his smile broadened, and he looked up to meet my eyes. "Well, that didn't feel great either," he said, standing straight again and holding his hands out placatingly. "How about we not kill each other today? I come in peace."

"Bullshit!" I stepped back. "Are you here to take me back to Andrei, so he can get back this precious little ring?" I held up my hand, waving the finger that wore it. "It doesn't miss either of you." I lunged toward him again, teeth flashing, but Lucy stepped between us and firmly grabbed my hands.

"No, no! Wait, Rachel. He's telling the truth. Jase reached out to us and brought us here to find you. You have to hear him out. *Please.*"

My brows shot up. "Don't be a traitor. He killed and turned you!"

"Listen to him!" The desperation in Lucy's voice shattered my rage, but when her eyes softened, it gnawed at me even more. When she didn't budge, I retracted my fangs, stepped toward Tony, and turned to him. Both of my friends were solemn, nodding in unison. Rational thoughts slowly took over. Tony and Lucy wouldn't do anything to endanger my life. So, for Jase to be just feet from them told me something terrible must have happened.

I let out a slow breath and looked back at my greatest enemy. I reached out with my senses and felt for his intentions. While anger and irritation were there, the intent to *harm* me wasn't. But then again, he'd deceived and manipulated me before.

I allowed my powers to focus on his aura, and something shifted. It was like what I had felt in the church had vanished and was replaced by something too veiled for me to analyze. Whether or not he hated me, he wasn't there to kidnap me and drag me back to Andrei's mansion. What I felt was fear.

Fear?

"Okay. Start talking."

"Not here," he replied. "You looked like you were heading some-where." His eyes turned to the bag over my shoulder. "How about we go there? The more people around us, the safer. Right? Plus, I think we're about to get caught by some vampires. I hear running in our direction. I suggest we get moving. Your mother isn't joining us, is she?"

"Fuck no." I turned my attention to the property gates in the distance and heard what Jase did. "You guys don't happen to have a car, do you?"

Lucy nodded. "We just have to travel a few blocks on foot. Come on."

Tony moved forward and grabbed Lucy's hand, and they slipped through a small archway through the neighbor's property, so we could cut a few corners and get out of view. I tailed them, followed by Jase right behind me.

Jase's breathing down my neck made me feel uneasy, so I stopped, moved to the side, and ushered him to crawl through the archway. "After you," I said. "I insist."

Jase smirked. "You think I'm going to stab you in the back?"

"You might."

This time, he chuckled. "Oh, this trip is going to be fun."

I scowled. "How about this? I'll trust you a tiny bit. But if you try anything, *Jase,* I'll beat the ever-living fuck out of you ... again. I still have my revolver."

Jase flashed his white teeth, wider this time, before he bit his bottom lip slightly. "You have my word, angel. I won't do anything to warrant a beating."

Jase with that fucking nickname.

"Good, because if she doesn't, I will, asshole," Lucy snarled at him as she poked her head through the archway. "What are you guys doing? Let's go."

I gave her a quick nod and rushed her way, crouching down into the archway and onto the other property. As we walked across the lawn and over to the other side of the road, I felt Jase's hand grip my shoulder in a light touch.

"Listen," he said, forcing me to swing around to face him. "Truce?"

I pinched my brows together. "Absolutely not. But … maybe I'll hear what you have to say for the next hour. I still hate you."

Jase didn't smile that time, but his nostrils flared like he was holding back an insult. "That's fair." He looked over my shoulder at Lucy and Tony. "Where are we heading once we get in the car?"

"Normally, I'd be able to venture out of the city on my own, but given that I just sent my mother flying across the room, we need to travel a little further before we stop," I said. "And I know just the place."

CHAPTER 22

RACHEL

We drove through the city for over thirty minutes before we arrived at the bar, and thankfully. The place was busy enough that we could enter without being noticed. The wine bar wasn't a place my mother knew I frequented. We'd be safe for now.

Tony went to the bar to order some bottles of much-needed wine, while Lucy found us a table near the back. She quickly sat between Jase and me and crossed her arms, her face promising violence if he did anything funny. I kept my right hand concealed from Jase's sight and even rotated the obsidian to the inside of my finger. Tony joined us and set down four glasses and two bottles—one white and one red.

After pouring our wine, I took a deep gulp before looking at one of the banes of my existence. "Alright. Start talking."

Jase raised an eyebrow before taking a sip of his wine. He chose the Merlot, like me.

"First things first. Rachel ... when you moved into the mansion, Andrei drugged you and implanted a tracker in your arm."

"Wait ... what?!"

"Jase! Way to rip the Band-Aid off, Jesus Christ," Lucy spat. "We agreed on the plane to wait until we were heading south."

Panic suddenly gripped me. "Where is it in my arm?"

Jase reached out and placed his hand on my bicep. "Here, but we can't take it out until we're away from the public. If we ditched it at the villa, that's the first place Andrei would go. It's made so that moment the temperature changes, it'll let him know it's offline."

I bounced my eyes between all three of them. "So he could know where I am right now?"

Jase nodded. "Last I heard, Andrei was at the mansion taking care of a mishap from the club. That was four hours after we caught a flight, so we had at least a head start, though we did have longer layovers than I had hoped. I reached out to a contact named Emily once we landed on a burner phone, but I haven't called her since then. I didn't want to take any chances. So, the moment we get going, we need to get off the main road and dig it out."

Dig it out? God.

Sudden nausea pulled in my gut, and anger strangled me. *That's it. That's how Andrei knew where to find me out here.*

"More shitty news," Jase started again, and I looked over to meet his eyes. "Andrei's been meeting with the Black Onyx Coven to use their resources not only to retake you and Valentina but also to use your blood to open a portal to the Upper World."

I choked on my wine. "Open a portal to the Upper World?"

Suddenly, the tracker seemed minuscule.

Jase nodded. "Yeah. A warrior angel named Ezrylos holds a weapon powerful enough to slay the Devil himself. An angel created the spell to hide Ezylos, so only angel blood can reopen the gate to bring him back." He paused, his eyes softening. "That would be you."

My brows shot up. "Me?" I whispered, glancing around to make sure no one overheard. "I'm half-human, half-vampire."

Jase leaned forward, his green eyes fixed on mine, as if searching for something. "Don't forget, your mother was turned by a creature born of both demon and angel. She was also a witch. That makes you a being of all three realms: angel, demon ... and human. You carry the blood of Heaven, Earth, and Hell."

I slumped back in my chair, horror souring the wine in my stomach. I knew what Kylan was and how his powers and blood transferred to my mother, but I had never thought about it like that.

I looked over at Tony. "Say something," I asked. "Do you believe this shit?"

"Fuck. I don't believe anything anymore, but that's what he explained on the flight here. We might need to trust our gut with this one," he said, taking a big gulp of wine himself as if he, too, wanted to drown out the reality of what was happening. "Not only that, but some of my contacts in other covens reached out. They told me that Black Onyx was recruiting hundreds of witches from other regions, especially those who went rogue, to join their ranks. Their goal is to ensure they have a loyal coven ready at their disposal. With Valentina back, they're scared."

Nerves gripped my stomach. *This keeps getting worse and worse.*

"My mother has a gem she intends to use against them. Apparently, this was a two-hundred-year war that got put on hold when they placed Valentina under that sealing spell. The clan at the villa is gathering an army as we speak. I was supposed to leave tonight to help recruit other clans and allies," I said. "They're planning to launch an attack on the Lemurian Quartz and Black Onyx, with innocent humans right in the middle of it all." The idea of it made my stomach plummet into an ice bath. "The gem she has will tear down all magic...."

Lucy's eyes went wide. "Jesus Christ, we're kind of fucked."

Jase reached out toward me, but I moved my hand away, wondering why the fuck he was trying to touch me. Once he realized his mistake, he pulled back. "Andrei, Meredith, Jackson, and I attended a meeting with the Black Onyx. They're a lovely group of cultish psychopaths, by the way," he said sarcastically.

A small smile reached my lips, but I held it back.

"During this meeting, Andrei negotiated with Gerald to track down the angel. Once he finds you, he'll wear the ring to access his magic, but he needs your blood to activate the pentagram and summon the angel. The angel's blood is what makes the spell work. Once the angel appears, he'll be holding a sword—his blade is covered in runes that enhance its power. He'll order the angel to kill Lucifer because if the Devil dies, he won't be able to claim our souls anymore. We'll be free from him. But there's more...."

Jase's voice shifted, and my stomach dropped.

"What else?" I asked, panic creeping up. Lucy squeezed my hand, grounding me, but I kept my eyes on Jase.

"He ..." Jase's jaw tightened, his hands twitching, almost like he wanted to punch something. "Andrei made a deal with Gerald to put you back under Andrei's control. If he returns with the sword and the ring, they'll give him the authority to take you—to lock you away in his lair ... and keep you there. Forever."

All the air in my lungs froze, and the room spun. Andrei left a clear warning the last time he invaded my thoughts, but locking me away as a prisoner? That fucker knew better than to try.

The threat of that cage was real.

However, I thought about one thing. Given Andrei's level of obsession with me since that night in the alley, it was very likely that he would do anything to keep me within his grasp. Yet why did he let me go when he tracked me to South Station?

Tony's warm arm slipped around me and pulled me close, easing the panic that choked my breath. Lucy squeezed my hand gently.

"We wouldn't have come if this literally wasn't life or death," Lucy said. "But Andrei's been acting strangely over the last month and kept trying to get me to behave more like a … vampire. He wanted me to join his clan because he knew I had access to you and thought he could use *me* to get to you." Lucy ground her teeth, fangs threatening to slide free. Tony placed his free hand over hers and rubbed his thumb over her skin as if trying to soothe her. "I refuse to be a tool in that fucker's game, and you know I'd never do anything to put you in danger."

I squeezed Lucy's hand. "That's because you're nothing like them, and no one, especially Andrei, can ever change that. Just you coming here proves that your heart is still there. You're still *you*."

I looked over at Jase again, who was watching Tony slide closer to me. Jase had the strangest expression. It was like he was *jealous* of Tony's closeness to me, his eyes momentarily locking onto where Tony rested his hand on me. The mask of indifference slid over his features, and he took another drink of his wine.

"Okay," I said, turning to him, but a thought dawned on me. "Wait, does Andrei know you're in Venice?" I asked carefully.

Jase's wicked smile grew as he raised his glass to his lips again. "Probably. Although I think my brother might be a bit preoccupied. I may or may not have allowed a little local pack of wolves to take over his club." He bit his bottom lip again. "And they may or may not have blown it up and killed Meredith."

"You what?!" I shouted, drawing several eyes to our table. "What the fuck were you thinking?"

Jase leaned back, raising a brow as he crossed his arms over his chest. "I called in a favor with the Bayou Perot wolves and had the Black Diamond Club blown to dust and rubble." His tone was light, almost bored, like he hadn't just poked a beast that could wipe us all out. "Bought me enough time to snag two items from his safe, recruit these guys, and get the hell out of New Orleans."

My mouth fell open, and words utterly failed me. Instead, I reached for the second open bottle on the table and poured another full glass of wine. I should have felt angry that Jase destroyed Andrei's livelihood and murdered one of his friends, likely sparking a war with the werewolves. But something else was bothering me about the whole situation, leaving me with more questions.

"You spent four years stalking my every move so you could manipulate me into releasing my mother from her tomb, including turning Lucy into a vampire." Lucy raised her middle finger at Jase. "Then, after you slit my throat, you and Andrei tried to kill Valentina with the ring's power. What exactly changed to where you would not only betray your brother, but also bring my two friends to Venice and warn me about the coven's plans? What the hell is your goal with all this? You have *nothing* to gain." I moved my hand up and showed him the ring again. "You haven't *once* tried to take this from me since you saw me on the sidewalk, yet you spent two hundred years waiting for it to resurface."

Jase ran his fingers through his messy hair, and his eyes turned again to look into mine. Immediately, my body relaxed, and a calming sensation washed over me, as if I were floating in a warm pool of water.

I mentally shook the feeling away and kept staring at him. "Well?" I asked, tapping my fingernail against the glass. "I'm waiting for an explanation."

Jase took another drink before his green eyes met mine over the rim.

"Let's just say my *motivations* have changed."

I rolled my eyes. "Right, now you don't want to save your soul from good ol' Lucifer fucking with it for eternity?"

Jase smiled, and instead of pouring himself a glass of wine, he took the bottle and chugged the remaining bit down. After the last drop, he placed the bottle back on the table. "Andrei isn't who I thought he was. Turns out, he's even more insufferable. As much as I *tried* to entertain the fantasy of starting over with him, I've realized something—I'm better off without a family. Always have been and always will be. Let him stew in his mess; he deserves it. I can't overlook the trail of sins he's left behind—or the fact that he expects me to jump into the madness that is his deranged little clan."

My eyes widened. "You're fighting already?" I mocked. "That isn't my problem."

Jase narrowed his eyes. "*He's* made it your problem now. I need to get to this angel first before he does, or it isn't just everyone around him who will suffer. You'll be the first to beg on your knees to your favorite coven to be free from Andrei's tight leash. His attempt to kill the Devil will only spark a war between the realms. I don't want to kill Lucifer. If I can destroy the pentagram so Andrei can't summon the angel, then Andrei has *nothing*. It's a win-win between us. We work together, and then when all this is over, we can go our separate ways and pretend we never even met."

I pinched my brows together. "What do you need me to do, exactly?"

"Just a tiny drop of your blood, straight from the vein so I can activate the pentagram. And it's gotta be fresh."

Why does he always need my blood to unlock things?

He reached into his pocket and pulled out a bronze key with a strange symbol at its center. "This key will allow us to get inside a cave where the spell takes place. The Book of Shadows in my bag will walk us through what we have to do. If you help me destroy the pentagram circle used to summon the angel, I'll make sure Andrei never touches you again. You can keep the damn ring for all I care. I just don't want Andrei to have it. His hunger for power and prestige will only worsen, and *no one* wants that."

I heard every word Jase said, but my attention was fixed on the key. I couldn't look away. It seemed simple, but it wasn't. The energy radiating from it hit my skin like an electric charge. I hadn't felt that kind of power before—it was ancient, warm, and alive.

Tony's voice broke through, pulling me from my trance. "The cave he's talking about is in Greece. So, we need to drive as far south as possible and then take a ferry to Athens. It's too risky to fly since Black Onyx has allies that could report our whereabouts. It's easier for Rachel to use her compulsion ability on individual law enforcement and ferry officials over an entire airport security."

I blinked, my gaze going right back to the key. It took me only a few seconds to make my decision. "Alright, fine. I'll help you," I said, looking up to meet Jase's intense eyes. "But after this, you and I are done. For good."

CHAPTER 23

RACHEL

After swapping my emerald-green blouse for a plain black T-shirt, we headed to the car. Tony was already in the driver's seat, Lucy beside him, and once I settled into the back with Jase, we pulled out onto the road.

Since he was the only one of us who had driven in Europe before when he'd visited his nonna and cousins, it made sense to let him navigate us south. And since I refused to trust Jase anywhere near my best friend, I made the ultimate sacrifice.

The car was ridiculously small, cramming us in the back like a can of sardines. This drive would be nearly impossible without touching him.

"Well, Italy is pretty," Jase said suddenly as Tony pulled off on the main road. "All the times I've visited, I never came this far north."

He's trying to make small talk. No thanks.

I inched closer to the window, ignoring him.

"You're really going to ignore me this entire trip?" Jase said, but I kept my gaze locked on the road.

Tony must have heard Jase trying to talk to me, and being the best guy friend I had, he turned up the music to drown him out.

"Jesus," Jase mumbled under his breath, shifting his gaze to his own window.

I turned to him. "Just because I'm agreeing to help doesn't mean I want to talk to you. In fact, the idea of chatting with you makes my insides hurt."

Jase pressed his lips together, irritation rolling off him in waves. The energy leaching from him made the hairs on my arms prickle. He wanted to snap back, to tell me exactly what he thought, but he kept the words behind his teeth.

Good.

"Thank you," I said, shifting my gaze back to the window. Outside, a beautiful display of stars stretched across the dark sky. By now, Darius and my mother were probably out searching for me, not knowing I had already left the city. Guilt coiled in my stomach. I hoped they didn't punish Luka for holding Valentina back while I escaped. But I had no choice. My mother had turned on me. I couldn't go back.

"Rachel?" Lucy called, lowering the music. "How are you feeling right now? I mean, not about what Jase told you, but we're taking you from other dhampirs. It can't be easy, leaving without saying goodbye to them."

I sighed. "No, it's not. Especially leaving Luka. I finally found freedom, a family that didn't control or dictate my every move. I mean, yeah, Valentina tried, but I made it pretty damn clear that I wasn't her tool to use." Leaning back, I rested my head against the headrest. "Seeing the others, knowing I wasn't alone in this world ... was surreal. I had a family, a real family, who understood me."

Another thought crossed my mind, making me instantly irritated. I let my head drop to the side to look at Jase. "Not a surprise to you, though. Right? You worked for the Black Onyx, so you knew I wasn't the only dhampir."

Jase was quiet, his jaw tensing before finally answering. "Yeah, angel. I knew."

The way he responded fucking irked me. It was like he was pleased that he knew something I didn't. I leveled an icy glare at him, letting my eyes glow a little from my magic for emphasis. Jase just raised a brow at me.

"I still can't believe you guys have been talking this entire time," Tony interjected, his eyes looking at mine in the rearview mirror. It was like he sensed the tension building in the backseat and needed to deflect it.

"Sorry," I said. "I probably shouldn't have even called Lucy, but I had to talk to someone. I needed to know what was happening with Andrei."

"Why?" Jase asked suddenly, pulling my attention back to him.

I frowned. "What do you mean, 'why?'"

Jase's expression softened. "I mean ... why the hell did you care what Andrei was doing?"

I let out a sharp laugh, shaking my head. "Are you serious? Gee, I don't know. Maybe because—"

"Oh, it's right here," Tony cut in, drawing my focus back to him. "I pulled this location up on my maps at the wine bar. There's a field not too far where we can ditch that tracker."

Thank God.

Relief crashed over me. I wanted the damn thing out. Now that I was aware of it again, I could almost feel it itching under my skin. But also—why did Jase even ask that?

As we veered off the main road, we pulled into a field and parked near a wooden fence. Jase quickly reached into his backpack, pulling out a hunting knife.

"Alright, maybe we get out of the car, so we don't get blood on the seats," Jase suggested.

"Ah, fuck," I muttered, throwing the door open. "I get that I'll heal, but I'm not immune to pain. I hate it."

I stepped out first, marching toward a grassy embankment hidden from view. The balmy night air settled over me as I shrugged off my thin leather jacket, letting it hang loosely in my hand. It's a good thing I changed. I really liked that blouse.

When I turned, Jase was suddenly there, inching closer. He was so close that our noses nearly touched.

His scent hit me then, the same one I remembered from the church. My heart pounded. And I fucking hated it.

"Maybe Tony can do it," I said. "He—"

"He's not touching my knife."

"Last time you used something that sharp, you cut me with it."

"Barely," he said. "You healed in, like, two seconds."

I opened my mouth to argue but decided against it. We needed to get this thing out and keep moving. Fighting was pointless.

"Fine. But back up a little, please. You're practically on top of me."

Jase smirked at that, and my stomach did that stupid flip I didn't ask for.

"How about I distract you instead?" he suggested. "You seem nervous, and if you flinch, it'll hurt more. Trust me."

I clenched my jaw. "Fine. Distract me."

Jase's lips turned up in amusement as he moved even closer. "You know," he said, grabbing my wrist and stretching out my arm, "the first time we met wasn't in the church."

I blinked. "You did stalk me for four years. I kind of figured that wasn't the first."

He shrugged, rubbing my shoulder as he searched for the tracker. His rough hands were surprisingly gentle as they moved over my skin.

"Give me a second. Andrei mentioned to Jackson that he planted it right below a freckle he thought was cute." His thumb pressed beneath my single freckle, pushing down until I winced. "Right there."

My stomach churned. "How did I not notice that?"

"It's deep enough to be undetectable unless you're looking for it."

I swallowed hard. "Alright, keep talking to me while you cut it out," I said, doing my best to suppress the surge of anger rising in my chest. The last time he held a knife against my skin, he slit my fucking throat. I couldn't let myself dwell on that. It wouldn't do me any good to want to rip his throat out the entire trip.

Tony cleared his throat. "Maybe I *should* do it—"

"I got it," Jase snapped, then quickly recovered, pressing the blade against my skin. "Uh ... we danced together, actually."

"What?!" I barked right as the knife bit in. "Fuck!"

Jase held me steady as he worked, our bodies so close it felt like we were practically hugging. The cold metal of the knife tapped against the tracker before he carefully angled it beneath the device. Slowly and carefully, he began pushing it upward through the tissue and muscle. A sharp sting followed, and I shut my eyes, drawing in a shaky breath. "Holy shit," I cried. My jaw tightened to the point of pain, trying to take my mind off the digging agony. My entire arm felt like it was on fire, and blood dripped onto the grass in rivulets. On top of that, my skin tried to knit itself back together to seal the wound, making my arm itch on top of the searing pain.

"Sorry," Jase said as blood ran down my arm. I looked up at him. He narrowed his green eyes, concentrating, and I could tell he was trying not to inhale the scent of my blood. "There."

He moved the knife away and reached into the wound, carefully gripping the sharp end of a square device the size of my thumbnail and pulling it free from my flesh.

"Got it." He held it up, and I hurriedly stepped back, creating a fair amount of distance between us. "Take a look."

Once the pain had subsided and he was no longer touching me, I held out my hand, and he placed the slightly bloody tracker in my palm. "I can't believe he did that," I said. "I mean, I knew Andrei was obsessed with knowing where I was at all times, but it was naive of me to believe he *wouldn't* go this far."

All of this reassured me that I had made the right choice to forget that monster completely. The dream of me in the cage and now finding out Andrei did this? This was the true nature of the man I didn't just fuck but I *kissed* in that bathroom before we parted ways. This manipulator would stop at nothing to own, *not love*, someone.

"Want me to destroy it?" Jase asked, but I shook my head.

"No, I got it." I gripped the device between my fingers and squeezed, shattering it with my vampire strength. I walked further into the embankment and dropped the pieces into the dirt. My eyes dropped to my sticky, bloodied skin.

Although my powers healed my flesh, my arm was a red mess. Jase wiped the knife on the grass before walking back to the car. Tony watched him with an odd look, as if he was suddenly very much aware of who he'd invited on this trip.

Hopefully, he's not thirsty. I can't deal with another blood addict like his brother.

"Here," Lucy said, tossing me some tissue she grabbed from her purse. "We can stop somewhere with water to clean you up better."

I nodded. "Are you okay?" I asked her with a side smirk. "You're kind of eyeing my arm like you want to lick it."

Lucy giggled and walked over to me. "Naw, I'm good. You smell like you always have to me. Besides, I fed before we left Louisiana. I'm good for a few more hours. More importantly, are *you* okay? I know you got the pain over with, but learning that Andrei did *that* to begin with ..."

Shrugging, I said, "I will be, but right now, I feel like hitting something ... or someone." I forced a smile to reassure her I was *mostly* okay. "This entire time, Andrei's been watching me because of that thing inside my arm. It makes me want to rip a hole in the earth and bury him alive. But having you and Tony risk everything to be here keeps my rage in check. If we're going to stop Andrei and the coven's insane, cocked-up plan, I need to keep a clear head."

"Well, if you need to vent or blow off steam, tell me. I took sparring lessons with Jackson and this other guy named Stephen back at the mansion. I'm pretty good now." Lucy grinned at the shock on my face. "Don't bottle up your emotions, bestie. I'm a part of this until the end and will always be here if you need me or Tony. We love you, okay?"

Tears burned behind my eyes, and I nodded again, trying to keep them back. "God, I missed you."

"Same." She smiled, her expression softening before she turned and walked toward the car. She paused for a moment, placing her hand on Tony's shoulder, and then climbed into the passenger seat.

After I cleaned off as much blood as possible, I turned to look at Jase, who was trying his hardest to ignore me. While I stared at him, Tony started the car and pulled us back onto the road. Jase wouldn't look at me anymore, acting as standoffish as I was when we first started driving. "You danced with me?"

Though he turned away slightly, I still caught the curve of his lips as he smiled. "Twice, actually. The first time, you probably remember. Granted, you were pretty fucking hammered, even for a dhampir."

I cocked my head slightly to the right and wracked my brain for any possible times that Jase would have gotten close to me. That's when a hazy, drunken memory came to mind—Andrei's club.

"You son of a bitch. I thought it was Andrei dancing with me. You smelled just like him," I said. "And the other time?"

"The second time, you wouldn't remember. Wendy used a spell on you to make you forget."

Hearing her name brought out both anger and sadness. I couldn't believe that bitch lied to me for so long. Of all the betrayals in my immortal life, hers was one of the worst.

"Wow," I said, struggling off the memory with a side smirk. "All that work, all that planning, just to lose it all in that church like a little bitch."

The smile I gave him caused his smirk to fall; that was all I needed to see.

CHAPTER 24

JASE

It was just past midnight when we pulled into the small gas station on the outskirts of Fermo. It was tucked away in a wooded area just down the road from a car dealership. The lot was empty, allowing us to pump gas without having to interact with anyone. Once Tony stepped out to fill the tank and grab snacks for him and Rachel, I rolled down the window to let the night breeze brush over my skin.

A group of human teenagers came up the road, walking down the sidewalk past the gas station. I made eye contact with a scrawny male, offered a smile, and perhaps let a little of my fangs show. When he realized what I was, he urged his friends to walk faster and quickly disappeared up the road.

"That's a dick move. Stop scaring kids," Rachel said, and I turned to look at her. She huddled against the car door with her leather jacket draped over her left shoulder and across her chest. "You must be getting hungry if you're harassing a small fry."

The taunting tone of her voice grated on my nerves. She was testing me, seeing if I was no longer the monster she met in Boston. Of course, she'd be wrong to assume I had changed in the slightest.

"Oh? Are you offering?" I replied, enjoying seeing her shift uncomfortably. Her eyes didn't break their gaze with me, though, challenging me more. "I mean, it's only fair since you drank from *me.*"

Rachel's eyes narrowed, and the blue color took on an icy glint. She didn't like that comment, and Lucy's shoulders visibly tensed..

"Naw, I'm good. I've already had one Dimitriou brother drink from me. I think I'm set for life."

Sudden annoyance hit me, and I did my best to not clench my jaw. *I knew he drank from her, but being reminded of it made my spine lock up.*

I barked out a laugh to hide my irritation. "Dimitriou isn't my last name."

"Ooh, that's right, you have a stage name. Andrei said you guys changed your surname years ago. What was it, anyway? He never told me."

The thought of Andrei drinking from her, let alone Rachel mentioning his name, sent another wave of anger crawling up my neck. Now I couldn't stop thinking about it. I hated how much that fucking bothered me.

"Our *real* family name was Bakirtzis."

"Hmm, what does that mean in Greek?"

I smiled. "Coppersmith."

"Huh, that's not very fitting. Your father was a fisherman," she said, curiosity getting the better of her.

"Ironically, my grandfather *was* a coppersmith, but Papá wanted to take a different path. Mamá loved our last name since she worked with copper pots to make healing potions. It actually did fit perfectly."

"Hmm," Rachel hummed but then pressed her lips together, contemplating my answer. "So, why pick 'Halpert' as a last name?"

"I used to fuck a woman back in the States with that last name before I joined the coven. I thought it flowed nicely with Jasen," I said, watching her shift uncomfortably at my brazen remark, and I did my best to read her from that response. "Eventually, we went our separate ways, but after I became a vampire, I paid her a visit. She was furious as hell and fought me, of course, but in the end, I gave her a sort of *parting* gift. If she couldn't have my dick anymore, she would have eternal life."

Her lips parted, and judgment took over her features. Rachel wanted to snap back, but she just glared at me instead. My intention to get a reaction out of her had worked.

Two can play at this game, angel.

But that look on her face bothered me to no end. I couldn't tell what she was thinking. An educated guess would be that she wanted to gouge my eyes out.

"Damn. You really are a dick," Lucy quipped, turning around to face us. When she saw the look on Rachel's face, Lucy smiled. "I'd be careful if I were you. I honestly think she will kill you when you're not looking."

I cocked my head and leaned against my door, the breeze ruffling my dark hair. My gaze burned into Rachel's glowering eyes. "If you have something to say, angel. Then say it."

Rachel bit the inside of her lip before sitting up to better stare at me. "You're such a lonely bullshitter, you know that? You steal someone's name and humanity and call it a 'gift.' Then you fuck one of my best friends to pass the time until the Hades Blood Moon, which you failed royally, by the way. You claimed it was all for obtaining my mother's power, but I'm not buying it. All you do is use people and discard them like they're trash. If you're trying to get anyone to feel sorry for you, you're wasting your time."

She raised a brow at me, her smirk sharp enough to cut through me.

"And let me guess. You think that casually dropping your past conquests and brutal violence would get under my skin? No, all it did was reveal more and more about your intentions."

"Holy shit," Lucy laughed. "You really shouldn't have said anything to her, dude. Rachel is notorious for calling out bullshit."

I didn't even glance at Lucy, not with Rachel's beautiful eyes burning into me.

"I bet you've spent the last two centuries filling that yawning void in your chest with one meaningless hookup after another," Rachel pressed on, trying to provoke me.

It was working, goddammit.

"Are you afraid that no one will pay attention to you if you don't brag about it?" she asked contemptuously. "You keep everyone at arm's length because you're afraid they'll see you for who you are." Rachel crossed her arms over her chest, the jacket falling from her shoulders. She spoke with mocking pity in her tone. "All that charm and immortality, yet trying to convince me or yourself that you're not completely alone."

"Watch it," I seethed through my teeth, not even realizing I had drawn out my fangs as anger burned into my chest.

"Are you exhausted yet, pretending that you don't care about how you hurt people or care about them in general?" she continued. "Naw, I think you *do*, somewhere deep in that soulless pit in your chest. You're dying for someone to see you and extend a loving hand to *you*. If the meaningless sex with anything with a hole gives you comfort, so be it."

It felt like she dug her claws deep into my insides and twisted them into a whirlpool of ice and blood. My hands balled into fists as my temper simmered to a near-boil under my skin.

"Pretty hypocritical of you," I bit back. If she wanted to pick a fight, I'd give her one. "You forgot I watched you for *four* years ... haunted every step you took, not like some damn puppy on the streets. No, I was inside that hotel, watching you work ... following you home, and watching you sleep. Loneliness is a cold bedfellow, angel. I've seen you touch yourself on those nights, slipping your fingers into your wet pussy until you came. And if you weren't doing that, you were fucking some stranger the exact same way you accuse me of doing. Don't claim I do anything for attention because I know you're the same as me."

"Oh my God," Lucy whispered, her eyes now on Rachel, as if anxiously waiting to see how she'd respond.

Rachel's jaw dropped like I had slapped her. Her eyes glistened, and I thought she'd start crying from how angry she looked. "You were watching me *in* my home?" Her heartbeat picked up until it was pounding against her ribs. I was sure that even Lucy heard it.

"It's not important anymore. At least I didn't kill you in your sleep or when you were preoccupied with a toy." I smiled. "But yes, I watched you sleep, dress, eat, and fuck. If you think I feel bad about that, guess again."

Rachel whipped toward me faster than I could blink, her fist aimed at my jaw. I seized her wrist mere inches from my face. My other hand shot out and grabbed her left hip, yanking hard enough that she slid on the leather seats onto her back. I pounced on her, my body pinning her down while my right hand gripped her throat.

Lucy snarled and lunged over her seat, but I held her off with my left hand. "Hijo de puta!" Lucy shouted, trying to pry my fingers off her wrist so she could hit me.

The tiny car rocked violently with our collective struggle, and if anyone were to walk by and see it, they'd assume something lecherous was happening. The sound of Tony's footsteps approached the back door.

"Let them go!" Tony growled through his teeth over the commotion. I looked up to see the gun he brought from his apartment drawn from his holster and pointed at my chest. "These bullets are wooden. Don't force me to go back on my word and shoot you in the heart. Let them fucking go."

Lucy's sharp nails dug into my skin as she hissed, fangs out. Rachel's eyes widened as she thrashed beneath me. The friction was maddening, and my mind wandered into dangerous territory.

Rachel was daring me to call Tony's bluff. He wouldn't shoot me, not when Rachel's life was on the line.

I released my hold on them and carefully leaned back, easing the pressure on Rachel's hips. I took a few breaths to settle my rattled nerves. "Don't ever, *ever* try to strike me again, angel," I warned, folding my arms over my chest.

Tony remained outside the car, gun lowered slightly, and watched us carefully.

Smart move.

Lucy took a breath as well, sliding back into her seat. There was a slight rasp, and Rachel immediately sat up. "Lucy? Did that wear you out? Jase has enhanced strength, so it's almost impossible to kick his ass properly. Here, you need blood."

Goddamn, woman. I knew what she was doing. She didn't have to strike me to inflict pain. Rachel knew she had another more effective weapon in her arsenal.

Her fangs emerged as she sank her teeth into her wrist, dark blood dripping from the wound. The scent hit me—so fucking divine. The veins under my eyes pulsed with hunger, aching to lunge forward and taste it for myself.

She then held her arm up toward the front of the car. "Drink up."

It wasn't her fist to my face I would lose control over ... it was this.

When Lucy saw the blood, her eyes burned crimson, and she sank her fangs into Rachel's wrist.

Well, fuck. While Rachel's body relaxed and she closed her eyes, my dick stirred to life. The hardened flesh pressed achingly against my jeans as I watched her friend feed. *Jesus.* The scent alone pushed me into a new level of frenzy that I had to force down.

"Okay, are we good now?" Tony asked. I nodded, and he holstered his gun and opened the driver's side door.

No, Tony, we're not fucking good.

A sudden ache burned in my stomach, sending a lick of pain up my throat. The hunger I've kept at bay reminded me that it was still there, waiting. If I didn't feed soon, I was going to murder someone.

Lucy's eyes opened and went to my face, almost like she was rubbing it in. After a few moments, she pulled her mouth from Rachel's wrist. "We need to find a place for Jase to feed, too,"

Lucy said, giving me a stern, judgy glare. "All that strength from Valentina turning you and years of being a villainous dick, you're one tantrum away from proving everyone right by how much of a loose cannon you really are." While Rachel's wrist healed, Lucy licked a smear of blood from the corner of her mouth.

"He's not drinking from an innocent human," Rachel growled, glaring at me.

I'm getting the goddamn third-degree from everyone here.

"And I'm not letting him drink from you, either," Tony said, turning around while pulling up his sleeve. He held his wrist toward me.

I didn't want Tony's blood, but after that scuffle where I had Rachel pinned down, he wasn't about to let me touch her again.

"I'll drive once you're finished. You can give me directions while you rest," Lucy said. "Rachel will manage him."

Tony nodded.

"You take more than necessary, and I will drown you with my mists before ripping your head off," Rachel warned, but I only smiled at the threat.

Tony shoved his wrist closer to my face. "Drink, asshole."

Sighing in resignation, I leaned forward and sank my fangs into Tony's wrist. While his blood tasted fine, it wasn't what I wanted. The scent of Rachel's blood took over my mind, as well as the visual of Lucy feeding from her. I knew it was only a matter of time before I took her blood for myself, even if she fought against me.

CHAPTER 25

ANDREI

"Though it's nighttime, remember to keep the necklace I gave you at our layover in New York under your shirt," Liam explained. "The sunstone needs to be flush against your body at all times." He turned to Jackson. "If you feel the sun burning your skin tomorrow when you first step into the light, it means the stone needs to be re-enchanted. I'm not sure how long the spell lasts; I haven't done this in a long time."

"That's reassuring," Jackson said, rubbing his necklace under his T-shirt.

Jackson didn't trust Liam at all, and I didn't blame him. He'd been in my clan long enough to know that a witch always had ulterior motives. Liam was an outsider to us, but we needed a witch for this mission. I had my own reservations about the man, but as long as he followed *our* rules, then Liam could continue to breathe.

I moved away from him and leaned against the stone bridge crossing over one of the canals. Closing my eyes, I let the warm breeze dance over my face and neck.

"It's been over two centuries since I last felt the sunlight," I said, opening my eyes to take in the water and the passing gondolas. "God, New York in the daytime was incredible."

Jackson came to my side and turned his handsome face up toward the sky. "Back in 1975, I had just moved to New York City to audition for Broadway. One day, I met a woman named Martha McAllister, who offered to give me a tour of the city. She was a member of the cast at the theater. Later, she introduced me to the director, who encouraged me to audition for a small part in the upcoming opera. We spent the day together and walked through Central Park. I still remember the bench where we sat, coffees in hand, as the sun set behind the trees. Fuck, I miss those sunny days."

"What happened to Martha?" I asked. Jackson told Meredith and me about his past, but I had never heard that story.

"She got married in 1978 and moved out to Virginia to teach. She had a couple of kids and died in 2016 from an illness. I checked in with her about a year after you turned me. Martha sounded happy, really happy, which I was glad for. She was a lovely woman. Don't get me wrong, Drei. I love being a vampire, but I've missed the sun. It reminds me of her and the chance she gave me."

Jackson wasn't the only one with fond memories of our brief human lives. As a child, I spent so many hours in the sun, helping my mother plant in her garden or assisting my papá with bringing fish to sell. Mostly, I enjoyed the time with Mamá. Papá ... far less so. But I remembered what I had gained from sacrificing my soul: power, wealth, and control. If someone had the power to offer me immortality again, I would take it.

"According to the GPS, the hotel is only a few miles outside Venice. We can walk there and have the rental car dropped off," Jackson said as he moved away from the bridge railing. Liam was typing something on his cell phone.

I nodded. "Alright, that sounds good. But we also need to feed soon. It's almost ten, and I haven't fed since we left New Orleans."

"Does Venice have a network of blood suppliers here?" Liam asked.

"Unfortunately, the closest network is in Mestre," I replied, "and we don't have time to waste. We need to get to Mira."

Jackson swung his backpack over his shoulder and gave me a quick nod. "Alright, let's drop our shit off and go hunting."

⁓ele⁓

Once we checked into the hotel, we changed into more upscale clothing and placed our documentation in the safe.

"Have you ever been to Italy?" I asked Liam, watching as he adjusted the cuffs of his white dress shirt. The top button was open, revealing a black stone necklace around his neck. I had never noticed it before and wondered if it was something of significance.

"Never," he replied. "This is actually the first time I've been out of the country. My family bounced around a lot in the States but never overseas. Once I joined Black Onyx, they had me get a passport ... you know, just in case."

Jackson exited the bathroom wearing a sleek blue suit with a black tie and gray shirt underneath. "How did the coven feel about you coming to Venice with us? Deadly vampires for hire and all?"

Liam chuckled. "Helen wasn't *too* thrilled about the idea, but they understood you found a lead and needed my magic to help." He turned to me. "But I need to know why you decided to keep the information about the tracker in Rachel's arm from Gerald. You've known her location for months. If I'm going to lie to my coven, I need an explanation."

My lip curled into a sneer. "Helen and Gerald want me to deliver Kylan's ring after we leave Italy. I refuse to hand it over to them. I couldn't run the risk of them assigning another witch to this. Your power is necessary for all of us to succeed."

We still didn't trust Liam, so I wasn't sure how he would handle the explanation. My apprehension vanished when he subtly smiled and nodded in response.

"I get it. I've been involved since the museum heist. If Rachel still has the ring, and your brother and she are heading to that cave, you're going to need my magic specifically to stop them."

I nodded, hoping his confirmation would ease Jackson's remaining doubts about Liam's motivations. His upbringing may have taught him to despise our kind, but he was now crucial to my goals.

"Speaking of the little runaway," I said, opening the tracking app on my phone. I zoomed in on the coordinates and noticed that the timestamp had been refreshed hours ago. It showed that Rachel's last location was just outside the home she'd been staying in almost two hours ago, a few miles south of the city.

"Is she on the move?" Liam asked.

"No, something's wrong," I said, closing the app and reloading the program. A notification popped up on the screen when it rebooted, and my jaw tightened.

Offline.

I stared at the GPS screen, the pin no longer blinking. "It only goes offline when there's a major temperature change," I muttered, trying to make sense of it. I glanced up, feeling my chest tighten. "It's not in her body anymore."

A deep, controlled breath escaped me as fury boiled beneath my skin. "Looks like Rachel dug it out." Another thought, even more infuriating, hit me. "I guess I was right to assume Jase got here before us. He would've told her."

Jackson didn't hesitate to say the only *other* explanation. "Or she's dead?"

The thought shook me, but I couldn't let myself go there. Though I couldn't feel Rachel like usual, something told me she wasn't gone. The bond was weakening, yes—fading, like someone was tampering with it. I could still sense her, but the connection was thinning with every passing second. My anger rose, burning hotter than before and causing me to dig my nails into my palm. It was a struggle to control this rage. I didn't like other people messing with *my* things.

"You've looked at that map a million times," Jackson reminded me. "We know where she's been, so all we need to do is go to the villa, kill a few people, and force the survivors to tell us where they went."

I shook my head. "If Jase has made contact with her, he'd do it without Valentina's knowledge; he knows the risk. Which means *she* could still be there. Or someone who may know which way they're heading."

"Do you plan to kill them, too?" Liam said. "If you put down 'She Who Walks with the Devil,' you'd secure your power position within Black Onyx. Believe me."

"Yeah, right," I bit out. "You've never met the damned woman. It won't be good if she realizes we're coming for her daughter. Valentina will unleash hell on our heads."

"This trip keeps getting more and more interesting," Liam added. "Valentina will slow us down. She also could have the ring."

When I looked at Jackson, I immediately noticed the concern in his eyes. "What do you think?" I asked, watching his gaze flit between Liam and me.

"Honestly, Liam might be right. If Rachel fled, Valentina would be the first to track her down. She'll pose a roadblock for us. Let's get to the villa, see who's still there, and take care of it. If we find the ring while doing it, even better."

I nodded. "Alright. Let's feed, and then we can pay a nice little visit to that lovely home." I looked at Liam. "Witches have always been self-righteous pricks. So, I'm only asking this once: are you willing to do what it takes to help us? To kill if you must ... even humans?"

Liam crossed his arms over his broad chest and grinned. "If it means we are a step closer to that angel's sword, then yes, I will kill anyone who gets in the way."

⁕

Venice was the perfect playground for those like Jackson and me. The city was filled with locals and tourists out for the evening, taking in the architecture and beautiful canals. We blended in perfectly. The more crowded it is, the less likely it is that anyone would see someone get snatched off the streets. Humans cared too much about themselves to notice strangers. That made hunting so easy.

As the city lit up with nightlife, we headed deeper into the Dorsoduro District, watching each group of people as we passed. The area was alive with the sounds of music, the smell of saltwater and spices, and the rhythmic beat of human hearts. I paused along a canal's edge and looked out at the water. Though I was sure someone would realize I was undead, no one seemed to notice. Humans believed that if they ignored us, we would leave them alone. Ignoring a wolf in a city of sheep was foolish.

Beside me, Jackson casually leaned against the wrought-iron railing, his tall frame cloaked in a black leather jacket. His black locs fell over his shoulders while he listened to a gondolier singing as he passed beneath us. He sang along with the man, the timbre of his voice clear in the night air. The gondolier looked up at Jackson and offered a deep bow before resuming his opera. The couple in the boat was so engrossed in each other and their wine that they didn't notice the beautiful voice was coming just above them. A fiery burst of hunger clawed at my throat.

It was time to eat.

Liam was a few feet away, fingers tapping against his thigh, as if he felt the pulse of the city itself. He brushed his brown hair back, and his eyes glowed excitedly despite the growing darkness. Several women had glanced at him while we walked, but he paid them no mind.

"Liam," I called. "Grab a bite to eat at that restaurant across the road, and we'll meet up with you in thirty-five minutes."

Liam looked around. "You sure?"

We walked over to him so no one could eavesdrop. Jackson smiled. "Trust me, you don't want to watch. It's a lot bloodier than what's in the movies."

Liam chuckled. "Alright, but don't kill anyone here. If they catch us within the city limits, it'll be fucking hell, and the coven will demand that we leave. Plus, if the women hear about it, they'll flee."

"Well, I can't promise anything," I teased before nodding to Jackson to follow me. Liam sighed and walked in the opposite direction.

Jackson and I moved through the narrow cobblestone streets toward the smaller shops and restaurants. Strings of white fairy lights crisscrossed above our heads, lighting up the walkway and over the crowd of people. Musicians stood at the street corner playing violins that drowned out the laughter of those seated at the outdoor tables.

Though I didn't need or miss human food, I still enjoyed the aromas of timeless recipes. I inhaled slowly, savoring the scent of rosemary, the tang of lemon gelato, and the richness of squid ink risotto. The piazza's central fountain sparkled like liquid silver under the lights, and the beauty was almost enough to distract me from the burning hunger.

Almost.

"There are plenty of people around," Jackson muttered. "Let's pick one and take them to the back, where no one can see. We'll have to use speed, but I doubt anyone will notice." He ran his hand over his mouth. "Fuck, I hate doing this."

I scanned the area, taking in the servers and tables nearby. There was one table off to the side, near a small garden, with a young woman sitting alone in a red floral-printed dress. She typed on her phone with her elbows on the tablecloth, utterly oblivious to her surroundings.

"There," I said, gesturing with my head.

Without a word, Jackson used his vampiric speed and ran to the woman. In the blink of an eye, he pulled her out of the chair and carried her toward the back of the building. Her phone slipped from her hands and hit the cobblestones, shattering the screen. I looked around one more time to see if anyone noticed. When no one looked our way, I hurried after him, kicking the broken phone out of sight.

Jackson was holding the struggling woman as I approached. I grinned down at her, letting my fangs show prominently. The woman's eyes widened, and she thrashed even harder.

"Shh," Jackson whispered. "I'm going to pull my hand away, but if you scream, I will snap your neck and dump your body in the sea. Understand?"

The woman stopped struggling; the fight drained completely, but fear shone in her eyes.

"Are you alone?" I asked, kneeling in front of her. She nodded. "Good, you know English. We'll not kill you. We only need your blood, nothing else. I promise you."

I looked at Jackson. "Lay her down gently."

Slowly, Jackson removed his hand from her throat and laid her flat on her back. The woman let out a quiet sob while she closed her eyes, and a few tears ran down her cheek. I moved over her, straddling her hips to keep her pinned. She was lithe with long, shapely legs, and her skin had a warm olive tone.

I went still for a moment. While I had drunk from the vein after Rachel left, this was the first time I'd done it to an unwilling person in a long time. It felt different. Hunting prey wasn't as exciting anymore. If anything, what we were doing had become repulsive ... but we needed blood, and vampires couldn't deny their nature. This was supposed to be easy—natural.

While Jackson slipped his hands under her armpits and pulled her up on his lap, I leaned in, fangs scraping against her neck. As I sank my fangs in, I felt the rush of blood enter my mouth. It was like fire in my veins, igniting every one of my senses.

Fuck. The woman tasted divine. Since Rachel, no other blood would satisfy me like hers. But this ... this was close enough until I could get Rachel back.

As I drank, she tried to kick and resist but kept quiet, more tears streaming down her soft cheeks. I wrapped my muscular arm around her back to lift her slightly, pressing my body into hers. Jackson ran his hand down her arm before gripping her wrist and pulling it toward his mouth, sinking his teeth in.

Once I felt satisfied, I released her and climbed off, using tissue from my suit pocket to wipe my mouth and chin clean and ignoring that flicker of anxiety that we had to leave soon before anyone noticed. Jackson continued drinking from her for another thirty seconds. I watched him close his eyes, and he let out a satisfying moan. "Fuck," he said as he pulled his lips free from her wrist. "I needed that more than I thought I did. Though I didn't mean to take that much."

Jackson had always been careful, unlike me. He often felt guilty for taking from an unwilling victim. He never had issues finding a woman who would gladly let him drink from them in New Orleans. I saw the conflict in his eyes. Blood dripped from the woman's wrist and onto his pants. The woman's warmth was gone, and her breathing became ragged.

"We've taken more than enough," I said, watching the woman's eyes flutter. "We might kill her. Remember what Liam said?"

Jackson nodded, lowering her arm back to the ground. The woman's current state told me we would have plenty of time to leave the city limits and get to the villa before she could regain enough strength to get help. We'd be long gone before any authority could track us down. I took another tissue from my pocket and handed it to Jackson.

"Wipe the stain on your pants as best you can, and then prop the woman against that wall," I said. "A server on their break will be able to find her soon enough."

Once Jackson had cleaned up his mess and tucked away the unconscious woman, we hurried away from the restaurant and down the road to where Liam had gone. A few minutes later, he joined us, and we returned to the hotel to get the car.

After a twenty-minute drive, we entered a neighborhood right along the main river that cut through the municipality of Mira. The GPS on my phone guided us to a villa surrounded by a tall iron fence and towering trees. Two men stood guard, and from the looks of it, they were human.

Getting inside should be easy.

Liam walked up to the closed gate and placed his hand on the knob. A subtle blue light trickled on the surface, and he pulled back. "Shit," he cursed. "It's enchanted. I can feel the elements attached to it. It's made to keep *me* out."

"You?" I asked, walking closer to the gate with Jackson. "What do you mean?"

Liam turned to look over his shoulder at us. "Witches."

I nodded. "Alright, once we get through, we'll find a way to get you in." Liam looked back as the two human guards spotted us, and I smiled. "It's time to play."

CHAPTER 26

Valentina

Rachel was gone.

Just ... gone.

It had been three hours since she'd fought me and ran out the door, and not even a basic locator spell was working. Luka had held me back while Rachel made her escape, and Darius intervened before my temper got the best of me and killed the young man.

All eyes watched me as I passed down the hall after failing the third spell I tried, giving me a wide berth from my crackling rage. As I reached for the iron door handle, Darius grabbed my elbow. "We will find her," he affirmed, but I yanked my arm away.

"You think she'll willingly come back after what I just did to her?" I growled, my teeth clenched as regret tugged at my chest. "She has my ring, and I broke my one promise to her!"

Darius's dark brows furrowed, and he shook his head. "From how you're acting, you seem to care more about that ring than your daughter and some promise. I thought you were more capable of emotion than this."

A slow smile spread across my lips. "And you seem to have forgotten who and what I am."

Yes, I *was* capable of love. I loved Cyrus, but he died, and they locked me away, my soul wandering the depths of Hell before I managed to escape Lucifer and hide—until Rachel brought me back. When I awoke, I wanted to love my child.

"When I rose from that coffin and saw that Rachel had survived, I thought it would bring me joy, a sense of purpose. But instead, I'm left with a foul-mouthed, sarcastic, reckless child who can't even control her powers. From the moment I met her, all I've felt is disappointment. I've seen parents who loved their children, parents who risked everything to create them—parents who fought and laid down their lives to save them when the academy was attacked. Me? I tried to use compulsion on her, something I swore I'd never do, to ensure the ring protected me, not my own daughter. I've shown her that I'm unchanged and have little humanity left. There's nothing left!"

Darius's expression turned grim. He was judging me. Everyone in the hallway was judging me with looks of disgust. I didn't care; I wouldn't let guilt deter me from tracking down what was mine.

"All I want is that ring, and I have no idea where Rachel is going with it, and basic spells aren't working." I paused, knowing that what I was about to ask was far more dangerous than any spell I had ever done. "Darius, I need my book."

His eyes widened, but he stayed silent for a long time before nodding. "Follow me."

He brushed past me and opened the library door. I followed him inside to one of the shelves along the back wall. He pulled on a red leatherbound book, and a small cabinet opened beside the shelf. Darius reached in and removed my Book of Shadows. When

I had fled to the States with Cyrus, I left the book in his care until I returned.

Thank God he kept it.

Darius turned to me, but he kept the book near his chest. "There are plenty of other spells that don't need to come from this book. You told me how dangerous the magic inside these pages is. Don't risk it."

He was right; I could draw from countless spellbooks, but *my* Book of Shadows was tied to my bloodline. Its power resonated with my element. My mother, and her mothers before her, crafted every spell within the pages. Our coven in Romania killed her for using dark magic, which was forbidden. Her screams as she burned haunted my nightmares for years to come. The dark magic soon found me after her death, chasing my shadow, tempting me to use its power as she had. I was only nineteen when Mother died, and I was alone in a world that hated my existence.

Five years later, Kylan turned me into the first vampire—stripping me of the magic that flowed in my veins. Before I died my first death, I swore never to abandon the book my mother and ancestors had poured their souls into, regardless of its controversial contents. When I awoke as a vampire, I sliced the palm of my hand and let my blood, which was now mingled with Kylan's, soak into the book's ancient pages. That blood was an offering to the Shadows, to my family's magic, to seal away the power I had been born with until I could find a way to use it again.

Being hunted down and turned by Kylan was not by chance. I was hand-picked to be his progeny; it was a direct command from his king. Lucifer came to me in a vision shortly after Mother died, claiming me as his future Queen of Hell. He'd sealed my fate before

I even met Kylan, destined to be his bride. Of course, I immediately refused. Having his minion turn me into a monster was only part of Lucifer's punishment for telling him *no*.

But it was only the beginning. Before Kylan disappeared, he brought me a black stone ring set in bronze, a gift from Lucifer. He'd forged it from Kylan's blood and would allow me to access a trickle of magic, thanks to his angelic heritage. There was a price, though. If I wore the ring, it meant that I accepted Lucifer's proposal and that when my end came, I would be his *forever*. The temptation to regain even a fraction of my magic was too strong, so I agreed—a gift with conditions from my future husband.

Darius cleared his throat, pulling me back to the library. He placed the book in my hands, and a cool sensation, almost like a stream of water, began to move through my fingers and up my arms. A lump formed in my throat, and I swallowed. I hadn't asked for my book since my return, even though I felt it calling for me every single day. I hoped I didn't have to use it, but I needed more magic than what was coming through my ring on Rachel's finger. Without my true power, no spell would be strong enough.

"I know what you're going to do," Darius murmured, brushing his fingers against my cheek. "Please. Don't."

I shook my head. "You have to let me. Our cause is too important. I need to summon him."

He nervously swallowed, his Adam's apple bobbing. I didn't need to read Darius's mind to know how he felt. His love and devotion were apparent, but I'd been promised to another long before Cyrus and him, and he knew it.

Someone who he feared more than anyone.

"Alright," he said, "but I won't be here when you open that gate. I'll stand outside. I have to protect my family out there. Those dhampirs especially. Don't pull *him* all the way through—"

"I know," I reassured him. "Go."

He gave me one final glance before abruptly leaving the library and slamming the door behind him.

Now alone, I hurried to the center of the room and kneeled on the hardwood floor. I placed the book on the ground and opened it. A tightness squeezed my dead heart as I flipped through the fragile pages written by my mother and my ancestors before her. I found the spell I needed. If I were going to cast a powerful spell, I needed some help.

My fingers trembled as I touched the surface of those pages, running over the black ink. The spell was written in an ancient language, the words so smudged and faded that they were nearly impossible to understand. I reached into my pocket and pulled out a pocket knife and a small hourglass. After pricking my index finger, I squeezed out a thick, black-red bead of blood and drew symbols onto the floor.

"Spirits of the coven, bound by the blood and the waters," I chanted, my voice steady despite the thrum of nerves under my skin. The symbols on the floor began to glow. "Hear my call, *old mothers*. Rise from the depths of shadows. Awaken from your slumber. I summon thee to my sacred circle by the lines of lineage and the power of our blood." The spell spilled from my lips like a hymn of praise.

The room became as cold as a northern wind, the veil of death parting for the spirits who listened. Intense, nearly blinding golden light shone from the symbols on the floor and the book.

"Arise, matriarchs of my bloodline."

There was an icy chill that blew over my skin, like the sigh of a corpse, and my great-grandmother, Katalina, emerged from the light, her outline forming as if by invisible hands. Her long obsidian-black curls framed the face I knew well, with some strands pulling into thick braids adorned with silver beads. Her deep-brown eyes bore into mine, both stern and filled with warmth I hadn't seen in over a thousand years. Another form manifested into my grandmother, Daciana. Her willowy frame, steel-colored hair, and knowing smile solidified. The judgmental gleam in her eyes never wavered, even in death.

Finally, my beloved mother, Nicoleta, with her auburn curls and bright blue eyes, stepped through the parted veil of light. A ghostly pallor had stolen the warm beige tone of her skin, robbing her of some of her beautiful, vibrant appearance. Tears threatened to spill when I saw her, but I steeled myself.

"Valentina, my dear girl, why have you summoned us? What have you done?" my mother asked, worry flitting across her eyes.

I looked at the three women before me and smiled. "I need your powers," I said. "For only a few minutes."

The ghostly women laughed at me.

Of course, those fools would.

I raised my left hand and moved my fingers in a waving motion. Purple mists shot through and danced over the circle of light, tying their spectral forms to this plane, so they couldn't flee to whatever dark hell Death took them to.

"Stop!" Katalina shouted. "This is forbidden."

"Since when has that ever stopped our family before?" I mocked. "I know what I'm doing."

My hands moved together quickly now, using more of my mists to seal any magic the women may have still possessed within the veil. My grandmother was shouting, her hands raised in fists. But I could no longer hear her or Katalina. Their voices were of no use to me, only their power.

My child, do not do this. You know the risks far too well. This ritual is beyond what we practiced. Do not be foolish. You can't control him.

My mother's voice rang clear in my head, but I ignored it. I pulled hard on those tethers of energy, snapping them into my own power, still alive through Rachel and the ring. *Thank God.* Closing my eyes, I began to chant again, a new spell harnessing the magic of the long-dead. I felt their energy grow strong within me. The tethers wove into a thin, delicate rope of our blended powers.

There wouldn't be much time; I had to do this now.

Keeping my left hand raised, I used my right to flip the book's pages to another chapter, a different spell. The images on the pages grew darker and more unnerving as I looked through them. My stomach flipped as my eyes landed on the spell I needed. The snarling face of a horned god at the top of the page.

Forgive me, Mother, I called out in my thoughts, knowing she would hear me through our shared gifts.

My relatives could no longer move, let alone speak. The spell held them in a frozen state, like sculptures. I closed my eyes, reaching deep within my wells of magic for that dark power I was born with—the kind that would have had me burned at the stake.

My fangs protruded from my gums, and I pricked the thick pad of my palm, smearing the blood across my skin. I pressed my hand against the page. My collected power surged to the surface, searing my veins. A sharp tug in my chest sent my body into a wave of pain.

"Shit!" I felt as though an icy fire was consuming me from within.

After a few seconds, the pain abated enough for me to move my hands from the book to the floor. The golden symbols that held my family continued to glow, holding that rope firm. I pushed all my magic, including my ancestors', into the parted veil.

"King of the Unyielding Darkness, heed my call. Rise from the depths of the Underworld, where the shadows crawl. By blood and flames and broken souls, I summon thee."

I opened my eyes, and my water magic took root. It rose from the floor in great misty columns above me, brushing against the ceiling. The clouds slowly circled the room, tiny droplets peppering the furniture and onto my upturned face. I quickly picked up the small hourglass and turned it, the blue-colored grains dripping slowly. Years ago, the hourglass was enchanted to snap a spell, no matter how strong. Once time ran out, so did the magic, and all connections would be severed.

"Lucifer, the Morning Star, bearer of tainted light, rise before me on this night."

The lights in the library flickered rapidly before dimming, casting the room in a murky darkness. The glowing light of my summoning spell remained steady. Then I felt it. An icy, clawed hand reached through the veil and wrapped itself around my throat. But it wasn't a threatening pressure, more like a possessive hold one would have on a lover.

"My beloved Queen," his cold voice purred in the empty room. Lucifer's voice was like a wave that gently lapped over me. Lust, power, and need consumed my blood, and his overwhelming presence pushed me back until I was lying on the floor. I held still as his other hand skated over my body, caressing every curve and sensitive spot.

"Stop," I hissed, pushing at his hands, but his grip stayed firm on my neck. The bastard wanted me to submit, so I stopped moving.

"Much better. Now, why did you summon me, my love?" Lucifer asked, voice booming with authority.

"I need to locate my daughter." Suddenly, fear overcame me. Mentioning Rachel to the entity that nearly destroyed his realm when I fell in love with Cyrus wasn't the best idea. But I had no choice. "If she intends to remove *my* ring, I will lose my magic, making it impossible to track her down. My powers aren't strong enough to do anything to find her right now. I need them returned to their natural state. Please. Make me a true witch again. Give them back."

Lucifer's lips were close to my ear, even though I couldn't see him. His warm breath tickled my cheek. "Now, why would I do that?" he asked, laughing coldly. "With you being mostly powerless, it's so much easier to control you. Until you're back by my side for eternity, your full strength is mine."

"You bastard."

A surge of laughter echoed in my ears. Muffled shouting followed; the tethered spell holding my family members had slipped a little. They were slamming their fists against the light that held them, trying to reach me, to protect me. But I didn't want protection; I wanted my damn magic back from Lucifer.

Even though he claimed me as his queen, I was not *just* his mate; I became a servant of his realm. When I foolishly put on his ring, I bound my magic to Hell. My powers, once a gift from the Upper World, no longer belonged solely to me. Lucifer tethered them to his command, along with my soul. The fragment I still possessed remained untarnished, but even that was slipping from my grasp.

A glance at the hourglass showed me that the top half was almost empty. Time was running out. Rachel likely would remove the ring soon, leaving me blind to where she was going. Relying on a damn trinket to access my birthright was pathetic.

"My darling queen, I am so close to taking you back I can *taste* it. No longer will I have to wait for your eventual death to have you. Unfortunately, it's not time. There is turmoil in the Underworld that requires my attention. But until then, I'm watching you."

Fury clenched at my jaw, and rage burned up my spine. *Goddamn you.*

"Don't bring Him into this," Lucifer chided playfully, reading my thoughts. "He is too busy sitting on His hands while I disrupt the precious 'balance of life' as those sycophants above screech about." A slick slide of his tongue ran over the skin between my breasts. The rope of power holding my mother and the others began to fray. "I'm coming for you, love. You'll be where you belong soon enough."

No.

There was a heavy pause, as if Lucifer was listening to something. "First," he started again. "You need to address a problem outside."

The last few grains of sand fell, and Lucifer and my spellwork vanished with a crack. The water magic above me collapsed, soaking me, but not the book. I looked around. The images of my matriarchs lingered for a moment. Their expressions were of horror and fury. My mother reached out but vanished like a wisp of smoke in the wind, leaving me alone. I was no closer to getting my full magic back.

"No!" I screamed. "Goddammit!" I picked up the still-dry Book of Shadows and hurled it across the room. It slammed against a shelf, and several pages broke free and fluttered to the floor. Rising to my feet, I wrung out as much water as I could from my clothes and hair.

I had barely taken a step toward the door, when it flew open, and Darius raced in. "Valentina!" he shouted. "We have intruders on the grounds!"

Panic seized me, and I ran toward him, taking his hand. "What's happened?" I asked as we ran down the hall toward the front door.

Darius said nothing as he threw open the front door, and we raced into the night air. I saw movement at the front gate, and a handsome, young-looking man with wavy brown hair was holding his hands high. Red magic poured from his fingertips and brushed against the shield. He couldn't get through.

"One foolish witch is trying to get inside? Kill him!" I ordered.

"Over there," Darius hissed, pointing ahead.

Near the garden, shadowy figures emerged a few yards away, dragging something across the ground.

Oh no.

Tati was being dragged across the grass by the throat and, even with her immense strength, she couldn't break free. I looked at the man holding her, and a familiar face came into view.

Andrei.

CHAPTER 27

VALENTINA

"You!" I hissed. "Let. Her. Go."

Andrei grinned. "Let him inside, and I will." He gestured to the gate with his free hand.

"You have a death wish, don't you?" I said through my teeth, but then my eyes immediately caught another figure on the other side. It was a tall man with deep-brown skin and long locs that almost reached the middle of his back. His towering body hovered over another hostage. Alessandro.

"We figured you would say no. Andrei warned us you'd gladly sacrifice everyone here if you had to."

I shook my head. "What are you doing here? How did you even find this place?"

I cast my eyes around the property, looking for Jase. Was he here, as well, looking for Rachel?

My vampire powers sparked to life, and my fangs slid past my lips. Darius growled next to me, his rage as tangible as my own.

"Andrei," the tall man holding Alessandro called out. "Do it."

Andrei raised his fist and slammed it into Tati's back. Her screams pierced my ears. Darius and I both shouted for him to stop before I took another step forward.

"You use your power on us, Valentina, and I rip her spine clean from her body."

"No!" Alessandro screamed, trying to crawl toward Andrei and his mate, but Jackson had a firm grip on the back of his neck. "Kill me. Kill me instead. Not her, not my mate."

"Open the gate, and we won't dismember and force-feed her body parts to you," Andrei growled, his dark eyes looking like the empty sockets of a skull.

I ran my hands through my damp hair, and for once, I didn't know what to do. Alessandro and Tati were vital members of Darius's clan, and he was about to watch her die.

Why am I hesitating? One vampire's life isn't enough to keep me rooted. What the hell is wrong with me?

The inner turmoil within me raged like a typhoon, and my thoughts spun with every solution I could think of. I should attack. So, why couldn't I take that step?

"Darius," I said, debating how to stop this. I couldn't use my speed because Andrei would kill her before I reached them. Compulsion was also too risky. "What can we do here?"

It was clear that Enzo and Charles were dead. I compelled the men to fight to the death against any intruder who breached the gates. No local vampires would attack the villa, as Darius was friends with all of them. So, how did Andrei discover this place?

"I'll open the gates," Alessandro cried out. The man holding him let him stand. "I may be a vampire, but I can access the spell since I live here. Any of us can do it."

"Don't!" I shouted. But he hurried over and pressed his hands against the barrier, uttering the spell to break the shield. There was a shimmer of light, and the magic disappeared.

"Thank you," the witch said as he crossed the threshold. With a flick of his wrist, Alessandro's neck snapped, and his body fell to the ground. I lunged forward, closing the distance between myself and the two men. Alessandro would heal instantly, and then we could save Tati.

But what happened next was something I had never seen a witch do before, and it left me frozen. When Alessandro attempted to stand, the witch threw out his power, wrapping his body in red mists. He pulled Alessandro off the ground and held him several feet in the air. Then he started stripping Alessandro's skin from his muscles, inch by inch. He was flaying him alive.

Oh my God.

He screamed, his healing factor trying desperately to stitch him back together. But then the male witch threw his arms down, reducing Alessandro's limbs and body into a puddle of blood. The red liquid splashed across the gravel, leaving a blackened mark in the pristine garden.

It wasn't me or Darius who screamed in horror but Tati. The heartbreaking wails that came from her would haunt me for eternity.

Though it was a risk, she tried to pull away from Andrei's hold on her spine. Andrei, seemingly stunned, pulled his fist from her back, and she fell to the ground. When the gaping hole sealed, Tati rose and staggered to the steaming pool of her beloved. The witch watched as she fell to her knees, one hand gripping her chest like her heart was shattering beneath, the other shakingly touching the puddle of blood that was once her mate.

"He ..." she gasped. "He did what you asked! We did nothing wrong. Wha—why did you kill him?"

The witch cocked his head as he looked down his nose at her. "Because," he purred, "the Black Onyx has *very* specific instructions when dealing with your kind. I'm merely doing my job, vampire."

Before we could move, he flicked his wrist and destroyed her, too. It was over in an instant. Tati's entire body, down to the last strand of her long black hair, dissolved into blood, splashing into Alessandro's mark on the ground. I clapped a hand over my mouth, stunned at this witch's cruel magic. Darius groaned, clutching the sides of his head while shaking with rage and sorrow over the loss of his clan members and his friends.

The man dusted the remaining magic from his hands and turned to grin at Andrei. "You're welcome."

Andrei's fangs flashed in a gnashing snarl of frustration. Clearly, he wasn't happy with what the witch had just done. Even Andrei's other vampire friend looked utterly sickened.

"Liam, what the hell?" Andrei hissed.

Liam shrugged coldly, as if he were devoid of any regret.

And now, their leverage is gone.

While the three men distracted themselves, I unleashed all my powers—elemental and demonic. My eyes burned crimson, and blue mists leaked from the corners. My fangs gleamed as I hissed. I summoned a ball of water and flung it at Andrei. He dodged, but the blast soaked his hair. The damn witch, Liam, charged at me, hurling a wave of red mist toward my chest. I raised a shield, but the impact slammed me to the ground.

"Well, well," Andrei taunted. "There are others inside that house ... with heartbeats." Something in Andrei's voice made my spine lock up. "Maybe we should catch one of them. That'll make you cooperate." I heard his footsteps disappear toward the villa, followed by his friend's.

No!

Darius roared and took off after them, for he would die for those inside that house.

As I moved to stand, Liam was on me. He grabbed my throat and lifted me off the gravel. This little brat was stronger than most witches; I'd give him that. But he was no match for me.

Grinning with feral delight, I seized his wrist and crushed the bones. Liam screamed in pain and attempted to hold me, but his useless hand fell away from my throat. When I stepped away, he threw another wall of red power at me, but my water shield forced it back.

We stood there, mere feet apart, watching each other. I burned with hatred, watching the witch's hazel eyes laced with pain and calculation.

I will rip this bastard into bloody chunks and throw them into the canals.

I threw my power into his mind with lightning speed, seizing control. Liam cried out, grabbing his temples. He tried to flush me out, but my mind-reading magic was unbreakable.

Or at least, I thought it was.

"Wow," he said. "That's some powerful magic you've got there." His own magic pressed against mine, shoving it back.

Though Liam was blocking me, it slipped for just a moment.

"Cave?" I said. "Rachel's heading for a cave in Crete with Jase?"

Even with my grip on his mind, Liam sneered. "You read the thoughts I wanted you to know. She's not safe, but don't worry. We'll take care of her when we catch up. For now, I'll enjoy taking that incredible power from you, sweetheart—right after I kill you."

I laughed. "Good luck with that." I spun and bolted for the front steps, hearing the sounds of Darius and the others fighting inside the house. I needed to reach them. But just then, a surge of red power slammed into my back, knocking me off my feet. I hit the ground hard but quickly sprang up, whirling around.

"Attacking someone from behind is poor form, boy," I seethed. "Didn't your mommy teach you any manners?"

Liam rolled his shoulder back as he marched forward, blatantly ignoring me. "Imagine the hero I'll be once I kill the infamous Valentina Vasile. Black Onyx will worship me. Maybe I'll even take Gerald's place."

I steadied myself, power crackling at my fingertips. "Oh, a young lad like you still has so much to learn."

Liam raised his hands as if ready to block my next move. "Well, why don't you teach me, old hag?"

Hag? Kylan turned me at twenty-four!

I lunged for Liam, not even bothering to use magic or my vampire powers, and slammed my right fist into his left cheek. I felt the bone beneath crack, and fresh blood leaked onto my knuckles. Liam's head jerked to the side, and more blood leaked from his nose.

Before I could bury my fangs in his exposed throat, his hand—the one I had crushed moments before—clamped down on my forearm.

"What?" I gasped, looking down at the healed appendage gripping my arm.

He healed.

"What are you? No witch should be able to heal a bone that fast," I snarled, but my voice betrayed my confusion.

His lips turned up. "Oh, I'm a witch, but let's just say I inherited some *fortunate* abilities from my father." Liam dug his nails into my skin until I winced. "You'll find I'm harder to kill than most."

My fangs flashed as I grinned, trepidation turning in my gut, and blasted a concussive pulse of water against Liam's chest. The force sent him crashing into a thick oak tree that bordered the wall a hundred feet away.

Try getting up from that, you entitled brat.

I rushed for the open front door and slammed it shut once inside, using several runes to seal it so Liam couldn't follow. "Darius!" I shouted, running into the kitchen, where I heard the commotion of chaos. He was still exchanging blows with Andrei and his friend, only now Gio had joined the brawl. I scanned the area and saw Ava lying on the ground, her arm sliced and bleeding, but she was alive.

Luka came charging in from the other entrance, throwing his magic toward Andrei, who had Gio in a bear hug. Andrei cursed and released him before grabbing his skull.

"Gio! Grab Ava and go!" he shouted, using his free hand to keep the other vampire at bay. I knew where they needed to go. The villa had a secret tunnel built beneath the main house. It led to a small inlet inside a cave connected to the river. A boat was waiting to take people away to a safe location. They all knew that one day, they would have to flee again. It just came far too soon.

Gio carefully gathered Ava into his arms and sprinted out of the kitchen, his footsteps fading in the chaos.

"Luka, hold for them as long as you can," I instructed. Darius was no longer in the kitchen, but a loud crack came from the front door. *Oh, God.*

Luka only nodded as he dragged Andrei and his friend to their knees with his telepathic powers.

I raced out of the kitchen and down the hall. "Darius!"

"In here. Hurry!"

Darius was in the library, gathering weapons from behind some false cabinets.

"That witch will be inside any second," I said, knowing I couldn't seal *every* door. Even if I could, the rune spells would never be as strong as the ones around the perimeter. "Where's the stone?"

He slung a bow across his back before running toward another shelf that concealed the Tear. Darius opened it quickly and grabbed the stone, handing it to me so I could tuck it into my jeans pocket. I grabbed a dagger hanging from the wall before turning around to gather other weapons. I spotted my Book of Shadows lying a few feet away, some pages knocked askew.

I gathered my book and shoved it into the weapons pouch, which I grabbed off the shelf. "Darius, go find Gio and Ava. I'm going to get Luka," I ordered. Darius hesitated momentarily, then he nodded and sprinted toward the back door, where he found the hidden tunnel entrance.

Another deafening boom echoed through the house. Liam was close to getting inside, and I needed to save the dhampirs. I reentered the kitchen. Luka was panting, his face dripping with sweat from his mind-holding power.

"I'll take it from here," I said, touching his outstretched arm. "Meet the others. I'll be right behind you."

"But—"

"Don't argue with me. Please. Just. Go." I pushed my compulsion power to my throat, coating the vocal cords in absolute control. Luka understood what I was about to do and dropped his power, which I replaced with one word: "Stay."

The other vampire was immobile, but Andrei managed to look at me and smile. It felt like we were back at the church, and Rachel had come into her compulsion abilities against him and Jase.

"Well," I said, "here we are again."

Andrei grinned wider, his eyes flashing with something unsettling. "Are you going to kill me now?" he asked, fangs bared.

"I have no choice. You'll find her if I don't."

Andrei's stare grew more intense. "Rachel's safer with me, and you know it."

I held my tongue. As much as I wanted to defend my child, I knew Andrei did, too. Through the wild darkness in his mind, I saw he cared about Rachel, even if he didn't know how to *love* her.

No matter. Neither Rachel nor my ring would fall into their hands. I had to kill them. I summoned a spear of water to impale the men's hearts, but before I could unleash it, an explosion rocked the kitchen, throwing me into the living room. Every wall around me cracked, and debris rained down on my head.

Liam appeared from the dust, red death magic pulsing at his fingertips. He looked like a man possessed. Before I could react, Darius raced toward me, seized my wrist, and yanked me to my feet. A jagged piece of broken metal from the coffee table dug into my skin, scraping painfully along my hip as it tore at the fabric of my sweater.

I winced as I watched the chaos of the crumbling villa.

And then we ran.

CHAPTER 28

As we sped south down the quiet Italian countryside, my hands kept curling into fists—fury and blood-soaked rage burned in my chest. My anger roared at me to return to the villa and unleash my wrath on those men, but I couldn't. If we delayed any further, I'd lose Rachel forever. Andrei was determined to find her by any means necessary, and for the first time in thousands of years, there was someone stronger than me—Liam—and I didn't know how a mortal could be so powerful.

What the hell is he?

The night seemed to swallow the world around us as we drove, with only a sliver of the crescent moon casting a faint glow over the hilltops. Since we fled the villa, there had been an uncomfortable silence between Darius and me. I knew him well, but Rachel and I disrupted his clan's lives four months ago, and now, because of us, he'd lost everything.

Before we headed south, Luka, Gio, and Ava were ordered to head to Rome, where Darius had a contact who would take and keep them safe. Luka and Gio had bowed to me, and Ava threw her arms around us both before the three vanished into the night. The hug made my chest tight.

I was clinging to the hope that once we found Rachel, we could reunite with them and resume our agenda of destroying Black Onyx. Until then, we had to be cautious and wise in our next move.

I turned slightly left to glance at Darius, shifting in my seat. His jaw was tense, the muscles there ticking, while his entire focus remained on the road. He gripped the steering wheel so tightly I could see the metal beneath it bowing. Thankfully, after having suffered heavy blood loss from the fighting and the villa's collapse, Darius's wounds seemed to be healing. Still, the hollowness of his eyes and the gauntness forming under his cheekbones told me he wasn't as whole as he appeared. I knew the desperation to feed well, lurking beneath our bones like a starved beast.

It was there for me, too—the gnawing hunger in the pit of my stomach, the scorch in my throat. It would have to wait for now. The task at hand was more important. Retrieving my little rebellious daughter, who fled with the ring that didn't belong to her, along with her fated mate who she had no clue about.

Jase *cannot be the one to tell her.*

"Do you think Rachel's alright?" I asked quietly, breaking the thin, icy silence between us. "She's never fought with me like that before, and the cave she's headed to … I'm familiar with it. There's a power there that will destroy us all."

I wondered why Jase would even take her there.

What is he up to?

Darius didn't look at me, but he pressed his lips into a tight line before saying, "She has a head start, and it's pretty clear she's smart enough not to get caught. Let's just hope she keeps the ring on because we'll need your powers to keep us safe until we catch up."

It grew quiet in the car for a while, with only the engine's hum to fill the void. Given the late hour, there was only the occasional flicker of other headlights or distant houses. My mind drifted back to the villa—to the chaos, Tati and Alessandro, the dhampirs—that *fucking* witch.

Darius's voice pulled me out. "My head ... is spinning. I know we have to keep moving, but if I don't feed, I'm going to crash this fucking car."

I turned to look at him. His face was paler than an hour ago, and there was a slight tremor in his white-knuckled grip. The hunger was weakening him too quickly.

"Pull over. I can give you some blood—"

"No!" he snapped. "You can't force me to do that anymore. That includes what you've been doing to me. We could lose control."

"I'd never allow that," I assured him. "But we have to get as south as possible to make it to Athens. We don't have the means to fly there, so driving is our only option. Once we're on the boat, we'll be safe, and we can find a lonely soul to feed from *together*. I won't force you."

He looked hesitant but answered with a quick nod.

As the miles passed, I watched Darius's hunger grow to a near-fever pitch. Suddenly, his spine stiffened, and the steering wheel screeched under the stress of his grip.

He's not going to last without something.

His dark eyes slid to mine, and there was a fierceness in that gaze—he wasn't hungry for just blood. His heated gaze roamed lower, hovering over my thighs. I clenched them together, tingles flaring to life in my core. When vampires were hungry, it awakened the beast-like primal side, and it would become a frenzy of blood-lust and arousal. The craving to kill and fuck was the only driving force for my kind; it was what made us feel "alive."

The car suddenly felt like it had shrunk, drawing our grow-ing desire together. We needed to find a blood source before we crashed. I shifted away and looked ahead. Up ahead, about a hun-dred yards from us was a maroon-colored sedan parked on the side of the road. My suppressed cravings surged and wrapped around my throat like a rope.

"Right there," I said. "We feed, get back in the car, and go. No more stops."

He didn't need me to tell him twice.

Darius pulled the car over a few feet behind the stopped vehicle and cut the lights and engine. Our enhanced vision showed a young man with dark-brown hair and tanned skin stepping away from the lifted hood. He wore a simple plaid T-shirt and jeans with a ball cap over his long, wavy hair. He didn't seem afraid of us, just frustrated. Smoke rose from the exposed engine—he was stranded.

I gracefully slid out of the car, Darius following close behind. Hearing our approach, the man lifted his head, eyes widening in surprise. Hopefully, the shadows would conceal our dirty and slightly torn clothes.

"Buonasera, signore. Ha bisogno di aiuto con la sua macchina?" I asked him if he needed help with his car, keeping my voice smooth and friendly. I didn't want to reveal my eagerness to snare this prey, so a playful, warm smile crossed my lips. "Uh, English?"

The man's eyes examined the two of us and nodded, yet he looked momentarily confused. "Eh, sì ... yes," he gestured to the raised hood. "Do you know anything about Nissans?" He threw his arms up in defeat. "I've tried everything. And Soccorso Stradale won't be here until almost dawn."

The sound of his heart rate quickened as he closed the lid over the smoking engine. The stranger didn't know, but I was already inside his head, slowly increasing his fear. It made the hunt so much more exciting.

Like the viper waiting in the grass, I struck first. The man didn't have time to react before I was on him, grabbing his wrist and slamming him against the hood. He tried to struggle, and I felt his joints pop in my grip.

"Relax, handsome," I purred, forcing him to look into my glowing eyes. My power seized him completely, and his eyes softened, body succumbing to the compulsion. Once he had gone completely limp, I pressed my body against his, with Darius looming over my shoulder like a hungry wolf.

I could already smell the blood beneath his skin, warm and coppery, and my stomach tightened. My fangs extended, sharp and ready, as I pulled the man's collar down, exposing his throat. His eyes fluttered closed.

Darius didn't hesitate. He moved to my right and sank his fangs into the man's neck with a soft growl. I followed suit, taking my share from the other side. The man gasped and twitched, but it was no use. His blood was ours now.

The taste of his life force sent a pulsing sensation between my legs—rich and virile. His heat became mine as the steady rhythm of his pulse filled me with sharp, immediate satisfaction. But that wasn't enough. I needed more, so much more.

My hand slid from the man's chest, and my body pressed against him as I drank deep and rough. Darius growled softly. He, too, became lost in the sensation. There was a raw, animalistic energy between us—hunger and *need*.

When I heard the first stuttering beat of the man's heart, I managed to withdraw my fangs. Darius followed, and the young man crashed into the dirt, barely conscious.

We didn't kill him ... yet.

I licked the last few drops of blood from my lips, savoring the taste, and Darius stepped away, wiping his mouth with the back of his hand. I leaned against the car's hood, my head tipping up to look at him.

"God, I need to fuck you," Darius professed, his eyes skating down my body as I raised a brow at him. The feral, dark need was consuming him. He still had unfinished business with me.

I reached for his dirt-caked T-shirt, gripping the fabric and yanking him toward me. His blood-covered mouth collided hard with mine. The kiss was brutal, desperate—making my pussy throb and drip. His hands were everywhere, like he couldn't touch me enough.

Darius grabbed the waistband of my jeans, quickly unzipped them, and pulled them down along with my underwear, leaving me exposed. He cupped my ass before lifting me higher on the car. I wrapped my legs around his waist, thighs hitching on his hips. With me caged, Darius unzipped his pants, pulled out his cock, and started pumping it. As my head tipped back, he slammed inside me with a vicious thrust.

"Oh, fuck!" I cried out as he stepped on our victim's spine, cracking it while raising us even higher, hitting all the right spots.

Well, he's dead now.

After hunting down prey, vampires' senses became incredibly heightened, but to fuck right after a feeding ... that was truly extraordinary. This was precisely what I needed to take the edge off of what happened. While I felt guilty for causing the young man's death, it was all necessary to catch up to my daughter before my failed progeny did. My mind whirled with so much awareness as Darius continued to ram himself deep inside of me again and again. The fury in his movements felt like he wanted to wreck me, and I would have gladly let him.

"My God," he moaned loudly, "you feel fucking divine."

His pace quickened to a maddening beat that erupted euphoric ripples through my body. His cock filled me up completely, pulling back only enough to thrust back inside, harder and faster, with no intention of stopping. Frenzied sex like this made me feel so in tune with my body that I almost felt *human* again—in the most ironic way possible. He'd awakened every sense, every dark emotion.

Everything.

There was no affection for how we did this or a moment of tenderness. Darius's grip on me would have cracked bones and ruptured organs had we not been vampires. I was his prisoner, surrendering to the surges of pleasure that thundered through me.

My cries echoed through the night, cutting through the stillness of the open fields surrounding us. Pleasure, sin, wickedness—all pooled together, filling my emptiness.

"Right there," I pleaded, feeling the body of the car dent against my back from the force. My release was close, my throbbing core clenching more rapidly. My head tipped back as I bit into my bottom lip to contain my composure. If I let go now, the world would shatter. All that mattered was the fresh blood, the distraction, the depravity of it all.

I shook as Darius kept me pinned against that car, each thrust more brutal. The windshield started to crack, and the lid buckled and caved beneath me. My eyes fluttered closed, my breaths growing heavy despite not needing to draw air.

In a flash, Darius unhooked my legs from his waist, withdrew himself, and flipped me around before grabbing my hair and yanking my head back. He then drove back in with such force that the glass shattered, blue fragments littering the car and the ground. It almost felt like a punishment for breaking our gaze. More cracking came from below as he shifted his stance atop the dead man's body, bending me over.

His left hand grabbed my thigh and lifted my leg, perching it on the bumper for deeper access. I was coming undone with the filthy way he fucked me, and yet felt I was ascending to the heavens—even for a moment.

"Oh my God," was all I could say as I parted my lips to draw another breath. His hand suddenly left my leg and wrapped around my throat, tightening its grip as he pushed me closer to the peak. "Don't ... don't stop."

Darius was now animalistic by how he rocked against me, glass and metal shattering around us. He was as close to the edge as I was. All I needed was—

"Oh, fuck!" the scream ripped from my throat as my head fell back, panting as I shuddered. Waves of endless bliss pounded through me, stealing every lingering rational thought. His pleasure followed a second later, and he groaned as he emptied himself deep inside me.

The high from our ecstasy seemed to drag on forever as Darius held me. As I regained my bearings, I realized that, though I was eager for another round, we had to go. There was a dead body and a smashed car, and we were wasting time. Pressing my palms against the car, I eased away, telling Darius to follow. He stepped off the man's corpse, and we noticed a large pool of blood soaking into the ground.

"Unfortunate," I mused as I rearranged my clothes. "Let's move on before someone sees us."

CHAPTER 29

ANDREI

I *should have killed her. She didn't even have the fucking ring!*

"Drei?" Jackson's voice snapped me out of my spiral, pulling my attention to him. "I need your directions. I don't know where the fuck I'm going."

Nodding, I rubbed a grimy hand over my blood-splattered shirt. Needles pricked over my shoulders and neck at how filthy I was. The urge to rip the damn thing to pieces was nearly unbearable. Forcing the thought aside, I focused on the overwhelming sight of blood staining my suit.

Once Liam collected our bags from the hotel and our travel identifications, we headed south. While Jackson drove, the GPS app on my phone pinpointed the last known location before the signal cut off.

"Yeah," I finally answered. "While the villa collapsing on our heads was a setback, they can't be that far ahead. Hopefully, we can track them down on the highway before we reach the airport. Of course, none of this would've happened if Liam hadn't gone and killed our leverage and blown up the damn house."

My fists shook with sudden rage, and I was half-tempted to reach into the backseat, rip out that smug asshole's heart, and gnaw on it for a few hours. Before we left the States, I thought Liam would cooperate, especially since I had threatened his sister. But every so often, it seemed like he had his *own* agenda, especially after how uncontrolled he was at the house. Witnessing his power made me realize we might have been way over our heads bringing a witch with us.

Not to mention that the Black Onyx members didn't play by the same rules as other covens.

My eyes turned up to the rearview mirror to glare at Liam, who looked utterly unfazed. He was twirling a piece of his cloak as he peered casually out the window.

"Sorry for what happened back there," Liam said, glancing at me and meeting my stern gaze. "I usually have more control over my power, but Valentina was going to kill you. So, I had to do something dramatic. What can I say? The woman has thousands of years of fighting experience; I did what I had to do."

"And yet *you* survived," Jackson remarked, glancing in the rearview mirror at him, a dubious look in his brown eyes.

"Good thing she was more focused on saving herself and the rest of that clan," Liam replied, before turning back to the dark world rolling by. "At least we discovered something we didn't know before. Rachel isn't the only dhampir. Quite a secret they've kept from everyone. The Black Onyx will love that. Unless they've known, too. In that case, we'll be commended for reporting it."

I was about to reply, but we were getting close to the last place the tracker had gone offline. Though she had removed the chip, we hoped to find clues pointing to where they had taken off.

"Exit here," I said, showing Jackson the screen. "It stopped at the field near that building." I pointed again, indicating the road he needed to take.

As we veered off the highway, Liam started humming some unrecognizable melody. I lifted my hand to fix my hair, grimacing as bits of stone sprinkled onto my lap. The same prickling tension rose, and my jaw muscles tightened.

Don't do anything reckless. I need my little dove back into her cage.

After driving a few blocks westbound, Jackson pulled the car onto a small paved road leading to several homesteads and an irrigation ditch.

"Here. Pull over."

When the car stopped, I shoved open the door and sauntered onto the grass, scanning my surroundings. The breeze shifted, brushing over my face as I moved closer to a secluded, most likely family-run vineyard. After stepping over a broken-down fence, a scent hit me, and I froze. It was that mind-numbingly delicious scent that always drove me into a frenzy. The smell of dirt was dominant, but I knew her blood was everywhere.

"She took it out around here," I said, using my heightened sense of smell to focus on the scent trail. Clearly, she had discarded it—the only way to lose the connection. But I needed confirmation first. "There." I pointed to the shiny metal piece in the grass. Rachel's blood was more potent now, the scent making my fangs burn against my mouth and the veins under my eyes swell.

Jackson and Liam walked up from behind me as I bent down to pick it up. She hadn't only removed it but also crushed it in two, the metal pieces now reddish-brown. The tracker wasn't the only thing soaked in blood; it was all over the grass and dirt, leaving me pleasant little reminders of her.

"The blood's drying. Who knows how far ahead they are? *Shit!*" I tried to push the weight of the situation aside. I knew how to snare my little rabbit, but now I had to punish her more for this.

And my brother.

I grinned, tapping the call button and lifting the receiver to my ear. The ringing made my cock twitch in my pants. I didn't care that Jackson and Liam were nearby—I wanted to play with her. If I could snatch Rachel's mind again, like I had with the cage, it would be easy to hold her down until I had my hands around her thin little throat.

A distant chiming sound interrupted my filthy thoughts. The three of us exchanged glances before Liam jogged toward a cluster of bushes several yards away. He kneeled and crawled between the branches.

"Looks like your dhampir ditched her phone, too!" He carried his voice over the field, raising his arm past the brush. Her cracked phone was in his hand, the caller ID lighting up with my incoming call. The ringtone sounded warped, though. She had tried but failed to destroy it completely. Liam tossed the phone toward me, and it landed in the blood-soaked dirt at my feet. I carefully picked it up, something lethal simmering beneath the surface, like an oily ink coating every vein.

"What about the guardian bond?" Jackson asked. "Can you tap into it and see where she's going?"

"Without her hearing my voice I can't get inside her head. Under normal circumstances, I should be able to feel her, at least, but ever since we landed, it's been faltering. She must have a blocking spell or something on her." I grated my teeth. "Dammit!"

My anger flared into a white-hot rage, and I squeezed her phone until the metal crumpled. With a grunt, I threw the device toward the parked car. The phone slammed into the side, leaving a massive dent in the driver's door. The car rocked to the right from the impact before settling back on its tires.

"Come on, man. Calm the fuck down," Jackson spat. "We already know where they're going. Now, with her mom searching for her, too? Someone will fuck this up. As much as you want to throw a tantrum out here, we don't have time for that shit. We have to get on the road now if we stand a chance of getting ahead of them. The Black Onyx has a plane ready. There's no way they'll get there before we do. It's possible that they don't know we have a witch with us, and they won't take every precaution. We can still come out of this on top."

Unfortunately, Crete had stopped direct flights to the island ever since vampires became public knowledge. Now, we had to fly to Athens and go through a screening process before getting on a ferry.

Liam walked back over, humming that infuriating tune again. His fingers played along the keys of an invisible piano, and I had half a mind to snap them all off.

I didn't know if it was because I was smelling Rachel's blood again, and I didn't have her in my arms to take what I wanted from her, but tension slowly pressed down on my body again. The night felt heavy, thicker with haunting shadows, and every goddamn thing seemed to mock me.

And my clothes are filthy. I need to kill something to make it right.

Maybe I needed to feed from somebody at this point before I cleansed this world in my fire.

My mind spiraled into a dark frenzy. Control was my greatest strength—no one would take that from me. Liam's hand fell on my shoulder, and my eyes moved to his face. "Don't lose your cool now, boss," Liam said, almost like a purr. "At least Valentina's not too far ahead. Once we close the gap between us and her, I'll be happy to wrangle her and keep her in line until you get your dhampir back."

I glared back at him. "How do you propose we 'wrangle' the original vampire, who still has fucking magic on top of her demonic powers, into submission?"

"A binding hex."

"Binding hex?" I tilted my head. "How's that work?"

"It's an old spell the Spirit bloodline forged hundreds of years ago, allowing you to bind a body to your will through metal links, regardless of its species. My father stumbled upon it as a young man. He taught me when my powers first developed." His smile broadened. "Not only will we be able to control her, but we can then suppress her element. She won't be able to fight back."

Jackson shot Liam a strange look from behind then turned to me to make the call. I could tell he didn't like the idea of capturing Valentina and possibly missing Rachel. But Liam's magic was powerful and fucking insane—it *could* work. The rage in my blood simmered down to a low boil. I shook my head, trying to clear the agitation fogging my thoughts.

"Fine," I said. "Maybe taking Valentina first could work in our favor. Rachel might be more cooperative if we had her mother."

As we were about to leave, Liam bent down and placed his hand on the grass where Rachel's blood spilled, closing his eyes. "We can do a locator spell on Rachel, too, you know," he said, looking up toward us. "It's what I'm good at. We just have to have something of hers."

I gave Jackson a look before I nodded. Instead of performing the spell right then, Liam gripped the bloody grass and ripped it from the ground, stuffing it into his cloak pocket. "But first, I have Valentina's blood from her ripped shirt after the explosion. We'll start with that spell first since she's closer." He stood and gave me an odd look. "It's a shame you lost your magic when you turned, Andrei. Having the power to find something you lost is quite a feeling."

Who the hell…?

My jaw clenched tighter, my teeth grinding at his remark. But before I could react, he smiled broadly. "We'll find Rachel, I promise. With my help."

My spiraling mind finally began to relax. Liam was right. Of course, he was. Everything was fine. We'd find them. And when we did … I'd make sure Rachel couldn't slip away from me again.

CHAPTER 30

When we arrived in Bari, it was a little after four thirty in the morning, and every muscle in my body ached. Luckily, Tony's relatives on his father's side owned an inn there.

Tony mentioned his cousins had inherited the inn from their great-grandmother, who lived in Bari until she passed away two years ago at one hundred. Most of his family, including his father and grandmother, had moved to the United States before he was born. Had they stayed, he would have owned part of the property as well as a vineyard in Tuscany.

The upside to staying here was that it wasn't far from the ferry that would take us to Athens.

"Even though Nonna loved our family locanda," Tony started, breaking me free of my thoughts, "she knew Dad had better opportunities in the US. And Bisnonna Chiara understood that. When Dad got married and had me, Nonna moved back to retire," he explained as we rumbled down the highway. "My cousins were the perfect choice to take over. We're part of a group chat, and they keep me updated on the business."

As we pulled into the parking lot, I saw an old wooden sign hanging beneath an ornate iron post, illuminated by a small golden LED light. *La Locanda di Manetti.*

"Both Andrei and my mother know your last name. Are you sure this is a good idea?" I asked.

He smiled and shrugged. "Do you know how common the last name 'Manetti' is here?" he asked, chuckling. "It's like 'Smith' or 'Jones.' Besides, even if it weren't, my family would protect us if things went sideways. They've known about all this shit and what I do long before vampires became public knowledge almost a decade ago. Fighting and gathering intel wasn't something I learned from the coven; that came from my grandparents."

That surprised me. Tony never mentioned how he knew so much about the supernatural, but it made sense now. The Black Onyx had always been overly cautious about who they hired. Every guardian had to "audition" per se and demonstrate the skills needed to bond with a dhampir. Yes, the magic bond had linked my strength to him, but he still had to know what he was doing in the first place.

We exited the car, and Jase, who had been a fucking stone wall this entire time, grabbed our bags and walked toward the front entrance. From the corner of my eye, I caught Jase staring at me.

I wish I knew what he was thinking. The broody staredowns make me nervous, and I'm way too fucking tired and hungry to deal with it. I need food.

The building's architecture looked more modern than the other places I had seen since arriving in Italy. Tony explained that his family had rebuilt it after enemies destroyed the original site during World War II.

Once inside and into the hallway, I looked down. The stone floor looked like it could have been the original, with long, curved cracks throughout, that seemed to have marked the test of time. Along the wall were softly lit sconces on earth-toned walls, creating a warm, cozy atmosphere.

"Wow," Lucy said as she looked around with me. "This place is gorgeous. Lune de Blanche seems so cold compared to this."

"Right? Chad would have a conniption. He prides that place more than his own cock."

Lucy threw back her head and laughed, and I swore I heard Jase snort from behind me.

"Maybe when we get back, I'll visit the hotel and tell him."

If we can go back, I mused bitterly. But I shook the thought away as we followed Tony to the front desk.

The elegant wood and marble desk smelled a little like lavender, and I saw bundles of dried purple flowers hanging on the walls. A small silver bell and a sign welcoming guests in several languages were on the desk. This place was a balm on the nightmare that the day had been.

Tony pressed a small button on the wall next to the desk. The sign read, in Italian, "Please Ring Innkeeper In Case of After-Hours Emergency." A minute later, a tall woman hurried down the stairs to our right. She wore a rose-pink T-shirt and black leggings. Her features made me guess she was in her mid-twenties, with long, shiny black hair, a curvaceous figure, and medium-bronze skin. When she saw Tony, her eyes grew wide.

"Antonio! Cosa ci fai qui? Hai chiamato mia madre? Quando sei arrivato?"

Tony's eyes lit up, and a grin spread across his face. "English, Giulia. Not everyone here speaks Italian. These are my friends. We're just in town for the day." He took a step closer and pulled her into a hug. "God, it's great to see you."

After Tony released their hug, Giulia looked at us and smiled, warmth radiating from her aura. "Of course. Hello. Come with me to the kitchen, and we can talk." Her accent was prominent, but her English was flawless. "You guys are lucky. I was just getting up to start opening."

She led us down the hallway toward a closed door labeled *La Cucina di Chiara*. Jase followed closely behind me, doing nothing to lessen our tension. He was always in my space that it made me feel uneasy. I didn't dare glance back, though—his silence told me he felt it, too.

"I'm guessing Nonna is still asleep?" Tony asked once inside the kitchen. The smell of freshly brewed coffee greeted my nose. *God, yes, please.*

Giulia shook her head. "No, she's visiting the vineyard this week. She also came down with a cold, so I'll be running things until she feels better. Nonna's supposed to be retired and taking it easy, but you know her. She loves to stay busy." Her brown eyes looked over to me before smiling. "He sent pictures over the last eight years. You must be Rachel."

I nodded, forcing a smile. Something about Giulia knowing my name—given my history—made me nervous. Tony said they knew everything about the supernatural world, but did she know about *me*?

"Oh, yeah. Sorry. This is Rachel, and this is Lucy and ..." His eyes skated over to Jase, who had his leather jacket zipped up to his neck and his arms folded over his chest. Though he was a vampire, Jase looked ragged as fuck, like he hadn't slept in days. Dark circles framed his green eyes, and his disheveled hair fell into a messy tousle over his forehead, like he had rolled out of bed. "This is Jase Halpert. He's the vampire stalker I told the family about."

Jase's eyes narrowed at Tony, and I had to turn away to hide my amusement. Since we left Venice, Tony developed a knack for getting under the man's skin. Jase dragged a hand through his hair, clearly trying to rein in his irritation. I felt a strange, unwelcome flutter in my chest. It was maddening how someone so thoroughly aggravating could look that goddamn sexy.

It must run in the family.

"The stalker..." Giulia said, tilting her head to study him. "If you misbehave in our family's business, I'll toss you in the sun and lock you out."

Oh, I like her.

Jase struggled to suppress a smile at her threat, but he failed miserably. "I'll try to behave."

Lucy cleared her throat. "Nice to meet you," she said, extending her hand.

Giulia smiled and shook it. "He told me about you, too."

A slight shift in the room's atmosphere occurred as Tony coughed, his cheeks flushing. He avoided meeting her gaze. "Anyway, do you have any rooms available? I saw a few cars outside. I know it's last minute, but we just need a place to stay for a day. Our ferry's sold out until tomorrow."

Pleasantries aside, my skin prickled with anxiety. Valentina was out there, likely hunting me, and there was a good chance Andrei was already heading this way from the States. I couldn't let my guard down—not even here. Tony was exhausted, and admittedly, I felt fucking terrible, so sleep and rest weren't the worst decision we could make. I went to the coffee machine and poured myself a cup.

"Two rooms is fine," Tony explained, his unease focused on Jase.

"Perfect, 'cause that's all I have left. Summer tourism is at an all-time high right now," Giulia replied.

Tony and Giulia quickly fell into conversation, English mixing with Italian as they caught up on family news. Lucy came over to stand next to me, and I handed her a mug of coffee while examining every shadow in the dimly lit kitchen. Jase still loomed by the door, brooding again over God knows what.

As comforting as a storm cloud.

Lucy took a long drink of coffee, her eyes fluttering closed for a second. "Thank God vampires can drink coffee," she said. "Hey, what's going on with Captain Mopey Ass over there? I'm half tempted to punch him just to change the look on his face."

I snorted into my coffee. "Please do it."

"Tony," Lucy called out, her tone slipping into her usual sarcasm. "Rachel and I will share a room while you and Jase bond over your mutual distrust of each other."

Jase smirked faintly, but his eyes moved to me, lingering too long for comfort.

Ten minutes and two cups of coffee later, Giulia escorted us upstairs to the rooms. They were small but clean, with padded leather framed beds and lace curtains that swayed from the single open window in the warm evening breeze.

While Lucy dressed, I peeled off my T-shirt and bra, practically groaning in relief. Slipping into my pajamas, I joined Lucy in the bathroom to brush my teeth.

We stood side by side, and my eyes turned up to hers in the mirror. She was biting back a smile, barely holding it in.

Needing to know the joke, I spat out the foam and arched a brow. "What's so funny?"

"Oh, I just thought it was pretty comical that two supernatural creatures with fangs brush their teeth and wear jammies," she replied. "We're nothing like the movies." I don't know if it was because we'd been driving all night and morning and the deliriousness got to us, but we suddenly lost it. We laughed so hard that tears streamed from my eyes, and she doubled over.

God, I missed laughing with her. After a few moments, we managed to get ourselves together, clean up, and climb into bed. My ribs ached considerably, but my heart finally felt lighter.

I needed that.

Once settled on the bed, I curled my knees up to my chest and leaned back against the headboard, waiting for her to talk first. Sure, we caught up occasionally during our brief calls, but it wasn't like this. This is what she and I did back in New Orleans. We had slumber parties with junk food and chick flicks. I didn't care that I was two hundred years old. Nothing is better than nights like that with your best friend, enjoying all the joys of girlhood, since I never had those experiences as a kid with the coven.

In the past, Lucy repeatedly suggested we find a place together, but I knew I couldn't. I was still a dhampir in hiding, and I couldn't risk fucking it up by her seeing something when I let my guard down. It also put her at risk.

Not anymore...

"What was it like for you?" I asked. "My experience at the mansion wasn't yours. I'd like to know what you thought of it."

She shrugged. "It's complicated. Andrei's an asshole, and when I see him, I'm going to punch him in the fucking face, but he did help me a lot after Jase turned me. There's still so much about the supernatural world that I don't understand. Especially regarding vampires. And he tried to help me adjust to this new life, even though the prick was trying to indoctrinate me into believing humans were less than." She let out a slow breath and leaned back on her bed like I had. "Jackson was cool, though. He has an amazing voice."

My stomach sank at what she said. Lucy had to navigate this mess without me there. Now, I saw her as a different species, but even after everything, she was still Lucy—my best friend, whom I wished I could've saved.

"I've only been able to see my mom twice since Jase turned me," she continued. "Andrei, or one of his men, had to be with me both times. Not because Andrei was afraid I'd run off and do something stupid, but because he didn't want me to hurt her. They were there to hold me back if my control slipped and I tried to ..."

Well, tonight was full of surprises. Andrei was still Andrei, but the fact that he cared about Lucy and Gabriela's safety was kind of shocking.

"I ... I didn't know that," I said. Lucy shrugged, and that was the end of that conversation.

Over the next hour, we filled each other in on what we couldn't talk about over the phone. I learned that my best friend was doing her best to adjust to this new, terrifying life. We both hoped that once all this bullshit was over, we could return to doing all the things we used to do together as if nothing had changed.

Maybe actually get that apartment together. We could look at places near the French Quarter.

When I noticed Lucy was ready for a light sleep, my stomach growled, reminding me I hadn't eaten in hours.

I rolled over and checked the time on my phone. It was a little past five, and I was no closer to falling asleep. Sliding out of bed, I shut the curtains for Lucy before the sun could rise. Careful not to make a sound, I tiptoed past her and slipped into the hall. Giulia was on one side of the inn, typing on a keyboard, while the guests remained upstairs, still asleep. My pulse quickened as I hurried down, each groan and creak of wood adding to my anxiety.

Once downstairs, I padded down the hallway toward the kitchen.

Before we went to our rooms, Giulia informed us that we were welcome to raid the fridge, as they were expecting merchants to deliver fresh supplies later in the morning. I pushed open the door and went inside. Now that she'd opened the inn for the coming dawn, I got to take in the surroundings. The kitchen was quaint, with copper pots hanging over a large gas stove. There was also a wood-burning oven that looked well-used. The smell of bread and seafood faintly clung to the air, and I could imagine Tony's great-grandmother cooking meals for her family and guests here. Ignoring the pang of loneliness in my heart, I went over to the stone sink, smooth from years of water and working hands.

I grabbed a blue-tinted glass and filled it with ice-cold water. My magic fluttered to life as I took a deep gulp, relishing in the flow within my veins. I leaned against the counter, the storm in my chest still brewing.

"Couldn't sleep?" Jase's smooth voice cut through the dark room, and a shiver snaked up my spine, causing my body to stiffen. Fuck, we were alone for the first time since the church.

I turned sharply to find him standing in the doorway. His broad shoulders filled the frame, and his green eyes locked right on mine. It was impossible to slow my racing heart as I took in the sight of him, especially as my eyes wandered down his torso.

He was shirtless now, wearing only black cotton pajama pants that hung loosely on his hips. A male vampire in pajamas was an odd fucking thing to see. Worse was that he looked beautiful—and so *human*.

I swallowed, trying not to roam my eyes over his very chiseled abs. "What are you doing here?" I asked defensively, holding the glass tighter than necessary before turning away to look out the small window over the sink. It was still dark outside, with the horizon slowly turning pale with the approaching sun, and I looked like a damn idiot who was obviously trying not to stare at Jase.

"Vampire," he said, walking deeper into the kitchen. "Sleep isn't really part of the deal, remember?"

Shit.

"Yeah ... gotcha," I said. The back of my neck prickled, alerting me to Jase's presence behind me. His aura wrapped around me in a chokehold.

"You shouldn't be alone."

Jase's tone sounded like a scolding father, and my temper kicked up a notch. I turned to face him, anger burning. "I don't need you to babysit me. Or hover. Or ... whatever it is you think you're doing."

His nostrils flared. "Do I have to fucking remind you that we have no idea where Andrei, or your mother, for that matter, is right now? Have you forgotten that he is still tied to you through the guardian bond? He could easily tap in at any time and feel all the anger running through your veins right now."

Exasperation added to my temper. "But he can't actually find me, though. No tracker. So, we're probably fine."

His intense glare made me realize that wasn't his point.

"I have my *own* plans, and I don't need any of you fucking it up for me before getting to the cave. So yeah, regardless of your missing tracker, I'm not risking it."

If I wasn't pissed when he walked into the kitchen, I sure as fuck was now.

I took a step closer, my anger outweighing common sense. "And what do you care? You tried to kill me four months ago. You turned my best friend, and before you explained what was *actually* going on, Andrei warned me that you were coming to kill me."

His expression hardened at those words.

I never ended up telling Valentina about those visions, but the last one shook me to the core. It threw me for a loop when Lucy and Tony showed up in Venice with Jase in tow on an entirely *different* agenda.

The memory of the last time I saw him replayed in my mind—Jase's hand around my throat, the bite of his knife across my skin. Then the other image that appeared in my dreams from that night was drinking his blood. Ever since then, my mind had been a mess, tangled in this reckless, stupid madness I couldn't shake. Jase somehow imprinted it into my brain.

My voice dropped, not wanting to alert Lucy upstairs. "You don't get to act like my protector now. Where the hell did this sudden concern about my well-being come from, anyway? Because if I die, you can't get your precious blood to stick it to your brother?"

A faint smile touched his lips, his flawless white teeth gleaming like pearls. "Yeah, that's exactly it. I just need your blood to get into that pentagram and destroy—"

"Oh, fuck that dumbass spell."

Before I could blink, Jase's hand shot out, fingers curling around my throat. He didn't squeeze. It wasn't painful—but the dominance in the gesture was absolutely there. It was just like Andrei. But ... *not*. My breath hitched as his thumb brushed against my skin like a silent warning.

"Be very, very careful how you speak to me, angel," Jase warned, his voice low and dangerous. "You forget I stalked you for years with you not having a fucking clue the entire time. I watched you train with Tony almost every weekend. Granted, you're pretty damn fast, I'll give you that. But I promise you, you're no match for *me*. I will break you if I have to. That angel's sword in the cave will give Black Onyx unlimited power, and they will go on a rampage to kill anyone who ever opposes them or their plans. Andrei will do the same, if not worse. And you"—he eased off my throat, looking at the pulsing vein beneath my jaw—"have a very smart mouth. My deranged brother may have thought it cute. I have no tolerance for this shit."

My heart was pounding so hard that I could hear blood rushing in my ears. Jase wasn't touching me anymore, but he was in such close proximity that it sent my stomach churning. To be honest, it also did something molten between my legs.

What the fuck is going on?

We both stiffened, a strange tension hanging between us. Then something happened—the faint warmth from the weird mark on my belly started to spread, pulsing in the same rhythm as my heart. My throat felt thick as I swallowed, watching his eyes glance at my lips before returning to mine.

As angry and confused as I was, I wasn't afraid of what he'd do to me. And *that* terrified me the most.

"Move," Jase said, finally breaking the very awkward silence. "I'd like some water, and you're standing in my way."

"Gladly." I needed to get away from him. I quickly stepped to the right while he moved to the cabinet to grab a glass.

The absence of him in my space was as jarring as when he'd grabbed my throat. I moved further away, wrapping my arms around myself.

While Jase filled his glass and brought it to his lips, I asked, "Why did you watch me?"

He set down the glass and slowly turned to me. "You know why," he said, his voice smooth, but something dark lurked beneath the surface. "I needed your blood to awaken Valentina."

I shook my head. "I'm talking about before. The Hades Blood Moon happens every two hundred years. You found me four years before making your move. Why stalk me for so long instead of just showing up to take me before you needed to? Why come into my apartment like a fucking creep?"

Jase's lips curled into that infuriating, lopsided grin again. "I enjoyed New Orleans. I'd never been before," he answered, cold amusement in his eyes. "Four years is nothing to our kind, as you know. But you kept me entertained. Every move you made, every decision, was way too fascinating. A supernatural creature, all alone, trying to live like a human." He stepped closer again, his scent pressing onto me like a shadow. "Yeah, I'd watch you when you were home alone ... or not. I listened to you laugh with your friends and how you breathed at night when you were lost in dreams. It was ... *hard* to look away, angel. You *tried* to be normal in an abnormal world. One thing I did learn, though, is you're not as righteous as you pretend to be. Like I said earlier, you're a lot like me."

I reared my head back and scoffed. *No, the hell I'm not.*

He leaned in just enough so the coolness of his breath brushed against my cheeks. "I didn't just learn your routine. I *studied* you. And I liked what I saw." His lips spread into a cruel grin. "You still haven't figured it out, have you? You never were just a target. You were my favorite distraction until the time came to spill your blood."

My jaw dropped as Jase stepped back, finished his water, and headed out of the kitchen, leaving me standing there like a damn fool.

Though his words sent my temper roaring, they also stirred something low in my belly—a dark, sensuous thrill that should stay buried. But no matter how hard I tried to shove it away, I couldn't silence it.

CHAPTER 31

ANDREI

Once we were back on the highway at almost two a.m., Liam reached into his pocket and pulled out the blood-soaked fabric from Valentina's sweater. He held the torn cloth in one hand and a bundle of bloody grass in the other. I watched from the rearview mirror as he closed his eyes, tilted his head back, and started quietly chanting. Before I lost my elemental magic, I never learned how to cast location spells, as I found them meaningless. I wanted to gain status as a talented doctor who cured illnesses. Reputation was important, even then, and my magic helped facilitate that. Mother used to scold me about my ego.

What the hell did she know, anyway?

"How does a locator spell work?" Jackson asked. I found myself curious as well. "Can you sense her presence and follow a trail? How do you find her?" I caught Jackson's gaze in my peripheral vision, and I turned to look at him. His dark eyes regarded me with skepticism for Liam and this *plan*.

Something felt off, and we both sensed it.

Jackson had been wary of Liam's involvement since we left the States, constantly watching him or arguing with every instruction or suggestion he made. And honestly, I couldn't blame him for it. Jackson wasn't just my best friend but my right hand in the clan's business. He always had the family's best interest at heart, so if he saw any red flags in Liam, I trusted his instincts.

After what we witnessed at the villa, I understood. The witch held no mercy or empathy for vampires, especially the two he slaughtered in the gardens. His magic was unlike anything I had ever witnessed, and who knew if Liam would turn that gruesome power on *us*? But it didn't change the fact that we needed the psychopath.

Liam's magic was our only chance to get Valentina and, in turn, Rachel, using her blood to crack open the seal that would release Ezrylos. The guardian bond's strength was waning from the growing distance, and without the tracker in Rachel's arm or a way to project my voice into her mind, it left me blind.

Irritation had me gripping the steering wheel until the metal groaned, and my knuckles cracked.

There was a crackle in the air, and Liam's eyes finally fluttered open. Then he looked in the mirror at us. "I can't reach Rachel. She's either too far away or blocking the magic somehow. My guess? It's the ring. I think as long as she wears it, I can't pin her location down." He paused and looked at me. "Valentina, though, is a different story. She's closer than we thought. I saw a sign off the highway that said 'Trattoria Fiorente.' They didn't stop there, but they're in the area. I can feel it. We should be able to pin down the road and city they're passing through and catch up."

Jackson curtly nodded, looking at me again. "I'm on it," he said, unlocking his phone and opening the GPS app. After a few seconds, he said, "It's a restaurant in Rimini. About thirty minutes ahead."

I grinned, pressing down on the gas pedal until the speedometer needle jumped. "Then it's time to cover some ground and catch up."

⁓ele⁓

Liam tilted his head, eyes half closed as his fingers hovered above the bloodied fabric. The way his brows pinched, it looked like he feared the scrap might burn him this time. Liam's lips moved slightly as he chanted, red magic glowing under his palms. After a few seconds, he opened his eyes and smiled. "I can sense them close by, but luckily for us, she's not moving fast."

"Alright, Jackson, keep an eye out for that car," I said.

Jackson was already leaning forward in his seat, searching the dark road, while his eyes narrowed on every car we passed. "I haven't stopped looking since we found the tracker," he said, a hint of irritation in his voice.

"Good." Every second we wasted was another chance for Valentina and that man, Darius, to slip away from us. I refused to let Rachel escape me again. Once I had her back in my lair *and* in my bed, I would never let her leave. The pretty collar I had for her would make her mine forever.

As we drove, the road turned into a two-lane street winding down the coastline of Italy, while the moon shed its cold light over certain parts of the ocean, creating ripples of white across the infinite black.

"Hey, Drei," Jackson said, pointing to a car not too far ahead. "That might be them. When they took off from the villa, I didn't get a good look at the car, but the license plate had matching letters. Liam, what do you feel?"

Liam's magic seemed to grow brighter, and his eyes opened to look with us. "Yeah, it's them."

Here we go.

"Everyone have their seatbelts on?" I asked, my grip tightening on the wheel as a thrill coiled in my chest. "Hang on."

As I got closer, I positioned the car directly behind them, and then floored it, ramming us into their bumper. The Maserati jolted forward, skidding across the asphalt. While they fought against spinning out, I drove into oncoming traffic, forcing another car to crash into a nearby guardrail. Then I jerked the wheel, smashing the bumper into the driver's side door.

Liam grabbed the handle above the door to brace himself, while Jackson shouted a colorful stream of words at me.

I probably should have warned them about that part.

The car groaned as I slammed against the side again, sending them careening off the road. It hit several jagged rocks before crashing into a thick tree. The Maserati crumpled like a tin can, sending shards of glass and metal into the air.

"Let's go," I said as I pulled the car over and swung open the door.

Jackson was already out of the car, running toward the wreckage. Liam followed with an eerie calm. The witch raised his left hand and flicked it to the side, fingers splayed. A swirl of silver magic shot from his palm, twisting into a glowing chain about ten feet long. As he drew closer to the wreckage, the chain glowed brighter and brighter.

According to Liam, that magical chain would keep Valentina nice and docile while we hunted down her daughter.

What a perfect little weapon.

As we approached the wreckage, we saw how badly damaged the Maserati was—the impact would've turned a human into a bloody pulp. Darius slumped over the steering wheel, half-ejected from the car, with shattered glass scattered across the smoking hood. The crash knocked him out cold. We had maybe minutes before he healed and tried to save Valentina.

When we walked around to the passenger side, she was already crawling out of the side window, glass slicing her skin. Her left leg shattered, the broken bones sinking into the bloodied, healing flesh. Fresh blood matted her red hair and coated her mouth and nose.

"Not so fast, sweetheart," Jackson growled, grabbing the back of her neck and pulling her out of the car. She tried to fight back by raising her torn hand to conjure magic, but Liam threw the chain at her head. The chain brushed against Jackson's hand, causing him to hiss and release Valentina. The collar of silver encircled her thin throat and snapped closed. Then the collar grew tiny tendrils of light that traveled down her body like twin snakes before wrapping around her wrists.

Valentina thrashed against the chain, and nothing happened when she tried to summon power again. Even her eyes stayed their blue hue, and her fangs had vanished. She was powerless.

Thank God.

Liam moved around her, yanking the chain to tighten the bonds as a devilish smirk spread across his face. He wrapped the end of the chain around his left wrist, securing it into a cuff. "It's unbreakable," he said, grinning like a cat who caught a bird. "I suggest you stop flailing around."

"What the hell is this?" Valentina tried to pry at the collar, but tiny electric sparks bit into her fingers, causing her to gasp.

"While we all appreciate you wanting to save your daughter," I purred, my voice low and dangerous as I approached them. There was still a large gash on her forehead, knitting itself closed, and more blood dripped down her face. "I need you to cooperate and act as bait to get her back."

Her gaze met mine. Though sharp, pain and fear were etched on her features. "I'll kill you and your lackeys the second I remove this chain," she hissed. "I'm not helping you do anything." Her head turned to Liam. "And you. I'll make sure your death is slow and so painful that even the angels will feel your suffering. You'll be my favorite kill."

I'd never seen Valentina's defiance before ... not like this. The fire in her eyes reminded me of Rachel, fierce and stubborn. It would be fun putting her in her place. *Tame the lioness to catch the cub.*

Jackson kicked her legs out from under her, sending her sprawling forward into the dirt.

"Where's Rachel?" he asked calmly. Jackson had a much gentler temper than I did. "If you tell us that, we won't have to torture you for answers. Believe me, Liam seems a little too excited to play with you."

Or maybe not.

Liam stepped forward, the chain in his hands pulsing again with an unnatural light. A flash of fear in Valentina's eyes gave her away. She tried to scramble back, but Jackson was faster, pinning her down with one knee pressed into her back.

"Don't touch me," she spat, her voice breaking as Liam looped the chain over the collar and pulled, choking her. "I don't know where she is! I read Liam's mind back at the villa and know Rachel is going to that cave with Jase. She ran off hours ago after we fought. My daughter is hiding from me as much as she is from you."

Jackson removed his knee, and Valentina rose, her fingers digging at the collar. She no longer cared that the magic burned and bruises were forming around her throat.

"The magic is unbreakable," Liam reminded us, his tone tight, as if he was holding back from choking her more. "She won't escape unless I say so."

Valentina's breaths were ragged, her face pale and streaked with blood. But her anger burned strong. "I think you've underestimated her. Rachel's hatred for you and your brother runs fucking deep. She'll do everything possible to elude you and every piece of shit from your clan. Leave her—"

"And yet she's with Jase," I said, watching her eyes turn dark. "I'm sure that was a surprise to you when you saw it in Liam's mind. My brother betrayed me to get to Rachel first, and I have no clue why. Right now, I'm trying to save our souls from being Lucifer's playthings. The sword in that cave is the only way to do it. I need Rachel's blood or yours."

She shook her head. "Then take mine."

I smiled and leaned down until my face was level with hers. "I knew you'd say that. Unfortunately, we still need the key and the book that my brother stole. Plus, you wouldn't be as much fun. Then again, you did make me destroy my family and reputation, so maybe tormenting you will be enough entertainment until I have my pet back."

Valentina's eyes darkened again with rage. "You'll never find her," she whispered. "She's too far ahead. I'm thrilled knowing she evaded you."

My frayed patience snapped, and I struck her across the cheek, sending her crashing to the ground. I looked down at my hand, a surge of anger rushing through me. As depraved and violent as I was, I'd never hit a woman—not like that.

Liam's eyes locked on Valentina, who was climbing to her knees, and his jaw tensed. His usual calm was gone, replaced by something darker. I guessed the psychopath had his limits to violence.

Jackson moved closer, his hand partly raised as though to protect her from me. "Drei ... what the fuck?"

I didn't explain myself. Guilt stirred in what little conscience I had left, and I looked away. *I'll apologize later.*

"Stand up," I growled before turning on my heel and walking away from the wreckage. Behind me, Valentina shouted at Liam to release her while he yanked the chain, prompting her to stand.

"What do we do about that guy?" Jackson asked, catching up to me and glancing at the smoking wreckage. Darius was still unconscious, but his wounds had vanished. "Also, what the fuck is going on with you?"

Liam cleared his throat, interrupting us. "May I?"

"Do it," I said. Liam uncuffed the chain and handed it to Jackson. He strode to the broken tree and selected a thick branch from the debris.

Valentina screamed and tried to run toward the car, the chain choking her back to the ground. "No!" Tears streamed down her cheeks, which made me stiffen. *Tears?* "Liam, no! Don't! I'll kill you. I'll kill you! Darius! Darius, wake up!"

Ignoring her screams, Liam grabbed Darius by the hair and yanked him out of the windshield. When his back hit the hood, Darius's eyes fluttered open. When he saw Liam, his fangs emerged, and he went to strike. The witch used the momentum to pull his elbow back, and then impaled Darius's chest with the branch, piercing his heart and exiting out of his back.

"Darius!" Valentina's cries turned to shrieks as blood gushed from the man's mouth. He turned to look at her. "Darius, I'm sorry. I'm sorry for everything."

"Val ..." he gasped, skin graying. "Protect the others.... I ... love ..."

His body collapsed into ash, the wind scattering it across the car. Liam brushed the grime from his hands and walked toward us, unfazed by the scene behind him. Valentina's screams echoed across the forest, piercing our ears like a thousand knives.

CHAPTER 32

VALENTINA

I felt like I was being consumed by Hell, my essence burned by eternal flames and ice. Yet I was still alive.... If you could call an undead monster *alive,* sitting in the backseat of a dented car. I wasn't in love with Darius, but he was still my friend. He was still someone I cared for deeply. Honestly, he was my oldest friend.

Liam had no reason to kill him.

Andrei, Jackson, and Liam sat quietly, all three staring at the road ahead, while the chain around my throat felt suffocating. It was too tight. I almost felt like it would squeeze even tighter every time I tried to pry at it.

As if it were punishing me for wanting my freedom.

While the pain of losing Darius still burned, I had to do what I did best: bury that grief and shove that humanity from my heart so I could figure out a plan on how to escape.

The chain, though, wasn't the worst of my discomfort; Andrei made me sit next to Liam, and far too often, I caught him looking my way, studying me.

What's his issue with me?

"What element do you possess?" I asked. Maybe some information about his background might help me fight the bastard. I watched him shift in his seat to look at me, but his eyes were solemn. "I've been around a long time, Liam. What you did back at the villa—was new, and even for me … quite unsettling."

He inhaled slowly and leaned back, his deep hazel eyes catching the faint light filtering through the back seat.

Now that we weren't fighting, and I was this close, I could get a better look at him. He looked no older than twenty-five, with light, wavy brown hair and a smooth jawline. Handsome, I'd give him that. But there was something ominous and deadly within him that made my head spin and my skin prickle. And it wasn't just that he had liquefied two vampires before my eyes.

"Spirit," he said at last.

Well, that surprised me. Spirit witches weren't exactly known for their dark side. They were the balancing force in the pentagram—the light that grounded our power.

"It was magic I never really understood as a kid," he continued, his voice lowering a bit as if he only wanted me to hear. He hesitated, though, pressing his lips together in a grimace, like he had tasted something bitter. "My father … he hated it. Thought it was the weaker link. He'd tear into me every chance he got, made me feel like I was nothing but an inconvenience to the family."

He paused, his jaw tight. The forced calm of his voice barely masked the hatred and frustration in his eyes.

Talking about his family wasn't the turn I thought this conversation would go, but I would listen. If I were to kill him, I needed to find his weakness.

"One day, shortly after I turned fifteen, my parents had had enough," he said, his tone flat, but venom laced his tongue. "They threw me out on the streets to figure it all out alone, just like that. No warning, no help. I had these powers I didn't know how to control, and no one was around to guide me."

His eyes darted around, looking as if his father was in the car with us, drawing out the pain he'd inflicted all over again.

"Ten years later, I moved to Atlanta from my hometown of San Diego. My sister, Elena, let me crash on her couch and eat whatever was in her fridge while she was at school. She never even told our parents I was staying with her. But she hated magic—refused to use it—and we made this deal: as long as I was under her roof, I couldn't use mine, either."

"That sounds miserable," I said. It truly did. But I also pitied him. He had unmatched power with no one to guide him. "You had power, yet they denied you your true self."

Empathy, compassion. Make Liam believe you actually care.

Liam leaned back, his expression softening just a little. "Well, eventually, I found something that worked for me—I didn't need a fucking coven or anyone in my family to feel free. I had no rules or expectations. Just freedom. In time, I learned my powers on my own, but in *my* way." He barked out a short, hearty laugh, shaking his head. "I don't know. But I started missing that family link. I couldn't ignore how lonely I was. It was as if the heavens themselves parted and shone down their light on a lost little soul. Then I found the Black Onyx. Or, I guess, they found me."

"In Atlanta?" I asked.

He nodded, and his lips twitched into a faint smirk. "It wasn't that long ago, actually. They gave me a job, a purpose. Then Andrei and Jackson tasked me with helping them, and I guess the rest is history."

Talking to him like this felt odd, almost like we were old friends reacquainted—like there wasn't a blade poised to strike his heart at the perfect moment. Yet I played along, fostering his trust for his inevitable demise.

"But the Black Onyx, Liam?" I pointed out. "Come on. They're the worst of them all."

Liam let out a low laugh this time, dimples appearing as his eyes lit up. "Well, I wouldn't say that. They're a little weird and unhinged, sure, but they helped me. I guess I'm more like them than I thought. Once you get past the surface, they're just looking for peace and balance in the world—"

A laugh escaped me now, and I grinned widely. "Oh, yes. Witches with no laws, wielding magic as weapons when someone doesn't agree with them. They've killed indiscriminately for far too long. Witches were never meant to have that kind of power. You misuse it, and karma will eventually come for you."

His brows shot up. "Right. Just like you, then."

"Me?"

"You're a vampire. You're the last person to judge someone for how they use their powers. Your undead heart had to forfeit magic to become the queen of bloodlust. Instead of trying to get it back, you embraced the darkness."

"Oh, please. It's not like I had a choice when my soul was ripped from me."

"Didn't you, though?"

I narrowed my eyes at him, unsure where he was going with this. But my insides burned. No one had ever talked to me like that.

"Purgatory," he said, and my brows shot up.

"What about it?"

He shrugged. "A vampire doesn't truly lose their soul, right? What wanders in Purgatory isn't the soul itself, not entirely. It's more like an echo—our essence, our intelligence, the fragments of what made us human. But your soul? It's still tethered to you."

I scowled at him. He didn't know anything about me.

"For every good deed, every moment of humanity, that tether pulls your soul just a little closer to your dead heart," he continued. "You tell your progeny they lose *all* their humanity when they lose their souls, but that's not entirely true."

"Excuse me, you—"

"You're a little liar," he berated, his tone shifting. "Tatyana created Purgatory for a reason—to keep a vampire's essence intact, to offer the chance for redemption. The idea was that if there's ever a cure for vampirism, the soul wouldn't be completely lost. It would return to the body when it was ready to move on."

"That's a pleasant story," I said dryly, but my eyes looked to the front so as not to give myself away. I knew all this, but how did he?

Though Andrei and Jackson had the music blaring and caught up in their own conversation, they had to be listening to what Liam was saying.

"It doesn't explain why witches lose their powers when they turn," I said, looking back at him. "If the soul's still there, shouldn't they be able to use their magic?"

That was one question I never understood, and Kylan never told me. If I knew the answer, I would have burned the world to get it back. I was aware we all had a link to our souls when they left the body, but no matter how hard I tried, I could never use my magic unless I was wearing my damn ring.

"They can," he said simply. "But the tether is weak. Magic is tied to essence, not just the body. Most vampires don't realize their powers can be accessed if they strengthen that connection."

I raised an eyebrow. *Seriously, how does this witch know about any of this?*

Maybe he'd tell me.

"And you know this how?"

"Because I've seen it," he said, his voice dropping. "Witches turned into vampires regained their magic. And not by some fucking ring. Vampires who found their souls drawn back by something stronger than death itself."

"What's stronger than death?"

"Love," he said, his gaze locking with mine. "A soulmate can bring a soul back completely. No longer tethered to some other realm. It's rare, but it happens. And when it does, it changes everything."

Yes. The same thing would happen to Jase and my own daughter. The thought made me sick that they were bound together. Jase was going to destroy her. She wasn't a full vampire, so her powers would always be within reach. Jase, though. By denying his mate, no matter how much I hated that they were fated, I was taking away his chance to be free from the curse I had placed on him, even if he had demanded it back then. But Rachel could be the reason Jase would get his magic back on his own.

"The emotions are there," he continued, and once again, I acted curious and intrigued. Liam was still my enemy and a stranger—I wouldn't tell him I knew most of what he was sharing.

"They're muted, tangled in the void left by the string of power. That's why it's unique when a vampire loves. It's raw. It's real. And when it's strong enough, it can call the *entire* soul back, binding it to their mate."

I held his gaze for a moment, my mind racing, then forced myself to look away. I took a few deep breaths to settle my growing agitation and turned back to him. Though I had to sell the lie, I was anything but calm. *Seriously, how the hell does he know all this?*

Kylan had been the only one to ever tell me about the tether, about how the soul wasn't truly lost but hung in limbo, waiting in a residual loop. He'd spoken of soulmates, their rare ability to call a soul back, binding it so deeply that even death couldn't sever the connection. I'd never told anyone about that conversation ... well, except for Jase. When it happened that night in the church, when his soul under the Hades Blood Moon connected to my unborn child, promising a future when she was a woman, I knew then that what Kylan told me was true. I never believed it until that night because I had never witnessed it with my own eyes.

"Nice theory," I said, a smirk playing on my lips. "Too bad that's all it is—a *theory*."

I kept my tone light and dismissive, as if his words hadn't added a million other questions about this man and what vampires who held witch magic were still capable of.

Liam's lips curved into a slight smile, his face calm, yet curiosity shone in his eyes as they looked over me. It was as though he felt my unease and somehow found it entertaining.

"Enough about all that," I said, trying to shift the conversation away from the talk of soulmates. "Are you honestly planning on giving me back to the Black Onyx? Collect your little reward?"

A wide smirk stretched across Liam's face, crinkling the corners of his eyes as he let out a playful laugh. "Well, maybe not *now*," he said. "One conversation and I find you fascinating. If I give you to them, I might not learn more about what's in your pretty little head."

Is he flirting with me?

With a slight shake of the magical chain in Liam's hand, the part around my neck loosened a bit. "Maybe," he continued, "when all this is over ... I just might keep you."

CHAPTER 33

ANDREI

We only drove for another hour before pulling into a parking lot of an empty beach. The car's headlights shone through the darkness, faintly lighting up a sign near the sand. Thankfully, the sun hadn't risen yet. Though Jackson and I still had those enchanted necklaces to walk in the light, Valentina didn't have that luxury yet. He was afraid that if he did that for her, he'd make it too easy for her to run if she somehow broke free from the chains.

Right then, our priority was our strength. Even though vampires could feed on each other, Liam was the only human with us, and we all agreed it was best to pull over and take what we needed for another day. We didn't have the time to hunt tonight. We hadn't fed since before attacking the villa, and we were beginning to feel *depleted*. The lack of blood caused my hands to press against the steering wheel, and my mind felt too hazy to focus on anything, let alone drive.

It also didn't help that Valentina's bratty little mouth was fraying my nerves.

"I don't think it's wise we drink from him," Valentina hissed stubbornly, but Liam chuckled quietly to himself instead of looking offended.

"We don't have a choice unless you want us to attack and feed from some innocent jogger this morning," Jackson said, twisting in his seat to look back at her. Under the circumstances, he surprisingly stayed calm. "You're looking paler than usual. All that healing after the crash took a toll."

Valentina's eyes narrowed, her fangs glinting as she sneered. "Then give me *your* blood."

Her resistance surprised me. For much of the drive, Valentina and Liam seemed civil, but then again, after going so long without food, even the kindest of us could turn violent.

On the other hand, Jackson hated contention and had a far better temper than I did. While I would've choked her by now, he only smiled, a curve of his lips that somehow diffused even the worst tempers. After giving her a brief nod, he bit into his wrist, holding it out to her. "Alright, sweetheart. Drink."

I caught a quick glimpse of the beach ahead of us. It looked like maybe a storm was rolling in. There were distant rumbles of thunder through the cracked window, but something seemed to gnaw at the back of my mind. It wasn't just the weather that filled me with unease—something else lingered there, like a sense of danger making my skin crawl. I wondered if it was the bond between Rachel and me. Were we closer to her than we thought? Was she in trouble?

Valentina shifted, sitting up straighter, and her gaze locked on Jackson's wrist with stubborn pride and hunger. Right as she leaned forward to take his wrist in her mouth, Liam's hand darted out, his fingers brushing Jackson's arm to push him away.

"We agreed before we stopped that it'd be better if she took it from a human," Liam said evenly. Though he had a calm and collected tone, something about it made me look at him twice. "If she tries to take too much, I'll use my magic to stop her. After that, the two of you will take what I have left before I pass out."

The idea of three vampires feeding from one human was insane. For anyone else, it would've been a death sentence, but Liam wasn't just *anyone*. The magic he wielded was unlike anything I'd ever seen. Maybe he *would* survive what no one else could.

Valentina's gaze stayed on him as he rolled up the sleeve of his black hoodie, exposing his wrist. "It's quite an honor, actually," he said teasingly. "The great Valentina Vasile feeding from me." He bit his bottom lip, his eyes darkening with something I couldn't quite name—something that again put me on edge. "Take as much as you'd like. Once I feel myself dying, I'll give those chains around your neck a little tug. If you don't stop, I'll strangle you until you pass out."

Her eyes burned with rage, her jaw tightening as her bound wrists shifted in her lap. Her reaction only made Liam's grin widen, as if her anger amused him. He raised his wrist closer to her lips, almost brushing against them. "Go on," he murmured. "I don't have fangs to cut myself like Jackson. You'll have to do it."

The air inside the car grew thick. Valentina tapped her foot nervously against the floor, or maybe she was getting close to snapping. I understood her hesitation. Feeding from a witch wasn't like feeding from a human. It came with the risk of absorbing bits of their power, even temporarily. It could have dangerous consequences. For the first time, something rare flickered across Valentina's face: genuine fear.

Letting out a sigh, she viciously bit his wrist, her bound hands clawing at his skin.

Liam's head tipped back, his throat exposed as his arm snaked around her waist, pulling her closer to his hip. His lips curved into that same arrogant smile; her defiance amused him.

I exchanged a glance with Jackson, and once again, he looked uneasy. Watching her feed from Liam felt wrong. Maybe it was a good thing we had her go first. If she survived, perhaps we would, too.

"I need to make a call to the States," I said, breaking the silence. "Jackson, go ahead and feed when she's done. If she doesn't stop in a few minutes, pry her off."

With a nod from Jackson, I switched off the engine and exited the car, feeling the breeze from the ocean sharp against my already chilled skin. I inhaled deeply, attempting to clear my head. There were so many dark thoughts in my mind, a thick fog that demanded attention. I was wearing out.

Walking toward the water, I pulled out my phone, momentarily closing my eyes. I tried to reach for the bond that tied me to Rachel, but there was nothing. The empty ache in my chest flared again, replacing it with a cold fury that wouldn't simmer down.

Lifting the phone, I dialed Alexei, the vampire I left in charge of the mansion and clan. It rang once before he picked up. "Andrei. Fuck, man."

"Great," I muttered, already bracing for bad news. "What's going on?"

"Well, did you see the news?"

I shook my head even though he couldn't see. "Let me guess, the wolves?"

"It's more than the Bayou Perot Pack this time. It's not safe for you to return right now. The mansion is still standing, and we haven't let them in, but they're issuing a warrant to search the place. Hendrick's turned over your contracts stolen from the safe to the Five-Point Order, and the human government is, unfortunately, getting involved in our affairs and cooperating."

"Fuck the Five-Point Order," I said. "Those people are in those contracts, too. If they want to point fingers and bring down my clan, I'll bring them down with me."

"It doesn't matter at this point. Right now, they're calling in everyone, and I mean everyone, to discuss their next move. The only hit they have right now is you and Jackson. The rest of us, I don't know."

Jackson and I knew this was most likely the repercussions of what Jase had done, but I didn't think it would happen this quickly.

One thing was sure: once we got that sword, the ring back, and Rachel, they'd soon find out how far I was willing to go to break down every wall they'd built to keep the peace between the species. If they wanted a war, I'd give them war.

"I'll call you in the morning. In the meantime, keep the mansion on lockdown. No one leaves or enters. Understand?"

"Yes, sir."

I clicked off the call and dialed Helen next. This wasn't a phone call I was looking forward to.

"Hello?" her voice rang out, but it sounded like she was busy, loud banter echoing in the distance.

"Helen, it's Andrei Dimitriou."

"Did your lead pan out? Did you find them?" she asked. "The last I heard, the jet was fueled up and ready for you."

"Unfortunately, we couldn't find Rachel in time, but we managed to find and subdue Valentina. She doesn't have the ring, but we can use her to get Rachel to cooperate once we reach Crete. I guarantee she has it."

She cleared her throat. "Already fucking this up," she berated and then sighed dramatically. "Remember our agreement. If you don't return with that ring and the sword once you use it, our deal is off. You can kiss your freedom goodbye, and those hunters will have a field day with you and your entire clan. We don't give a shit. Find the dhampir and take care of it. If you can't get the ring back from her, just use Valentina's blood to get the sword, and we'll send a team to track Rachel down. We're running out of time."

I bit down on my tongue, trying to hold in what I truly wanted to say to her. But we needed the Black Onyx's help, so until then, I had to play nice.

"That's the plan," I said, now gnawing on the inside of my cheek. "For now, we need to feed before we get on that plane. Your newest recruit from the Atlanta division, Liam, has been more than happy to let us drink his blood. Once we reach Athens, I'll update you."

There was silence on the other end before Helen spoke again. "What are you talking about? We don't have an Atlanta division. Who the hell is Liam?"

Everything around me froze like the world was turning, and my stomach gripped tight.

"Andrei? Are you there?"

"Um ... yeah, I—no one"—I looked back at the car—"just someone we met on the way. I'll call with an update later."

I clicked off the call and narrowed my eyes, watching Liam exit the car and walk over to me and onto the beach. "Don't take too much. Jackson got carried away, but it's your turn."

He held up his wrist, and I looked down at the smeared blood along his skin. What was happening?

Who the hell is this guy?

Immediately, I lashed out to grab his throat and demand answers, but Liam caught my fist and twisted it. I felt my bones crack and tried to shout for Jackson, but the witch placed his hand on my head and started to chant.

The blackness in my head began to pulse crimson.

"You're okay. You're okay," he said calmly. "I think you're a little confused and tired. Take it easy."

As my head spun, my nerves settled, and I looked back at Liam.

"I need you to feed. Got it?" he said again.

I looked down at his wrist and shook my head, feeling my body settle, and for a moment, I couldn't remember how I even got on the beach. I looked down at my phone, and the call log was still open.

"Oh, um, I called Helen. The plane is ready for us. We need to get going."

Liam smiled and held his wrist up to my lips. The scent of his blood caused the veins under my eyes to swell. It smelled intoxicating. "That's it ... drink," he said in a soothing voice, like he was lulling me to sleep. "Drink."

I nodded and grabbed his wrist, my fangs digging into his skin. My entire body melted as I drank, falling forward and into his arms. He caressed my hair and allowed me to take in the euphoria from his blood. At that moment, calm washed over me, and all was peaceful and good in the world.

CHAPTER 34

JASE

After becoming a vampire, I noticed that you had to be very patient when hanging out with humans. While Lucy and I didn't sleep, we had to account for the other two to wake up hours later. But Lucy never came out of the room all morning and afternoon to join me, appearing as though she actually chose to sleep. Tony had already had his morning coffee and lunch, but he mentioned he had to make some calls to the States and speak to Giulia before we could leave. After the kitchen incident with Rachel, I spent the early morning trying to find something else to do. So far, it had been reading a mystery novel about a man who could speak to Death. I checked the time on the wall above the front desk.

It's almost four in the afternoon. Wake up.

I'd be lying if I said that being so close to Rachel last night didn't mess with my head. The minute I approached, her scent put me in a fucking tailspin. It didn't matter how hard I tried to shut down the feelings—every instinct screamed at me to rip her clothes off and fuck her right there on the countertop. To stake a claim on my *mate*.

Grabbing her throat was the only thing I could think of to tame the beast inside me. It was oddly soothing. Keeping her still and in my presence was enough to regain control of my emotions. Insulting her, too, kept me from doing something even more reckless.

Knowing that the celestial powers fated our paths while she remained ignorant slowly destroyed me. The wisest—or most sane choice—would be to walk away as soon as we destroyed the summoning circle and ruined my brother's ambitions. But the longer we spent time together, the clearer it became: walking away from Rachel Hardmann might not be an option.

No, fuck that. Rachel hates me; she'd be thrilled if I disappeared unless I tied her up and dragged her with me. Shit, that might not be a bad idea ... What the fuck am I thinking? Tony's rapid footsteps interrupted my thoughts as he rushed down the stairs.

"Jase," Tony called out. "Turn the TV on. Now."

I set my book down and hurried into the lobby, grabbing the remote on the coffee table and switching on the TV. The local news station flickered to life and appeared to be broadcasting a live feed from America. The stream showed the Louisiana Division leader of the Five-Point Order standing behind a podium in Jackson Square with dozens of microphones set up before him.

"What the fuck is going on?" I asked as Tony came into the room.

He came beside me, phone in hand. "I got a text from a friend back home. Rachel and Lucy are packing right now. We gotta move as soon as they come down and check in somewhere else until the ferry leaves tomorrow morning—my cousin won't be safe if we stay here."

Luckily, the station had English subtitles under the Five-Point Order's division leader's dubbed-over voice.

"As of last night, we have uncovered years' worth of secret contracts between supernatural entities within our city," the man announced. "The Four-Fold Accord has been broken. I have received word from the other Five-Point state leaders, who have confirmed it's not just affecting Louisiana. The bombing of the Black Diamond Club was just the start of these revelations. Thanks to the Bayou Perot Pack, we have received documents accounting for hundreds of assassinations, blackmail, and illegal blood trade contracts as proof. We've deployed the Sanctum Order, our national enforcement division, to track down those responsible. Last night, we received word that two vampires of interest may be traveling to Italy. Once found, they will face trial and prison—but those guilty of violent crimes will be executed on sight. Our world forged the Accord to uphold peace and sanctuary between the species, and neither we nor the human government will tolerate such a grave offense."

My jaw dropped, and my mind raced. While I was a rogue vampire and did my best to stay out of range of politics, I learned enough to know exactly what that meant. The Sanctum Order wasn't just some enforcement group—they were a *lethal* force, each member forged into the perfect weapon. Each state had its division of the Five-Point Order and supernatural law enforcement that worked with Sanctum.

They were an elite hunting team comprised of two military-trained humans, a former coven leader, a vampire mercenary, and an Alpha werewolf. They ensured there'd be no bias, and the hunters acted as one unit. The team apprehended only those possessing crucial information and brought them to their Boston headquarters for questioning.

"Well, shit," I hissed under my breath. Those motherfucking werewolves. I'd made a deal with them. They were supposed to take their revenge by looking *into* his contracts to use the information for their own strategic move—not handing *everything* over to the goddamn government.

What the hell are they planning?

"All this over what? A vampire mafia boss playing dirty?" I said. "Like that's never happened in the history of mankind."

Tony turned to me. "Technically, this is your fault, too. Nothing good ever comes from involving werewolves. Trust me."

I flashed him a sneer before my attention turned back to the television. Tony had flipped through several stations, seeing what other coverage there was on it but then stopped on one of them. There was footage of the villa property where Rachel was staying, with flames rising high over the trees and surrounded by flashing lights, and neighbors being interviewed. At the bottom of the screen, the text mentioned that no one was home at the time of the incident.

Shit. This has Andrei's name all over it.

Tony cleared his throat. "Well ... we can now assume Andrei is already here. Fuck." His gaze shifted to me. "It looks like they're reporting it happened at eleven last night, so it's possible they've either passed us or are already in Crete. So, yeah, we don't have a choice but to lie low somewhere else until tomorrow. We can't risk Andrei tracking us down here if he has enough resources to dig into my family."

"I thought you told us Manetti was a common family name," I reminded him.

"Yeah," he said. "That was before he, or someone looking for Rachel and Valentina, blew up an entire villa."

I nodded and looked around. Luckily, no human guests were in the lobby. The creak of wooden stairs pulled my attention. Rachel and Lucy hurried down, their bags slung over their shoulders.

"Jase, whatever shit you have, pack it up. We're leaving. Now," Rachel said sharply with her messy bun atop her head and tank top strap sliding slightly off her shoulder. "We'll hide out somewhere else until tomorrow morning. I don't know how much information Andrei has on you or your family, Tony, but it's a good idea to get out of here just in case he's not far behind."

Tony nodded. "Yeah, I said the same thing. I'll talk to Giulia."

Why was Rachel's attitude such a fucking turn on? My dick twitched at her expression as she glared at me. I wanted to punish her for it.

"Andrei may be the only one we need to worry about. It's not like the hunters themselves know where *we* are," I said, though the knot in my stomach suggested otherwise. "Hunters in the U.S. can't come to Europe without approval from their division *and* the EU."

If they know about Andrei, they could know about her.

Tony nodded, and then turned to Rachel and Lucy. "Andrei is scary enough. Let me talk to my cousin. She may have some ideas."

Rachel nodded, gripping her bag tightly. "Tony, I'll go with you to talk to her. I want to say goodbye, too."

Brushing past them, I rushed up the stairs. Frustration seemed to pour into every vein in my body. The fact that we weren't even in Athens yet made me nervous. Then I thought about it. Even if Andrei was already in Crete, he didn't have the key or the book. He still couldn't do shit.

We ... I still have the advantage.

I shoved my arms through my black hoodie, pulled the hood up, and packed the rest of my clothes. This was getting more and more complicated by the damn minute.

Ten minutes later, Tony and Rachel left the locanda, with Giulia watching from the doorway. After a quick goodbye, they jumped into the car. Rachel scooted as far from me as possible again, and I rolled my eyes, leaning back into the seat.

The sun had barely peeked over the tree line, but thankfully, thick rain clouds dulled its intensity. As soon as the sunlight disappeared behind them, I pulled off my hoodie. Over the last decade, car manufacturers started using UV-protective film on windshields and windows—our rental was one of those models. We were safe as long as Lucy and I stayed inside until sundown.

"Okay, Giulia has a friend who's traveling overseas right now, but they have a beach house not too far from the ferry in the Camerini Beach Front," Tony started. "We hang out there tonight, get another good night's sleep, and catch the nine a.m. departure to Greece."

This was going to be a long trip.

———

The music from Tony's playlist was the only element of this car ride that eased the tension. While he and Lucy chatted, Rachel and I were dead silent. No surprise there; the woman wouldn't even look at me. I tried reading a book during the first leg of the trip, but the words quickly lost meaning, and I tucked it away after an hour.

The world flowed by in a monotonous sea of greens, reds, and grays, which meant absolutely nothing to me. My focus kept dragging toward the infuriating woman, who was mere feet away. Rachel sat as far away from me as physically possible, her arms crossed like a fucking shield. Though she did her best not to acknowledge *my* presence, *she* was all I could feel. The way she pulled at me was infuriating. All I wanted to do was bury my hands in her hair and taste her skin.

Knock it the fuck off, I berated myself, trying to clear my thoughts.

I shifted in my seat, glancing out the window to avoid looking at her because she pressed further toward the door every time I did. If that were even possible. I was pretty damn sure she was trying to fuse with it.

My mind wandered back to the train station, replaying every word Valentina said to me. It didn't matter that Rachel and I were fated. Fuck what that woman said. It didn't matter that my instincts screamed to protect her—to be near her. I'd spent four years watching Rachel, never making a move, even though the beast in me demanded it. I sure as hell wasn't about to kowtow to that annoying bond just because fate had a twisted sense of humor.

"What the fuck is your deal?" Rachel's voice cut through my thoughts but was low enough not to reach the front seats.

I rolled my head to her. "What the hell are you talking about?"

"The kitchen," she said sharply. "What the fuck was that about?" her tone was sharp enough to get under my skin. "Before—" Rachel's mouth clamped shut, her fingers twitching against her thigh as if she was physically holding back another smartass remark. "I never thought, in the two hundred years of living, I'd have to worry about some broody, self-serving vampire coming along and destroying everything." She tilted her head, the muted sunlight making her hair glow a deep gold. "First, Andrei storms in and destroys any semblance of a normal life. And now *you*. I swear, I think fate hates me."

My lips raised into an arrogant grin. "The kitchen? Nothing happened in the kitchen. You were blocking me from getting to the sink." My tone was flat, dismissive.

Her lips thinned. "Really? You grabbed my throat, you asshole. But then you ..." Rachel's nostrils flared, making it crystal clear she was dancing around the *other* tension brewing between us last night. There was something there. I felt it, and I knew Rachel would rather die than admit she felt it, too. My heightened senses were going haywire in that damn car. I could smell the arousal between her legs.

Of course, instead of saying something to ease the chaos between us, I opened my mouth and made it worse. "The amount of strength I'm using not to rip that ring off your finger, take your blood with it, and do the spell bullshit myself is astronomical. I'll take the risk of the blood not being fresh...." My voice trailed off. If Rachel wanted to see me as only the villain, then I'd give her a villain.

The ice-blue of Rachel's irises flashed into something dark, violent. "Try it, dick."

I narrowed my eyes, matching her threat. "Lucy will try to kill me, and I'd hate to make a mess. I'll wait until we're not sharing a car with her."

Her laugh was humorless and cold. "That sounds like a good time. It's been a while since I got to brawl with an asshole male vampire. Did you know that before Andrei jumped me, I ripped off a bloodsucker's arm who tried to bite me? You probably did, now that I think about it, since you were likely watching from some dark corner like a fucking alley rat."

Rachel raised a brow at me, daring me to react. I carefully leaned back, determined not to show how much she'd gotten under my skin.

Unfortunately, that night, I *wasn't* in that alley. If I were, I would have stopped Andrei from ever meeting her.

Lucy must have heard Rachel because she glanced over her shoulder at us. "If you two are going to have some dramatic lovers' spat, can you wait until we're not on the run?"

Rachel glared at her. "Bestie, you're supposed to be on my side. We're not having a spat. Jase is being a self-entitled asshole, and it's his fault we're all on the run in the first place."

Lucy chuckled like our banter was adorable before returning to Tony. "We're going to have to figure out how to handle what's going on in the States after all this. It may not be safe right away for us to return with what's going on with the hunters. If they know about Andrei and Jackson, it won't be long before they figure out we're involved somehow, too. Rachel's name is in those contracts."

Tony nodded. "Well, hopefully, if all goes well, maybe we can use that angel's sword to negotiate her freedom. They only send out the Sanctum Order if the suspect poses a threat. Right now, we're stopping a vampire from possibly disrupting the balance of the universe and summoning an angelic entity to Earth. I'd say they better fucking reward us instead of arresting her."

"Maybe," Rachel said. "We can't be naive enough to think the Five-Point Order won't figure out soon that dhampirs exist—that vampires can have children with the right spell. Lucy's right. If the Bayou Perot Pack handed over those contracts, they would have seen the one on me. Next, they'll dig into the Black Onyx and uncover what they've been hiding. They're the reason the world believes Valentina Vasile is dead. Five-Point will soon learn she's not. Until things settle, going back to New Orleans might not be an option."

It was silent as that point sunk in with all four of us.

"Besides, we don't even know if my blood will do shit to activate that spell to raise that angel to begin with. Right now it's just a *theory.*"

Tony gave her a nod and readjusted his hands on the wheel. "Alright," he started, "once we get to the beach house, let's hang until dark, and then go into town for food. Once we get a good night's sleep, we'll head to the port for the last stretch to Athens."

Rachel nodded and sat back again, looking out the window.

I wanted to reach out, make her fucking look at me again, and talk about the real reason why I invaded her space in the kitchen, but I couldn't. No fucking way I'd ever admit that to her, though I knew at some point, I'd lose all self-control and unleash something on her I'd been suppressing for the last four fucking years.

CHAPTER 35

RACHEL

According to Giulia's map, the beach house wasn't too far off the autostrade, and only thirty minutes from the ferry.

Taking this route was the safest option to stay off the main road. The house we were searching for was the perfect place to hide for the night until we could take the ferry to Greece tomorrow morning.

My only assurance was that the tracker was no longer in my arm. Andrei may have felt my emotions through the guardian bond, but he couldn't *find* me. And he couldn't trap me in my mind again.

Thank God.

Because we still had an hour before the sun finally set, Lucy and Jase covered themselves in their hoodies and gloves as we prepared to exit the car.

As Tony crested the hill, I looked out over the trees. There was a small white beach house at the end of the street behind them, nestled against a sandy bank. We pulled into the driveway, and when Lucy signaled she was ready, we climbed out of the car.

The beach behind the house was so serene, with only the sound of waves crashing against the shore. Fading sunlight bathed the house's stone walls, casting a soft orange glow on the pearl-colored stucco.

"Giulia couldn't reach her friends—so we may need to break in unless we can find a key," Tony said as he stepped onto the porch. He squinted through the window, looking inside. "But at least we won't be disturbing anyone." He looked away from the window and then back at us. "They aren't supposed to be back until August second."

Tony examined the front door and pointed at a coded lockbox hanging from the handle. "Ah, perfect. We won't need to break a window. Lucy, you're up."

Lucy nodded and walked up to it. She hefted the metal in her hand before crumpling it like a goddamn soda can. The little door popped open, and she fished out a silver key.

"I could have done that, too, you know?" I muttered under my breath. There was a smothered snort from Jase to my right, but I ignored it.

Tony opened the door, and we stepped inside. The smell of the ocean mingled with a fainter, lingering scent of musk, likely left behind by the owners, wafted in the air. Near the back, the windows were slightly ajar, letting in the cool sea breeze. The house was immaculately clean and clearly well-maintained by a housekeeping crew.

My shoes squeaking on the polished tiled floor echoed through the hallway before we reached the living room and flipped the lights on. A heavy silence pressed down on me. The house felt like a warm family home—not a place where a group of supernatural creatures would sleep.

The hairs on my neck prickled, and I looked over my shoulder. Jase was right behind me, close enough to aggravate me but not enough to touch. His clouded aura was like a fucking storm, threatening to break open at any moment.

"Let's relax for a bit. After dark, we can grab some food and a drink somewhere," Tony suggested with a sigh, collapsing onto the couch. "I saw online there's a club with a kitchen in Brindisi, about two blocks from the ferry we're taking tomorrow. Probably the only thing open by the time we get there." He ran a hand down his face. "Fuck, I slept like shit last night. Took me forever to even fall asleep."

Dark circles shadowed his eyes, and with every movement he made, he looked heavy with fatigue. Guilt gnawed at my chest as he sank deeper into the cushions. The poor guy had done all the driving so far and was the only one in our group who truly needed a good night's sleep.

Jase, unfazed by the mention of rest, casually walked into the kitchen, poking around in cabinets and the fridge as though he had a right to do so. He wasn't going to find any blood bags tucked away in there.

Lucy raised an eyebrow, her voice low as she spoke to Jase. "After we get back from dinner tonight, you and I can keep watch. Make sure no headlights are coming down the path. You take the first shift."

Jase nodded and turned to Tony. "We should leave at dawn," he said. "The ferry doesn't leave until nine, but it'll give me and Lucy enough time to go through the company's vetting process for vampires to enter a ferry with humans." His eyes slid over to mine, like he expected me to object. "Let's just hope everyone made it out of the villa and Andrei is empty-handed."

And just like that, Jase went from watching, staring, and making me uneasy to reminding me that maybe there was still a trace of humanity in his dark, lonely mind.

⁓ele⁓

We didn't get out of the house until almost ten, but it was fine. Tony had crashed on the couch around seven for a two-hour power nap, unbothered by the noise we made coming in and out of the rooms. About an hour before we left, Jase headed down to the beach to stick his feet in the ocean and enjoy the summer night breeze on his face. We still hadn't spoken much since our argument in the car, and honestly, I was relieved to have some space between us.

For tonight, we wanted to forget all the bullshit surrounding us. I needed to feel normal, even for a few hours.

Lucy and I got dressed for the club, and I did our makeup. I chose black shimmering eyeshadow that made the blue in my eyes practically glow in the dark, paired with a pink-nude lip. Lucy opted for wine-red lipstick and black smokey eyeliner that made her look like a damn goddess. I wore a flowy green summer dress that I had packed for Ireland, while Lucy changed into jean shorts and a black corset-style tank top that accentuated all her gorgeous curves.

Between laughs and inside jokes that left my sides aching, it was the first time in a while that I could just breathe. There was no chaos or danger.... It was just us.

When we stepped out of the bedroom, the room fell silent. Tony turned beet-red, suddenly focused on his shoes as he bent down to grab them. Jase, though—he swallowed hard, his eyes dragging over me before locking onto mine. Something about the look in his eyes sent a shiver through me. His jaw muscles tensed, seemingly battling an internal torment. I forced myself to look away, pretending I hadn't noticed. And just like that, the moment was over, and we headed to the club.

Once past security, Tony pointed to the green neon-lit sign of the nightclub right above our heads. "An hour, max, and then we need to head back and get some sleep."

It'd been a long time since I had been to a nightclub. Before Andrei essentially kidnapped me and coerced himself into being my guardian, Lucy and I had a favorite spot in New Orleans. If one of our days off fell on the weekend, we would wear glamorous makeup, tease our hair, and dance all night. Most of the time, it was a lot of fun. Dancing was a good outlet for me. It allowed me to release all my frustrations and loneliness into the music's rhythm.

I didn't miss it now. Some nights would be a sensory overload, with flashing lights, the intense bass, and the din of bodies packed way too tightly around me. My vampire nature would make it a lot worse. I could sense *everything*: the heat, the sweat, the energy my intuition would pull from people. I didn't want to read their intentions, but with all those bodies and the onslaught of their emotions, I couldn't control it—an endless wave I couldn't escape from.

A knot formed in my stomach, and I took a breath to settle it. We didn't have many choices for food venues tonight. Most restaurants had closed early because of the new regulations after vampires became public knowledge. There were always exceptions, though. Like in the States, many nighttime businesses welcomed the latest surge in clientele. Nightclubs were exempt from the restrictions. They had enhanced security to keep humans safe, and some even served warmed bottles of blood for vampires. Other clubs catered to blood sharing, but the one we walked into wasn't one of them.

Once inside, everything hit me, and I immediately regretted it. *Yup, tonight is a bad night for me.*

The pungent scent of sweat, alcohol, and perfume clung like a thick fog. Blue and white lights pulsed over the crowd in a hypnotic pattern. The bass pounded against my heart, and drunken laughter and shouts mixed with the music. This place reminded me of Andrei's club back home. I'd been shitfaced, but it was the only way to deal with the chaos of that place, and everything that had happened that led up to that night.

How did Andrei deal with this shit? Being an owner—well, former owner now—meant dealing with this every single night. *No, thank you.*

Tony, as usual, remained unfazed by the noise. He scanned the room, searching for an open booth or table. Lucy was already tying her thick hair into a messy bun in the reflection of a mirrored column. The gesture tugged at my heart, and though I still felt uneasy, I smiled at her. Being a vampire hardly changed a thing about her. During the car ride, she told me she often snuck out of the mansion to go to one of the government-run clubs to feed—on voluntary humans, of course. Lucy never went hunting for unsuspecting people.

I glanced behind me to look at Jase. He was, as always, unreadable. He leaned against the wall near the door, his sharp features half-hidden in shadows. Those eyes looked over all the writhing bodies like a predator selecting his next meal. Jase may have fed from Tony yesterday, but now, with that heated look in his eyes, I knew it wasn't enough to hold him over until we reached Athens. Some vampires could go at least a day before their next feeding. It seemed he was a lot like Andrei, needing someone to snack on every ten hours or so.

I should have assumed it instead of cutting him off Tony's wrist before he took too much. Even after he pushed my friend away, my gaze lingered on him longer than intended. At that moment, there was something about Jase—an invisible pull, something magnetic around him. And it was very fucking annoying.

Jase's presence was dangerous, alluring, and it was beginning to stir something in me I didn't want.

And the bastard knew it.

"Let's order something at the bar!" I shouted, my voice barely rising above the music. "I don't see an open table."

A brush of intent rolled over my shoulders, and I glanced around. The humans nearby were uneasy about our presence. Not that we were foreigners but that we were *outsiders*. Humans and vampires still didn't mix well in public spaces, regardless of the laws put into place—the façade of order and safety. Here, it was even more obvious who didn't belong. Lucy and Jase seemed to be the only vampires in the club. Several people walked past to the dance floor, giving my group a wide berth. Their instincts warned them to stay away. As for me? They likely assumed I was one of them—a weak, unsuspecting human.

Oh, if they only knew.

We walked over to the bar, finding a gap in the crowd. It was as if, on cue, people around us suddenly had somewhere else to be. Some shot Tony and me anxious glances, but we ignored them. A young man with dark tanned skin and a perfectly combed pompadour was busy making some drinks. His black name tag with yellow text read "Adrian," and he moved with the grace of someone who had seen it all. The man remained unbothered, even with the undead waiting for him at the bar.

I liked his energy.

When Adrian approached our group, he smiled broadly before focusing on Lucy. "Cosa vi posso offrire?" he asked. Lucy hesitated, shooting me a confused look. Adrian's thoughts clicked instantly. "English?"

She nodded, and Adrian handed her a drink menu printed in English, but his movements faltered when he looked at Jase.

I could see the calculations in his head as he fully understood who stood at the bar. Lucy quickly spoke up. "I'll have a mojito, extra mint, please."

Adrian reached under the bar and pulled out a different menu marked with a single red drop.

"Of course, and if you want, we do have—"

Lucy shook her head, smiling warmly at the bartender. "Just the mojito, please."

Adrian blinked once in surprise before nodding and putting away the second menu. He then turned to Tony.

"A bottle of Moretti, please," Tony ordered, sliding a couple of euros across the counter. "Actually, can we see the food menu, too? Is the kitchen still open?"

Adrian nodded and pulled out a black leather menu. "Sì. It's open until one."

Tony slid the two menus over to me. "Rachel, do you want anything?"

I read through the menus quickly, letting out a defeated sigh. My anxiety still tugged at me but I decided that one drink wouldn't kill me. "I'll have an Aperol Spritz and the fried calamari." My Italian was really rusty, so I was grateful for the English translations underneath the items.

"Jase?" Tony asked. "Anything for you?"

Jase shook his head.

Adrian raised an eyebrow but wrote the order down on a notepad. Our group dynamic clearly confused the bartender, but he handled it well—which was probably for the best. He walked to the other end of the bar to put in our order and help other customers.

Right at that moment, Jase came to my side, intense silence rolling off him in waves. Of course, he didn't order anything. He hadn't said a word since we pulled up to the club.

At least order a blood product, for God's sake. He's completely on edge from thirst.

I should've let him drink more from Tony. Regardless of my fear that he'd take too much, I didn't like this version of Jase. Being around him now felt almost more dangerous than how he behaved back in the church.

At least there, he showed me exactly who he was. But now? I couldn't read him at all. That obscurity over his intentions scared *and* annoyed me.

"You're not drinking?" I asked, hoping that the concern in my tone didn't provoke him. I wasn't expecting an answer until his voice echoed close by my ear.

"Alcohol dulls the senses, angel. Even for us. You should know that." His voice felt like silk against my ear as I turned toward him, his lips curling into that infuriating smirk again. "I prefer to stay alert tonight." His smile faded, replaced by something colder. "You never know if someone is watching you, ready to grab you when your guard is down. And no, I'm not hungry ... at the moment. You can quit looking at me the way you've been doing since we left the beach house."

My eyes narrowed at him. "Well, I suppose you would be an expert on *that*." I couldn't get a sense of what he was thinking beneath that threat. Something shifted significantly between us since I tasted his blood—and I found myself being drawn closer to him, in spite of his arrogance and fucking audacity. I hoped, in time, it would fade, and I could go back to hating him again.

"Suit yourself," I said, turning back to the bar and away from those piercing green eyes. My focus needed to be on anything other than *him*. Fuck, why did he smell so good? My eyes swept over the bar—drinks made, a mix of Italian, English, and other languages were melting into the throb of house music, and people were danc-ing behind us. Any of this should have been a welcome distraction, but no, my mind stubbornly kept going back to wondering what stupid Jasen Halpert was thinking.

Lucy shot me a look as Adrian returned with our drinks. She grabbed her mojito and took a long sip before speaking. "I'm going to dance for a bit," she said, sliding off her stool. Lucy then gave me a playful smile. "I suggest you join me *after* you eat, or we might be mopping up blood tonight. I've seen you when you're hungry."

She headed to the dance floor, blending into the crowd. At least Tony was still here with me.

"Alright, I'm joining her until my food is ready," Tony said suddenly. Before I could protest, he disappeared after Lucy. *Traitor.*

"Great," I muttered, taking a sip of my Aperol. "Just what I wanted."

"Don't act too excited," Jase quipped, a touch of dry humor in his tone. He leaned in closer, giving me zero space to avoid him. I tried to move back, but the counter's edge bumped my lower back. He'd caged me now between him and the bar.

"Why the hell are you hovering over me?" I asked, taking another sip of my drink. My throat was tight, and the smell of his cologne was goddamn delicious.

Jase's eyes locked on mine, and a lump started to form, strangling my breath. The look on his face was unnerving—piercing. Though he and Andrei shared similar jawlines and hair colors, that was where the comparisons stopped. While Andrei was incredibly handsome, Jase was breathtakingly gorgeous.

Stop thinking about his dumb face.

"I don't know. If you die or get kidnapped, I can't stop Andrei. I figure someone has to keep an eye on you," he said, sounding amused. "Might as well be me. You have a real talent for disobedience—and reckless stupidity, and I feel like I'm the only one who can rein it in."

"Oh, I'm sorry," I snapped back, sarcasm dripping over every word. "I'll try harder to be a good girl while we race to stop your brother from bringing about the end of the world."

Jase's smirk widened, and to my surprise, he laughed a little. "I never said you had to be a good girl." Those words flowed from his lips, and my mouth parted, heat rising between us despite his body being as cold as fucking ice.

I had to shake my thoughts away to think about my comeback.

I didn't have one.

"Well." I swallowed. "It's unlikely that something will happen while I sit here and eat fried squid."

Jase went to respond, but Adrian returned with a small plate of calamari, and Jase pressed his lips together instead.

Thank fuck. My stomach growled as the savory food hit my nose. I scooted away from Jase's looming figure but felt his eyes on my back as I settled on the chair to eat.

"What?" I snarled, looking over my shoulder. "Do you want a bite of my food or something? Do I need to order you a blood pack, so you chill the fuck out?"

He raised an eyebrow. "Bitchy isn't a good look on you."

"Looks like my plan to be repulsive to you is working," I muttered, biting into a crispy tentacle while letting the aioli drip down my mouth. "I'm glad you're getting the hint."

Every muscle of his seemed to tense, but he didn't move away from me. Trying to ignore his looming presence, I continued to eat my food.

He was way too damn close.

Before Jase could respond, Lucy came out from the crowd, her black hair hanging in pieces around her face. She looked impossibly gorgeous in that frazzled state.

"What did I just walk into?" she asked, her dark eyes darting from me to Jase. The look they shared caused me to pause.

What the hell was that?

"Rachel, you're too stressed. Dance floor. Now," Lucy ordered. "Whatever you're bottling up, you need to let it go."

Before I could answer, Jase held out his hand to me. "I'll take her."

Is he serious?

"Good enough for me. I'll see you out there. Tony will be back from his smoke break, and I need to find him before someone snatches him up." Lucy set her empty glass on the bar counter and danced back into the fray. I stared after her, dumbfounded.

"Come on, dance with me," Jase said, his mouth close to my ear. "We've done it before. Twice."

I frowned. "Against my will."

Jase's smile widened. "That's not a 'no.'"

I hesitated, staring at his hand. He was wearing black gloves now, and as my fingers brushed against his, a flood of memories hit me. But it wasn't from the masquerade ball Wendy erased from my mind but from the night in Andrei's club. Jase had been dancing behind me at the time, preventing me from seeing him. He wore Andrei's cologne, pretending to be him. Except that wasn't the only thing I remembered. Jase was sitting at the club bar before that. He wore the same gloves and intense look as he stared at me across the bar. That night, I was only a conquest and tool for a sadistic plan to awaken my mother and steal her ring. I didn't know then that I was staring into the eyes of a killer—a stalker—my worst fucking nightmare.

Jase waited for me to respond. When I didn't, his voice hardened. "I won't ask again. This isn't a request."

I pulled my hand away and turned back to the bar. I finished the last few pieces of calamari before grabbing my drink and slamming back the remaining liquid. Lowering the glass, I glanced at him. "One second."

Adrian was busy, but the second bartender, a slender Black woman with long braids draping over her right shoulder and wearing light pink lipstick, came over to collect the empty plate and take my order. I ordered two vodka shots, knowing that would be the quickest way to get through the night. She filled the shot glasses and slid them toward me. Jase reached for one, but I snatched them up and downed them back-to-back.

"Two more, please," I called, ignoring Jase's indignant face.

"Rachel," he scolded, his voice sharp with disapproval.

"Don't worry," I waved him off. "Alcohol is like water to me. I'll be sober within the hour. Perks of my heritage, remember?" I took the two shots and then turned to face him. I wished alcohol would have more of an instant effect, but I barely felt the softest tingle of a buzz in my head. For now, it had to be enough. "Okay, let's go."

Jase's jaw tightened, his expression hardening. His tense demeanor only lasted a moment before it softened, and he looked down at my outstretched hand. Then he took it gently and led me to the dance floor.

The music was at near deafening levels, and the pulsing beat mimicked my own pounding heart. I moved back to put some space between us and swayed to the rhythm, but it didn't last long. As the music hummed in my chest, Jase's hands settled on my waist, pulling me in. His body moved against mine, matching the pace of the music. My body was acting of its own accord, moving with him, leaning into his touch. It could have been the alcohol taking a more potent effect than I realized—or the tension between us since last night in the kitchen.

Or, to be honest, since that night in the church when his blood touched my tongue. The thought made me stumble a little.

"Angel," he said, his breath like ice against my ear. "Can you handle yourself, or will you need my help to walk by the end of the night?"

As if to emphasize his question, Jase pulled me even closer. His hands roamed over my shoulders, back, and hips like he wanted to memorize every curve of me. The flicker of emotions in his eyes told me he enjoyed this and hated it.

"You don't get to judge me," I shot back, arching against him.

"Oh, I think you're doing plenty of that yourself," he replied, his hands shamelessly trailing up to my chest. "Those perky little nipples are a clear sign that you're enjoying this, and you fucking hate it."

How dare—

I wanted to slap him for that remark, but the way he said "nipples" did something to my restraint that I *didn't* hate. A sudden pulse of wetness formed between my legs, and I pressed against him further.

Goddammit. Alcohol and stress are making me lose all self-control.

I was now hyper aware of every sensation between us—his gloved hands, cool breath, cologne, and energy radiating off his body. It was all too much, but I didn't care. I wanted to forget the fucked up world outside those doors and let go.

As I swayed my hips, the mark on my stomach flared, almost as if it were burning. I relished the sensation while our bodies moved in sync. The music—"The Sound of Silence" by Disturbed, remixed into a dubstep-techno beat—filled the crowded room, and the lights swallowed us whole.

My head fell back, and my eyes closed, shutting out the crowd. Jase's hand pressed against my back, keeping me upright. The vodka's effects were more potent now, clouding my mind, so I kept my eyes closed, lost in my bubble. My intuition ability was mercifully quiet as well.

Jase's breath skated over my exposed neck. Then his left hand slid down my back and cupped my ass.

And I let him do what he wanted. *Again.*

"Jase," I breathed, my eyes opening. He carefully removed his gloves and ran his hands through my hair before gripping it at the scalp possessively.

The realization quickly settled in my mind. A yelp escaped my lips as Jase yanked my head back, pressing his mouth to my neck. A wave of goosebumps covered my skin, and my pussy throbbed.

"Fuck," I swore, feeling his lips graze so close to my pounding vein. "Don't you dare fucking bite me." The sharp warning caused him to pause. His lips pulled away from my neck, and when I thought he was going to step away from me, Jase released my hair and spun me around so my ass pressed against his crotch. Jase was fucking hard for me.

My breath froze in my lungs as his cock pressed harder against me, twitching as I ground against him to the beat of the music. While one arm slid over my waist to keep me pinned, his other hand moved to the front of my dress before slowly lifting the hem, his fingers trailing to the seam of my underwear, sliding his fingertips beneath the fabric. Prodding. Testing. He wanted to see how far I'd let him go.

It feels so good. He's making my skin burn. I've never felt this much desire. I need to make him stop.

But I didn't want it to stop.

"Fuck it," I said, my alcohol-fueled bravery taking root. I leaned my head back, so my mouth was closer to his ear. "Yes."

The dance floor was dark, with only the strobing lights above. We were just a pair of intertwined shadows in a sea of rhythm. The crowd was so dense that no one would suspect what we were doing. Slowly, Jase eased his hand down between my legs. My wetness was soaking the fabric of my underwear, and I was sure I'd soon be dripping down my inner thigh. The tips of his index and middle fingers parted my opening, gently massaging where I needed it most. My lips fluttered as heat pulsed through my body. I could barely think. The arousal, music, vodka, his scent—it was all too much.

"I could already smell your arousal for me at the bar. Stop pretending to be afraid of me."

"I *am* afraid," I said honestly. But it wasn't because I thought Jase would kill me. It was because my feelings for him were suddenly shifting. Being so close to him now made it almost impossible to pretend they weren't. The desire for Jase to ram himself inside me and fuck me into oblivion was burning me alive.

As I leaned back against his chest, his fingers slipped inside me, his other hand wrapping around my stomach to keep me flush against him. Stars filled my vision as he pumped in and out while his thumb pressed and circled my clit. God, he knew all the right spots—how to pleasure me. That made sense since he watched me for four years. Watched as I touched myself on those lonely nights.

I can't believe we're doing this.

And in public.

And while his brother could quite literally walk through the door at any moment.

My heart pounded against my ribs, and I knew Jase could hear it. My body and mind betrayed each other. Shame and arousal warred within me, but I no longer knew which one I was angrier at.

I reached up and grabbed the back of his neck. His cologne and the delicious scent of his blood were driving me mad. The buzz in my head made me feel like I was about to collapse.

"I've got you," he whispered, fucking me harder now, faster. By now, some people likely could see what we were doing, but I didn't fucking care. I wasn't dancing anymore; I was shaking, barely hanging on as pleasure swirled through my body.

"Oh, fuck," I cried out as my orgasm crashed through me. I sank my teeth into my bottom lip to stifle the moans, but it was useless. My moans remained muffled as I shook against him.

"Jesus, your cries are fucking beautiful," Jase said, pressing his lips to my jawline and trailing down. "But try not to scream too loud."

As my pleasure started to fade, his teeth sank into the crook of my shoulder. That sensation unleashed a renewed wave of euphoria that stole my breath completely.

I bit down harder on my lower lip as he fed on my blood, my drenched pussy clenching around his fingers as he thrust mercilessly. The music was a dull roar in my ears, and nothing existed outside of Jase's rough touch.

Yes, I told him not to bite me only minutes ago, but as he drank from me, that hesitation melted away completely. *This* was *so* different from Andrei. He only fed from me for control, pleasure, and the addictive taste of my dhampir blood. What Jase had just done was different. I couldn't explain why; it just ... was.

His fingers slowed like he was savoring every fucking second of me clenched against him. Jase's fingers felt like heaven.

"More," I said. No, I *begged*. "Take more."

Jase's lips pulled into a smile against my skin before he sank deeper into my vein. Euphoria gripped me like a vise. By now, the haze of vodka wrapped me in a fog of ecstasy, losing myself in it. Jase *owned* my body then.

My eyes fluttered open, and I saw Lucy approaching us through the throngs of oblivious humans. The sensation of cold water splashed over me as I grabbed Jase's wrist and pulled his hand out from under my underwear. Understanding the hint, he pulled his fangs out of my neck. There was a sudden feeling of loss as he moved away. When Lucy reached us, her eyes went wide as she saw my healing puncture wounds and the bloodstain on my dress straps.

"Holy shit," she said, glaring at Jase behind me with murder in her eyes. "Do I need to kill him?"

I shook my head, which made the room spin. "No," I told her. "He ... I ..." I wanted to tell her I'd let him. "I need some air."

I pushed through the crowd toward the back door near the bathroom. No one noticed me as I ran by. I didn't want to look back.

When I touched the handle, I felt two hands grip my shoulders, spinning me around. Jase's eyes, those emerald eyes that seemed to swallow me whole, looked dark and intense. He pinned me against the wall aggressively, pressing against my body as I attempted to free myself. His expression was so unreadable that a feeling of dread pulled at my stomach.

And then he kissed me.

And I let him.

CHAPTER 36

JASE

Rachel melted into my body, but as she did, guilt gripped me by the fucking throat. I took her blood while she was wasted, and the monster in me didn't want to stop. I had to have her—all of her—even if she resisted and fought against me.

But right now, she didn't. Rachel kissed me back, the taste of her mouth blending with the sweetness of her blood on my tongue.

Her hand slid to the back of my head as I pressed into her, fingers tightening in my hair at the scalp. *Fuck.*

I was so fucking hard for her, my dick painfully straining against my jeans.

One of my hands reached down and cupped her ass, lifting her up on the wall while our bodies remained flush. With my knee between her thighs to keep her still, my other hand gripped both her wrists and pinned them above her head while I continued to taste her mouth, like it was made for my lips.

Over the last four years of watching Rachel in the shadows, I'd imagined what it would feel like to have her lips against mine. I only had a taste of that when she drank from me, but nothing—and I mean nothing—could compare to what was happening now.

As we kissed against the wall, my mind told me to stop. Why was Rachel so eager to kiss me back? Was it because she was drunk, or was it because of the bond's influence? I'd earned nothing from her. She *shouldn't* want this.

And neither should I.

The screaming voice in my head begged me to let her go. But then the burning sensation of the rune on my stomach flared to life, silencing it. It was a cruel reminder that our paths weren't ours to choose—whether it was an angel, fate, or some twisted cosmic joke that did this to us. There was no escaping my feelings for Rachel, no matter how hard I wanted to fight them.

This wasn't me. I didn't do *love* or relationships. For years, I believed my soul was gone forever. Valentina ripped the humanity from me when I asked her to turn me into a vampire. How could I possibly feel so strongly about someone?

If Valentina was telling the truth, how much of my broken soul would be present right now to allow the possibility of something happening between Rachel and me?

The more she moaned against my mouth, the more guilt squeezed me.

Doubt ultimately won, and I broke the kiss, releasing her, and pulled away from that warm mouth. Then I stepped farther back, my eyes taking her in. Regardless of her swollen pink lips and heaving breasts, the way she glared at me warned me not to try it again. Rachel still had her back pressed to the wall, and her hands trembled slightly. I couldn't tell if she was mad that I kissed her or pulled away so quickly. Maybe she believed she repulsed me.

Quite the opposite. It took all of my willpower not to grab Rachel and fuck her right there in front of everyone.

A heavy silence hung between us, and my quickened breaths matched hers as I watched her expression turn into an even deadlier scowl.

She wanted to slap me.

Maybe even kill me.

"Get back on the dance floor without me," I ordered, my voice cold and distant.

There. I made the decision for you.

"This was a big fucking mistake," I added.

I didn't want to see the look on her face as I hurried away from her, heading outside to calm the fuck down.

The cool evening air greeted me as I stepped onto the concrete pad near the parking lot. I looked around, spotting a couple of humans hanging out on the covered patio. They had the same idea as I did.

The fresh air felt good, and I took a deep breath, hoping it would quell the raging storm in my gut ... and dick. I leaned against a crumbling alley wall, taking several more breaths to calm down. The taste of Rachel's blood lingered on my tongue. She tasted like sweet honey and power that threatened to undo me.

What the hell was I thinking?

The bond was a tethered chain, dragging me toward her, but this wasn't how it was supposed to be. Rachel deserved better than this—more than the beast I'd let myself become. And tonight, I'd let it win. Kissing her was bad enough. Drinking from her while she was drunk off her ass? I was no better than my damn brother.

The sound of footsteps against the nearby cobblestone walkway caused me to pause my thoughts. I didn't have to look up to know who it was. Tony and Lucy—Rachel's little shadows. *Did she send them?*

"Are you fucking serious?" Lucy hissed as she stopped in front of me. She crossed her arms, the glint of her fangs visible under the neon sign above her. "You drank from her, Jase? And even worse, in front of everyone. Thankfully, they were all too drunk to notice, or we'd be knee-deep in shit. But getting caught is beside the point. If you want to prove yourself to her, taking her blood in that state isn't the way to do it. That's how you lose her trust." She took one step closer to me, daring and bold. "Unless you're *trying* to drive her away."

I straightened, my jaw tight. "I don't give a *fuck* what either of you think. You're forgetting my true nature. I'm a vampire. Didn't Andrei and his clan teach you anything while you were under their roof? I've been undead for two hundred years. This is what we are: hungry predators. You can fight that shit all you want. But you are just like us now."

Lucy lunged at me, but Tony quickly raised his arm and pressed his palm against her chest, pushing her back. "You tell Rachel what Valentina shared with you, or *we* will," he warned. "It's taking a lot of fucking control for us to listen to your request and keep our mouths shut. Especially when you're losing control and biting her in public."

My glare burned into his as a growl rumbled low in my chest. "Careful, human. You tell her before I do, and I'll snap your neck before you even blink."

"Try it, asshole," Tony shot back. *Brave ... brave little human.* "Rachel isn't a damn toy. She's been through more shit than anyone else here. Her life has been nothing but betrayals and fucking trauma. She deserves the truth … now.”

Lucy's eyes narrowed, her voice a sharp whip. “You have until Athens. As Tony said, she's been through enough, especially with being lied to. We went along with this because that fucking tool you call a brother is going to hurt her. But it has to stop. If you don't tell her soon, *we* are going to.”

I balled my fists at my sides. “It's not your decision.”

“I'll make it my decision!” Lucy snapped. “She's going to figure it out eventually, and the longer you drag your feet on this, the more she will hate you for keeping it from her. Fuck, she'll hate *us,* her best friends, for knowing and not telling her the moment we found out … that is *if* your deranged ass is telling the truth.”

Their words hit me, but I'd be damned if I let them see how much it bothered me. Instead, I glared at them both, not backing down. “I'll tell Rachel when it's time,” I said finally, my voice low and stern. “But that time isn't tonight.”

I went to walk away, but Tony grabbed my shoulder, catching me off-guard and shoving me against the brick wall. “Listen to me, you two-bit mosquito fuck,” he growled. “You watched Rachel for years, *years*, and you still don't realize how vulnerable she is? How much she hurts all the damn time? Rachel grew up as a goddamn science experiment for a prejudiced magic cult. If I had known Andrei was working with those monsters, I would have never left her with him, and I will live with that regret for the rest of my life. Rachel has been lied to, manipulated, and used her entire life. By the Black Onyx, by Andrei, and by *you*.”

My body tensed at those words, but before I could open my mouth to respond, he kept going.

"I was her guardian for almost nine years. I tried to be as open and honest with her about everything as much as I could because I saw how secrets broke her heart. And those fucking witches forced me out, letting your brother weasel his way into becoming her guardian and adding another chain to that collar. So, I'm asking you, as one of her best friends, her *brother*, please don't keep this fated mates stuff from her anymore. Tell her, so she can make her own goddamn decision on her life, her *fate,* for once."

Unfamiliar guilt rendered me utterly silent.

Tony shook his head, muttering something under his breath before leaving me with Lucy. Her deadly stare bore into me, and I wanted to push it away.

"I've known Rachel for just as long," she said. "I've seen her loneliness, even before learning she was a dhampir. That woman deserves better than the hell given to her. You're going to break her if you keep this up." Her voice was softer now but no less firm. "And if you do, I'll make you wish you hadn't."

She turned and followed Tony back inside, leaving me alone in the alley with nothing but my guilt and the faint echo of Rachel's laughter inside the club that my vampiric hearing picked up immediately.

Laughter? What the fuck is she doing?

I hurried inside and down the hall, spotting Rachel on the dance floor. Now she wasn't alone. Behind her was some dickhead with medium-beige skin and a shaved head, his arm wrapping around her waist from behind ... like I had. The guy leaned in and nipped her neck with his teeth while his right hand slid up to try to grab her breast. *The fuck?* I was about to use my vampiric speed to run toward him and snap his neck, but Rachel had already spun around, her elbow coming up and ramming it into the guy's nose.

Oh, shit.

"Bitch!" the guy cursed, holding his bloody nose before he reached out to grab her. Before she could move, I rushed toward them, grabbed the offending wrist, and crushed it into pieces.

"You don't get to put your hands on her body and still have them by the end of the night," I growled. "No one touches her."

The man's wailing blended with the music and gasps from the dancers around us. When Rachel turned to look at me, her eyes were wide as saucers, and she gaped. Instead of thanking me, she slapped me so hard across the face that my head physically whipped to the side.

That one hurt. Fuck!

"I don't need you protecting me," she seethed. "I *had* him."

The guy continued to cry like a little bitch beside us and attempted to throw another hand, but I reached out and caught it, twisting his last good wrist and threatening to break that one, too.

"I don't care if you did," I seethed through my teeth, barely able to control my temper now. "I'm well fucking aware of your strength. This asshole shouldn't put his goddamn hands or filthy mouth on you."

"That's enough!" Rachel cried out. "I'm not yours, *Jase.* You don't get to decide that." I turned to look at her, and her bright blue eyes seemed to grab my sanity. "He's just a human. Let it go."

I shook my head, trying to ignore the fact that Rachel's pull on me might destroy us both. Fighting it felt pointless now, but letting these feelings go wasn't any easier. I wanted to protect her, to keep her safe from everything—even me. But deep down, I knew I couldn't. Not when I felt this way. Not when every part of me was already hers ... she just didn't know it yet.

Instead of breaking the guy's wrist like I wanted to, I slowly turned to him and bared my fangs, feeling the veins under my eyes turn dark.

The guy's eyes widened when he realized what I was and nodded. "Va bene, me ne vado," he said, turning to Rachel. "Mi dispiace."

I swallowed, released his fist, and stepped back, giving her another look. Tony and Lucy were watching us from the bar, horrified and frantically waving for us to get the fuck out of there. "Time to leave."

She nodded, her jaw set. I wasn't sure what she saw in my eyes, but whatever it was, she understood not to press me any further. For all her vulnerability, she was stronger than I'd given her credit for because the Rachel I had seen over the last four years wouldn't have caved so easily.

I took her hand and ran out of the club into the night.

CHAPTER 37

RACHEL

O nce we returned to the house, I walked over to the windows and slid them shut. After I flipped the locks, I gazed outside at the beach and the endless black of sea and sky. The sand appeared white with deep-blue shadows, painting another world on top of our own.

I was barely registering the scene before me, my mind returning to Jase. His eyes hadn't left me since we fled the club, and I did everything I could to pretend I didn't see him but failed miserably. The memory of what we did while dancing kept replaying in my head during the drive and the very slow walk back up the front steps. It was like a heated, twisted loop of images—his firm hands touching me, his fangs in my neck, the sensation of being claimed.

Frustration welled up, and I balled my fists—and thighs—I should have left the dance floor when things got too intense. Now it was all I could think about.

I *shouldn't* have allowed that to happen. But I did. Why?

Jase wasn't my friend. But as the question lingered, I had to admit the truth: I wasn't even sure if he was still my enemy.

Lucy vanished down the hall while the rest of us unpacked a few things we'd left at the door when we first arrived—water bottles, snacks, and anything else we could scrounge up for the night.

She and Tony have been extra cautious regarding Jase being around me.

It was likely because Jase bit me on the dance floor and Lucy was ready to punch him in the throat for that. They didn't want him to lose control again. I never told them that I gave him permission to drink from me. Granted, I was drunk.

"I'm not going to sleep, but I might close my eyes for a while," Lucy said, coming back into the room. "Not that it does much, but it can help with recharge, and we'll need our energy tomorrow. Staying up all night just because I can is also boring as hell."

"I'll take the couch," Tony added. "Rachel, you take the other bed." He nodded at Jase. "Just keep the lights off, and I'll fall asleep fine."

After discussing our plans for the next morning, I found extra blankets in the hall closet and set them up for Tony before heading back to the bedroom. Lucy changed into her sweatpants and tank top, slipping under the covers on the other twin bed. I noticed Jase heading toward the simply furnished office down the hall, decorated with beach-themed knickknacks and a chair facing the large window overlooking the sea. I needed sleep, too, but the sounds of the waves were more appealing. Remembering Jase's solitary walk earlier, I decided that was what I probably needed, too.

An hour passed before I got out of bed, my legs tangled up in the sheets before I slipped out the back door. I needed space to breathe, and being inside the house with Jase only twenty feet away wasn't where I wanted to be. The cool night air would clear my mind. The thought of the ocean and the waves crashing against the shore felt like the only escape from the constant battle inside my head.

Once outside, I walked down the wooden stairs and stepped onto the sand, the grainy texture pressing against my bare feet. I closed my eyes, breathing in deeply. The saltwater filled my lungs, the wind caressing me gently and pushing the loose strands of my braid from my face. I allowed myself to enter a meditative state, a familiar exercise the coven taught me to keep me grounded.

After a few minutes of deep breathing, I opened my eyes and glanced up at the office windows Jase had been brooding by earlier. He was no longer there. Although my anxiety had lessened, what happened at the club left me deeply conflicted.

"Taking another nightly walk sounds like a great idea. I'll join you," Jase said, his smooth, irritatingly calm voice causing an involuntary ripple down my spine and my stomach to twist.

Though Jase being here wasn't the worst thing, I let out a frustrated breath. "That would defeat the purpose of walking alone. You had your time earlier. It's my turn."

There was no way I'd admit to him or myself that his presence was oddly relaxing.

He laughed at my remark. A dark sound that only made my irritation grow even as my shoulders eased.

Jase had a nice laugh.

"You're not walking alone," he said.

I whirled around, eyes flashing with annoyance. "Sorry, *Daddy*, I need some space from you."

"Funny," he said, "considering how you let me finger fuck you on the dance floor. I doubt space is your top priority."

My chest tightened, and my cheeks burned red from embarrassment and something else. I bit my lip. "That was a mistake. Just like you said before pushing off me and leaving me standing there alone," I muttered. "It was a mistake that won't happen again."

His green eyes glinted in the moonlight like emeralds as he drew near. "I don't think you believe that for a second. The moans you made are a little contradictory to that statement."

I opened my mouth to argue, but Jase was right there before I could, his hand cupping my left cheek. The words died on my tongue as he suddenly crashed his lips against mine like he'd done in the club when he had me pinned against the wall. His other hand tangled in my hair, pulling my head closer as he deepened the kiss.

No. No. No.

I fucking hated that I liked it.

It was nothing like the kiss at the club, though. This kiss was rougher, more demanding, a silent claim that made every part of me burn with wanton need.

When he pulled back, I couldn't catch my breath. "Stop doing that. What the fuck do you want from me?"

"You." His voice was a promise, low and unwavering. "Just … you."

"Me?"

"Well, maybe not when you're being a brat, like right now," he smirked, and I gaped at him.

"Talk about contradictory. You kissed me at the club and then pulled back like I burned you, right before you ran away like a little bitch," I retorted, but then I instantly regretted how harsh that sounded.

His expression hardened as he wrapped his hand around my throat, pulling me closer. He slammed my body against his, gripping my hair tighter in his fist. The possessiveness of his hold sent a rush of heat through my body, igniting something deep within me. "For the longest time, I told myself all I wanted was to kill you," he confessed, his voice rough. "I thought I could convince myself it was revenge, but it was never about that. I'm not afraid to admit that anymore."

My heart raced in my chest as his thumb grazed the edge of my jaw. "Let go of me," I demanded, even though every part of me didn't want him to.

A wicked, slow smile tugged at his lips. "You really want me to?"

He traced my lips with his thumb, pausing as if savoring the moment. Then, with gentle pressure, he pressed down on my lower lip, parting my mouth ever so slightly. His feather-light touch sent a welcoming shiver straight down my spine again; his gaze locked onto mine. It felt like a storm brewing in the depths of his beautiful eyes, making my pulse quicken.

I glared at him, and my breath grew shallow. The anger I wanted to feel melted under the weight of his touch, and I swallowed hard. I couldn't even bring myself to respond. The words I wanted to say would be a lie, yet the truth would betray me.

"I thought so." His smile deepened. "Because you feel it, too?"

I shook my head, ready to deny everything. How could I admit what I felt to the man who had disrupted my life so severely not that long ago? This feeling of being drawn to him couldn't be real.

Jase's lips brushed mine again before I could stop him, and this time, the kiss was ruthless—leaving me fighting for air.

I told myself to push Jase away, to fight back, but my body had other ideas. Instead, wetness pooled between my legs. Before I could clench my thighs together, Jase's hand released my hair and slid down my body, and he ran his palm gingerly up my inner thigh, stopping right between my legs. His grip on my neck tightened just enough to keep me grounded, and I melted into him as he rubbed my pussy, my pajama shorts creating a barrier of friction to his touch. As the pleasure built, my hands fisted his shirt, pulling me closer.

"We're going to finish what we started in that club," he breathed against my lips as he released the kiss. "Lay the fuck down, angel. I have to taste you."

It was pretty obvious in his tone he wasn't talking about my blood. Slowly, against my better judgment, I kneeled against the sand and settled my back on the ground, the grains getting into my long hair.

Jase didn't waste a moment teasing me—I wanted him to take me immediately. It was as if he needed this more than anything and was ready to take it. He slid my shorts down my legs, taking a moment to admire me, and then he settled himself in between my thighs, his breathing heavy as he inhaled my aroused scent.

"You have no idea how much I have wanted to do this...." he professed. It was an unexpected confession. I barely had the time to draw in a breath, let alone say anything, before he used his fangs to snip the fabric of my panties and began feasting on my wet pussy.

Oh my God.

His tongue found my clit, circling it mercilessly and stimulating me in all the ways I loved. My finger knotted into his wind-whipped black hair, my eyes rolling back into my skull as I struggled not to scream in pleasure. It felt good.

So fucking good.

My body was entirely under his control, and at that moment, I didn't want to have it any other way. Waves of bliss rose through me, crashing against the very essence of my being. Soon, it became apparent that his tongue wasn't enough; he needed to touch me more.

Fuck yes.

Jase pushed two fingers into my soaked entrance and rammed them inside just as fiercely, almost like he wanted to both please and punish me.

My lips parted, but it was nothing but heavy gasps. I was shaking. My body was shaking beneath his hands and mouth. I needed him closer.

His mouth and fingers weren't enough. I raised my hips, grinding them into Jase's face and prompting him to take more of me.

And oh *God,* he did.

He brought me to the heights of pleasure that had one of my hands fly to my mouth, only to prevent a scream that would have undoubtedly broken from my lips as my orgasm struck. Unexpectedly, hard and fast. I squirmed desperately, lost in the whirlpool of pleasure that wouldn't release its hold on me. My entire body was trembling, but Jase didn't stop.

Instead, he seemed determined to draw out the pleasure as much as he could, reminding me I belonged to him at *that* moment. The pleasure dragged on and on until my vision swam.

Then and only then did he release me, his lips glistening beneath the moonlight.

A lingering thrill hit me as I came down from the high, reminding me that this wouldn't be the last time, no matter how much I didn't want to admit it.

I wanted more.

CHAPTER 38

RACHEL

I got *very* little sleep that night. I still felt Jase's hands on my thighs, his mouth, the way his tongue slid into me. My mind drifted in and out of restless dreams, playing out a hundred different scenarios for the morning. Would we talk about it? Should I tell Lucy what happened?

I shut my eyes as the sun poured into the room, deciding to pretend it didn't happen—at least until Jase and I were alone again. Then, maybe, we'd figure out what this meant.

The heat was already seeping through the cracked window, a reminder of how unbearably hot the day would be. I missed having two fans right in my face while I slept.

My hair was still damp from the shower I took last night to wash out the sand that had stuck to it; my natural curls were basically a ball of frizzy mess. I pulled on a pair of workout shorts and a black tank top, twisting my hair into a loose bun. Makeup didn't seem worth the effort—not when we'd be spending the day and most of the night on a ferry.

As usual, Jase and Lucy covered themselves to shield their skin, rushing to the car to sit behind the special glass. Once we reached the port, they didn't linger, disappearing below deck as soon as we boarded.

The nine-hour ferry ride was pretty uneventful. While Jase and Lucy stayed below until sundown, Tony and I spent most of the time on the balcony. A gentle sea breeze made the heat somewhat tolerable. It no longer bothered me as much while I looked across the endless blue ocean; its shimmering beauty calmed my thoughts.

Tony and I had a chance to speak alone for the first time in months. It had been one thing after another since we left Venice, and I hadn't realized how much I had missed talking to him. We fell into an easy conversation. He updated me on our coworkers at Lune de Blanche, and I told him all about the other dhampirs I met and how kind and generous they were. I silently pleaded to whoever was listening above that they were safe.

"What's going on with you and Jase?" Tony asked suddenly, catching me off guard.

Why the hell would he ask that?

Maybe Jase and I hadn't been as careful as I'd thought. The idea of Tony and Lucy finding out about what happened between us made me feel ashamed.

When Tony kept staring, waiting for an answer, I could only say, "I don't know."

It was the truth. I still didn't know what to make of everything that had happened. The club, the beach—it replayed in my mind. But I'd also be lying if I said I didn't enjoy it.

A lot.

Tony didn't press the subject further, and we quickly changed topics.

When the captain announced we were close to docking in Igoumenitsa, Lucy and I managed to grab one last drink together. Occasionally, I'd catch Jase watching me from the other side of the room. I wondered if he was avoiding me, too, or if he simply didn't understand why I was still so cautious with him.

We keep dancing around each other. At some point, one of us will break entirely.

"Lucy, I need you to do me a favor," I said, putting my glass on the small table between us. "You need this weapon more than I do. Take it." She raised her eyebrows as I carefully reached into my bag and pulled the Gunslinger revolver into my lap.

"Wait. Why are you giving me this?" she asked. "You said that only you can use the gun."

I shrugged. "The gun will only work for the true bearer. That's now you. All you need to do is recite, 'I invoke the rite of the Gunslinger,' and the spell will recognize you as its new owner. You're powerful enough, but you'll need a weapon like this if something happens."

Lucy stared at me briefly before nodding. Since no one was nearby to raise an alarm, I quickly slid the weapon across to her. She placed her hand on top of it and said, "Thank you."

With one quick glance around, she picked it up and tucked it into the waistband of her jeans. I smiled and reached for her hand, giving it a gentle squeeze. Lucy grinned back, and we tapped our glasses together before downing the rest of our drinks.

Tony came over and nudged my shoulder as we pulled into the dock. "Ready?" he asked.

We both nodded, and I watched Jase grab my bags with his own, so I wouldn't have to carry anything—an unusually kind gesture coming from him.

When he walked by, he stopped beside me, and in a rare moment of civility, he said, "I'd like to head to Fiskardo once we check into the hotel in Lefkada. I'll be back before you guys wake up. Then we can head to Athens."

I wondered about that, knowing Jase and Andrei's childhood home was only a few hours and a ferry ride from the hotel. It made sense for him to want to stop there.

"Yeah, I figured as much," I said, reaching for my bag, but he shifted to the side, not letting me take it. "Come on. I can carry my own bag, Jase."

He smiled faintly before replying, "I know ... but not today."

Once we picked up the new rental car and continued the hour-and-a-half drive to the hotel, Tony looked up in the rearview mirror at Jase. "I don't think it's a good idea for you to detour to Fiskardo. Let's just rest for a few hours and then keep going. We've stopped way too many times already."

"I'm going," Jase said. His tone seemed agitated as he ran a hand through his messy, dark hair. My heart fluttered, and a tight knot formed in my stomach.

Tony was right, though—we needed to keep moving. But I also knew Tony arguing with Jase was pointless. If Jase wanted something, he'd get it.

My intuitive ability sprang to life without prompting, reaching for Jase's intent.

Sadness ... and homesickness. Pain and guilt.

I experienced it all as if the feelings were my own.

Months ago, I wouldn't have felt a thing for the man I once called my enemy. But something changed over the past few days. We had changed. I didn't know if it was because I had opened myself up to him intimately or something deeper lurking beneath the surface, just out of reach. All I knew was that his face had haunted my dreams ever since the church. It was his face I saw when fear crept in. His face I thought of when heat curled in my stomach.

Now, standing this close, the pull between us was so intense I could barely separate my own emotions from his. And the strangest part was that I wasn't afraid of him anymore. I knew that with absolute certainty now. Instead, I was drawn to him—to whatever he was, to whatever *this* was.

"It's been over two hundred years since I've been so close," he reminded us. "I'm not asking for permission, *human*. You guys wouldn't be here if it weren't for me. Sleep, and I'll be back before sunrise."

Lucy sighed and turned to me to gauge my reaction. "Do they even run the ferries this late to Kefalonia Island? You won't get there until almost eight," she noted.

"I already looked into it," he said. "There are two ferries that leave at night specifically for vampires. Once the treaty reached Europe, they made it work for those who *couldn't* travel by day. It's not that convenient to stay constantly below deck. It makes people nervous."

"Gotcha," Lucy replied. "Well—"

"Rachel's coming with me, too," Jase said with a smirk, cutting her off, and my head jerked over to him. "She can make sure I don't get lost."

My stomach did another flip. Going to Jase's hometown wasn't some stroll on the beach with my friends in the house beside us; I'd be traveling alone with him.

"Rachel?" Lucy called, and I looked at her. "It's up to you."

"Seriously?"

Tony's nostrils flared slightly before he added, "Yeah. What do you want to do?"

Well, I wasn't expecting them to be so comfortable with me going alone with him. Especially after last night.

But something told me that Jase, alone in the place where his brother brutally murdered his parents, probably wasn't the best idea without someone there strong enough to reel him back in.

"Alright, fine," I said. "I'll make sure we're back before morning."

I couldn't believe I was entertaining this for Jase, of all people. But my instinct pressed harder against his aura, almost demanding that I do this. If something was drawing us together, being alone with him again might help me get some answers.

⁓⁓⁓

I lost track of how many cups of coffee the ferry staff served me, but I swore I could hear colors. I finished my drink and leaned back in my seat. Even though I had gripes about being dragged along, I knew in my gut that this visit was important for Jase. What happened to his family left a gaping wound in his heart that never stopped bleeding.

No matter what he's done, he deserves closure.

If Andrei had been sitting here on the same quest, I would have understood and supported that, too. I never had the luxury of a mom and dad raising me and treating me like family. Being raised by a coven of witches and guardians wasn't the same, so I couldn't even imagine what an actual loving home and family felt like.

Jase sat across the aisle from me, his head leaning against the glass and looking out into the sea. Though it was so dark out into the water now, aside from the small lights coming off the boat, he seemed focused on something out there. After we parted from Tony and Lucy, he'd been quiet, almost nervous. I kept fighting the urge to offer him a bit of comfort. Only a handful of vampires and a few human companions were aboard the ferry tonight, settling quietly in their booths. It made the atmosphere suddenly feel heavy.

This awkward silence has been fucking killing me. Why am I having such a hard time talking to Jase? I've been able to give him a piece of my mind plenty of times before. Maybe because he ate me out for dinner on the beach last night, and we still haven't talked about it, even after that long-ass ferry ride from Italy.

Not to mention what happened at the club. Since that night, something had changed in how I hated Jase—or *thought* I hated him. Now I wasn't sure what the hell I felt. On the dance floor, I was drunk off my ass; I wasn't thinking clearly. But at the beach house last night, I was stone-cold sober. We made our choice, fully aware of what we were doing and the consequences that could follow. Jase had also helped get us out of Venice and had been guiding us to this damn cave. But I couldn't figure out this "change of heart." He bombed the Black Diamond, stole the key and the Book of Shadows from Andrei, and protected me from that handsy asshole from the club.

Even though I had that prick. I already broke his nose, for fuck's sake.

I don't get any of this.

The crackling voice over the intercom jolted me upright. "Kalispéra, ladies and gentlemen. This is your captain speaking. We've enjoyed having you here with us today. We'll be docking at your destination of Fiskardo, Greece. Please watch your step when you exit. We'll have brochures at the far left table for any-one visiting here for the first time with restaurant and sightseeing recommendations come morning for those who can go in the sun. For your safety, please stay seated while we dock, and keep your belongings close until we come to a complete stop. The last ferry will leave at six a.m."

Rising slowly, Jase stretched, his toned stomach visible beneath his black shirt. My throat went a little dry, and my core ached. I averted my eyes and busied myself, putting my book back into my small backpack.

"Was it good?" Jase's voice broke through my thoughts, and I turned to look at him.

"Excuse me?"

"The book you're reading. Was it good?"

We had stopped at a local bookshop before heading to the docks. I was worried we'd have nothing to talk about, so I needed some-thing to occupy the time.

I smiled, feeling a little awkward, but held up the book, displaying its elegant gold-and-blue cover. "Yeah, it is, actually," I answered with a smile. "The main character's a total badass—a queen with uncontrollable magic. Once you get to the twist, you find out about this dark force threatening to destroy the planet, and the sexy love interest is kind of the perfect balance to all the chaos she's dealing with. I'm only a fourth of the way through, but I like it."

Jase smiled, and my heart flipped at how warm it was, even for an asshole like him.

"You like to read, too?" I asked, tucking the book back in the bag and zipping it closed.

Jase shrugged. "I did as a child. We didn't have much back then, but Mamá always made sure I got at least a book for my birthday. Andrei used to tease me about it. After I turned, I stopped reading for fun for a long time. I only started again recently when I had to kill time during the four years in New Orleans." A playful smile tugged at his lips. Though I wanted to scowl at the reference to his stalking extracurricular activities, I didn't.

Before I could respond, a chime rang through the boat, and everyone around us rose and made their way to the gangplanks. I stood quickly and moved toward the aisle where Jase was.

"Tell you what," I started. "When this bullshit's over, I'll lend you this. Plus, it touches on Greek mythology that you might enjoy."

Jase blinked his annoyingly lovely eyes at my offer. *What am I doing?*

Once off the ferry, we headed into the town. A loud mix of tourists and locals filled the streets as restaurants geared up for dinner, and the aroma of salt, fish, and spices wafted in the air. My stomach growled at the scent of food, and Jase snickered at the noise.

"While I don't particularly miss human hunger, I miss the food here. After all these years of picturing it, I can still smell and taste it." He flashed me another playful smile before adding, "Come on. My family's farm is only a mile away, and if we move *quickly*, we'll get there in minutes."

Jase moved to a shadowy part of a house and waited for me to catch up. When no one was paying attention, we used our vampiric speed and raced toward his old village.

∼℮℮∼

Most of the city had gone inside to have dinner with their families. Jase's jaw tightened as he drew a slow breath, steadying himself while we stepped onto the path leading into the woods toward the house.

"Are you okay?" I asked, moving closer to his side. His scent filled my nose and made my cheeks warm. The mark on my stomach itched again, causing me to rub the spot.

I'm so close to burning this damn thing off.

"Yeah. It's been ... a long fucking time. The village looks almost the same as when I was a kid. It even smells the same." He shook his head. "I mean, sure, it's changed over the past two hundred years, but somehow ... it's still here." A small silence lingered before he looked at me. "This way. My parents' house is down the road as it curves around the bend. Of course, it used to be a donkey trail. I don't know if the house is still standing, though."

As we walked, the silence stretched between us again. The stars glittered in the navy blue-black sky, and the sounds of the sea were soothing as hell. If I weren't with my *former* enemy, I'd find this adventure pretty damn romantic. This silence was irritating the fuck out of me, though.

"This broody persona of yours is driving me nuts, Jase," I started, spinning on my heel to face him as I walked backward. "You've been weird since the beach house, so why not indulge me and talk? Why was it so important we came to Fiskardo? I know you and Andrei were born here and that my mother … caused the murder of your family. But why come back? Wouldn't that reopen a dark, hidden wound?" Jase's eyes turned toward the night sky. I elbowed his side and offered an encouraging smile. "Come on. Talk to me."

"Closure, I guess," he replied and stopped. That was my guess, too, but to hear the words leave his lips was odd. I stood in front of him and scanned his face. In the darkness, I saw the grief, the pain that burned beneath his skin. This was the first time he showed an emotion that wasn't cold and cruel. He looked so human. "I want to see my mother's garden one last time. I want to know if it's still there after everything. When my normal life ended."

His anguish stabbed through me like a blade to the heart. Andrei had told me about that night—how he killed his parents, his wife, his child. But he never said what happened to Jase.

Jase had been there. He had seen the carnage. He *survived* it.

As a child, he had borne the scars of my mother's violence, her evil. And for centuries, he had carried that weight alone.

For once, I didn't know what to say.

As we approached the curve, a dilapidated farmhouse appeared near a grove of trees. Jase took a sharp breath and stopped.

"This is it," he said in a tight voice, his eyes looking up. "The dock where my father's boat used to be is gone, but everything else is still here. The house ..." His eyes lingered on the crumbling structure. "It looks like shit. But after a monster from hell tore through this place, I guess I shouldn't be surprised."

A signpost to the left of the building caught my eye, and I went toward it. There weren't any security cameras, and I couldn't sense any protection magic to keep out intruders. When I reached the sign, I noticed it was written in Greek.

Of all the languages I had learned throughout my life, Greek wasn't one of them.

"Can you translate?" I asked.

He came to my side and read the first few lines of the sign: "Welcome to the Bakirtzis Healing Garden. Growing wild since 1805. We preserved this garden to honor Aine Sofia Bakirtzis, a renowned healer in Fiskardo, and the good she did for her family and community. Please visit this place at your leisure, but do not remove any plants without permission from council members. —The Fiskardo Municipal Council."

God, the garden lasted this long intact.

Clearly, he shared the opinion, too. "Holy shit, they kept the garden after *two hundred years*," Jase said, shoving his shaking hands into his jeans pockets. "The witches and humans who lived in the village kept it safe."

"They must have loved her," I replied, motioning with my head. "Let's go look."

We walked past the farmhouse toward the back of the property. A fairly new shed sat next to a fenced garden that stretched the length of a football field.

My jaw dropped slightly. "This is stunning. She built all this?" I asked, moving to the fence and inhaling deeply to take in the herbal scents. "Marjoram, lemon balm, sage, and ...?"

"Sideritis, or 'Greek Mountain Tea,'" Jase answered, coming to my side. "There's a gate to go inside. Come on."

We walked down to a small iron gate that opened into the garden and entered. It was so quiet, as if a glass bubble had fallen over us. My magic tingled in my fingertips, and a strange peace filled my chest. I followed Jase deeper into the garden until we found a small bench surrounded by lavender and echinacea flowers. Jase swallowed hard before sitting down.

"Hey, are you okay?" I knew asking him that again was stupid, but I couldn't help myself. For some reason, I wanted to hear everything he was thinking—feel everything he was feeling.

He buried his face in his hands. "Even though I was only a kid when Valentina arrived, I never forgave myself for not fighting back. I had magic, but my fear left me vulnerable. I watched my older brother become a demon and slaughter everyone I loved. And I still did fucking nothing. Instead, I saw a nightmare unfold before my eyes, and I ran like a scared little boy."

I blinked. "You *were* a scared little boy."

When he didn't respond or even look up at me, I sat beside him, the narrow bench forcing my knee to touch his. "There was nothing you could have done. Valentina is a monster who ruined so many lives, and you suffered the consequences of her evil. But you survived. You made it out."

"Yeah, and I turned into a monster just like her. How's that for irony? My brother is a selfish asshole who was always after wealth and notoriety. But me ... I just wanted the nightmares to stop."

Jase stood suddenly, running his hands through his hair. The absence of his body next to mine gave me a weird sense of loss, a void of comfort. I watched him try to rein in those turbulent emotions, that endless grief that turned to ice.

The pain is like a choking fire in my heart. I can feel every ounce of the suffering he's dealt with for so long. He—my thoughts paused when the realization hit me like a lightning bolt.

I stood and approached him, grabbing his wrist to stop him from pacing. "You did all this so you wouldn't feel helpless," I said. Jase's eyes widened. "You wanted this ring, so you could never be vulnerable like you were that night. To never be weak and defenseless ever again."

Jase staggered back as if I had punched him, but instead of giving him space, I stepped closer to him, and my heart lodged in my throat.

Suddenly, as he stared at me, I did something I hadn't planned. I closed the gap between us and pulled him into an embrace. He was taller than me, but my arms held him tightly around his waist, my cheek pressing into his chest. I hadn't planned on hugging him; it was impulsive and even surprised me. God, this made me more anxious than our beach and club activities. As I questioned if I should release him, his body relaxed against mine, and my thoughts settled.

Breathe.

The fragrance of his cologne set my skin ablaze, and my head spun. His firm body pressed against me made me feel safe and protected, like I was no longer trying to console him but the other way around.

Jase took in a slow breath and ran a hand over my hair. When that happened, the mark on my stomach flared, and I felt my insides melt.

"I'm sorry for what my mother did to yours. No child should ever deal with that kind of trauma. You spent hundreds of years in hell because of her. And me. I'm so fucking sorry."

Jase stiffened under my touch, and I was sure he would shove me away for being in his space in that state until his arms wrapped around the tops of my shoulders, squeezing me back.

It felt right. But so goddamn confusing. I hated Jase for forcing me to leave New Orleans, yet he allured me as our bodies found solace in each other.

"I was supposed to hate you," he started, his cool breath brushing against my hair, "the child of the woman who destroyed everything I loved. You were just a way to get to Valentina, take that ring, and then kill you to punish *her* for what she took from me. I needed to put my damn guilt into the grave. But no matter what I do, I can't fucking stay away from you. I don't want to hurt you anymore. But even after all of this, I wish I knew what you were thinking."

I felt Jase's hands on my shoulders, and he gently pushed me away. His blazing green eyes locked with mine when I looked up. Lifting my right hand, I brushed my thumb over his cold cheek, and his gaze fell on my mouth.

"Rachel ..." he whispered. "I ... fucking hell." Jase leaned down and pressed his lips against mine. The times he had kissed me before were rough and desperate. This kiss, though, felt ... *awakening*.

It was like the world suddenly burst into light and color as I closed my eyes, wrapped my arms around his neck, and pulled him close. All my reservations about his very existence melted away. This unbearable attraction to him consumed my every thought, and I was no longer strong enough to fight it.

His kiss was beautiful, like finding peace after a storm, and tasted just like his blood did in Boston. It felt like warm sunshine, wind brushing through olive trees, and a sense of home—I needed more.

I opened my mouth to deepen the kiss. Jase groaned, swiping his tongue over mine. The coolness of his flesh was the perfect sensation against my heated skin. His hands slid down the curves of my back until he cupped my ass and pulled me against his hard cock. A fire burned in my core, and I pressed my hips against him, needing more of his touch, his passion.

God, why am I so turned on by this man?

Jase freed his lips from mine and moved down my neck, his tongue trailing a path. Then—a scrape of fang. My body stilled, and he pulled away. Worry was pretty damn clear in Jase's eyes as he looked at me. "You and Andrei drank from each other, and honestly, it pisses me the fuck off when I think about it. I wasn't thinking in that club, and while you gave me permission ... eventually, I felt guilty because you were drunk. So, if you say no, I'll stop."

I blinked. I wasn't expecting that. It was true that Andrei and I drank from each other, and there were times I wished he hadn't, like when he bit me in the hotel alley and behind the bar. But even after we started sleeping together, if I had told Andrei to stop ... I don't think he would have.

"For a selfish asshole, that's probably the nicest thing you've ever said to me," I joked. Blowing a breath, I broke my gaze from Jase and looked at the echinacea flowers swaying in the sea-scented breeze. The desire to feel his fangs in my skin was growing stronger and stronger. I pressed my forehead against his chest.

Fuck it.

"Do it," I said. "Take what you want. It's okay."

Jase cupped my cheeks and lifted my face to look at him. His emerald eyes locked on mine, searching for any hesitancy. When he didn't see it, he licked his lips. Then, like a serpent, Jase struck, burying his fangs into the crook of my neck.

I gasped at the pressure, but ... there was no pain. Instead, unrelenting pleasure erupted beneath my skin as he drank. My pussy clenched and throbbed at the sensation, and wetness soaked my panties. Jase moaned, his weight pushing us down to the ground. My back pressed against the grass as his hips ground against my aching core.

Fuck.

It was as if every inch of my body had suddenly come to life, lost in the sensation of that first bite. I could barely breathe, let alone remember my body's usual functions for a moment.

I needed more.

Much, much more.

As Jase took another pull of blood, my hands slipped down his chest to his waistband. Jase stilled but didn't remove his fangs from my skin. He nodded slightly, allowing me to touch him. I popped the buttons of his jeans free and pulled the zipper down. His cock, thick and long, sprang free.

Good God.

When I reached and grasped the hardened flesh, Jase shuddered above me, still feeding. My touch was gentle yet firm as I stroked him. He moaned again, and my pussy throbbed in response.

My strokes increased, and my head swam until my vision clouded. *I'm getting too light-headed.* Using my left hand, I caressed Jase's dark hair. Taking my signal, Jase pulled his fangs free from my neck. Much to my surprise, he licked the puncture wounds clean before pressing his lips against them.

"Rachel," he breathed against my skin as my hand moved faster. "I'm close."

"Good," I said, releasing his cock. With my legs, I pressed against his hips and used my strength to flip him onto his back. Now beneath me, I gave Jase a wicked smile before sliding down, my left hand gripping his hip. There, I took his cock in my mouth. After last night, I wanted to make *him* feel just as good as he made me. His hips jerked upward, driving it deeper down my throat. The taste of him was addictive. I wanted more of him; I wanted *all* of him. My tongue swirled over the head, tasting the slight salt of him as he grew closer to his release.

"Jesus … Rachel … Touch yourself…." His words faded as a groan replaced it, and he fisted my hair in a tight grip as his other hand clasped over my right arm so hard I felt the bruising. The delicious pain sent me spiraling right as I moved my hand from his hip to between my legs, rubbing my clit under the fabric. I could feel my release coming.

He hummed approvingly as my head bobbed up and down. His taste was drowning me, and I was glad to sink beneath the surface of his darkness, lost in the forbidden pleasure. He continued to rock his hips upward, his eyes rolling back into his skull as I drove him to his sweet release.

This is what he needed, too.

Jase let out a loud grunt, his back arching as his release spilled into my mouth, down my throat. I moaned as I took him in, draining every last drop. As he fell back onto the ground, I climbed over him, straddling his waist and taking his hand, replacing my fingers with his, sliding inside my pants. I ground myself over his wet cock while he touched me. I wanted him inside me, to fuck me so hard I'd scream, but a part of me was holding back. I wasn't ready to cross that line yet.

As he moved his hips with mine and his thumb pressed on my clit, bliss flooded my veins, and my body shuddered as the orgasm claimed me. Jase's free hand held me steady as my head tipped back and my cries echoed across the garden. Suddenly, there was a crackling sound, and I turned my head to look over my shoulder.

Jase still held me straddled over his hips but raised himself to look at the sound with me.

"Oh my God," I cried, struggling to reclaim my composure. Blue fire engulfed the nearest echinacea blooms. Jase sat up as I climbed off him, and we scrambled to our feet. He quickly tucked himself back into his jeans and zipped them up. "What the hell just happened?" I was still out of breath as we raced over to the flames. "You and Andrei aren't wearing the ring. How the fuck did you do that?" Reaching out, I ripped the plant that burned from the stem and dropped it to the ground, quickly stomping the heel of my shoe over it to smother the flames. I looked back at Jase, and his face turned pale.

"I don't have a fucking clue, angel. But we need to go before someone comes and sees this." His hands shook as he wiped my blood from his lips. I nodded and went to grab my bag. As we hurried out of the garden, Jase's hand took mine, his fingers weaving through. My skin flushed at the initial gesture, but confusion overrode everything else.

Whatever just happened, we'll figure it out after we leave this place.

Jase closed the gate to the garden, pressing his fingers to his lips and placing them on the iron. The gesture broke my heart, and I squeezed Jase's hand in solidarity. He came for closure, for forgiveness from himself or his family's memory. By the ease in his body language, I thought that he did.

"Aionía sou i mními," he whispered.

"What did you say?" I asked gently. Jase looked down at me, his handsome face written with anxiety, bliss, and relief. But there was also solemnity in his eyes.

"May your memory be eternal."

CHAPTER 39

Jase and I returned from Fiskardo before sunrise. After showering, our group left our hotel early for the four-hour drive to our destination. Finally, we reached the historic and breathtaking city of Athens.

Our destination was another hotel that catered to the supernatural, much like some other European tourist chains. The building had fortified windows that filtered sunlight to protect the vampire guests. All rooms had a stocked kitchen filled with blood bags and a feeding area with employed blood suppliers in case the bags were unavailable or rejected. Not everyone could stomach it cold.

They operated this *specific* location through Greece's supernatural government, which enforced strict protocols to maintain peace between species. The rules were nonnegotiable but necessary—they were the only way to keep the business going without attracting unwanted attention or reprisals from human officials or hunters. Thankfully, humans were allowed to stay there, too, but with conditions.

Tony and I had to sign waivers affirming that our stay was of our own free will. Jase and Lucy had to sign a waiver agreeing not to engage in unsanctioned feeding or face immediate execution.

Now that the sun was disappearing over the horizon and it was time to get ready for the evening, I loosened my bun, letting my hair fall to the center of my back. After combing out the tangles, I threaded a wavy strand between my fingers as I set the brush on the breakfast table and went to the balcony. The Temple of Olympian Zeus was visible from my room, with the golden hues of twilight washing over the ruins. The city was incredible. I couldn't believe I had never been allowed to explore the world, let alone such a magnificent country like Greece.

It was shameful, really. *Fucking Black Onyx assholes.*

I tried to ignore the growing knot of anxiety about us being so close to Crete now. The stakes were so much higher for us. For now, I wanted to pretend I was on a trip with my best friends before reality brought that dream to an end. This was the last stop.

And there will likely be a confrontation with Andrei if he's in Crete waiting.

Leaning onto the railing, I gazed at the temple again, its ancient columns casting long shadows over the people exploring below. The magic beneath the ground was insane, a natural flow that tied all the energies of life together. My power bubbled within me when we arrived here.

God, the view was beautiful.

Jase and Lucy were most likely downstairs at the hotel bar, having a drink laced with blood, while Tony ventured out to grab dinner since he was still safe to roam. They'd left me alone with my thoughts and this bottle of wine Tony had brought me before heading out.

I grabbed the glass from the small patio table beside me, swirling the red liquid before sipping. It was a dry flavor, but after three more, the subtle bitterness melted away to aromatic dark fruits—plums and blackberries mingled with a hint of oak. It was a fabulous bouquet that hit all the right spots in my senses.

I could drink the entire bottle.

The cooling breeze carried the aroma of local food mixed with the faint scent of the ocean. I inhaled slowly, letting the air soothe my nerves and ease the tension in my back and shoulders before exhaling. I'd been carrying so much stress since we left Italy, and it mentally exhausted me.

The sun dipped lower, sending rays of amber and crimson across the dark-blue sky. Our ferry to Crete wouldn't depart until late afternoon tomorrow, which was the best way to ensure we arrived after dusk. Thankfully, the world was different now, with vampires in society. They ran the ferries all night.

Once we arrived, we'd have to walk to the caves, and it wasn't safe for Jase and Lucy to be in the daylight since there was no guarantee of shade. Plus, we didn't want too many people seeing us, so it had to be nighttime—it was the only option.

I leaned forward, my elbows resting on the balcony railing, and my thoughts drifted to Jase. My stomach fluttered. We hadn't talked much since leaving the garden in Fiskardo, and the drive after was painfully quiet. We fooled around in that garden, resulting in him involuntarily using magic. Something felt so electric between us. It was both scary *and* exciting, if I was being honest with myself.

Closing my eyes, I let the memory wash over me—the pressure of his hands on my skin, the lust burning in those beautiful emerald eyes, and the taste of him. God, it felt so good. I didn't want to ignore the moments we had together anymore. Jase consumed my mind.

For the first time since leaving the villa, I wasn't thinking about Andrei in any capacity other than hoping we didn't run into him. Four months ago, we parted at the train station after he kissed me for the first time. It left something in my heart that made me so angry. I couldn't tell if it was lust, a warped form of love, or a combination of both, but Andrei revealed his true nature when he assaulted me through our guardian bond. He was a depraved demon who only wanted to control and oppress me. I was afraid of him now.

No ... I was *terrified*.

But what was also insane was that I was falling for his brother. Before, I was sure he and Jase were the same.

But I was wrong.

What would Andrei do to me and Jase if he found out? I couldn't tell if I was more scared of those consequences than being taken and used for that damned spell.

Or worse.

When it came to Jase, I'd spent days fighting against whatever the fuck was developing between us, denying the force that seemed to pull us together. I took another drink of wine and sighed, the last streams of sunlight bathing me with my eyes still closed. I knew the answer—resisting was pointless.

I wanted him.

Jase Halpert, the vampire who had been my enemy, had *kissed* me in the garden.

Not just kiss me …

His touch set my body and soul on fire. Something deep inside me ignited in his arms, as if I belonged there against him. Like fate had aligned our paths, no matter how ridiculous that sounded. The whole situation was still confusing as hell but not enough to stop me from giving in to whatever this was. Jase wanted to kill me not too long ago. Slit my throat even. He stalked me for years and turned my best friend into a vampire. Jase even asked a woman to infiltrate my life before the two of them destroyed it.

I should hate him.

I should want to *kill* him.

But I no longer felt either of those emotions.

When I opened my eyes, night started pulling its cloak over the land. Lucy wanted to explore the city with me, and we'd head out in about an hour. As I turned to leave the balcony and change, I slammed into a broad chest, almost spilling my precious wine. A rich scent filled my nose, and my cheeks heated.

Jase.

"Well, that was bold," I said, raising my head to meet his eyes. *God, the green in those eyes really could inspire poetry if I had a talent for it.* "The sun's barely set; you could have scorched that pretty face of yours."

A soft smile graced his lips, making my chest squeeze. "Well, I was waiting patiently."

"In the room?" I hadn't heard him come in. *Wait, isn't the door locked?*

"The doorway, technically."

I narrowed my eyes. "That's a little stalkerish, you know?"

He laughed. "I enjoy being stalkerish."

Silence fell between us for a moment before Jase stepped closer. I took an involuntary step back, allowing him to press me against the railing.

Jase's hand drifted up to my cheek and cupped my jaw. "Why do I feel like you're still scared of me?" he asked, almost *hurt*. I blinked. How could I answer that?

"It's ... it's not that I'm scared of you. Not anymore, at least. I'm afraid of ... *this*." I touched his chest. There was no heartbeat, of course, and despite his cold body, I sensed a warmth that drew me in. "Why *do* I feel like this when I'm with you?"

Jase's brows knitted together, and he shook his head. "Angel—"

"And why do you call me that?" I asked suddenly. I wasn't sure if I was trying to distract from hearing the answer, but this had also been on my mind since we met—that nickname—the one I initially hated but now craved to hear him say.

Jase stepped back a little and folded his arms over his chest. Another breeze swept his wavy black hair across his face, partially obscuring his left eye. When he didn't answer, I lifted my arm and delicately moved his hair away. It was long enough I could tuck it behind his ear. I let my fingers brush his cheek, and his head tilted slightly toward the touch.

"A Nephalem turned your mother," he finally answered. "You carry demon, human, and angel blood...."

I smirked. "Then why not call me 'demon,' given how you felt about me in the past?"

"Because"—Jase bit his bottom lip to keep the growing smile away—"the beautiful, angelic part is the only thing I see in you."

My pounding heart seemed stuck in my throat. I was so far from angelic.

As if he read my mind, Jase leaned forward, wrapped his hand around my neck, and pressed his lips against mine. Any air in my lungs vanished as his body leaned into me. His mouth tasted faintly of whiskey and some delicious, warm spice.

God, he knew how to kiss.

"Jase," I whispered against his lips, breaking the kiss. "What's happening?"

I moved away and pressed my hands against my stomach. The rune wasn't burning like it usually did, but it tingled. I lifted my shirt, and Jase's eyes went to the mark. I hadn't shown him yet. Every time Jase touched me, my shirt stayed on and covered the area. "I have—"

"I know. I have it, too." Jase raised his shirt and turned slightly. My jaw dropped. It was the same symbol, only closer to his hip, so I wouldn't have seen it until now.

My mind reeled with theories. The odds of us having the same mark should be practically fucking *zero*. "Is it because I drank from you in the church?" I asked. "It appeared shortly after that." But that didn't make sense. Andrei and I drank from each other, too.

"We ..." Jase swallowed, his expression blank. "Fuck. We need to talk."

I didn't like the sound of that at all.

Nerves rattled me as I brushed past him, stepping off the balcony and back into the room. Without thinking, I headed straight for the bathroom and shut the door behind me like a damn coward.

Jesus, what the hell am I doing?

I wanted answers, but why was I so goddamn scared of them now? I spent my whole life just wanting the truth—no more secrets. Yet I wasn't ready to face *this*.

There was a tap on the door, and I jumped. "This has to be some kind of punishment, right?" I said. "It *has* to be." There was silence on the other side. I rested my head against the wood. "Jase. You know what these marks are, don't you? Tell me what they mean."

"I …" his voice trailed off before the knob turned, and he opened the door.

Damn. I forgot to lock it.

"Your mother told me something at South Station while you were gone," he said, leaning against the doorframe.

My stomach twisted into a tight knot. *What?* "Wait. You were at the station?"

I didn't expect that. While I was being fucked by Andrei, I'd assumed that Jase was either gone or with Jackson and the others. Valentina didn't say shit about him being there, too.

He shook his head. "Andrei was supposed to distract you while I went to kill her and take the ring. It was supposed to be easy since she was so weak. Instead, Valentina told me something that made me change my mind. Well, to be honest, it freaked me out so badly that I ran. I didn't want to ask questions, so what I'm telling you is all I know."

Jase held out his hand, and without hesitating, I took it. He led me out of the bathroom to the bed. We sat down on the mattress, and I turned to him, waiting.

"I've never really put much thought into celestial power or cosmic influences," he began. "Sure, I believed there was an afterlife, like Hell, but since I'd never seen it, I wasn't sure until those demons attacked us. That pretty much shattered any doubt. But before then, I never thought too hard on the subject."

Nodding, I replied, "Same here."

Jase reached out and retook my hand, rubbing his thumb over my knuckles. "When your mother turned me two hundred years ago, something extraordinary happened. I'd never experienced something like it before or since."

My brows furrowed. "Tell me."

He swallowed. "The Hades Blood Moon somehow linked my soul with your mother."

My eyes widened.

"It didn't stay linked. There was this enormous force that slammed into my body, crushing me from the inside out. I thought it was part of becoming a vampire, but I was wrong. I thought I was dying and tried to fight back against whatever the hell it was. Then suddenly, it lifted, and I could move again. There was a snap, like a lock clicking into place, and warmth seemed to fill my body for a moment. When that happened, I didn't understand it at first. At the station the night you fled, Valentina told me that my soul wasn't connected to hers. I was linked to yours. I felt that rope of power...."

I shook my head. That was impossible. "I wasn't even born yet."

He squeezed my hand. "I know," he replied. "Some higher power chose us. They selected me for you. When I came to New Orleans, I couldn't stay away. I thought it was to learn about you, but it became so much more. Everything about you captivated me—your fiery temper, strength, bravery, and loyalty to the ones you love. I questioned why every day. That night at the church, when you drank from me, it happened again, that same feeling...."

My heart was pounding so hard I felt dizzy.

"Valentina told me I still have a soul, angel. That 'rope' was an anchor, linking my powers *and* soul to your essence. We're fated, or cursed, mates. However you want to look at it."

He released my hand and cupped my cheek instead. I wanted to say something—I even opened my mouth—but no words would come out. Jase's expression turned to concern as he watched me process this insane information.

When I stayed silent, he gently said, "Please, say something."

"We ... we're soulmates?" I asked. It was the only thing I could think to say. The coven had taught me about them growing up. Not everyone had a mate, but when they did, it was impossible to fight the ties that pulled them together. Even if one of them walked away, they would never find such a powerful love again. It sounded romantic as a child, but right now, I was fucking *pissed* that it had to happen to me.

I pulled away from his hand and stood, pressing my hands against my chest. Pacing in front of the bed, I reeled under the weight of what he told me. Then I stopped in front of Jase and, without a pause, slapped him so hard across the face that his head jerked to the side.

"Fuck you," I seethed through clenched teeth. "I expected something like this from my lying fucking mother, but she isn't here for me to hit. If this is true, you should have fucking told me. You've had *months* to come to Italy and find me. Or even before we left on this insane road trip from hell! Almost an entire week! Goddammit, you knew before you even touched me, you ... you ..."

Jase sat motionless, seemingly awestruck that I had hit him again, his eyes downcast.

Slowly, he raised his head to look at me with heated eyes. "It's like you want me to punish you," he said, licking his lower lip. "I warned you about hitting me, and yet you keep fucking doing it."

"Well, you deserved it every time." *The audacity of this man.* I couldn't believe it.

I stepped back when Jase jumped to his feet. He grabbed my arm and spun me around so my back pressed against his chest. His left arm snaked under my shirt and across my stomach, right over the rune. His fingers gently caressed the raised symbol in slow strokes as his right hand grabbed my throat, pulling my head toward him. Jase's hard cock pressed against my ass, sending molten heat between my legs. My breathing grew ragged.

"Don't think I regret any of this for a second," he growled through his teeth.

"But I do—"

"Liar," he said, chuckling in my ear. He knew I was full of shit. Finding out I had a fated mate was enraging, but it enticed me to the core. It was a mix of wondering if anything I felt for Jase was real or just part of some universe-magic bond bullshit. Whatever it was, I loathed and loved it.

In his arms, right then, I didn't want him to let go. Jase's arms gave me such a sense of peace and belonging. Every shred of doubt in my mind burned away, and I allowed myself to melt into his touch while he buried his face in my hair, slowly breathing in my scent.

"Do you want me to let go? Because I really don't fucking want to," he asked.

No, I don't. Please, don't let me go. The words rang clear as a bell in my head, yet I couldn't speak them. He knew the answer, though. His grip tightened around me possessively.

"Does it burn, too?" I asked instead, focusing on that soothing touch of his fingers on my mark. "When you think of me?"

Jase nodded in my hair. "Every goddamn time. It's like a searing pain that drives me to insanity. The only time I find relief is when I'm around you."

Closing my eyes, I leaned further into him, feeling his body relax. His fingers moved away from the mark, sliding down my stomach and slowly inching under my pants.

It was just like the club, but we were alone now. There was no barrier to stop us, no more guilt to drive me to run away.

The coldness of his fingers sent shivers down my spine and goosebumps over my skin, moving toward my wet heat. Jase's hand settled in between my thighs, and he groaned against my neck. I was so fucking turned on that I thought I was going to go crazy.

Before Jase could slip his fingers inside, I turned, causing him to pull his hand away. Confusion crossed his face.

God, he's hot when he's confused.

I stepped away, reaching for the hem of my shirt before lifting it over my head and dropping the fabric onto the carpet. I wore a lacy black push-up bra, the clip at the center squeezing them together in an alluring swell. Jase's green eyes roamed over my body, taking in the sight like a starved man finding sustenance for the first time. He nibbled his bottom lip as he reached for me, sliding the straps from my shoulders. Moving closer, he pressed his lips against the curve of my neck.

"Yes," I whispered as his sweet kisses trailed up my neck, pausing by my ear.

"I'm not going to be able to stop myself, angel," Jase confessed.

"Good, because I don't want you to."

Instantly, he wrapped his hands around my arms and pulled me in. His left hand then gripped my ass, guiding me against him. Jase's teeth grazed my heated skin with playful nips, each one sending shudders through my body. His cool breath skated over the crook of my neck before he bit down, and I ascended into fucking heaven.

Oh fuck....

My head tipped back as Jase drank from me. Every part of my body surrendered to him as he fed. He grunted low against my skin like he satisfied a long-buried need. The bite was painful, but I loved it. He devoured me rough, ruthless, and desperate. But it wasn't enough. None of this foreplay felt like it was enough.

"Get on the bed," I ordered, and his fangs pulled away from my throat. A playful smile touched Jase's lips as he backed away, his legs hitting the mattress. I watched him for a moment, taking in his features. The tug in my chest pulled, demanding to be close again.

He's the most beautiful man I've ever seen.

But he still had that damn leather jacket on.

It needed to come off.

Once he was seated, I climbed on top of him, caging his hips with my knees. I slid the silver tab of his jacket zipper down and pulled it off, tossing it across the room. The shirt came off immediately after. I paused, taking in his chiseled abs and flawless, sun-kissed skin. My breath hitched as I brushed my lips against his before pushing him back. My tongue trailed down the side of his neck and then glided over the contours of his chest. I let my fingers play with the strained fabric of his jeans, slightly pressing on the hardened flesh beneath.

"Fuck, Rachel," Jase moaned, his head falling back. He reached up to thread his fingers into my hair, gripping at the scalp. I felt the possessiveness beneath that burning hold, the desire, and I wanted to lose myself in those sensations.

Up until now, there had always been some restraint. Not wanting to act on this forbidden connection that was meant to be. We weren't fighting it anymore. I wanted to give Jase everything and, in return, to have him be mine completely.

I raised my eyes to him and pressed another kiss to his mouth, savoring that smokey taste mixed with my blood. Taking my time, I slowly moved my hands to unbutton his jeans. I lowered the zipper and skillfully worked his pants and boxers down past his hips and knees to pull his cock out.

Before I could move, Jase released my hair, grabbed my hips, and flipped me onto the bed, so I was on my back. We moved toward the center of the bed, his knees against my thighs. It was his turn to take control. Those eyes took me in like I was the most beautiful woman he'd ever seen.

"Jase," I whispered. And that was all he needed. It was like the leash had finally snapped, and we couldn't keep our hands off each other for a second longer. Jase wasted no time, ripping my black lace panties in two and throwing them aside. The bra was next. I was laid bare for him, revealing every inch of myself.

In a heartbeat, Jase pushed my legs apart while stroking his cock. He leaned forward, settling himself between my thighs. His length teased my pussy, sending a shocking pulse through my body. *Yes.*

I barely drew a breath before he thrust his hips, ramming himself deep inside of me.

Then I cried out, the world exploding behind my eyes, my vision swirling with stars. As Jase filled and stretched me, my hands went to grab him, to dig my nails into his back. But before I could, Jase seized my wrists and pinned them above my head.

Yes.

Only the sounds of heavy breathing and moans filled the room as we drowned in each other. The scent of *us* clung to the air, making my mind blur. Jase slammed his hips into me so roughly that the bed squeaked in time with his thrusts. He felt so good, so goddamn good. He was made for me. It felt like Jase was everywhere: my blood, my bones, embedded in every fucking cell of my body.

"Fucking hell," Jase moaned loudly, his words muffled as he kissed me. His tongue slid over mine as we devoured each other. I could barely breathe as I shoved my hips upward, allowing him deeper access. We finally had what we wanted the most ...

Each other.

"Don't stop," I pleaded.

"I won't, angel. God, I never want to stop." He grabbed my bent leg and pushed it out, spreading me wider. From that angle, he was hitting all the right places inside me. Jase didn't need to do anything—my body felt like it was on fucking fire.

That's when I felt it—the bond between us. My eyes fluttered open, and I saw our elements swirling around us—a vortex of violet and cerulean blue—Water and Fire blended together. It was beautiful and terrifying.

"Jase," I said, panic edging into my voice.

"Shh, keep your eyes on me, angel," he demanded, and my eyes returned to his. Whether or not he knew about the magic, he didn't care. His focus was solely on me. As Jase pounded harder, he lowered his neck to my lips. "Drink."

My fangs slid free, and I sank my teeth deep into his vein. Blood flooded my mouth, and I moaned against his skin. Holy fuck, Jase tasted like heaven on Earth. That sense of home returned in full force. I clung to that feeling, that completeness I'd been missing my entire life.

I felt him start to tense on top of me. We were drowning in pleasure, and I could feel the shuddering pulses overtake my body. I was hanging by a thread. Then Jase groaned my name ... and I came undone. Tingling waves rushed through me, moving between our bodies as Jase came, too, filling me up as I continued to take my fill of his blood.

There was a snap, and our blended magic disappeared. Lost in the sweetest of sins, neither of us wanted to let go, and only one thought came to my mind: things would never be the same again.

CHAPTER 40

RACHEL

As the small ferry departed the Piraeus Port and cut through the dark waters of the Myrtoan Sea, I found myself glancing at Jase more often than I expected.

The tables have turned. Now it's me who's the staring weirdo.

After last night in Athens, his demeanor had shifted; he was no longer broody and pretending not to give a shit about me. Instead, he smiled back whenever he caught me looking at him.

Since it was daylight, the four of us stayed below deck together this time. While Tony and Lucy lounged in the cafe and bar, Jase and I remained in bed, doing *very* little talking—or sleeping.

When night fell, Jase kissed me, slipped out of the room, and headed to the deck to gaze at the water. After we parted ways, I bought a much-needed snack and joined Lucy and Tony on the other side of the deck.

Tony leaned back against the bench and turned to me. "I'm glad the bastard finally came clean," he said, keeping his voice low. "I'm sorry we didn't tell you, but he said the 'fated' stuff needed to come from him."

I smiled at Tony and shrugged my shoulders. "Naw, I get it. It's still hard to make sense of everything, but I'm just fucking relieved you two don't have to be weird about it anymore."

"So, what does that mean for you and him?" Lucy asked, apprehension in her tone. "You're just going to accept it?"

My eyes went soft. "I'm not dismissing every fucked up thing he's done, including what he did to you. Right now, we're learning about each other, and once this nightmare is over, we can go from there." I pulled the Book of Shadows out of my tote bag and laid it on my lap. We'd shelve the relationship talk for the time being. We only had a few hours before we dock—

"Maybe you shouldn't have that out in the open, angel," Jase said while walking over, his voice carried by the wind and waves. I gripped the book between my fingers. The power within those pages was fucking wild, but the more I held it, the more it felt like it was a part of my essence. Maybe the parts I still wasn't sure how to use. But it sure spoke to me.

"If this is going to work, we all need to keep a level head when we enter that cave," I said, tapping my index finger on the cover. "All we know is what the Black Onyx told Andrei; those instructions were their agenda, not ours. It wouldn't hurt to snoop around these pages before we get there. I mean, we *are* conjuring a spell in a dark, spooky cave tied to Heaven and Hell."

Jase sauntered over to the bench. His lips pulled into a smile, but I saw the worry in those eyes. It was clear he wasn't sure how we could pull this off either, but he was trying not to show it.

When he reached the bench, Tony stood, and Jase switched places with him, sitting beside me. Tony and Lucy headed below deck, leaving us alone. I slipped my hand into his and squeezed gently. Although it was a daring move, by then, I believed we had overcome the initial awkwardness and uncertainty about what we wanted. Did he still get under my skin? Sure. But I think the little matching symbols on our stomachs were telling us to let all that shit go and finally trust each other.

"All we have to do is destroy the obelisk so that Andrei and the witches can't use it," Jase said. "I think the three of us with super-human strength are more than enough to smash some rocks."

Right then, the boat lurched upward, and I pulled my hand free of his and grabbed my stomach. Nausea roiled in my gut, and my legs instantly turned to jelly.

"Why, of all the human traits to inherit from my dad, did I get seasickness?" I groaned.

I put my head in my hands and tried some breathing techniques to ease the nausea. The world was trying to throw me off with how tumultuous I felt. Suddenly, the soft touch of his arm wrapped around my hunched shoulders, and icy fingers brushed against my skin. The smell of his cologne filled my senses, and my stomach settled a little.

"When I was a boy, I'd get sick on my papá's fishing boat all the time," Jase said softly. "He wasn't cruel about it, but I could sense his disappointment every time I threw up. Mamá would craft potions from her garden, trying to help. Most of the time, they worked. But there were still bad days." He smiled. "I guess there are perks now to being a ruthless vampire who doesn't get green in the gills, even temporarily."

I looked up at him. While his smile was cocky, his eyes softened at the memory of his mother.

"She was a Fire witch, wasn't she?" I asked. "Just like you and your brother?"

"Both my parents were, but she used magic to create potions for illnesses and to heal wounds. Unlike the raging wildfire my brother and I inherited from our father, it was a comforting hearth fire on a chilly night."

"That's why she had the garden," I affirmed, straightening and shifting in his embrace. It felt *good* to be held by him. Jase nodded. "This sentimental side of you is new. You're usually a cold, mean bastard."

Jase turned his head slightly toward me and smirked. "Yeah, well, don't get used to it."

I laughed softly then and confessed. "I kind of like it. You were lucky to have a mother like her. I can't say the same. Obviously, I didn't know much about Valentina before now, but over the last four months since she awakened, I've seen a mother I want nothing to do with, especially after she broke her promise and tried to get me to remove the ring. I hoped we would somehow become a family after we left the States.... Jase, even if she were to catch up with us and we were to start over, I don't want to."

"And you're not obligated to," he said. "Just because you share the same blood doesn't mean Valentina is automatically your mother."

I nodded. "I guess when you've destroyed countless lives, more than what *you* were even capable of ..." Jase raised a brow. "It changes too much of you. Maybe I was being really fucking naïve, but I hoped for her to be more like a mom. I hoped for *something*. But it's ridiculous for me to hold on to that belief. Her selfish darkness will rule over her heart for eternity. As much as she loved Cyrus and me, ambitions ultimately win."

Jase squeezed his arms around my shoulders, holding me tighter. "Maybe someday she'll see you for more than this weapon she thought she'd create. If not, then she doesn't deserve your love or respect."

Jase's expression was solemn before I asked. "What about you? Are you okay? Fiskardo opened a lot of wounds for you, especially seeing your old home turned into a memorial for your family."

I felt his lips press into my hair, and he inhaled my scent.

God, I can't believe I wanted to kill him just days ago.

Having someone who once caused me fear and now offered comfort was so strange.

"I mean, yeah, it was hard. Seeing the garden and the home we lived in where Andrei killed my parents. I wanted to burn it all down, but it would be a disservice to Mamá's memory. She loved us dearly. Although, I'm not sure she would be happy to see her sons become such monsters."

"You're not *that* much of a monster. I wouldn't be spreading my legs for you if I thought there was no hope of saving you from the demons that pull you to darkness." He smiled at that remark and I gave him a playful wink. "If this fated bond is real, which I think we both know by now it is, I have to believe there is hope for us ... hope for *you*."

He raised a brow and reached up, tucking my hair behind my ear. "I guess if the heavens believe I'm worthy of someone like you, maybe you're right."

Smiling shyly, I tried to look away, but his fingers tightened around my chin, holding me in place. "I don't feel bad for watching you all those years. I don't regret a damn thing. But you should want to kill me for it."

I nodded. "I did … but oddly enough, there's a weird thrill behind it, too." Jase bit his bottom lip at those words, and my stomach flipped.

When I looked back at the book, Jase scooted closer. "Okay, let's read it," he said.

Anxiety gripped my stomach. We still hadn't looked through the pages yet.

Opening the Book of Shadows, I noted each page was thick and worn, some letters barely legible.

Jase reached over and began flipping through the pages until we stumbled upon a colored drawing that caught my breath. An angel with medium-brown skin, long, thick hair, and stunning gold wings stared back at us.

"'This is the story of Ezrylos and Zahar,'" I read, my eyes straining slightly to read the text. Although the archaic script flowed through the pages, the text ran from top to bottom, not left to right.

This could take me a minute.

"'*In the days of dark, when the realms were young, there lived an angel named Ezrylos, chosen by the heavens and tasked with guarding the gates that lead to the Underworld. He bore a sword of celestial fire, engraved with the runes to the sole weapon forged to vanquish the dark betrayer.*'"

Jase leaned closer, his curiosity as piqued as mine.

I glanced at him briefly to meet his eyes before returning to the text.

"'Yet his heart belonged with that of Zahar, a being of light whose love knew no bounds. The fates conspired against them, for the decree demanded one's demise to seal the other within the cave.'"

I stopped reading as the realization hit me. *God, that's sad.* His mate sacrificed himself so that his love could live.

"'To seal Ezrylos in the cave, Zahar shed his sacred angel blood, which closed the gates and condemned him to eternal silence. That act was a last testament of love—a sacrifice of life. At the moment of his death, Zahar placed a key on his wings; it served as the last remnant of their bond and the power to unleash the ancient weapon.'"

I looked up. "Not the Fire key, right?"

Jase shook his head. "I don't think so. It would still be inside the cave."

My eyes dropped back to the pages as I flipped to the next one. The aged paper showed a sketched pentagram with a stone at its center, but the surrounding words were severely worn. "I think this might be the spell, but it's hard to read."

"The story is kind of romantic, you know? Tragic ... but romantic," Jase interjected, causing me to look back into his eyes. "To love someone so much, you'd sacrifice yourself so they could live. Love that powerful but at such a cost ..."

I nodded slowly.

"It's a reminder of the lengths we'll go for those we love, even if it means losing ourselves," he added.

I flipped through more pages, searching for anything else that could help.

"Let's get some rest for this last stretch before we get there," Jase said, shutting the book for me, but I gripped it at the spine and tucked it under my armpit.

"Alright."

His cool fingers touched mine as he helped me stand and escorted me off the deck and downstairs to our cabin.

Before we entered our room, Jase's hand grabbed the back of my neck, yanking me back toward him. He then spun me around, moving his hands around my upper arms. Once through the threshold, I tossed the book on my opened duffle bag before he slammed the door shut and pinned me against the wall, his lips crashing onto mine. We didn't even bother to lock the door. Though the window to the cabin was slightly ajar, I could still hear the sea and the ferry engine echoing in the night air. I felt his arm tighten briefly before his hand gripped my jaw, moving my chin up so I could look into his intense eyes. Those eyes that once harbored so much anger and hatred were now filled with desire and need.

My breath was rapid as Jase's cool breath skated over my face.

The silence between us spoke of everything we needed to know right before he kissed me. I welcomed the feeling with a soft moan before I opened my mouth to taste him.

Jase guided us back to the small twin-sized mattress, where he sat down and positioned me between his open thighs. He pulled my body closer and gently glided his hand from my back to my chest. My lips parted as he cupped my left breast and ran his thumb over my peaked nipple. I gasped against his mouth, arching my back at the intense sensation. That simple touch was enough to send a wave of shudders through my body.

My hands grabbed his jeans, and I quickly unbuttoned them, pulling his cock free. I gripped his length, relishing in the throbbing need there. Jase grunted at the sudden motion, his body tensing against mine. Without a word, I broke the kiss and quickly slid my pants down. With a swift motion, I straddled him, digging my fingers into the muscles of his shoulders. One of his hands drifted to my panties, pushing the thin lace of my underwear to the side.

"God, I'll never get enough of you," he groaned as I eased myself onto the tip of his cock. I was already throbbing around him, aching to have him inside me as I slid lower down his shaft. My legs shook, a small moan leaving my lips. Finally, I leaned down and kissed him again. "I need you. Fuck, I need you *now.*"

Jase grabbed my hips and, with a thrust, seated himself deep in my pussy. Hard and fast. Claiming every fucking inch of me. His free hand found the back of my head, forcing me into a kiss that stifled the scream burning in my throat.

The pleasure was mind-numbing. It felt so right, so perfect. It was like his cock was made to be inside me.

"Just like that," he praised me, and the words swirled inside my head. "Look at you, so desperate to take my cock."

I began to move my hips up and down, my wetness coating him and my inner thighs. Finally, his head pulled back from mine, tipping backward as pleasure flooded his face. The ferry rocking gave me extra momentum to take him even deeper.

"Four years, angel," Jase said. "God, the images of you touching yourself. I pictured myself there every time, wishing it was me fucking you. I watched others touch what was mine, even if, in those moments, I didn't know it yet. Now I get to have you just like this, with my cock buried inside you, claiming you as mine." He bit his bottom lip. "All fucking mine."

I bounced on his lap, my whole body begging me not to pull back. I felt his hands eagerly trail over my body again, as if he wanted to memorize every curve, every line. It was a heavy contrast to the way we fucked as I breathed heavily, struggling to stay silent. That had never been my forte.

My head fell back as Jase leaned to lick the column of my throat. His fangs scraped over my skin, leaving goosebumps in their wake. A part of me wanted his sharp teeth to tear through my flesh, to lace this pleasure with pain, but he refrained. Instead, his left hand focused on moving my hips against him. A pulsing wave hit me deep in my core as we moved together, threatening to explode at any point now that I could barely hold back, especially with the way he continued to breathe heavily against my throat.

"Rachel, I'm close. Ride me harder, angel. Fuck," Jase panted. It was as if I was under his command—right away, my movements grew faster, harder, more needy. His thick cock stretched my walls to the point of delicious pain. I'd feel it once we finished and before my body would heal.

I knew it would be only a few thrusts away before we both reached our climax.

"Oh, God. Jase," I cried out as an orgasm rippled through me, causing me to shake in his arms. A tremor ran through me, mixing with pleasure as I struggled to breathe. Jase grunted as his release chased after mine, filling me up. Deep purple mists spilled from my body as my pussy clenched on Jase's cock, cloaking us in shadows.

Holy shit.

I opened my eyes and let out a sharp laugh when I saw the magic covering the sheets and walls around us, lighting up the space in purple hues.

I've never had it do that before.

Jase looked around with me and threw back his head, rich laughter echoing in the room. The sound was so carefree and... *happy.* I looked down at him and wrinkled my nose. "What's so funny?"

"Just observing how shit is changing. You suck me off and I burn a small plant in my mother's garden. When you ride my cock, your magic comes rushing out like that." I gave him a little smack on his chest. "We probably should be careful before we destroy shit, angel."

"You might be right," I replied, and then met his eyes. "You know, I've never seen you laugh like *that* or genuinely smile, for that matter."

Jase pressed his lips together, as if stubbornly trying not to show emotion again. Instead, he leaned forward and gently kissed me on my swollen lips. "I've never had a reason to until now."

CHAPTER 41

RACHEL

When I opened my eyes, I found myself alone in bed. I felt the hum of the ferry's engine, but we had to be close to shore by now. I sat up and swung my legs over the mattress, wondering where Jase had wandered off.

After putting on my clothes and shoes, I walked to Tony's room, knocking a few times with no response. I then used the second keycard he had given me and stepped inside.

"Tony?" I called out quietly. "We're going to be docking pretty soon. Are you up?"

The moment I switched on the light, my stomach dropped. Although no one had ransacked the room, something felt off and out of place—a faint, yet unsettling scent lingered in the air. I couldn't identify it, but every instinct in me screamed that something was very, very wrong.

Did Tony have someone else in here besides us earlier? I'd always had vampiric senses, but identifying scents wasn't my strong suit. It wasn't like Jase or Andrei's abilities.

I'm just overreacting. No. I have to get Jase.

I went into the hallway and back into our room to see if Jase had returned. Then my eyes turned down to my bag.

The book was gone. I know I put it there.

Jase must have it.

Next, I pivoted toward the stairs, heading down to the bar.

"Hey," I said. Lucy looked over from the bar and raised her wineglass. "Finally, you're joining us. Tony just went out to grab a smoke. I'll get you a glass of wine. What do you want?"

The last thing I wanted was for Lucy to freak out over what could be nothing. "Where's Jase? Did he come down here?"

She nodded. "For like a half second. He went to find you in the room, but you weren't there, so he went looking for you. Probably upstairs. You had to have missed him." Lucy cocked her head and gave me a strange look. "What's wrong?"

"Um ..." I looked out the window toward the sea, only seeing the top of the deck by the railing. "Not sure. I just need to find Tony or Jase. I'll be right back."

I hurried to the stairs leading to the upper deck, looking around and inhaling deeply, hoping to catch Tony's cigarette smell.

"Tony?" I called out, looking around. He wasn't there. "Jase?"

I twirled around to my right to head to the other side of the top deck, right as a hand cupped around my mouth, muffling my scream.

My instincts roared to life, and I started fighting. I kicked, head-butted, and did everything I could to break the attacker's hold, but a muscular arm snaked around my stomach, tightening with every movement. That same scent from the room hit my nose.

I felt thick, sharp nails dig into my stomach, and dread washed over me. "Shhh," a familiar voice purred in my ears, causing my entire body to grow still. "You were reckless," Andrei said. "I'd think with having an ancient key and a sacred Book of Shadows, you'd have kept it a little more secure than you did."

No. No. No.

"So," he said, loosening the pressure on my mouth. "Tony's safe. Don't worry; he's sleeping on the other side of the deck, but if you scream or fight me, I'll toss him overboard."

I felt sick. Utterly sick.

I nodded because I wasn't a fool. Andrei had always been a psychopath, and he would, without hesitation, hurt someone I loved to get what he wanted.

Andrei dropped his hand from my mouth and slowly turned me around, forcing me to look up into his haunting, dark eyes.

He bit his bottom lip, and his eyes went to mine before his hand came up softly and cupped my cheek. "This is so much better than those visions. Isn't it? Touching you in the flesh? I must say, though, that guardian bond we have, it's fucking sensational."

I shook my head. "Fuck the guardian bond. You're here now, so why not break it? I'll do whatever you want if you do."

Andrei flashed his white teeth and stepped forward, gripping my chin with his fingers and forcing my gaze to stay on his. "Now, that wasn't a very nice thing to say. I know you'd do whatever I asked if it meant keeping your *mother* alive as well." My eyes grew wide. My mother? "She might be an all-powerful vampire, but her powers are a little suppressed at the moment. I could easily cut her gut open and watch her insides fall to the floor before I stake her through the chest if it meant having you back as my prize. But I need you to obey me. So, first, we have a little trip to take together."

Andrei looked out into the water and pointed. My enhanced vision cut through the gloom, and I saw what he was pointing at. My mother was lying on the deck of a small fishing boat, which was moving at the pace of the ferry. Jackson sat at the helm while another man I didn't recognize held a small gas lamp to give me enough light to see them fully. Beside Jackson was my blue back-pack, which had the Fire key inside.

"The Book of Shadows is in there, too," he said, as if he'd sensed my thoughts. "You lost, sweetheart. It's time you accept defeat, so we can finish this."

We were so close. But we got too comfortable and dropped our guard. *God-fucking-dammit.*

Andrei turned to look back at me, but I grabbed his shirt, jerked him closer, and then slammed my forehead against his. I wasted no time sprinting for the boat's edge, but Andrei snatched my collar before I made it over the railing.

"Do you have a death wish?" he growled, pulling me back and into his chest. "You can still drown, and Valentina will die in two seconds before you reach the boat with one order from that witch over there. Don't be stupid."

Two seconds. That is all it would take for Jackson or that other guy to stake her and toss her body over that boat and into the water.

"Fine!" I said through my teeth. "Just don't hurt her."

Andrei moved past me and climbed to the top of the railing, balancing on the bar, while Jackson moved the boat closer to the side. I reached out and let Andrei grab my hand to pull me up, and then he wrapped his arms around my waist. Together, we jumped off the ferry and onto the fishing boat.

"Hey, kiddo," Jackson said, forcing a smile. He didn't want to be there, and I didn't need my ability to see it. Annoyance shone in his eyes as he looked at Andrei. At his feet, my mother lay unconscious, wrapped up in some spell. Glowing silver chains bound her wrists, ankles, and neck, pulsing with power.

"Who the fuck are you?" I said to the man watching us quietly at the right of the deck. He had ashy brown hair and features that made him look like a young college frat boy.

The guy smiled. "Liam. We never did get a chance to meet. I joined the Black Onyx this last year. They thought I'd best tag along with your friends here, so everything went smoothly."

I rolled my eyes and sat in front of Andrei on a wooden bench, much to my irritation. The deck was small and cramped. "You sure know how to pick your friends. Are you sure you really want to risk your life for these assholes? You can't trust Andrei for shit."

Liam smiled. "Well, the pay is pretty generous. I think I'll go along for the ride." He paused and smiled. "Oh, and in case you get any reckless ideas, compulsion doesn't work on me. Trust me, your mother has already tried and failed. If she can't, I promise you, your attempts will fail." With a wave, he walked toward the boat's bow, disappearing from view.

Get fucked.

Jackson smiled apologetically before heading inside the small cabin. He revved up the small motor, churning water and pulling us away from the ferry. I closed my eyes, not wanting Andrei to see the tears threatening to spill.

We were so close.

Andrei forced me to settle between his long legs, burying his lips into my hair. I would have melted in his touch four months ago but not after that last vision, when he invaded my mind and put me in that cage. He wasn't the same man I opened my legs for willingly back in New Orleans. Andrei was never a saint, but he had never crossed my boundaries like that before, and it was horrifying that he did it so effortlessly.

I moved uncomfortably, trying to shift away from his embrace before his hand touched the hem of my pants. "I missed this," he said, touching my stomach and breathing in my scent again. This time, when he inhaled, he paused, and I felt his body stiffen from behind me.

Within seconds, he grabbed my shoulders, spun me around, and slammed me onto the floor of the boat. The wood from the bench cracked under the force, showering me in splinters. I felt Andrei's hands grab my hips.

"Get off of me!" I screamed, scratching and clawing at his face, but he pressed his hand firmly against my chest to keep me pinned.

"You smell like ..." His nostrils flared, and his fangs came out. "No!"

Andrei pulled up my shirt and skated his hand down my stomach before undoing the button of my pants. I tried to summon any magic, but my terror snuffed it out.

"Stop!" I screamed again. I scratched at his arms and drew blood from his skin. Part of me hoped that Jackson, or even the new guy, would hear and step in to stop Andrei.

No one did.

I closed my eyes as Andrei's fingers found my opening, rubbing just enough to coat his finger with my wetness before bringing it up to his nose and inhaling. "What the fuck are you doing?" I hissed.

Steeling myself for the worst, I looked up into those demonic-looking eyes, watching them grow dark red and the thick veins under them bulge. Andrei grabbed my throat, squeezing hard while he hissed.

Shit. He smells Jase on me. He knows.

CHAPTER 42

RACHEL

The door of the cabin slammed open, and Jackson ran to where Andrei had pinned me. He shoved Andrei hard, breaking his hold on my throat. Once I had room to move, I scrambled on all fours, scooting away from him. Jackson shifted, and I thought it was to prevent me from running, but he was putting himself between us.

"Calm the fuck down! What the hell are you doing?" Jackson shouted, his fangs now out, too, challenging him. Liam also came around the corner, standing next to where Valentina still lay. He didn't do shit, though, only stood there with his arms folded and an arrogant and amused grin flitting across his lips.

Would either of them actually protect me from him if it came down to it?

I crawled closer to Valentina, pushing past the asshole Liam, and placed my hands on her wrists. The chains were glowing when my fingers skated across them, and I dug under the cuffs, trying to pull them off. Instead, the metal seared my fingertips, and I jerked them away.

What the hell is this?

"You ... you had sex with Jase?" Andrei seethed from behind me, and I looked at him, meeting his deadly eyes.

"Ah, shit," Jackson cursed, but he kept his hands raised. "I doubt Rachel would—"

"Yes," I blurted out confidently, my eyes never leaving Andrei's. "Yeah. I fucked your brother, and I loved every second of it."

Poking the beast was pretty idiotic, but watching how angry it made him—his walls falling apart—made me feel justified. He had no right to feel betrayed. Andrei shattered whatever relationship we had by manipulating my thoughts within the bond and assaulting me.

Andrei took another step closer, but he stopped, and his eyes suddenly softened. "Why?"

I shook my head. No way in fucking hell I'd tell him the truth. "Boredom," I lied, watching his expression shift to skepticism. He didn't believe me.

"Boredom," Andrei repeated, his dark hair blowing slightly in the wind. "I see...." His voice trailed off before taking a few steps and sitting on the edge of the bench that he'd just smashed with the force of my body. His eyes took on an unsettling calmness as he sat there, staring at me.

Silent Andrei was never a good thing.

Jackson looked around before going over to Andrei. He kneeled and touched his chest, forcing Andrei to gaze at his best friend. Jackson was probably the only one who could tame him.

"We are five hours away from sunrise. This plan won't work if your brother beats us to the caves. We don't have time for this. We can let the two of you kick the shit out of each other once we get to Crete. For now, calm the fuck down and let it go."

It was a good thing Jackson was Andrei's little bestie. Or his head would be rolling down this deck by now. That was how angry Andrei was.

Surprisingly, Andrei nodded and settled on the bench, no longer in a blind rage. I didn't want to look at him anymore, so I moved closer to my mother and wrapped my arms under her shoulders, pulling her upper body and head to rest on my lap. I leaned back and watched the stars as we made our way to the island.

About an hour later, we pulled into the port in Heraklion. The city was asleep, with only a few lights flickering in the darkness. Jackson grabbed the Book of Shadows and flipped to the map that showed a direct path to Mount Ida.

"The Dikteon Andron Cave is right on the slope of the mountain," Jackson said while Andrei gripped my upper arm to pull me away from Valentina. Liam moved over to her and effortlessly lifted her over his shoulder. The chains binding her rattled a bit as they hung loosely over his chest. Whatever spell had Valentina subdued like that, it was powerful as hell. We walked down the dock toward a narrow road that led into the town.

"What about the Door of the Veil?" Andrei asked.

"It's supposed to be deep in the cave, away from the tourists, and concealed by magic. We can find it since we now possess the key," Liam said. "If we have any issues, I'll use my magic. I'm not sure how far that will get us, but it won't hurt to try."

"Fine," Andrei said. "Wake Valentina up. Now."

Liam gently laid Valentina on the ground and touched her head. A black swirl of magic swept over her body, and she groaned. Her eyes fluttered open, and her face filled with horror after realizing who was there.

"Rachel!" she cried out, attempting to run toward me, but Liam swept a hand over her fingers, and the magical chains tightened around her wrists and squeezed around her neck.

That motherfucker.

"I can't use my magic. I'm sorry," she said, her eyes glaring at Andrei and back to Liam.

"Welcome back to living, Miss Vasile," Andrei said. "Did you enjoy your nap?"

Valentina hissed, showing her sharp fangs, but the only effect they had was the three men laughing at her attempt to intimidate them.

"This really will go more smoothly and painlessly if you cooperate," Liam said. "And don't even think of making a move against me, dhampir. A flick of my wrists, and I'll squeeze these chains so tight that they sever her pretty little head."

I shook my head. "You sick fuck."

Valentina scrunched up her face and balled her hands into tight fists. These men had no idea of the wrath they were about to face when she broke free from those chains.

Jackson looked back up at the path. "We need to hurry. If we don't get to that cave before Jase does, we might not get this shit done before the sun rises."

Andrei nodded. "Before we do, though, I still need something." He glanced at Valentina first. "Not that I don't trust those chains, but if she were to break free, I can't risk the two of them using their powers on us."

He looked down at my right arm in his grip. He released it and instead seized my wrist, bringing my hand up between us. The ring glinted in the light of the streetlamps.

"Give me the ring. Or I'll follow through with my promise to kill her, just like I should have done in that church. When she dies, I'll feel nothing."

I smiled. "But then you lose your leverage," I reminded him.

"Then I'll hang by the shore until Tony gets here and chain him up, too, exactly like Valentina. You know I will."

My anger flared to life. "Still jonesing for this stupid devil trinket? Jesus Christ, you're like a starved dog. Desperate for any semblance of meaning in a wasted immortality. You're nothing but a power-hungry asshole who has nothing to his name but pain and hatred. What a disappointment you've become, *Dimitriou*. This ring will do nothing but tear you apart, and I hope it hurts."

A deathly quiet filled the air, and Andrei's eyes glowed with red hues beneath the dark brown. He squeezed my wrist hard, making the bones pop and creak under the strain. Though it fucking hurt, I didn't flinch.

"Give. Me. The. Ring." Andrei nodded once, and Liam jerked the magical chain, choking Valentina to the point of gagging.

Goddammit.

"You're a weak man," I said, pulling the ring from my finger. He pried it from my hand and shoved me into Jackson's arms.

"Good girl—"

"Shut the fuck up," I seethed.

Andrei paused before a smirk pulled at his lips, and he slipped it on. A rush of power pulled from my aura onto him, the ring sizing to his finger with that crackle of energy.

Andrei closed his eyes, and his fangs slid free. There was something so erotic in his face then, like he relished in the flow of dark power more than he did fucking.

After the ring's power settled, Liam pointed to the small parking lot beside us. "Alright, let's steal a car and get out of here."

We walked around the lot before Liam spotted an SUV that could fit all of us. He touched the handle and used magic to pop the lock without triggering the alarm. Once we settled in the car, Jackson gave us the all-clear, started the engine with the help of Liam's magic, and headed out to the main street.

"That road should take us to Mount Ida," Liam said, pointing to an upcoming intersection. "I'll navigate from back here."

It was mostly silent for the next hour. While Jackson drove, Andrei and I sat beside each other in the back seat, with Liam and Valentina in the row in front of us. Every so often, Valentina would look back at me, and we'd share a look of understanding. The last time we saw each other, we had fought, so much anger brewing between us. But at that moment, I knew that once these bastards released us, she and I would work together to fucking kill every one of them.

There was always the uncertainty about whether we should summon Ezrylos or destroy the summoning circle if things went wrong. Now that nightmare was already upon us, and I didn't have a clue how to get out of it.

The weight of my bloodline felt so damn heavy under my skin. Not only that, but if anything happened to Jase, my mother, or Tony and Lucy, I would never forgive myself.

It's all too much.

I closed my eyes and rested my head against the back seat, the coolness of Andrei's skin against mine causing a ripple of nervous energy to flow through my body. The ropes of anxiety banded around my ribs loosened a little when I pictured my friend's faces instead of focusing on the man beside me.

Soon, we arrived at the two paths leading to the cave. Jackson parked the car outside the perimeter to avoid detection by the security guards. Liam and Andrei gathered the supplies, and we headed toward the paths.

"According to the Book of Shadows, the hike will take twenty minutes before we reach the mouth of the cave," Liam explained, holding the book close to his chest while still gripping the chain that bound Valentina with his other hand. "The paved path on the left means we won't have to do any rock climbing. Jackson, Andrei, keep your senses open to any night hikers or security."

After Liam ensured he had the necessary spell supplies from his backpack, we started the trek to the cave. Liam led us up the mountain, while we trailed behind, Andrei keeping a firm grip on my wrist. There were a few moments when Valentina lost her balance, slipping on rocks, or when Liam pulled too hard on the chains. That fucking asshole, Liam, was going to be the first to have his head ripped off when I got my hands on him. The tang of magic fluttered between me and the witch, which I prayed he didn't notice was coming from me.

Though I had so much more to learn, my magic had grown over the last four months while training at the mansion. Even my dhampir abilities were stronger. Being so close to another witch made my magic flare to life, like a protective response to a threat. My vampire nature also responded to the magic beneath our feet, making my skin crawl, and the beast within my mind growled in agitation.

The area has a lot of power. Even if Zeus's birth here is purely a myth, the magic is real and saturated.

"What's making my skin itch like this?" Andrei asked.

"Yeah, I feel it too," Jackson added.

"The cave's magic repels anything unnatural, and vampires fall into that category because of the source of your power," Liam explained. "But since I have the Fire key, its power lets us enter and remain here without the cave rejecting those with vampiric blood."

"Well, we need to go faster because this is fucking awful," Jackson snapped.

"Hopefully, once we're inside the cave, it'll let up," Andrei noted.

When we reached the end of the trail, I noticed that someone had pulled a large metal gate, complete with several padlocks and chains, across the mouth of Dikteon. The area had several security cameras in place. Andrei gripped my arm and moved us past Jackson and Liam, carefully avoiding detection. The chains and padlock were simple metal, with no hidden wards. Liam reached out and closed his eyes, chanting a cloaking spell I remembered from training with Black Onyx as a child. It made sense why Andrei and Jackson would bring this witch along. Even though they knew I wouldn't risk Valentina's life, having another witch do their dirty work made the process much smoother.

Please, I silently begged whoever or whatever was listening. *Please let Jase, Lucy, and Tony get here soon.*

One thing that comforted me to know: Jase had memorized the map.

There was a calm ripple of power beneath the ground as it moved through Liam, dancing in the air between us. Deep-black mist flowed from his body when he opened his eyes and spread across the ground. The cameras vanished in the thick fog, and Andrei quickly grabbed and tore apart the chains and padlocks before pushing the gate open.

Jackson, Liam, and Valentina hurried inside the cave, while Andrei stopped and turned toward me. "Listen," he whispered, closing the gap between us. "I don't care what happened between you and Jase. You know damn well who you belong to. When all this is over, you'll return to New Orleans with me, and we'll make everything right. You know just as much as I do that no one else will take care of you like I will. I can offer protection that no one else can. Stop fighting me on it."

I blinked. *He can't be serious.* "You're the one I need protection from," I said. "Back at the train station, I thought what I felt for you was real. For a moment, I saw you as more than just a monster bent on capturing me and hurting everyone you came across. I wanted to love you. I really did. But all I feel now is hatred and betrayal for the first man I gave my heart to in decades. You're no different from the Black Onyx—the assholes who kept me on a leash to use and control me. I do not belong to you, Andrei. I never did, and I never will."

Andrei tightened his jaw and gripped my arm again, twirling me to face the cave. "Walk."

The cave was massive, with stalactites and stalagmites covering the walls. Although it was pitch black inside, my enhanced vision allowed me to make out the interior layout.

"Okay, Liam, give me the key. Let's see where it leads us," Andrei ordered.

Liam's jacket rustled as he pulled out the pouch with the Fire key and handed it to him. "Go ahead."

After Andrei took out the key, a soft light covered the metal, throwing long shadows up the rock formations, making them look like jagged fangs. The glow looked like the flame from a candle, and as Andrei turned, the tip of that magic started shifting, directing the light deeper into the cave. At the same time, I felt a tug at my heart, pulling me forward. Something was calling out to me from the darkness, like a song of ancient power.

The cave's darkness wasn't normal. It had a tangible aura that set my nerves on edge. The feeling of being watched by countless curious entities overwhelmed me, as though they were eagerly awaiting any intruder to walk into their sacred space, ready to sink their teeth into our flesh. My heart beat faster with every step as terror threatened to swallow me whole.

"Are you okay?" Andrei whispered, as if he gave a fuck. "Your heartbeat is almost deafening in my ears."

"Leave her alone," Valentina said, distaste in her tone. "You're bothersome enough as it is."

That earned her another yank on the chain, but we grinned at each other. Suddenly, the key's light flared into a brilliant flame, blinding us momentarily.

"What the hell is happening?" Jackson cried out.

"My guess is that we're near the Door of the Veil," Liam replied. He looked around and pointed toward something shining thirty feet ahead. "The key is reacting to that pond."

When my eyes adjusted to the light, I saw what he was pointing at. Several jagged stalagmites were concealing a small pond. My chest tugged again, even though my vampire nature rebelled against it.

"Rachel, you're going to get rid of that water with your element," Liam said. "And let me warn you now. If you use your Water *against* us, I will show you exactly what I can do with Spirit."

I may not be able to get into Liam's head and control him, but I sure as fuck felt his intention then. He put the images in my mind at exactly what he'd do to me if I fucked this up.

"Okay."

I stepped away from Andrei and moved toward the pond. Thankfully, he didn't follow me but blocked the exit, so I couldn't run out. I kneeled at the water's edge and looked at the glassy black surface. It seemed harmless enough, but the energy was undeniable. My Water magic stirred beneath my skin, eager to be released. Cautiously, I dipped my fingers into the water. I felt a strange sensation, like liquid magic had lain dormant for centuries, guarding something that should never be disturbed.

Liam stepped forward with the Book of Shadows, with Andrei beside him, using the light from the key to read the page he had opened. "According to the book, The Door of the Veil is underneath the pond. Get started."

Without acknowledging his entitled tone, I stood and backed away from the water. I raised my hands and focused on all the teachings my mother had given me since we arrived at the academy, allowing purple mists to flow from my fingertips.

"Rachel?" Andrei said in a warning. "Remember, we have your mother's life in our hands."

Get fucked. I moved my magic around, letting it dance in the air.

"Focus. You've been practicing this magic for months," Valentina reminded me, acting like no one else was here but us. Not that we both wanted to give them what they were forcing us to do, but we knew the consequences if we didn't. Getting us inside was our safest move.

I groaned. "Maybe if you weren't always on my ass about how worthless I was with my powers, I could focus better." My magic hummed again, as if urging me to hurry. "Let's see what happens." I looked over my shoulder at Andrei, Jackson, and Liam. "You all should back the fuck up, or we might be limping out of here if it backfires."

Mists poured from my hands and moved across the ground toward the pond. The mists touched the water, and ripples appeared across the smooth surface. Soon, violet fog shrouded the pond, and my arms grew heavy. Splashing and churning waters echoed in the cave as my magic melded with the pond.

Liam stepped forward with the Book of Shadows cradled in his right hand, his left hand raised.

"Water of blood, heed the call," he said, reciting the spell. "Lift the veil and reveal the door of the heavens. Obey and open the gates of righteous light. Only the Burning of Angels will ignite the depths."

A tremendous roar echoed through the cave, like a thousand rivers crashing against the walls. Andrei threw his body over me, and we fell to the ground. Jackson cursed in the darkness. Instinctively, I tried to shove past Andrei to protect Valentina, but he wrapped his arms around me, holding me back. The roaring water seemed to last forever before an explosion of purple and black mists shook the cave. In the distance, I heard several rocks crash to the ground. After a moment, I raised my head to look at the pond.

"Well, would you look at that?" Jackson said with a hint of disbelief in his tone. "The water's completely gone." He turned to me, a grin spreading across his face. "Little dhampy, you did it. Nice work."

Looking back, I noticed an ornate bronze and copper door at the bottom of the pond, surrounded by carvings of winged beings and a lock laden with runes. Andrei helped me to my feet before carefully approaching the door.

When he left me alone, I hurried over to Valentina. Thankfully, Liam didn't pull her back with the chains. "Are you okay?" she asked me, and I nodded.

"You?"

"Not until we're out of here," she said. "Keep focusing on that power—"

"This is the Door of the Veil," Andrei interrupted, running his hand over the door. "The rune above the keyhole matches the one on the key."

Liam then instructed him to open the door.

Andrei reached down, slid it inside, and turned it. The key glowed brighter than before, and its magic vanished into the lock with a wisp of flame and smoke. There was a clang of metal, followed by silence.

Then we waited for ... anything.

As we all stepped forward, the bronze doors began glowing, illuminating the cave before vanishing. There was a collective gasp as the door opened, revealing underground granite stairs.

"Alright, so there's that," I said, brushing dirt from my jeans. "Go on, Andrei, you can go first." I shot him a seething glare.

Andrei slipped the key back into the pouch, tucked it into his pocket, and then seized my upper arm. "Thanks, but Valentina goes in first."

Liam pulled on the chain around her neck, forcing her to walk down the stairs.

My mother descended into the cave with Liam right behind her, and they disappeared into the murky darkness. As I waited to hear her voice, anxiety dug its nails into my stomach.

"We're okay!" she called, her voice echoing from the hole.

"Alright, get your asses down here!" Liam shouted. "Just watch your step. There's evidence of a previous cave-in near the stairs."

Jackson went down first, using the headlamp to illuminate the steps, and then Andrei and I right after. When we reached the bottom, the room glowed with quartz crystals that appeared to have been activated by the opened door. A circle of blue-white marble pillars surrounded the enormous cave. On the floor was a carving of a giant pentagram. The top of the symbol pointed toward an obelisk carved from black stone with veins of gold running cross its surface. At the center of the obelisk were runes etched around a small hole.

I sniffed the air and grimaced. "It smells like stale dust in here. "—I turned to Andrei—"and old blood."

"It's likely from the angel who had to sacrifice themselves to seal the door," he replied, pointing toward the cavern's edge where a pile of dusty bones lay. The wings rested further away, indicating that something sharp had severed them and fallen away from the body. I drew a sharp breath.

"I assume that's the angel from the story—Zahar. That angel must have cut off his wings and then ... killed himself," I said. "It's as if the celestial part of them took longer to deteriorate, so they still have flesh and feathers." My stomach knotted as I sensed the immense yet dormant power of the space. It felt like the stone tower lay sealed in a slumber, meant never to be awakened.

Like what the witches did to my mother....

"Rachel?" Valentina asked. "What's wrong?"

Shaking my head, I replied, "It's nothing. This place is just really fucking creepy." I looked over at the witch. "What does that book say to do now?"

I didn't want to help Andrei get the sword before Jase and the others got here, so we could destroy the obelisk, but I knew that if we didn't make progress, every second was one step closer to them hurting us. Maybe now, if we summoned the angel and got that sword, at least we'd live another day and figure out a new plan that wouldn't leave us all hopelessly fucked.

Liam didn't answer. Instead, he walked to the edge of the pentagram and studied the carvings on the ground. "Jackson," he finally spoke. "Grab your switchblade. Andrei and Rachel, search the wings for anything *unusual*."

Andrei and I went to the angel's body and carefully sorted the dust-covered wings. My nose wrinkled as paper-thin flesh crumbled in my hands as I searched. The feathers were still in pristine condition and silky to the touch. The sacrifice this angel made to conceal this place made my heart hurt. Zahar loved Ezrylos so much that he was willing to die to keep him safe.

"This feather will be different from the rest," Andrei said, kneeling over the left wing. He looked up at Liam. "You said part of the spell involved a special feather of the angel's mate. Right?"

Liam nodded. "It didn't say which one, but your guess is as good as mine," Liam said. We turned to look, and Andrei was holding up part of the severed white wing. Only ... it wasn't all white.

"I'm guessing it's that orange-tinted feather," I said, stating the obvious.

"That'd be the one," Liam said, glancing at the book. "According to the witch from the Black Onyx who was here during the initial ritual to seal the angel within this cave, the power was so strong that it sparked an electric current through his mate, creating a unique item to house the energy. That power concealed itself into something that couldn't die when the rest of the angel's body did."

Andrei plucked it out and gently placed the wing back on the ground. "Hold out your hand," he said.

I did as he asked, and he placed the feather in my palm. A small rush of power pooled in my hand. Something in my blood roared in warning, making my hand tremble.

Before giving any further instructions, Liam sliced my finger with Jackson's knife. "What the hell?" I cried out, but he squeezed, making my blood drip from the wound onto the curved border of the circle.

I looked down as a bright light illuminated each line of the pentagram. A forceful boom echoed from the design, sparking with energy.

Liam handed the switchblade to Jackson and glanced at the ancient pages. "Now you can walk inside. Once you reach the obelisk, place the feather into the opening. After that, step aside and stand at the center of the pentagram," he instructed.

Carefully, I stepped inside, followed his instructions, and then moved back.

"Jackson, now give her the switchblade," Liam said.

Hesitantly, Jackson walked over and placed the knife in my hand. "Don't kill anyone with it, alright?"

Nodding, I looked over at Valentina. Her safety and mine were more important than me stabbing someone ... for now.

"Alright, now cut your palm and drip your blood into that divot in the middle. We need more blood than what I squeezed from your finger," Liam instructed. "If this book is right, the pentagram will light up again, and the blood will flow into the obelisk and the feather. In theory, your angel blood should activate the summoning magic."

"And then what?" Valentina asked, looking at Liam. "You're basing all of this on the fact that the Black Onyx gave you some book you trust will summon an angel? Do you think that whatever comes out of that circle won't try to kill us? It's dark magic. We should leave." She turned to Andrei. "If you ever cared for Rachel, you wouldn't risk her life like this. I don't care if she has angel blood to break this spell. This is wrong, and you know it."

Andrei's eyes turned venomous. "No one wants to play with the dark powers that be, but you and I know that killing the Devil saves us from becoming his little toys someday ... and that includes you, too."

Valentina's eyes grew wide. She knew she was promised to Lucifer, and it was true that if this angel could kill him, maybe she would let it happen when the time came. But was she willing to sacrifice the life of a daughter she fought so hard to have all those years ago to do it?

"We're running out of time," Liam said. "Cut your hand now, Rachel. Do it, or I will tighten these chains, and you can hope Valentina's head doesn't snap off from the force."

Liam yanked the chain, pulling Valentina across the dirt before she lost her balance and fell to her knees, trying to keep the metal from biting into her skin and cutting off her air.

"Stop!" I shouted.

"Do it!" Liam ordered, his eyes flashing red.

What the fuck?

A hostile aura surrounded us, the walls beginning to shake. A sinister darkness grew, dimming the crystals' light into a murky gloom. Something harrowing and dangerous rose in Liam's power that I hadn't felt until now. Whatever magic was within him, my intuition couldn't detect it. Like Wendy, Liam concealed *his* true magic, and it wanted to decimate everyone in that room if we didn't comply.

Shit! Shit!

"Alright. Fine!" I said, desperation in my voice as I held up my hands. "I'm doing it."

My stomach dipped, and every instinct shouted at me to stop. I couldn't destroy the stone anymore, but we could end this if I could get the sword before Andrei did.

"One ... two ... three!"

I pressed the blade against my hand and yanked across my palm—a biting fire bit into my skin, and warm blood pooled from the wide-lipped wound. Liam nodded, and I turned my hand so that the blood poured onto the ground. As the blood splashed, the ground seemed to rumble beneath my feet. The five pentagram points suddenly flared to life in a deep-blue hue. The star's light began to shift toward the obelisk's base.

When the light touched the obelisk, it traveled until it reached the opening where I'd placed the feather. There was a thrum of power and a heartbeat of silence. Then pure golden light burst from the stone and rocketed through the cave ceiling, breaking through the mountain and into the sky. Rocks and debris fell around the pentagram in heaps. I felt my eyes roll to the back of my head and fell to my knees.

"Rachel!" Andrei and Valentina both shouted simultaneously, but I couldn't move. I could only open my mouth and scream. It was as if all my strength was being pulled into the pentagram, fueling the magic.

After what felt like an eternity, the magic stopped pulling on my body, and I opened my eyes. Something landed in the dirt before me, and I saw that Liam had tossed me the Book of Shadows.

"Read it," Liam ordered. "Read it now."

Andrei grabbed the back of my neck, forcing me to stay on my knees. The pentagram's protective spell was gone, and he could cross the circle. "Read the spell."

I nodded, knowing he wouldn't hesitate to torture me, not when he was so close to his goal. Opening the book, I turned the pages to the summoning spell. The incantation was beneath the sketch of the cavern. I started reading.

"The gates of the heavens heed the summons. Ezrylos, the Upper World's gleaming glory against the darkness." I stopped, tightness crushing my chest. This was wrong. This was so wrong. Whatever we were doing was going to destroy us.

"Don't stop now," Andrei said, the floor beneath us trembling. "Keep reading."

I shook my head. "Blood ... blood of the three realms harkens you to this earthly plane." My voice was trembling now, barely able to read the spell as fear strangled my throat. "Come forth, angel of war!"

The light from the obelisk pulsed faster and faster as magic spilled into the cave. With a final boom, the light faded, the obelisk went dark, and the gold veins were no longer visible. The pentagram's power waned, and Andrei wrapped his arms around me as I collapsed in the dirt, softening my landing.

"Shit. Please tell me you're okay," he pleaded as if he was worried about me.

"I'm okay," I said, trying to escape his embrace. "Just ... just exhausted. I can barely move." My lungs felt heavy.

Something shifted behind us, and my eyes widened when I turned around. Standing above us was a man of incredible height, with russet-brown skin and deep brown eyes that glowed like lit coals. His golden wings were almost blinding. Golden armor covered his body with a silver sword etched with strange runes and symbols at his side. His face was pure menace, and he raised the sword to point it at Andrei and me. "Why have you called down the angel of war, Devil's child?"

Ezrylos ... Fuck me.

Before I could explain, the angel's gaze shifted past me toward the perimeter of the cave, where the decaying body of the white-winged angel lay. The golden-winged angel lowered his sword, his eyes growing wide before he ran toward the body, collapsing to the ground beside the severed wings. Ezrylos gripped the weapon and placed his other palm on the white wing. All we saw was his back, his golden wings curling around the fallen angel who had sacrificed his life for him centuries ago. His mate, Zahar. The angel leaned back, his gaze fixed on the ruined ceiling above, and released a thunderous cry that boomed through the air, shaking the walls until they splintered and more rocks rained down around us.

The moment the angel stood, his wings stretched so far they almost touched the cave walls. Once he turned, the ground began to shake.

"What's going on?" I asked, turning to Liam. "What's happening?"

The wall beside the angel cracked and crumbled, and we all quickly ran from the projectile debris. When I looked up, Ezrylos used his wings to block the stones from hitting him.

"Rachel, watch out!" Valentina cried and leaped forward, gripping my arm to pull me away as a three-headed creature crashed through the wall, aiming to pin me beneath its claws.

"What the fuck is that?" I screamed, terror threatening to knock my legs out from under me.

Andrei and Jackson ran our way and turned around. Andrei's hands were out front, and his fire magic hovered over his fingertips. "That, love, is a Cerberus."

CHAPTER 43

RACHEL

"Cerberus?!" I screamed as I looked around the cave for a weapon. "What the fuck?" My eyes darted over broken, jagged rocks. The creature stepped further into the cave and a sulfurous scent wafted around us. My eyes burned, and I felt my magic roil in response to this evil entity. Even the beast within my head roared with rage and *fear*.

"Liam, take these goddamn chains off of me, so that I can fight!" Valentina shouted at him. The young witch looked sick with horror as he took a step back.

The coward was useless.

We would have to rely on Andrei's Fire magic and my Water element to hold off the Cerberus. Ezrylos was watching the beast crawl out of the ruined wall, his sword still only dimly lit with power. It looked like he had no intention of helping us.

It was like he'd sent them to kill us.

Andrei unleashed a wave of searing heat at the beast, melting the rocks beneath its massive paws. The Cerberus leaped high, evading the magic, and launched itself at Andrei. It crashed into his body, sending them both flying across the cave. Jackson ran after them, his fangs and sharpened nails flashing as he tried to get to his friend.

Fuck. We'll have to work together to get out of this alive. Then I'm going to fucking kill Andrei and that goddamn witch.

Summoning my mists, I manipulated its shape into something manageable and as sharp as ice. I sprinted to where Andrei grappled with the dog monster and jumped onto its back, driving two water knives into its flesh.

Okay, this is getting easier.

As it shrieked, I tried to crawl up, aiming to grab one of its heads. The other two were preoccupied with trying to turn Andrei into a chew toy.

I didn't see its serpent-like tail whip around behind me. Its heavy force slammed into my body and knocked me to the ground, cracking two ribs. A burning, ripping pain tore through me as the beast's razor-sharp claws sliced into my left arm. I looked up to see a huge dog head come barreling down to take a bite out of me.

"Fuck!" I screamed, kicking my left leg to fend off the teeth. A ball of molten lava smashed into the Cerberus, knocking it back and setting its black fur aflame. Ezrylos growled as the beast rose and lunged for him instead.

Okay, maybe I'm wrong about those creatures working with him.

The sword flared to life, and the creature howled in rage, claws swiping at the angel. *Looks like he'll have no choice but to help now.*

"There's another one!" Jackson shouted as he rolled to his feet, a gash across his brow. My head whipped to the hole, seeing another equally fucking ugly monster emerge, its fur just as black and odious as its twin.

Valentina desperately tried to pull off the chains around her wrists, her fingers tearing against the binding magic. Her face was pure panic as her eyes found mine. Her intention flooded my senses. She was terrified for me. Her desire to protect me, her daughter, drove her to madness, and my heart cracked again.

"Rachel!" a familiar voice shouted into the cave, and I spun around. Jase stood at the edge of the pentagram circle, blue flames rising from his outstretched palms. *Thank God.*

Right then, the second beast charged at him, and he sent the fire crashing into its body. He sprinted toward me, wrapping me in his embrace. His scent washed over me like a warm pool, making me suddenly feel renewed.

"Where are Lucy and Tony?" I asked frantically as we pulled away from each other.

"Lucy's with Tony outside the cave. She'll protect him," Jase said, pushing a tangled lock out of my eyes. His gaze grew cold as he looked at his older brother, who watched us.

"Protect her at all costs. Understand?" Jase growled with every word, the demand in his voice making my knees weak. Andrei blinked in surprise but nodded. Jackson was with Ezrylos, fighting against the burnt Cerberus. Liam was still standing on that platform like a useless idiot, and Valentina began clawing at her chains.

The brothers launched into a combined attack with waves of amber and cerulean dancing around them. I summoned more purple mists but didn't hold back my vampire power this time. I threw the leash off my beast and let her roam wild in my bones, my very blood. My eyes shifted to blue-black, and the intense power melded with the violet of my water magic. My heart pounded with the exhilaration of my combined energies, and my wounds healed instantly.

I had control over this. I *was* in control.

I lifted my right hand overhead and concentrated on the weapon I desired—the power of the dhampir and the witch. A halberd formed in my palm, and my fangs slid free behind my lips. A surge of energy filled the space, and the second Cerberus cocked all three heads in my direction, ignoring Andrei and Jase.

"Come here, doggie," I crooned, ice in my throat. "Mommy's got a stick for you."

The middle head bared its dripping fangs at me, knocking the men over with that giant tail. Its head weaved like a cobra before charging at me.

Let the water of life and the power of death pierce the monster. I chanted this mantra silently as I lowered the weapon, sliding my left hand up the shimmering staff and gripping the end with the other. As the beast closed in, I shifted my weight and swung the halberd, letting the blade slice across its flesh. I kept the momentum and moved the weapon in a figure-eight pattern at lightning speed. Black blood splattered on the ground as I forced the Cerberus into retreat, deflecting the claws aimed at my throat.

The three heads shrieked, making my ears ring, and it reared on its hind legs as I forced it back against the cave wall. Seeing the opportunity, I imbued more power into the spike, transforming it into a spear. Then, using every ounce of my vampire strength, I drove the weapon deep into the beast's chest, cracking bone and sending more reeking blood spraying into the air. I gagged against the intense sulfur and rot that poured from the thrashing body.

Then I yanked the spike free and let the twitching dog collapse, its three heads staring blankly at me.

Disgusting.

I glanced over my shoulder, and Jase had the other monster trapped in a ring of blue fire, while Andrei slowly turned the stone beneath its claws into molten lava. Jackson was sitting against the wall, his hand pressed to his side as a slow crimson bloom spread under his hand. I couldn't see Ezrylos in my peripheral, but eyed Liam collapsing on his ass, watching everything while tugging on a black necklace around his throat.

I took one step toward him and my mother—one step.

And everything went to Hell.

Liam suddenly bolted to his feet, a deranged, wicked smile on his face. His left hand was still on his necklace, and he raised the other in my direction.

"No!" Valentina screamed. Jase's head whipped to me as Liam's crimson magic speared right for me. I dissolved the halberd and replaced it with a wall of violet-blue ice. His magic crashed into mine, and the wall fractured.

"Shit!" I shouted, pushing more magic into the wall, but the cracks kept spreading. Jase screamed my name with so much fear in his voice. My vampire strength held, but my magic was starting to sputter. I didn't know if I'd be fast enough to evade the energy if my ice wall fell.

It trapped me.

My wall shattered into shards of purple snowfall as my eyes locked onto Jase's. A fire ignited deep within me—not just the will to fight for myself but for him—the one the stars had chosen as my mate. I didn't know what that truly meant or how I felt about it, but at that moment, I wanted to fight for him. For us.

Suddenly, a massive figure blocked my sight, and a hand shoved me several feet back, my back and head smacking the ground so hard that white spots covered my vision. When I recovered, I looked up. Liam's magic had pierced Ezrylos's chest, and the sword fell from his hand. As the angel dropped to his knees, Liam moved in front of him, grabbed the weapon, and drove the blade through Ezrylos's back.

Everyone, including the surviving Cerberus, stopped. My hands flew to my mouth. *Oh my God.*

The angel groaned. His right hand stretched to those white wings—to the long-dead mate he loved so much. "Zahar."

The angel's skin turned gray, and his body fell into dust. His golden wings, now dulled, landed on the ground. Liam cocked his head to the right, a sinister smile tugging at his mouth as he looked down at what he'd done. The shining sword also lost its color, turning steel gray, and the runes vanished.

Liam spun on his heel and returned to my mother, who seemed rooted to the ground. As he walked, he let out a sharp whistle. The creature trapped in fire bounded over the flames and trotted toward Liam. The one I *thought* I killed also rose and ran to its master. "Come, Jinx," he called to it.

"What the fuck?" I whispered, too confused to say more.

"Come here, boy," Liam called again. "I could have let this go on longer, but I couldn't risk you hurting Jinx and Saber. My pets. I already lost Nyxen. To gain your trust in that museum, I had to make that sacrifice, killing one of them."

What is happening? Andrei came to my left side. Jackson, now healed, slowly walked to my right, fangs bared. "Why? Why did you kill the angel? You weren't supposed to do that … dick."

Andrei hissed and started to move toward Liam, but the witch held up a hand, his hazel eyes flickering to black. "I wouldn't do that if I were you, *Dimitriou.*"

Jase's hand slid over my wrist, gently pulling me back behind him. Liam's eyes flashed to us, and my spine locked up in pure terror. Ice coated my veins, and my gut burned with fear. Horrific intentions poured from Liam's body.

He wasn't a witch.

Something was always off about him since the boat; I just didn't know what.

"Are … are you a demon?" I asked.

The Cerberus called Jinx moved in front of Liam, caging him in a protective stance. Liam let out a low, indulgent laugh, his fingers drifting back to that damn necklace. "Demon? No, I'm not a lowly servant. I find that offensive, Rachel."

Valentina let out a heavy sigh and shook her head. Liam moved to her and yanked on the chains, knocking her down to her knees.

"This was all too easy. Andrei's fascinating obsession with you made him the perfect tool to get here. Plus, I needed a Fire witch to turn that key. We hit a few snags along the way, but the results are the same. My father always hated me, and now I get to gloat over the fact I've killed his favorite son, saving you all the doom and gloom of his presence here on Earth and this pesky war. Father loved Ezrylos the most, always thinking of me as the weakest of his children. Guess I proved him wrong."

Brother? Is Liam an angel?

"So, what?" I snapped. "All this was because you have fucking daddy issues?"

"Rachel!" Valentina warned, her voice strangled by the collar. "Don't provoke him. Get out of here!"

I shook my head. "Not until this whiny bitch releases you from those chains."

Liam laughed again before yanking hard on the necklace, snapping the black chain free. He tossed the broken pieces aside, and dread replaced the terror in my body. Liam's face began to shift and melt, like wax too close to a flame, and he *changed* before our eyes.

His brown hair darkened, growing in waves that reached just below his ears before turning black as midnight and absorbing all light. The smooth lines of his face sharpened, and his jaw hardened into something predatory. His cheekbones rose as he smiled, carved as if from stone. His softly tanned skin gleamed unnaturally, flawless, and unearthly.

He was hauntingly beautiful ... like a god.

When he stepped closer into the light, his warm hazel eyes chillingly transformed into a burning green, shimmering like gemstones. I felt the weight of an ancient, incomprehensible power as he loomed over us.

As the cave grew silent, Liam's eyes rested on my mother.

"A demon is a servant. But an angel of darkness demands submission." His gaze pierced mine, locking me in place.

"No fucking way...." My voice faltered as the man who had once been Liam yanked Valentina against his broad chest, pulling her into his arms. Jase's hand gripped mine fiercely, anchoring me against the mind-numbing horror before us. In my peripheral vision, I watched Andrei's eyes grow wide, and his hands curled into tight fists.

"I could never hurt *her*," he said, his thumb brushing gently across Valentina's cheek. "But that angel was the only one standing in my way, and *he* needed to die." His smile broadened with pride. "We haven't officially met, Rachel." I felt the burn of his stony gaze when he redirected his attention to me. "... I'm Lucifer. The Morning Star."

CHAPTER 44

JASE

I have known terror. Ice-cold terror that stole the strength from my muscles, froze the pulsing blood in the heart, and strangled the screams. My brother embodied that feeling when he killed our parents and went after me.

But the Devil ... was so much more frightening than Andrei ever was. My hand squeezed Rachel's, and she gripped back with equal strength, as if to assure me she was there. Andrei was a few steps ahead, while Jackson stood on Rachel's right, frozen in fear with us.

Lucifer smiled, running a long, sharp nail down Valentina's arm in a delicate caress. "Well, you've become quite the captive audience. Good. We can get started."

He raised his hand and snapped his fingers. A black metal chain shot from the ground and wrapped around Rachel's upper body, yanking her toward him and out of my grasp. She collapsed on her knees before him, thrashing against the chains that kept her arms tied down.

"You fucking piece of shit!" I growled, my fangs bared. "I'll fucking kill you!" I charged toward him, each step fueled by a primal rage to protect her. My vision tunneled to Lucifer's arrogant smirk.

"Andrei," he said calmly. "I need you to restrain your brother for me."

Andrei spun so fast I barely saw him move, his arm reaching out to grip me by the throat. His eyes were deep red, the veins bulging beneath them. He shoved me backward, but I seized his wrist and shoulder, yanking him forward so my forehead smashed into his. Using my heightened strength, I threw him off-balance and kicked him in the ribs, sending him flying back. A grunt left his lungs as he slammed into the cave wall, the impact splitting it in several directions.

Surprisingly, Jackson made no move to attack me. His dark eyes met mine, and he gave a slow, deliberate nod. *Approval?* It shocked me, which left me wondering what the fuck my brother did to turn his best friend against him.

My attention went back to Rachel as she shouted over the chaos. "Jase, no!" she cried, the chain slowly winding up her chest toward her throat. "He'll kill you."

The fear painted across her face halted my steps.

Andrei was slow to rise but made no move to grab me again. It felt as if … he was waiting for something.

Shit.

Lucifer snapped his fingers again, and multiple chains materialized, keeping Valentina anchored to the floor. He turned toward me with that familiar predatory grace all of us monsters possessed. He raised his hand and used a slow, languid flourish to address us again.

"This is ridiculous. What exactly was your plan, Jase? Did you think you could make a heroic rescue to overthrow the King of Darkness? I mean, it was *very* bold of you. I'll give you credit for that. But allow me to show you some pointers."

I growled, my fangs bared and ready to tear this fucking bat's throat out.

Lucifer spread his arms wide before swinging them together, his palms clapping with a deafening crack that boomed in my ears like thunder. My head swam from the force, and I pressed my hands against my ears, feeling blood squelch beneath my palms. The fucker busted my eardrums.

"Fuck!" The ringing in my head was all-consuming, and the world seemed to tilt beneath my feet. That's when another concussive blast hit me square in the chest. An invisible current seized my body, icy claws wrapping around my arms and throat and freezing me entirely. My feet felt encased in ice. Panic flared in my guts. I couldn't move.

"Jase! Jase, are you okay?" Rachel's screams sounded so muffled in my head. My ears itched fiercely as the perforated eardrums began to heal.

Shouting erupted beside me, and Andrei's and Jackson's curses echoed through the cave. I couldn't see what was happening, but I heard a scuffle cut through the hum of Lucifer's power. From the noise, I could tell Jackson was grappling with Andrei, trying to get him to calm down.

"Come on, man, please snap out of it. You can't let that fucker get in your head," Jackson pleaded.

There was a snapping, popping noise, and Jackson fell to his knees, a force of blistering energy shoving him down. Andrei stalked forward, pushing past Jackson, and summoned a ball of fire. The heat was unbearable, and I was sure the rocks would melt any second.

As he passed me, he threw it at Lucifer's head.

Thank fuck.

But it was pointless. Lucifer snatched the flames mid-air, closing his fist around the magic like he was snuffing out a candle. The embers dissolved into nothing, and the asshole laughed. *Fuck.* I could only stare at the Devil and hope the chaos from the cave reached Lucy. She'd stayed behind below the hill, just as I ordered. Tony would have only slowed us down, and she refused to leave him behind, choosing to stand guard in case any more enemies came up the trail. Right now, though, I needed her to ignore that order and get the fuck in here, or there'd be nothing left of us to save.

We were so fucked.

"Oh, come on. This is a little too dramatic for me," Lucifer mocked, wrapping his arms tightly around Valentina's waist like the beast couldn't bear to be away from her. His eyes burned with hatred as he moved closer to us, dragging Valentina behind him like a dog on a leash. "All of this fighting is just going to wear you out and get you killed." He paused, lips curling into a wolfish grin. "Let's calm down and have a civilized adult conversation instead."

His gaze shifted lazily to Valentina, who thrashed against the chains. "How long?" she asked. "How long have you been on Earth, disguised as someone else?"

He reached out and tucked a red strand of hair behind her ear in a slow, intimate gesture. "Ever since Jase brought you back to life with Rachel's blood in that church. You see, the moment they broke the spell, I climbed through the gates with my demons. Remember, darling, that blood oath you made allows me to come and go as I please so long as *you* live. Since then, I've played a little role in manipulating Andrei to hire me to work with his clan, creating this faux character named Liam, and making them all believe the Black Onyx assigned me to them. They don't even know I exist. Nor could anyone see me unless I allowed it."

Valentina's breath hitched, and she tried to move away, but he only squeezed tighter on the chains.

"My love, I've been watching you since you awoke in that crypt. I am the Devil, of course; I see every dark heart that roams the world. But since I couldn't step into this pentagram or use that key, I needed Andrei to do my dirty work. In time, his weak mind succumbed to my power. His obsession with your daughter was the driving force to get you back. Granted, I may have helped grow that obsession through my power. Now, he's practically unhinged for her."

Using my dwindling strength, I turned to look over my shoulder. My brother was kneeling, nails buried in the dirt and rubble. Andrei's face was pure rage, but he couldn't move anymore. We were all trapped.

"You bastard." Valentina's voice drew my eyes back. She scowled at him before spitting in his face. Rachel's jaw dropped, a ghost of a laugh in her mouth, despite the shit we were in.

Instead of lashing out, Lucifer wiped his cheek with the back of his hand and then wiped it against his pants. "Oh, my queen," he purred, tilting his head. "You're going to give yourself wrinkles if you scowl like that. I don't think you want to ruin that beautiful face of yours, do you?" He reached out, wrapping a crimson lock around his forefinger to brush it from her face. "A queen must be untouchable." His voice sounded like a velvet caress. My stomach churned in revulsion, and Rachel's face reflected the same sentiment. "Poised, breathtakingly beautiful, and absolutely *mine*." His eyes turned to a deep midnight green as he leaned to whisper in her ear. "Save that energy for when I fuck you."

Valentina's eyes burned with defiance, even when her body stilled under his hands. "I have told you for thousands of years that I will never be yours. Ever!"

Lucifer smiled at that. "Ah, that fire," he mused, his fingers trailing down her cheek to her jaw. "It's what makes you so exquisite. It's why I chose you. You're constantly fighting me at every turn, yet here you are. Completely at my mercy." He leaned in, his lips barely a breath away from her ear. "Do you feel it, love? What the two of us will become together?" She jerked her head away, but his hand slid to the back of her neck, holding her so firmly she winced. "Hate and scream at me, and try to run—I *welcome* it. None of that *fucking* matters, because at the end of the day, you'll always end up right here." He pressed his forehead lightly against hers, his voice dropping to a low whisper. "With me. Not Cyrus. Not Darius." He smirked. "I took care of that one for us."

Valentina's eyes turned dark, but all the rage inside her would still do nothing.

Rachel remained frozen like the rest of us but turned her head to look at me. I wanted to run to her—to save her — but all we could do was watch.

"Not even these chains can hold you tighter than I already do, my queen," he purred before twirling her around and placing his grip on her throat. "Now that everyone is where I want them, it's time for the next step of my plans."

"What do you want?!" Rachel cried out. "She already rejected you once, you fucker. You killed the angel and destroyed that sword's power. What more from us do you want?!"

Lucifer reached into Valentina's pants pocket and pulled out a stone with his free hand.

"No!" Valentina screamed. "That doesn't belong to you. It's mine!"

Lucifer held it up to the dim light of the illuminating crystals in the cave. "This stone will temporarily break down the elements, severing all power on Earth. Unfortunately, now that I'm here in the flesh, I'm not entirely immune to getting hurt. We can play a little back in the States with the covens. I guess it's a gift for Valentina. She's been dying to enact her revenge on the Black Onyx Coven for years. And I'm tired of those fucking witches killing my vampires ... the children that will soon unite in the Underworld with me."

It was then that I realized Lucifer wasn't going anywhere. He was on Earth to stay, for now at least.

I looked back at Andrei. His head was hanging low, his disheveled dark hair covering his face. "Andrei, now's the time for us to settle our feud once and for all. Help me fight this fucker."

He raised his head, and my blood froze. Andrei's dark eyes, our father's eyes, were pitch black, the veins prominent again. Something moved behind those eyes, like smoke.

"Ah shit," I cursed. "Jackson, I need you!"

"I can't even fucking move," Jackson groaned, but our eyes locked, and we both knew the same thing. Lucifer's smoky power fully had a hold on Andrei.

Lucifer's Cerberus advanced toward me, its hot, reeking breath skating over my cheeks. It took all my resolve not to look away as it advanced.

"Andrei, I have a task for you," Lucifer said, standing straight.

"Of course, my king," Andrei replied, swaying a little as he climbed to stand. Burning fear ate at me, and I thrashed harder. This version of my brother was more horrible than when I was a child in that shed.

"Once we've settled these matters, you'll bring my beloved pets home. Don't forget to feed them. They enjoy the souls of murderers for dinner and animal abusers for breakfast. My servant, Charon, will assist you with whatever you need," he said. "Someone needs to guard the Underworld while I'm gone. And it may be *a while*."

No. No fucking way.

"He's not doing shit for you," I warned. "Let us go, or I swear—"

"You'll do what?" Lucifer taunted, those twin pillars of smoke behind his back dancing. "You knew, deep down, that something was off with me. Jackson suspected it, as well, but you couldn't quite figure it out, huh?"

The beast was so close to me now that a glob of greenish slobber dripped on my arm.

Gross.

"Not to worry; I have other plans for you and Rachel."

My eyes narrowed at the Devil, no longer caring about the deadly creature's teeth next to my face.

With a sigh, Lucifer released Valentina's throat, the chains rattling as he stepped forward. The twin pillars writhed faster and solidified, morphing into enormous bat wings. Crimson and black flesh that pulsed with a tangible, unholy aura. Atop his head, black, curved horns formed, the points reaching to the back of his head.

He flared his wings wide as he shouted, "Kneel!" The compulsive power in his voice slammed against all of us except Andrei, and my knees slammed into the rock floor, pain searing up my thighs and back. Rachel was also dragged to her knees and forced to face me, panic wild in those blue eyes. She tried to speak, but no words came.

We were mere feet apart, yet I couldn't reach her.

Lucifer sauntered toward us with grace, bending his knees to rest his elbows on his thighs, eye level with us.

"You never told your brother, did you?" he asked, shifting his eyes to Andrei, who walked to his side, eyes still black. "Andrei won't save you. My power has taken root within him, and he will obey my every word, but he is still aware of what's happening. I can't wait to tell him this next little secret."

I shook my head, knowing exactly what he was about to reveal.

"Andrei, I know you fucked this pretty little thing, but I have bad news. She's fated to your brother. They're soulmates." Lucifer flashed his white teeth. "This is why you stopped feeling her through the guardian bond. Jase's connection was snuffing yours out."

Rachel's eyes widened, and she shook her head right before staring into Andrei's penetrating, heated gaze. When I looked up, Andrei's expression had changed. Though his eyes hadn't returned to their usual brown, the deep hurt in them suggested he was close to fucking tears.

"Impossible," Andrei said. "It's not true."

"Oh, but it is," Lucifer breathed. "They even know it. Jase has known this entire time since he's been living under your roof. I'm guessing he told Rachel about it during the brief road trip down here because, by the look in her eyes, she seems to have accepted it. In fact, she loves it."

"Lucifer, stop!" Valentina shouted. "I'll go with you. I'll be your fucking queen. Just leave her alone. Leave them all alone!"

"Oh, that's rich, coming from you, sweetheart," he said, standing up and turning slightly to face her. "Aside from Jackson, you're responsible for everyone's misery in this cave. You turned these poor brothers into monsters. Murdered their parents. You created a hybrid for your own selfish needs by fucking a human man when I had *forbidden* it. Funny enough, that's the reason we are all still here. My queen, albeit perfect, needs to be punished for her actions. You see, I have a secret myself."

Lucifer looked back at us before walking toward Rachel. I struggled to break the spell that bound us, but I couldn't move to save her. The Devil's blackened nail extended, and he pressed his finger under her chin, raising her face to stare directly into his eyes. His other hand touched the hem of her shirt and lifted it.

"Don't you fucking touch her!" I growled, but Lucifer only smiled and touched the rune on her stomach. Immediately, I felt mine burning to life, drawing out the power between the bond. My insides felt like they were on fire, stoked by my desperation to protect her.

"When that Hades Blood Moon occurred four months ago, a tether of power reforged their lives together," Lucifer continued. "The first link occurred two hundred years ago, as her mother lay on the floor of the church after Jase had consumed her blood. The fate of the Underworld and the Blood Moon's lunar influence bound their souls together. Oh yes, your little brother never lost his soul. It's there, nestled inside. Valentina was enraged at the idea of her child being fated to another, especially *him*. To have Rachel's choice stripped away and tied to one of her enemies."

My eyes widened, and dread gripped my stomach. I hadn't felt nauseous in centuries, but right then, I wanted to be sick.

"Shall I read the meaning of the runes to you all?" Lucifer mocked. "*By the stars and the moon bathed in blood, let two souls become one*. Poetic, isn't it? As the stories all say, I, too, was once an angel of great power before my father cast me out and trapped me within the Underworld to rule as its king. But he didn't strip me of all my celestial powers. One gift remained—to grant *unique* souls their destinies ... or fate, so to speak." His bemused smirk deepened, sharp as a blade. "Do you understand now? *I* was the one who tied the two of you together. Not some sanctimonious Upper World angel. *Me.* A fitting punishment for your mother's ... deception."

No ... he's fucking lying. I really was going to be sick. "You like to talk, don't you?" I choked out.

He moved closer to me now. The black energy rolling off him was suffocating. "It helps that you and Rachel understand everything. You're not only bound as fated mates because of me but by *Hell* itself. Your souls? They belong to *me*. Ring or not, I own you. If you deny each other, you could perhaps escape the consequences. But something tells me it's already far too late for that."

I didn't want to look at Andrei's face. I could feel the murderous rage emanating from him. Lucifer's hold over him was the only thing keeping him from killing me.

Lucifer turned his piercing gaze solely on me. Fury ignited in my chest, my magic raging and desperate to burn the smug motherfucker in front of me. The feeling was searing and all-consuming within my soul—a soul I didn't know I possessed. "Especially for you, Jase Halpert," he continued, his voice dropping to a low, taunting whisper. "Your love for this woman burns brighter than any star in the sky or flame in Hell could conjure. I've seen countless souls across eternity, yet yours stands apart. Rachel may not feel that love yet, but you ... you'll endure damnation and eternal torment to keep that love alive. However, since I am *benevolent*, I will offer a choice." Lucifer stood between us now. "Keep the fated bond, and your souls will remain together, but when death comes, I will take your souls to the Underworld. If you want to be free, I shall remove those marks from your body, but you'll never see each other again, nor will you ever love another again."

"Oh my God," Rachel breathed.

Lucifer made a face like she'd just insulted his entire existence.

But she wasn't paying attention to him. Her eyes locked onto mine, and something in her expression knocked the air from my lungs. She shook her head, and I wished like hell I could hear what was running through her mind.

"Jase ..." My name barely made it past her lips.

I held her gaze, keeping her from looking at the bastard beside us. She had to focus on me. Not him. Not what was coming.

As if Rachel could read my thoughts, she shook her head. "Don't," she said softly, yet her voice was pleading. "I ... I don't want you to."

I knew how I felt about her, but even with her begging me not to deny that fate, I still didn't know how she truly felt.

Her head slightly turned, and a tear fell from her eye, dripping down her cheek. "I don't know how I feel," she said, keeping her eyes locked on mine. "But I know that whatever this is, I'm not ready to let it go."

My gaze looked into hers, brimming with tears for me. "I would gladly surrender my soul to the shadows of Hell if it meant I could see your light every day for eternity. You have given me a reason to feel alive again—a solace for the broken parts of me. I choose you, my angel. I will always choose you."

Andrei growled.

"Mmm," Lucifer murmured, standing straight. "That was easy—"

The crack of gunfire filled the cavern, cutting him off—a bullet whipped overhead, slamming between Lucifer's eyes.

As he staggered back and fell, the binding power lifted slightly. Rising to reach Rachel was like moving through thick mud. Somehow, I managed to grab her, pulling her up.

"What the hell was that?" she asked frantically.

Before I could answer, Lucifer was already on his feet, brushing debris from his legs. The cave walls started to shake as he flared his monstrous wings. There was a flash of movement by the stairs that led out of the cavern. Lucy charged inside the pentagram, Rachel's Gunslinger revolver in her right hand. She took cover behind a large stalagmite.

There was another crack as the magic slowing us down finally fell, and I lurched forward, my fire sparking back to life. Rachel took a deep breath beside me, and cooling mist brushed against the side of my face.

Lucifer straightened, a grimace twisting his godlike features as his dark energy swirled around him like a raging storm. The hole between his eyes sealed, black tendrils pulling the flesh together, and the bullet clattered harmlessly to the floor. His green eyes shifted to that blood-red shade I knew too well, sparkling with indignant fury and something akin to amusement. "Well," he said. "That was rude. Ironwood stings, you know."

Lucy sprinted forward with her vampiric speed, but this time, Lucifer was ready. Lucy took another shot at his head, but he quickly dodged the bullet, which smashed into the wall behind him. When she came close, her arm pulled back with a knife clenched in her fist. Lucifer seized her arm and wrenched it until the weapon dropped to the ground.

"Lucy!" Rachel screamed, throwing her hands out and sending two spears of water at Lucifer. He released Lucy's arm and batted away the oncoming magic. Jackson grappled with Andrei, throwing punches to subdue or knock some sense back into his head.

From my peripheral, Tony appeared and sprinted to where Ezrylos fell, and the sword lay. Tony's fingers closed around the hilt and lifted it as he ran toward Rachel. Though the wielder was dead and the runes gone, I hoped it could still do some damage. Lucifer's smoke-like energy rushed past my head, and before I could cast a shield, it struck Tony, slamming him back into a column of stone. The sword slipped from his hand and skittered across the ground toward Rachel. We looked at each other, and she took off for the weapon. Lucy followed, taking a defensive position over Tony. She fired two more shots at Lucifer.

Valentina remained anchored to the ground, completely immobile. She screamed at Lucifer to stop, to leave her daughter alone and take her instead. The collar around her neck dug deeper into her skin, and thin streams of blood oozed out.

As I turned to help Tony, Andrei was on me, his fiery fists swinging for my head. I dodged and glanced over his shoulder to see Jackson sprawled on the ground, alive but stunned, with a smoking wound on the side of his head. Andrei's possessed eyes locked on mine, empty and strange.

"We know what happened the last time we fought," I taunted, conjuring flames in my hands as I ducked his blows. "Either get a hold of yourself or I'm putting you down again." We clashed in a blaze of heat, brilliant flames locking in a dance of death. The surrounding space began to shimmer, and the ground beneath us glowed.

Jackson lunged at Andrei from behind, the wound in his head now healed. Though he was a blur, Andrei reacted faster. He spun fast, raising his right arm across his body, and lashed out, sending a whip of searing heat across Jackson's chest. With a grunt of pain, Jackson fell back, a large smoking gash slicing through his shirt and skin. He rolled to his feet and snarled at Andrei.

"Focus on Lucifer!" Jackson coughed, his voice strained as he healed. "I'll take care of Andrei."

I barely had time to register his words when Rachel's voice cut across the chaos. "Jase!"

I turned to see her grab the sword while Lucy helped Tony to his feet. With both hands wrapped around the hilt, she staggered a little, like the weight of it was too much. Once she steadied herself, she took on a warrior's stance, wielding the sword high.

Lucifer paused when he saw her. His expression darkened, the smirk fading into something colder. "That won't kill me, sweetheart. Not anymore."

Rachel raised the sword higher, her grip steady now. Her ice-blue eyes blazed, unyielding in the face of evil. "I guess we'll see what damage I *can* do, then. Maybe scar that smug fucking face of yours."

She charged, the blade cutting through the air with an ethereal hum. Lucifer raised a hand, and a black-red whip lashed at her, but the sword cut through the magic effortlessly, meeting him head-on. The force of her swing knocked Lucifer back, slicing through his left arm and chest.

I summoned a ball of fire and threw it at Lucifer. He sidestepped the attack and raised a brow at me. "That was quite an aim. You almost got me," he taunted.

I grinned at him. "I wasn't aiming for you."

Valentina looked down at the weakened binding hex now severed by my magic. She whipped the broken chains around the Devil's arm, pulling him off balance. Rachel dipped low and sliced into his knee, making him fall. Lucy appeared from the other side, her fists finding their marks. The three women were making that bastard suffer, and I fucking loved it. I drew deep within my wells of magic, calling on the fire of all the stars. It was time to send this demon back to Hell.

For a moment, we had him cornered.

Then Lucifer let out a deafening roar, his power exploding outward in a wave that sent all of us flying backward.

My head cracked against the ground, momentarily stunning me, but I forced myself up. That was when Andrei tackled me, his arm locked around my neck. He had Rachel by the throat, and she was clawing at his hand. Lucy and Jackson lay unconscious, and Tony hunched over near the stalagmites. I heard his shallow breaths, his broken ribs dangerously close to puncturing a lung.

Fuck!

Whatever possessed Andrei had enhanced his strength. I went to use my fire again, but nothing happened. I reached up and felt his fingers, moving my hand around until I noticed he was no longer wearing the ring. It had vanished.

"Goddammit, Andrei! Fight it! You can't let this fucking bastard control you," I yelled, struggling against his grip around my neck. Rachel tried freezing his hand with magic, but the purple mists skated over him. The amplified demonic power possessing him was snuffing it out. We only had our strength, and it wasn't enough.

Valentina lunged for him, but the broken chains reconnected themselves, and a force yanked her back to the ground. Lucifer stepped forward, his grin back in place and his bloodless chest wound healing. "You tried, at least," he mocked as his lip turned up. "But it would never be enough."

Valentina pushed forward, but the chains tightened and wrenched her back. Behind him, the earth cracked open, splitting in two as a hellish red light poured from the depths. Flames licked at the jagged edges, their heat making the air reek with the stench of brimstone and scorched earth.

"Andrei," Lucifer called to him, "bring them to me."

"No!" Rachel screamed, thrashing against Andrei's grip while she attempted to slide the sword over to her with her feet.

"You're the only one who can kill me now, Rachel, so I think it's best you hang out below deck for a bit while I play house with your mother up here."

She shook her head. "How could I possibly—"

"Your arm," Lucifer said, and we all looked at her.

No. The symbols from the sword were etched onto Rachel's forearm like a bright red scar.

"Seems my brother, before I stabbed him, did one last thing before he died. Once he stops breathing, the sword tied to his powers dies with him. So, it looks like he passed that magic onto you ... a new vessel ... making you the next weapon to kill me. And we can't have that."

Fuck. Horror now gripped my throat.

"This all worked out for the best. I needed Andrei to fall into darkness, so he could guard the Underworld in my stead. Not only that, his guardian bond was perfect for weakening Rachel and pushing her to Jase. Get my fated mates together, only to rip them apart in the end. Such misery is *delicious.* Now that the symbols are on your arm, I'll have to hide you, or the Black Onyx will *really* come looking for you. I'm glad Andrei will have some company while I'm gone."

The pull of the Underworld intensified, dragging us closer as Lucy, Jackson, and Tony shouted behind us. Andrei didn't loosen his grip. His strength, fueled by Lucifer's will, tightened around my scalp, making it burn as he adjusted his hold and now dragged us by our hair. Hell's gate flared to life, its heat brushing against my cold cheeks. We struggled against Andrei's strength, but the darkness consumed us, swallowing us whole as we fell through.

The last thing I heard was the echo of Rachel's screams fading into the void.

When my feet hit the ground, I looked up. Andrei was no longer holding me, and I spun around, panicked.

"Rachel?!" I shouted, but she, too, was gone.

The Underworld was not a realm of fire and brimstone like the books said. At least, not where I stood. It was much more frightening than that. It was a world crafted from breathing shadow and ice. The ice-covered ground held no light; the air was thick with sulfur, and each draw of breath felt like iron coating my lungs. Distant screams and wails echoed off the pillars of black obsidian that peeked from the roiling darkness. It was so cold it burned my bones from the inside.

This place made nightmares look like pleasant thoughts.

As I cast my eyes around the world once more, there was a clearing of someone's throat from behind me. I turned around, and my breath caught.

There, standing in a sleek, black leather bodysuit, was someone I hadn't expected.

"Well," Meredith said, stepping out of the shadows with a broad, wicked grin that revealed her crimson-red lips. "The Underworld just got a lot more interesting. Lucifer has a brand-new favorite demon ... me. And I've been given some very specific instructions. Payback for killing me is going to be a veritable nightmare, sweetheart. Now we're going to play *my game.*"

ABOUT D.L. BLADE

D.L. Blade has always had a passion for creative writing, with a particular focus on poetry during her younger years. One night, after having a vivid dream, she was inspired to pick up her pen and write her debut novel, *The Dark Awakening*.

Initially, Blade had focused on writing young adult fiction, but she has since shifted her focus to adult fantasy, paranormal, and dark romance. Through her stories, she takes readers on a journey into a world of unconventional love, morally gray men, and villains who get the girl.

When she's not writing, Blade enjoys reading, spending time with her husband and two children, attending rock concerts, and exploring new restaurants in Denver. She dreams of continuing to create exciting novels for her readers, taking them on a journey through the magical realms that spill from the pages of her books.

ABOUT C.M. LOCKE

C.M. Locke is a passionate writer who has been crafting short stories and poems for many years. Though she is a first-time author in the book world, she has already honed her skills through her love of writing.

Reading is one of her favorite pastimes, and she has likely read over 100,000 pages throughout her lifetime. Whenever she has free time, she loves to curl up on the couch with a cup of peppermint tea and dive into a well-loved book or a brand-new novel.

Originally from Colorado, C.M. Locke currently lives in rural Missouri with her boyfriend and three beloved kitties.

www.ingramcontent.com/pod-product-compliance
Lightning Source LLC
Chambersburg PA
CBHW022012300726
48970CB00003B/849